CORANOX

E-ISBN 978-0-9862555-0-2

ISBN 978-0-9862555-1-9

First Edition

Fifth Exile LLC / Brookline, MA

Laestran Calendar (LC)

Terminology

1 tick = 1 standard (Earth) second	**1 turn** = 5 days
1 rep = 100 ticks	**1 half-cycle** = 25 days (5 turns)
1 arc = 100 reps	**1 cycle** = 50 days (10 turns)
1 day = 10 arcs	**1 year** = 6 cycles (300 days)

The first **arc** in the ten-arc day is known as new arc. The second arc is one arc in reference to how many complete arcs have passed; therefore, the last arc of the day is nine arc. Reps are referenced after the arc designation, as in three-arc sixty.

Every **cycle** tracks the two moons **Rhynon** and **Faerila**, representing a cumulative orbital period for both moons. Nominally, the first five cycles are known as **Exiles** (First Exile, Second Exile, Third Exile, Fourth Exile, Fifth Exile) while the sixth cycle is known as the **Reunion**.

Lunaprism

A color scheme known as the **lunaprism**, rooted in the mythology and astrology attributed to the two moons, establishes informal shorthands for each cycle over any two-year span. Odd years (e.g., 987) are known as **years of Rhynon,** and even years are known as **years of Faerila.** Within each of the two years, the cycles are assigned the following colors.

Cycle	Proper Name	Rhynonian Color	Faerilan Color
1	First Exile	Sky	Ash
2	Second Exile	Jasmine	Rose
3	Third Exile	Coral	Violet
4	Fourth Exile	Jade	Onyx
5	Fifth Exile	Crimson	Azurite
6	Reunion	Umber	Ivory

For example, in the fifth cycle of a year of Faerila, the phrase "previous sky cycle" would refer to the First Exile of the previous year, while "next ash cycle" would refer to the First Exile of the year after next.

Notation

Dates are written in the following format: Year.Cycle.Date.

For example, the date 987.3.17 would be officially known as the "Seventeenth Day of the Third Exile in the Year 987," while 987.6.02 would be "Second Day of the Reunion in the Year 987" or "Second Day of the 987th Reunion."

Colons are used in written notation to separate arcs, reps, and ticks, all of which are denoted with two digits, as in 08:72:94 or 00:12:63.

Seasons of Moriana

The following depicts the average time frame and interval for each season on the continent of Moriana:

Spring: 1.25–2.50
This season contains mostly cool weather. Toward the end of spring, frequent rain occurs, and the temperatures increase significantly.

Summer: 3.01–4.12
This season holds the warmest weather of the year. Storms occur less frequently than in spring but tend to be more severe.

Fall: 4.13–5.24
This season grants cool weather and the least amount of precipitation. Every once in a while a severe rainstorm will occur. Early snowstorms may occur during the early parts of the Fifth Exile.

Winter: 5.25–1.24
This season results in harsh blizzards. Winters can arrive early or end late, though usually by the start of the First Exile, the snow begins to melt.

CORANOX

TONY GAO AND BRENT PECKHAM

FIFTH EXILE / BROOKLINE, MA

Prologue

(975.6.41)

A light snow dusted the fields throughout the morning. Jardis had yet to emerge from the shadow of winter's tail.

Early in the day, merchant caravans from Calena arrived for just the second time during the Reunion. The people of Jardis always welcomed their presence, not only for the chance to restock supplies during the winter but also for the modest stir of activity they aroused in what was otherwise a dormant village in the northern Atherian Outlands. The traders and vendors of the caravan took positions around the large bell in the center of the village square and conducted their business into the early afternoon, when the tranquility shattered.

At first, the sight of a young woman running hurriedly from the east was only a mild curiosity to most of the people bustling about the square. Several merchants were even amused by the way her flowing faded blue dress clearly hindered her movement. Eventually, the villagers who caught a glimpse of the expression on her face realized that there was nothing frivolous about her sprint. The woman slowed down to speak to her friends and neighbors in an even but grave tone. This confirmed the urgency of the matter to them, and despite her warnings to remain calm, the word began to spread like wildfire throughout the square. Merchants exhibited varying degrees of pause before committing, in a hurry, to pack up their goods and flee south. Some of the women and children hastened for the safety of their homes. Whatever opportunity there had been to preserve the collective composure of the gathered populace dissipated into the suddenly foreboding frosty breeze.

Edith Sylvera weaved through the frantic scattering crowd until she reached the central raised-stone platform where the large brass bell hung. She paused absently to adjust the hem of her dress before yanking on a long chain that served as a pulley to swing a retractable wooden beam into the side of the bell. Jarred by the clanging, as Edith rang the bell several times, everyone in the square fell silent almost immediately. The few traveling merchants who had yet to flee continued to pack up their goods and stands, while all the residents of Jardis stopped in their tracks and turned their attention to her. Within ticks, many other villagers poured into the square from all directions.

From the eastern road came a man well into his fifties, dressed in simple yet neatly tailored, dark green robes. The crowd immediately parted to let him pass. At the south end of the square, a handsome, well-built young man with wavy blond hair and gleaming blue eyes emerged from the largest house in the village. In contrast, he did not appear agitated in the slightest. The two men joined Edith on the platform.

"Elder," she said to the older man, "we have confirmed raiders approaching from the east."

"Sebastian, what of our guest?" the elder asked the younger man.

"Secure in your house," Sebastian replied. "He wanted to help, but I insisted he return to safety."

"Good."

Elder Norman Potts stepped forward to address the people of Jardis who anxiously awaited his words. He raised his hands and straightened his back. The traces of stubble covering his face and his short, curly gray hair, sprouting from his tanned, bald head, gave the elder an unkempt appearance, but his smooth, firm voice had a reassuring effect on the crowd.

"Everyone, please! We must remain calm to keep our homes safe. As usual, Sebastian and Edith will oversee preparations for the coming raid. Please follow their lead in gathering your weapons and securing your homes and families."

A murmur swept through the crowd before the shouts began. The men of the village demanded more information, while the women searched the crowd, frantically accounting for the whereabouts of their families. The elder tried to maintain order but was unable to address everyone at once.

As she surveyed the growing panic from her position on the platform, Edith felt precious time passing. She ran over to the elder's house from which Sebastian had emerged, where several dull-pointed spears lay against its western side. Edith grabbed one of the crude weapons and raced back to the platform relatively unnoticed, as the villagers were focused on the elder or talking nervously among themselves. She looked around once more before repeatedly slamming the butt of the spear down on the platform, causing everyone in the square to start.

"Listen!" she shouted, curling her lip and waving her spear in the air. "We're going to tear those bastards to shreds!"

The stunned crowd uttered no reply.

Smiling, Sebastian drew closer to her, resting his hand over hers and lowering her spear.

"Not all of us are as bloodthirsty as you, my dear," he said.

Several villagers emitted nervous laughter at Sebastian's attempt to relieve the tension.

"Remember the protocol, everyone," the elder said.

"Let's not waste time," said Sebastian, spurring everyone to action.

The remaining merchants had already departed; each fled as quickly as the burden of his or her luggage would allow. Many mothers collected their children, leading them into their houses before shutting and bolting the doors, while Edith, Sebastian, and Elder Potts led a group of would-be combatants eastward. The Jardis militia stood in full strength with sixty-some able-bodied men and women, though not all had previously seen real combat. As his rapidly approaching old age made him ineligible for combat, Elder Potts now coordinated efforts to prevent a sense of isolation and defeat within the militia.

"Third time this year," Edith whispered to her husband. "How much more of this must we endure?"

She never hid her jealousy of Sebastian's ability to suppress his feelings of unrest from public display, an ability she strove to emulate. Sebastian saw a bolt of concern flicker across Edith's face that only he knew well enough to detect. He reached out and gave her calloused hand a quick squeeze, releasing it almost immediately so as to escape notice of the militia who looked to the pair for strength. Edith did not return his gaze, but nodded in acknowledgment, the muscles in her face relaxing visibly.

The elder marched just behind them, preoccupied with assuaging the fears of the stabler's eldest son, Dane Landsman. As the group approached the eastern storehouse, the largest of three such structures within the confines of the village, Elder Potts produced from his pocket a large iron key, which he used to unlock the door of the wooden building. Lit fortuitously by sunbeams sieved through scant cracks in the roof of the shack, a large crate, lying on the floor, was discernible amid the interior darkness.

"Help me distribute those," the elder said to Sebastian, striding forward toward the crate. The young man obliged and followed suit. The two leaders began distributing short swords and spears from the crate; the weapons were as dilapidated as the one Edith carried.

After arming ten more villagers, the elder instructed Sebastian and Edith to lead the advance party to the outpost.

"Certainly, Elder," Sebastian said. He motioned for Edith and the remaining armed militia to follow him outside and then to continue eastward.

The Sylveras could now see the bandits clearly in the distance. They were at least a kilometer away. Most of Jardis lay on open, flat land, making it easy to keep track of their movements. Furthermore, the bandits' dirty garbs stood out against the snow. Unfortunately, the terrain also made the area much more difficult to defend once the fighting broke out. Despite this disadvantage, the militia usually had ample time to rebuff wantonly aggressive bandits, and previous raid attempts had been easily repelled.

As the makeshift squad reached the outpost, Harrison Agilda, one of five men stationed atop the outpost tower, saw them and waved. He swiftly climbed down the ladder in front of him. Harrison's gait was slightly uneven, although he had never suffered any significant leg injury and maintained that it was simply the way he walked. A pair of well-worn spectacles gave his thin, youthful face a bookish quality, while his overall physique was toned by many long days in the fields. His attire was worn-out but efficient, as he was not ashamed of his poverty and made no effort to disguise it. He was well respected by the entire village, and it was of little surprise that he and his wife, Maya, maintained a close relationship with the Sylveras.

As Sebastian approached, Harrison seized him by the arm and clapped him on the shoulder.

"Are the children safe?" he asked urgently.

It was Edith who replied, "Yes. I had Maya take them to the Altons' house."

"Thank Creon," Harrison said with relief. Out of habit, he grabbed the well-polished iron locket around his neck. He had far exceeded his means to commission the small portrait of his daughter contained within; it was the one material possession he valued above all else.

He adjusted the bridge of his spectacles and squinted into the distance at the wave of figures moving through the fields. Noticing that they advanced very slowly, he said, "Looks like this may be a smarter bunch."

"The elder will be here shortly," Sebastian said. "We should be able to establish our positions soon."

"Well, we'll need all the help we can muster," Harrison remarked, turning his attention to the larger group of villagers coming up the path. "William and I counted at least fifty of them this time, some on horseback."

His voice wavered, betraying his stoic expression. Like Edith and many of others in their party, he did his best to contain his terror.

"We should start setting up our positions," he said. "Let's head out. Creon help us."

· · ·

By six arc, a soft breeze had set upon the village and its surrounding fields, as the sounds of battle began to subside.

Edith felt a throbbing in her head as she got up slowly and absently dusted herself off. She had been dragged a few meters by a horse during the skirmish. Her dress was torn on the outside of her right leg, but the snow had cushioned her fall, and she suffered nothing worse than a few scratches. The struggle knocked the wind out of her, but the rider had been much less fortunate. Only the lower half of the bandit's body was visible; Edith had heard the dull crunch as the man's head collapsed under the weight of the toppled horse.

She bent over, coughing and gasping for air. Her mind racing, she tried to focus on the condensation of her breaths to collect her thoughts. The bandits had broken through their defenses, but how many of them had slipped through to the west? She estimated that only about twenty reps had passed since the fighting broke out. Harrison … Harrison had returned with several others to pursue the bandits that had gotten through while she and Sebastian fought a large group of raiders near the outpost.

Where was Sebastian? She swiveled her head from side to side against the pain that was rattling her skull. He was about fifty meters away, fighting off two men who had cornered William Cadrene, a young goatherd. Sneaking up behind them, Sebastian dispatched both attackers with ease and rushed to check on William.

Edith began making her way toward them. Bodies were strewn all over the ground. Though it was difficult to distinguish villager from bandit, Edith recognized at least ten faces among the dead. Still dazed, she could not yet process the sight of so many torn and mangled bodies, people she knew and loved, writhing or lying lifelessly in the blood-soaked snow.

Before all was quiet, someone let out a final cry of anguish from behind Edith. Tall and thin, sixteen-year-old Thomas Polke clutched a sword tightly with both hands and stared at the crumpled body of a bandit at his feet. He was a meek youth of poor constitution, but this was not his first fight, and Edith saw a glint of bloodlust in his eyes.

"Edith." Sebastian laid a hand gently on her shoulder. "Are you all right?"

"Yes," Edith said, some vigor returning to her voice. "What about the others?"

"Harrison has not returned yet."

"We have to follow him."

Edith disengaged herself from her husband and began to run westward toward the village.

"Anyone who can still fight, follow me to the square!" she yelled. "We have to make sure they're gone!"

Sebastian scanned the surroundings as several villagers, who remained on their feet, took off after her. He was anxious to follow though knew that someone needed to stay behind to secure the outpost and tend to the injured. Gradually, he noticed voices he did not recognize and turned his head in their direction.

Two enormous white durions stood nearby, baring their teeth casually. The voices Sebastian heard belonged to the two men who stood beside the horses. The one doing most of the speaking was a bald, middle-aged man, his intonation even and unnervingly detached from the surrounding mayhem. The other was an imposing figure who appeared to be a military officer. He was clad in a resplendent and unblemished suit of gleaming white armor. A dozen well-armed men in unmistakable Coranthian Army uniforms accompanied the two.

Soldiers? When had they arrived?

Having caught Sebastian's inquisitive gaze, the bald man locked eyes with him.

"You, sir." The man raised his hand as he approached Sebastian. "Are you injured? Who is in command here?"

It took Sebastian a moment to find his voice.

"I am unharmed. The elder of this village is Norman Potts. I last saw him near the outpost to the east."

"The elder? Yes, I spoke to him," the bald man said without breaking stride. "We assisted your militia at the outpost. Your elder is safe, though somewhat dazed. He told us to venture west and seek out two men—Sylvera and Agilda. Are you aware of their whereabouts?"

He extended his hand as he drew to a halt. "Minister Verinda. Of the Interior."

Sebastian's eyes widened as they shook. "Lord Verinda, I am Sebastian Sylvera. I apologize for failing to recognize you."

"No matter, Mr. Sylvera. What of Agilda?"

"My wife left in search of him."

Minister Verinda nodded solemnly and turned to motion to the armored man, who had already followed him.

"And I apologize for not having arrived sooner," the armored man said. His blond hair was short and perfectly cropped; his chin, strong and clean-shaven; his fiery blue eyes, piercing. Sebastian found his face familiar though could not recall having ever met him. Unable to hold his gaze, Sebastian cast his eyes downward, whereupon he saw, carved deep into the armored man's chest plate, a stylized crimson crown, which finally revealed who stood before him.

"Your Majesty," he acknowledged, dropping to his knees.

To his surprise, he felt the king's firm grip on his shoulder, pulling him upright.

"Rise, now is not the time. If anything, it is I who ought to hang my head to you and your fellow villagers. We were unable to arrive before the raid began."

At twenty-five, Sebastian was already a leader among the people of his village and permitted himself occasional pride in that fact, but as he found himself, once more, face to face with Samsen Caden Coranthis, who, though almost a decade older, radiated more youthful vigor and charisma than Sebastian could ever hope for, he realized just how inconsequential he truly was.

"Thank goodness you're here," he heard himself say.

"Very good," the king said. "I shall leave three men and a doctor behind to tend to the wounded. Lead us back to the village, and we will sweep away any remaining bandits. Minister Verinda will return east to retrieve the elder. Do we have an understanding?"

"Yes, Your Majesty."

Without another word, Sebastian began to head west, wondering what Edith would think if she saw the dumbfounded look frozen on his face. He could hear the clinking of the king's armor coming from behind, followed by a shuffling of footsteps as Coranthian soldiers fell in line.

• • •

Maya Agilda sat at her well-worn dining table, nervously sipping a cup of tea. She anxiously watched her daughter, Madeline, and Edith's son, Reznik, as they sat on the floor. It had been some time since Edith had asked her to find Reznik and escort the children south to the Altons' house. With Madeline in tow, she searched anxiously for the boy, but was unable to locate him until just after Edith had rung the bell in the square. Finally, Maya found Reznik attempting to pull a wagon of firewood from the northwest. After forcing him to abandon his haul and dragging him back to her home, she decided not to take any chances and told the children they would remain there. Though the interim had been uneventful, it served only to put her even more on edge.

"Are we supposed to just wait here?" Reznik asked for the third time. He was six, same as Madeline, and had his father's blue eyes and blond hair, but his mother's thin lips and narrower face. As young as he was, he projected an air of quiet intensity that combined Sebastian's composure with Edith's confidence.

"Will you relax, Rez?" Madeline said. She kept herself busy by trying to rub off a cake of snowy mud attached to her tanned-leather shoes. Madeline was almost a mirror image of her mother as a girl. Both had cherry red hair, bright green eyes, pale skin, and slender features, though Maya's hair was neck length while Madeline's fell past her shoulders. "You know we have to wait until they ring the bell."

Before Maya could react, Reznik jumped up and walked to one of the front windows. He unlatched the shutter and pushed it slightly open to get a look outside.

"Reznik, stay away from the windows!" Maya commanded.

The young boy stared steadily to the north.

"I think there's a bandit outside," he declared.

At first, Maya did not believe him; bandits had never previously paid attention to any part of Jardis west of the square, because it was, even from a distance, readily apparent that the village's livestock and three storehouses lay to the east. When it occurred to her that Reznik would not lie or say things he did not mean under the circumstances, she bolted up out of her chair and rushed over to him. A quick glance confirmed that he was indeed telling the truth. She jerked him away from the windowsill, her heartbeat escalating.

"Mama?" Madeline's voice came meekly from behind her.

Maya's hands shook as she stepped away from the window and quietly closed the shutters. In a single motion, she grabbed Madeline and Reznik by the arms and dragged them both toward the back door. She fervently hoped that the men outside could not hear them.

"Madeline, Reznik, you have to run."

"Why? What's wr—"

"Run through the fields. Stay low and head to the Altons'. Stay together but move quickly. Are you listening to me?"

Maya turned to Reznik and stared penetratingly at him. "Reznik, I am entrusting her to you. I'll be right behind you. I have to distract them so you can get away, then I'll follow. Now go!"

Before either of the children knew what was happening, she had shoved them both outside, closing the door behind them and locking it from within. The two bewildered children momentarily remained where they were before Reznik stirred and took Madeline's hand.

"We should listen to your mother. Let's go."

Madeline was uncertain but agreeable. She nodded and allowed Reznik to lead her into the yoa field. The stalks, which grew up to twenty-five pegs in the summer, had been cut down during the harvest, though still allowed the crouching children to make their way through the field unseen.

From inside the house, Maya let out a brief sigh of relief. She knew she could count on Reznik to act quickly and decisively, and it gave her comfort to know that the children were out of harm's way for the time being.

But Maya had no time to rest; the bandits were getting closer.

She heard one say, "We got played for fools. That bastard said this side was lightly defended, but there ain't nothing here to defend."

"Nothing but shitty crops and old ladies rotting inside their huts," a second voice agreed. "I'm going to gut Harker for trying to put one over on us. If you help me, I'll split his take with you."

"Hah. I'll agree if there actually ends up being anything worth taking."

A horse snorted faintly somewhere farther down the road. Then came the sound of someone spitting a stream onto the ground, along with that of approaching footsteps. A man with a long scar running down his right cheek walked up to the front door of the Agildas' house and attempted to look in through several small cracks in the wooden door. With the shutters closed and curtains drawn, the interior of the Agilda home was almost completely dark.

"The hell are you doing, Weldon? Just bust it down."

The man with the scar, called Weldon, looked askance and said, "Bet nothing's in there anyway."

"Move."

A short man with an unevenly receding hairline pushed Weldon out of the way.

From inside the house, Maya heard a deep breath. Suddenly, the door caved in under the force of a huge club. Splinters flew as the short man gave an enthusiastic roar and continued to smash away until there was a gaping hole, big enough to fit a child. Light poured into the house as the short man gave a satisfied grunt. Dropping the club, he reached in to unlock the door. His hand found the doorknob and turned it. The door swung open, and the short man stepped into the house. He had barely gotten his other foot inside when Maya emerged from the corner of the room and drove a kitchen knife into the left side of his ribcage.

The man screamed and immediately dropped to one knee. His right arm was still wrapped around what remained of the front door, rendering him unable to attempt any sort of coordinated movement.

"What the hell?" Weldon exclaimed, jumping back and hurriedly reaching for a short sword strapped to his waist.

The short man's thrashing subsided as he lost consciousness. His weight pressed on the door, which came off its hinges. Wood, flesh, and bone toppled onto the floor inside the house. Weldon remained beyond arm's reach of the door, unsure of how to proceed, when he noticed Maya skittering around the body of his fallen companion. His eyes followed her as she ran to his right.

"Hey!"

Unsheathing his short sword, he ran into the house, wildly jerking his head in search of the peasant woman who had dared to fight back. He was greeted by half a kettle full of scalding water in his face. Involuntarily dropping his short sword, Weldon let out a pained squawk and stumbled out of the house, covering his burned visage. Maya darted forward and picked up the short sword. Raising the sword over her head with both hands, she stepped outside. Before she could strike, she heard a thud and felt a sharp pain at the back of her head. She let out a cry and fell instantly to the ground.

Maya strained her neck as she tried to look up. Her vision was blurry, and her head felt as if it had been ripped open. She was barely able to make out the two figures standing over her. Had there been a third man?

"Stupid bitch!" Weldon rasped. The harshness of his voice caused Maya's ears to ring.

She felt the hard toe of a boot ram into her side, and she groaned.

"She's mine!" Weldon said. "I'm bringing her!"

"Forget it," came a new voice. "I think I cracked open her skull."

Everything had grown very dark and very quiet for Maya. She ceased to hear them.

Weldon looked down at the limp body. Seeing that the woman would be of no use to him, he reentered the house and glanced around, looking half-heartedly for anything of value, but gave up without much effort.

"Let's just get out of here," he mumbled to no one in particular and wandered outside to find his horse.

Meanwhile, the third bandit, a thin man with a crooked beak for a nose, went inside and bent over the short bandit's bloody mess of a corpse.

He gave a low whistle and then gave Weldon a contemptuous look. "You useless shit, I can't believe y—"

The back door flew open and Edith entered, coiled and prepared to strike. The bandit whirled around in surprise before his lip quickly twisted into a condescending sneer.

"Hey, Weldon. Looks like—"

He was not afforded the time to finish his sentence. Edith was no longer brandishing her spear, which had snapped in half during an earlier encounter. The bandit standing before her, though, still had his sword sheathed on his hip. She saw this and charged straight at him. Before he could flinch or notice the set of agriclaws she wore on her right hand, she ran up to him and swung from below, jolting his nose upward into his brain. He fell dead on the spot, the center of his face thoroughly pulverized.

Weldon, who had been tending the horse, was taken by surprise for the third time in as many reps and was unable to recover. He never stood a chance as Edith barreled toward him with a petrifying scream, her shoulder-length brown hair flying wildly. A crow of terror escaped his scarred lips as he saw his death in her blazing green eyes. She jammed the agriclaws deep into his chest and kicked him hard in the stomach, yanking her arm to free the blades. Weldon fell backwards, clutching his chest and gasping in pain. Edith lunged again, slashing him across the throat. Choking on his blood, Weldon collapsed and died within a rep.

Edith tossed aside her makeshift weapon. She stumbled over to Maya. Her trembling legs gave way, and she dropped to her knees. Warm, sticky blood poured over her hands as she rolled her friend's body toward her. When she saw that Maya's eyes were rolled back to their whites, she lost control and began to sob.

"Maya ... Maya!" she wailed. "Wake up! Maya!"

Sebastian arrived shortly after the bloodshed had ceased. When Edith violently shook Maya's lifeless body, he immediately stepped in to pull his wife away.

"Maya? Maya!" Edith cried in despair.

Sebastian wrapped his wife in an embrace, simultaneously restraining and consolatory. Gradually, Edith's struggle subsided, though she continued to weep. Sebastian stood up and walked slowly back into the house, staring numbly at the two bodies on the floor.

After some time, Madeline appeared in the back doorway. Sebastian had immediately set out with King Samsen and his soldiers for the Altons' upon reaching the square and was surprised to hear from the children that they had only recently left the Agildas' house. He had told the Altons to head for the square, now the most secure location in the village. Reznik had gone with them, but Madeline insisted on joining Sebastian to see her mother.

"Uncle Bastian? Where's Mama? Did you see her?" Madeline asked worriedly.

Sebastian walked quickly to Madeline, took her hand, and began to lead her eastward, taking care to shield the girl from the sight of her mother's corpse, which was lying in front of the house.

"Your mother isn't here, Maddy. She left. Let's head back and find your dad, okay?"

Madeline nodded.

Although many of the houses had suffered damage, the square and its residences remained relatively untouched, with only traces of debris scattered about. Some children and pets were even playing in the square, oblivious to the horrors that had transpired. Sebastian noticed plumes of smoke to the north.

"Sebastian! Madeline!" Elder Potts walked briskly over to them as they approached. "I am glad to see you both!"

Sebastian gave Madeline a gentle nudge toward the other children. "Madeline, go play for a moment. I have to talk to the elder."

Madeline ran off obediently.

"Where is Edith? Is she safe?" asked the elder.

"Yes, I saw her. She's with … Maya is dead."

The flatness of his own voice surprised him. The elder initially seemed taken aback, but softened quickly.

"May her soul rest with Rhynon. I'm sure she fought to the end."

"I have no doubt that she did," Sebastian said with a sigh. He had not fought much, nor had the bandits he faced put up much of a fight, but he was completely drained, and his bones suddenly began to ache. "It's quiet, Elder. I take it they've gone?"

"We underestimated them," the elder said, visibly shaken. "They took … They broke into the northern storehouse."

"How much did they take?" Sebastian asked mechanically, although he already knew the answer.

"They burned it down," someone in the crowd volunteered.

Sebastian craned his neck to see that Minister Verinda was the speaker. Before he could reply, Sebastian heard someone call his name. A man wearing an embroidered dark blue cloak, similar in style to Minister

Verinda's, stood nearby, and Sebastian recognized him as the man he had locked inside the elder's house before the bandits arrived.

"What's wrong, Gustaf?"

"I need to show you something, Sebastian," the man said gravely. Although Gustaf Renault was typically well kempt, as men of his stature tended to be, his long brown hair and pale face were coated in snow and dirt. Sebastian noticed specks of blood dotting his friend's cloak.

"Lord Renault," Verinda said with surprise, "what are you doing here?"

"Minister Verinda, I could ask the same of you. I beg your pardon, but I need a moment with Sebastian."

Verinda frowned and nodded. "Very well."

Sebastian followed Gustaf as the latter led him out of the square. He immediately realized they were heading for the northern storehouse. His nostrils filled with acrid smoke as they approached the ravaged building. The fire had subsided, and little more than a smoldering ruin remained. Gustaf led him around the wreckage to the back, where two charred corpses lay over one another, permeating the air with the stench of burned flesh. Sebastian picked up a limb of a fallen tree off the ground and prodded the top body until it rolled over. It was easily recognizable as a bandit; a sheathed sword appeared through some leather that had melted into the corpse. The other was disfigured beyond possible identification. Based on the positions of the bodies, Sebastian guessed that there had been a vicious struggle between the two.

Gustaf drew his hand from beneath his cloak and held it toward Sebastian. "He must have followed some of the others and tried to protect the storehouse. I found this on the ground."

In spite of the damage it had suffered, Sebastian immediately recognized the item in Gustaf's outstretched hand. His stomach churned as he took the metal locket.

"I'm sorry, my friend."

Gustaf's words barely registered. As he managed to pry open the keepsake, Sebastian heard himself emit a despondent sigh when he saw that the picture inside was just as charred as its container.

In the distance, the bell in the village square began to ring.

"Damn it all," Sebastian muttered. "This is just …"

A rustling noise came from behind the two men.

"Who's there?" Gustaf shouted suddenly. He retracted his hand quickly inside his cloak. "Show yourself!"

A small boy walked slowly out from behind the rubble. He was as well-dressed as Gustaf, although his cloak was forest green. When the boy's face became visible, it was clear that his choice of attire was not the only thing the two shared.

"My apologies, Father. I just wanted to see if you needed my help, that's all."

Gustaf straightened up. "I told you to stay in the square, Renard."

"The children are playing silly games," Renard Renault said. "Besides, we all wanted to follow you."

Sebastian froze as Reznik and Madeline appeared behind Gustaf's son. The three children came to a standstill and immediately covered their noses as they approached the bodies.

"What's … that smell. What is that?" Renard asked in a muffled voice.

Gustaf walked up to Renard and took his arm. "I told you to stay put, Renard. Come, let's go back. Come on, children."

The three were eager to escape the stench and followed Gustaf without any complaint. Once the four of them returned to the square, Gustaf left them in the company of the elder and sought out Verinda, who had not stirred from his original resting place.

"You have chosen an unfortunate day to visit, Lord Verinda," Gustaf stated gravely as he walked up to the minister.

Verinda's lips pressed together as he rubbed his bald pate.

"I suppose that is one way to put it. His Majesty decided to investigate the recent report of a bandit collective firsthand. We thought we'd have more success tracking them closer to the Pelaros Woods. Had we only set out a day or two earlier …"

"The king is here?"

Gustaf skimmed the crowd instinctively.

"He's meeting with his soldiers. He should be along shortly," Verinda said.

Meanwhile, Sebastian returned to the square alone. He saw Edith sitting in the grass with her back to him, but decided Madeline was his first priority. She had just lost both of her parents, and it didn't seem right to him for her to find out from someone else. Slowly, he approached the crowd of children surrounding Elder Potts.

"I need to talk to you, Madeline," he said in a grave tone. She looked up curiously; he could not look her in the eye. Instead, his normally bright blue eyes remained dully fixed on the elder.

Nearby, Reznik and Renard watched as Sebastian led Madeline away from the other children. Renard's gaze drifted to Edith, who sat alone in the center of the square, staring at the ground. Gustaf walked up to her and spoke to her in a low voice. Edith's grief-stricken face fell as she learned of the passing of her two closest friends, leaving Madeline an orphan. Although Edith was exhausted and suffered from the bruise on her head, tears streamed down her cheeks. Gustaf removed his cloak and wrapped it around her shoulders and then sat next to her, unsure of what else to do.

Reznik's eyes focused on his father and Madeline. The little girl was bawling in Sebastian's arms and screaming for her father.

After a moment, she began to cry out, "Where's Mama? I have to tell her!"

Although the children were young, they understood death. Madeline simply had not learned of her mother's fate. Reznik knew. His mother had told him when she returned to the square, adding flatly that Harrison should be the one to tell his daughter, but Reznik had recognized the locket during the exchange between Gustaf and Sebastian at the storehouse. He kept silent, as did Renard, who always knew more than he let on.

Elder Potts took Madeline's hand, as he gently led her away. Sebastian managed an appreciative nod in his surprise. He was drained, both physically and emotionally, and no longer bothered to hide it. Reznik approached him.

"This … this is horrible," his son said. Reznik's gaze was steady, but his voice wavered with emotion.

Sebastian stood up. "Are you all right, son?"

Reznik nodded. "Yes, but Maddy …"

"You should leave her alone for a while, Reznik. Your mother will take care of her. Goodness knows she's much better at that sort of thing." He rubbed his chin wearily. "Stay with Renard for now. I'll come get you in a little while."

He ruffled his son's hair.

"Why do people do this to each other?" Reznik said. "Don't they know it's wrong?"

Sebastian considered the question briefly.

"Not everyone cares about right and wrong."

Reznik stared piercingly at his father.

Sebastian was not completely satisfied with his answer, but he decided to leave it at that. He gave Reznik a comforting nod and walked toward Edith.

Madeline sat in front of the bell as her cries slowly gave way to low sobs. The elder held a comforting arm around her tiny shoulders.

"But what else is there?" Reznik muttered to himself.

. . .

Several reps passed as a flurry of flakes fell from the sky. Suddenly, the elder stood and took stepped away from the bell as the magnetic figure of the sovereign strode to the central stone platform and knelt down in front of Madeline. He began to speak to her softly. All those in the square were captivated by the king's golden aura, their eyes fixed on the scene in front of the bell.

Madeline finally rose and timidly extended her hand at the king's request. He clasped it in his own and gently pushed a small object into her tiny cold hand. After he released his grip, she stared momentarily at her clenched fist before she bowed. He stood and, after patting Madeline gently on the head, gestured toward several nearby soldiers as he walked away.

Reznik ran up to Madeline. Her eyes, misty emeralds, pulsed inconsolably, searing his core with each quiver. "Maddy—" He was at a loss.

"I'm so sorry, Madeline," said Renard, following on Reznik's heels. Without hesitation, the older boy held her in a comforting embrace.

"Thank you, Renard," she sobbed, pulling away.

Reznik cleared his throat, but it took him several ticks to find his voice.

"Maddy," he finally managed, "what did the king give you?"

She extended and slowly opened her still-clenched right hand to reveal a large crimson pin enclosed in a shielded frame gleaming against her pale white skin.

"The Coranox."

Chapter 1

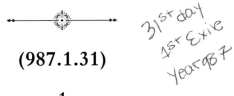

(987.1.31)

—1—

As he traversed Capital Circle, taking note of the vendors and couriers going about their daily preparations in the intermittent rain, Radley Lariban received the unequivocal impression that Corande's denizens were unaware of what had transpired at Elsin Point.

He strode briskly up to the northeastern gate of Castle Coranthis. Two imposing guards flanking the entrance were awaiting Lariban. They immediately saluted when they recognized the golden colonel's pin on his navy blue officer coat. Lariban continued toward the castle, the highest point in Corande.

Uninterrupted passage was a rarity for the colonel. Despite his rank and reputation within the Coranthian Army, he was often stopped for inspection, unrecognized by many soldiers. Lariban attributed this to his muted appearance—his hair was short and he maintained a clean-cut look, which complemented his nondescript features.

Entering through the gate, Lariban made his way south along King's Road, a cobblestone path sloping gently uphill toward the castle. Several nobles saluted or nodded in recognition as they passed him along the road. Horses from the royal mews grazed lazily on the large pasture to Lariban's right, occasionally trotting over to a nearby canal to drink. Halfway to the castle, he spotted a small squad from the Royal Guard sparring in the woods a short distance off the road. Again, there was no indication that anyone on the castle grounds had any knowledge of recent events. Lariban knew that would soon change.

Gradually, the Coranox on the banner affixed to the protruding castle walls came into view. The path expanded into a wide, sparkling white stone walkway, split in two by a central strip of garden and lined with lamp posts. As he walked, Lariban's eyes were drawn to the enormous marble statue of the late queen, Evangeline, anchored near the end of the garden strip. Past the statue, the path steepened sharply, leading up to the entrance. A guard positioned in front of two large wooden doors saluted Lariban as the latter approached. The colonel returned the salute. The guard turned and rapped the door's large brass knocker. An inviting draft of warm air greeted Lariban as the door creaked open.

The colonel had never before been inside the castle without an escort. Having arrived so early in the morning and well before the time of his scheduled appointment, he was free from the presence of the guards who typically hastened him along. This gave him the chance to pause and admire the elegant craftsmanship of the castle. Despite being significantly taller than the average Coranthian, Lariban found himself with plenty of overhead space, allowing him a panoramic view of the ornately patterned ceilings in the cavernous first-floor corridors.

As he reached the north foyer, he encountered four members of the Royal Guard, two on each side of a double concave stairway that flanked the Queen's Hall, a closed-off room on the ground floor. An enormous three-ringed glass chandelier hung from the ceiling, directly above the statues of Coranthia's progenitors: King Creon donning his crown and Queen Caliri wielding her scepter. Upon reaching the top of the left stairway, Lariban was surprised to hear voices emanating from within the King's Hall through the large, slightly ajar doors directly in front of him. After a moment's hesitation, he gripped the double-barred handles and entered. A herald fell in behind him to announce his arrival.

Toward the back of the room stood a two-tiered dais. The four men of the Royal Cabinet occupied the lower tier. Between them sat the king, who had the upper tier to himself. Presiding over the room behind an expansive raised table, with two advisors on either side, King Samsen Caden Coranthis sat in a high-backed chair that would undoubtedly swallow men of lesser stature. All five men were dressed in immaculate suits. The king wore white with a red cravat, while the Cabinet ministers, donned blue with gold cravats.

As the herald retreated, Lariban saw that he was not alone on the floor. Two older men stood in front of him. The one closer to Lariban was looking up at the dais. Streaks of gray ran perfectly parallel in his dark hair, meticulously smoothed over to project an air of wisdom and authority, despite the fact that the man looked significantly younger than his forty-nine years. He turned around and studied Lariban as if he had never seen the colonel before.

"Your Majesty," Lariban said with a bow, ignoring the man's gaze and facing the king. "My apologies for the intrusion."

"Colonel Lariban." The gray-streaked man ran his tongue over the name as if it had been pricked.

"Lord Eurich."

Lariban nodded in deference and received only a look of thinly veiled contempt in return.

"Colonel," Samsen's booming voice cut in—taking full advantage of the acoustics offered by the room—"I can now personally attest to your reported penchant for being early. If you wouldn't mind, we'll take only a rep or two more. You may stay."

"Yes, Your Majesty." Lariban bowed again and walked across the white marble floor to the side of the room.

King Samsen leaned back in his chair and said slowly, "As you were saying, Lord Eurich?"

"Your Majesty," Sebastian Eurich began, turning his attention back to the dais, "I must beg you once more not to hasten into this war. The Elsin incident can be concealed from the public. We can prevent the arousal of any uncontrollable panic—"

"I have already approved Lord Verinda's official report to be released to the public," Samsen said, gesturing to his far left at the Minister of the Interior. "What is its status?"

Martin Stanton Verinda, the senior Cabinet member, gave a slight nod, adjusted his black-rimmed spectacles, and replied, "I've already sent it to the Post, Your Majesty."

Eurich narrowed his eyes. "I must confess, Your Majesty, that this most certainly will not accrue favor from some of the lords who are more hesitant to pursue such an immediate disclosure."

Samsen leaned forward, raising his eyebrows.

"Ah, Lord Eurich, you mean to tell me that you'll have your subscribers follow your lead?"

Eurich scowled. "Of course not, Your Majesty. I am simply—"

"And you, Lord Gregor?" Samsen interrupted.

The king turned toward the other man on the floor and heaved a heavy sigh when the latter looked away.

"I'll not have you keep your silence," Samsen said, rubbing his modest beard. "What is your stance on this, Second Chair?"

The king's tone was more subdued than the one he used to address Eurich. Sixty-one-year-old Mathias San Gregor, former Minister of Agriculture and one of the senior members of the Assembly of Lords, exuded quiet confidence to which his detractors paid begrudging respect. Despite his advanced age and wizened appearance, he maintained a kempt appearance, sporting a short, neatly trimmed goatee, and wearing an elegant off-white robe.

The count permitted himself a slight bow, clutching the curved gold grip of a white cane in his left hand. "Your Majesty, I speak on behalf of no one but myself. I understand wholeheartedly the need to defend our country and honor, and stress that I am merely asking that the unrest in the Outlands not be ignored."

"Surely, in light of such circumstances, you cannot ask us to deploy troops to the Outlands to wrangle some highwaymen who are killing each other," scoffed Ferdin Velmann, the heavyset Minister of Defense who sat to Samsen's right. He spoke easily, almost lethargically, and had a habit of tinkering with the assorted jewelry he wore on his fingers and wrists.

"What of the reserves?" Gregor replied without any hesitation, raising his voice slightly, as he was known to do on rare occasion. "There should be no harm in sparing some of them to quell the fighting in the Outlands until some measure of order is restored."

Eurich muttered something to himself before darting his eyes in Gregor's direction, glaring without turning his head.

"Lord Gregor's proposition merits some consideration, Your Majesty," said the Minister of the Treasury, Weston Grandville, who sat between the king and Minister Verinda. Although he fought alongside Velmann and the king himself during the Coronation War, Grandville had lately come to be known for little more than his bookkeeping. He always presented himself diffidently, but few within the nobility dared to underestimate him.

The air grew heavy in the silence that followed. A look of thinly veiled smugness spread across Minister of Defense Velmann's round face.

"Colonel Lariban," he finally said, leaning back in his chair as his voice echoed across the room.

"My Lord."

Lariban stepped forward. Eurich and Gregor turned, both having forgotten that Lariban was present.

"You have come with word from Aldova. Give us the news you were charged to bring."

"Sir, as per your orders on behalf of the Ministry of the Defense, General Leynitz has issued the mobilization of half the reserve companies to Aldova. He and General Mortigan are planning to use them as part of our first offensive."

Velmann said nothing in reply, allowing the weight of the announcement to sink in. The intended effect came to pass; Eurich became visibly angry and swiveled to face him.

"Neglecting any form of consult with the Assembly? And of which reserves do you speak, Lord Velmann?"

Samsen's blue eyes flashed at Eurich's exclamation.

In an attempt to conceal his relish, Velmann made a deliberate examination of his fingernails, and without looking up, began to speak slowly, savoring each word.

"Lord Gregor."

"Lord Velmann." There was a sinking tone to Gregor's acknowledgment, as if he knew he would not like what he was about to hear.

Velmann continued, his full red lips twitching in a restrained grin, "As you can see, even our reserves are being called upon at this time. Our generals are working to strike first and respond with ferocity. To ask us to divert additional military resources to the Outlands at this time is inadvisable. Would you not agree?"

"You have me at a loss, Lord Velmann," Gregor said simply.

Velmann leaned forward, expecting elaboration, but, when Gregor offered none, he shrugged and slouched leisurely in his chair.

"Mathias." A soft voice came from Velmann's right.

The room turned to look as Elliott Havora spoke for the first time since Lariban had entered. The current Minister of Agriculture, Gregor's successor, was a thin, bespectacled man with straight blond hair. Havora cleared his throat before continuing.

"I appreciate your concern, but Lord Velmann is not entirely incorrect in his assertion that the unrest in the Outlands appears to be little more than in-fighting among outlaws at this point. We have no official reports of innocents being killed or villages being raided. If our upcoming mobilization were to be hindered in any way, this matter would impose a much greater urgency, but last year's harvest was bountiful and the caravan routes are secure. Perhaps now is not the best time to … Well, I don't see any immediate danger in ensuring the priority of the Amelarens. If these incidents become more severe, we will, of course, revisit this matter."

A look of surprise washed over Gregor's face; he had not expected Havora to say anything, least of all against him.

"I concede to the wisdom of king and Cabinet," he said with resignation. "The military has my full support. May our victory be swift and decisive."

This was not enough to placate Eurich.

"Your Majesty," he started, "I really d—"

"It is not to your advantage to address this matter any further, Lord Eurich," Samsen cut in coldly. "I have made my decision."

Eurich's mouth snapped shut. Once again, silence filled the room.

"Very well, Your Majesty," he said, visibly strained. "I suppose I have no reason to further delay the war preparations. Nevertheless, it is my duty to summon the surveyors and accompany them to Aldova."

"As is your prerogative and responsibility as First Chair," Samsen said with a nod.

"If you'll excuse me, then."

Eurich bowed hastily and turned to leave. Velmann permitted himself a wrinkle of his nose once Eurich's back was turned.

"I shall also take my leave, Your Majesty," Gregor said. "My wishes for our success." He took a few steps forward and bowed slowly and purposefully to Samsen, clearly emphasizing where his loyalty lay. After Gregor departed, Samsen and the Cabinet were left alone with Lariban, who had retreated back into the corner.

Grandville looked at Velmann across the dais and spoke in a low voice to ensure that Lariban could not hear him. "Your preemption is remarkable but altogether quite brash."

Reverting to normal volume, he turned to the king.

"Your Majesty, were you aware that this order had not been cleared with the rest of the Cabinet?"

Samsen arched an eyebrow. "I was not aware that my orders required clearance."

"Yes, Your Majesty." Grandville's tone was agreeable, but his gaze lingered on Velmann, who smiled back faintly.

Samsen wagged his finger in Lariban's direction. The colonel stood motionless, paying close attention to all that was transpiring.

"Colonel, you are also dismissed. You may retire to your quarters and await my orders for General Leynitz. Before you leave, however, I wish to ask you why you abstained from arriving and spending the night in Corande yesterday. Was there some sort of delay?"

"No, Your Majesty," Lariban replied, surprised at this question, though he stepped forward without hesitation. "I deliberately chose not to arrive last night. Had others recognized me, they may have suspected something of significance was brewing. I wanted to minimize any such speculation."

The king smiled slowly and nodded as he spoke. "Very good, Colonel. I must admit I find you to be very practical."

Lariban bowed and exited, leaving the king and his advisors.

Samsen drummed his fingers on the armrest of his chair.

"What of our fort at Tull Rock?" he asked. "How goes the construction?"

Verinda said, "It looks to be ready just before General Leynitz sets out from Aldova, as scheduled."

"Everything is progressing smoothly," Velmann chimed in.

"Very well."

Several reps went by as Samsen fidgeted in his chair before realizing that the others were waiting for him to conclude the proceedings. In an energetic voice, he said, "Well, let us get on with it, then. Lord Verinda, I wish to speak to you and Lord Velmann privately about the banquet. I will send for you later today."

"Certainly, Your Majesty," replied Verinda, dabbing at his bald head with a handkerchief.

"Gentlemen, I'm sure this stirs up memories of the Coronation War. Warlord Orlen tried to breach our borders once before. We drove his troops back into their savage lands. This time, we will take the fight to them." Samsen paused for effect. "I am not foolish enough to think that we are destined to conquer this continent, but when we are dealt such an unwarranted indignity and horrific act of brutality, we must let the barbarians know that our hold on these lands is inviolable. We *will* show them our might, and we *will* ensure that they will never again attempt any assault on our sovereignty. That is all."

"Yes, Your Majesty," the ministers chorused, and with that, the meeting was adjourned. There was much to be done, and the four men made haste to tend to their respective tasks.

—2—

In the southwestern quadrant of the castle, Adrian Lanford Coranthis lay on his bed, staring at the high ceiling of his spacious bedroom. The bed itself was massive; it could comfortably fit four and was the most lavish piece of furniture in his otherwise spare quarters. While extravagant, his quarters were relatively modest compared to other rooms within the castle.

A soft knock on his door interrupted his meandering thoughts. The voice of Garrett, one of the castle's butlers, eked through the door. "Your Highness, Lord Grandville is here to see you."

Adrian closed his eyes briefly, pressing his head farther into the soft quilting. His long, wavy blond hair fell freely over his pale face, covering his right eye and the small scar beneath it.

"Let him in," he said, the bed muffling his voice.

The door swung open and Weston Grandville entered. Seeing Adrian lying on his back, he quickly closed the door behind him.

"I can see that you are not expecting visitors."

Suddenly feeling rather bleary, Adrian angled his head and blinked slowly. "Weston. How was the meeting?"

Grandville frowned.

"Fine, fine." The prince sprang to his feet and moved to one of the round chairs across the room, turning it away from a small tea table. He motioned for Grandville to sit in one of the other chairs.

"It went as expected. Unilateral support is secure, at least officially. Lord Gregor initially had some different thoughts altogether, imploring we divert resources elsewhere, but …"

"But?"

Now seated, Grandville ran his hand through his short black hair. He disapproved of Adrian's overly informal tendencies, though was, himself, generally looser in manner when conversing with the young man. "Ultimately, he shares our views. Don't worry about it, Prince. Now, to our business."

"What's the occasion?" Adrian asked, though he could already guess.

Grandville glanced around, noticing the haphazard arrangement of Adrian's details: eight pillows randomly strewn across the bed, the door to the bathroom slightly ajar, and the prince's sheathed sword propped up against a small, dark brown wooden bookshelf on the floor in a corner.

"Is it really so difficult to employ a bit of tidiness?" Grandville chided, shaking his head.

"Surely you did not come to address my sense of decor," Adrian said dryly.

Grandville emitted a sigh and stared at Adrian. "I must inquire—"

He trailed off. Adrian waited for him to finish, his green eyes trained on Grandville, remembering a time when the minister's appearance was fresh and youthful, in stark contrast to what he saw before him: the haggard face and sunken eyes belonged to a man who seemed well beyond his forty-four years. The cumulative stress had not been kind to Grandville's physiognomy, though his demeanor remained as steadfast as ever.

"I must inquire whether you plan to deploy."

Adrian nodded. "I do."

"Then you must stay at Aldova," Grandville said firmly.

"And why is that?" Adrian's retorted without missing a beat. "You think I'm incapable of leading my own troops?"

"Your father and General Leynitz are planning a large high-risk offensive deep into enemy territory within the next cycle. Projections of casualties are potentially—"

"And what would I be were I unwilling to take that risk, Weston?" Adrian's lethargy had dissipated. He leaned forward in his chair. "I will defer command to the general when it is appropriate if my inexperience is the issue."

Now clearly agitated, he rose and waved his hand as Grandville opened his mouth to reply.

"The time has come for me to take charge."

"Prince," Grandville said calmly, "you will have many chances to prove yourself in battle. But for now, I'm afraid that this matter has already been settled. What I have come to convey to you is not a suggestion on my part but an order that your father has given—"

He stopped short as Adrian, visibly struck by these words, fell into his seat. Grandville sat patiently, never taking his eyes off the young man.

"That's it, then?"

"You are bringing no dishonor to your name, Prince. There is no doubt of your conviction." Grandville rose from his chair. "Now, if you will excuse me."

Adrian sat motionless in his chair. Only his eyes followed Grandville as the minister left the room.

The prince remained in his room for only ten reps, pacing and absent-mindedly scratching the small fencing scar under his right eye. As he stared across the room at his sheathed sword, he realized that he had been lingering for far too long in his thoughts; he had intended to wait only until he was sure Grandville had left the floor. Quickly donning a jacket over his buttoned shirt to make himself more presentable, he exited his room.

Years ago, a member of the Royal Guard would have been posted outside his door, but as soon as Adrian began attending the military academy at Tellisburg, he argued vehemently with his father against having an escort. To Adrian's great relief, Samsen finally relented; the prince could now travel freely without fear that he was being watched.

It was a short walk down the hall to his sister's room. A female attendant whom Adrian did not recognize bowed deeply upon seeing him.

"I'm sorry, Your Highness. The princess is away from her room at the moment."

"What? Do you know where she is then? Or when she will return?"

The attendant blushed.

"I do not, Your Highness."

Adrian shrugged irritably and strode away.

—3—

Nestled in a crook within the castle grounds between the banks of the Sarigan River and the looming southern wall of Castle Coranthis was the Royal Nursery, a row of greenhouses bookended by a gardener's cottage on the eastern end, and an expansive field on the western end. Several marble gazebos littered the field, which allowed people of the castle to enjoy the breathtaking scenery of the palace, water, wildlife, and impeccably maintained greenery.

Adrian stepped into the southernmost gazebo. Taking a thick handkerchief from his coat pocket, he wiped the residual moisture from the rain off the bench and sat down.

"What are you doing out here?" a voice boomed. Ferdin Velmann stood just outside the veranda, peering in at him with a frown. As he spoke, he tied the reins of his black zephyr, Silas, to the hitching post as the warhorse stood aloofly behind him. Zephyrs were generally medium-sized and agile, but Silas suffered the same affliction of corpulence as his owner.

"Just getting some air," Adrian replied. "Are you out for your morning ride?"

"As always," said Velmann. "I want to take in as much of this cool weather as I can. When spring arrives in full bloom, you won't see me out here for half a cycle."

"Ah, Ferdin. You fear no man, but pollen presents a different challenge altogether."

The minister chuckled throatily as he entered the gazebo and sat facing Adrian without bothering to wipe off the bench.

"You looked pretty out of it, Prince," he remarked. "An aetra for your thoughts?"

He paused.

"Never mind, I can venture a guess."

"Probably," Adrian agreed. "It should be fairly obvious."

"You're not a fighter," Velmann said, his mouth crinkling wryly. "There's no reason for you to drop everything and rush to Aldova. There are men better suited to that task."

"I can fight just fine, and you know it," Adrian grumbled.

Velmann stretched lazily and spread his arms, wrapping his elbows around two spindles of the balustrade behind him.

"That is not what I meant. You should not be so eager to put yourself in the way of unnecessary harm." Even as his words became loftier, the minister maintained his disaffected expression. "We have a strong and proud army, with soldiers as eager as we to deliver justice unto the Amelarens. As the prince, you need only channel your sentiments through them. They are your sword.

"You were on the front lines alongside my father the first time we fought the warlord," said Adrian. "It is only right that I do the same."

"Surely you jest, Your Highness." The Minister of Defense shook his head. "Do you think that is how you'd best serve the country? Of course not. You are the prince. Your responsibilities exceed those of a soldier."

Despite the other man's lackadaisical demeanor, Adrian could not refute his words.

"I was good for nothing else," Velmann continued. His lips curled briefly into a frown before reverting to their loose indifference. "I will add, though, that your father should have told you himself instead of dispatching Weston. I don't blame you for being upset."

Suddenly, Adrian felt silly and slightly embarrassed that Velmann had so nonchalantly seen through him. He had only just begun to concede that there was a layer of artifice fueling his misdirected frustrations.

"He would say what you've said: 'You're not a fighter.' And he's not giving me the chance to prove otherwise."

Velmann stared steadily at the young man. If he felt any sympathy or compassion for Adrian, he did not show it.

"I suppose I'm not helping. You came out here to cool off, and I'm just stirring the pot."

He stood up and continued to speak as he moved to unhitch and climb back atop his horse. His movements were surprisingly light and fluid given his significant girth.

"Will you attend the banquet, Prince?"

"No. Why would I bother with such a tacky affair?"

"My apologies. I also find them to be dreadfully dull. I will not be attending this time either. Lord Verinda sought a replacement speaker for me. I suppose you haven't heard anything about that."

Adrian shrugged. Velmann smiled cryptically as he turned the horse around.

"Try not to worry so much, Prince. It's not your time yet, but it will be someday. Now, with your leave." With that, he snapped the reins and rode across the fields to the north.

Adrian took a long, deep breath as he watched the trail of vapor escape his mouth and fade into the chilly stillness of the air.

He lost track of time as he recalled the report from Aldova, which detailed the discoveries at Elsin Point. The attackers had left Orlen's Mark everywhere; blood-red crescents were carved into the sides of what buildings remained standing, as well as the bodies of the male Coranthians. No female bodies had been left behind; the women had disappeared. Adrian did not want to think about their possible fate. Morbid curiosity stirred a desire within him to see these markings for himself. He had seen crude photographs in documents, but they lacked visceral impact.

He tried to imagine the reactions of the scouts who had discovered the scene at Elsin and felt anger swell inside him. Standing up abruptly, he drew his sword, Antilus, and swung its flawless aeron blade, deftly weaving it through the air. Gracefully shifting his feet, he pretended to maneuver around an enemy who was before him. Practicing his swordsmanship and footwork had become second nature and required little thought on his part. Whenever he grew bored of being stuck inside the castle, he took time to refine his strokes, which had gradually amalgamated traditional military stances with more stylistic flourishes.

His mind drifted back to his time at Tellisburg. He knew that he had been granted certain privileges and unearned accolades as he trained with other Coranthians at the academy. He resented the special treatment. In fact, it made him more abrasive to those around him. He neither needed nor wanted the help. He wanted to feel worthy of his achievements. He felt coddled, and the only way to change this was to be afforded the chance to prove himself. This upcoming war yielded the perfect opportunity, yet he was given no choice but to leave the fighting to the low nobles, the common folk, and the Outlanders.

Adrian darted forward and thrust his sword in a jabbing motion before quickly returning to his original stance and sheathing his sword. Breathing deeply, he stared past the green field toward the Sarigan.

"It's not my time yet," he echoed bitterly. "Is that so?"

Interlude

It was a cold but pleasant night. A man hobbled through the forest, perturbing the stillness. His vision was limited—as the moonlight only partially pierced the canopy formed by the trees—and occasionally he stumbled, but his pace never slowed. Ilarud Alcat had an urgent matter at hand.

Alcat emerged from the tree line onto the plains before stopping. The road, which weaved its way along the southern edge of the Volqua Forest, advanced straight ahead. Rhynon—crimson and nearly full—gave chase to the azurite crescent of Faerila in the starry night sky, though Alcat took notice of neither moon, nor the sight of the clear lake glistening before him. He held no appreciation for such things. Alcat briefly scanned the outline of the large fortress that lay beyond the lake before his eyes fell on a bonfire beside the lake, about a hundred meters away. Heading toward the light, his limp worsened as the cold bit through layers of leather and into his right leg. Years earlier, a runaway slave had stabbed him in the thigh with a wooden stake, and the injury had left behind heavy, painful scarring.

As he approached, Alcat could make out nine figures huddled around a gigantic slab enjoying a feast, the fire roaring behind them. His mood worsened as he realized that the entire Amelaren War Council was present.

"Orlen!" he shouted crossly. They heard him clearly, though no one acknowledged him, even after he yelled again.

When he was within ten meters, Alcat inhaled deeply and spoke in the most commanding tone he could muster. "Orlen! I demand an audience!"

The only one to stir was the chiseled man seated at the head of the slab, who asked, "Why do you disturb me on this hallowed night, Ilarud?"

"You know very well why I'm here! Who gave you the authority to start a war whenever you damn please?"

Orlen chuckled.

One of the war chiefs, Lebb, looked up from his charred rib of boar meat. Light from the fire wisped across his sun-tanned face, highlighting his pronounced battle scars and condescending sneer. "Have you lost your mind? Watch your tongue and know your place!"

Alcat ignored the remark and continued to stare at Orlen, who finally raised his head to meet his gaze with a faint smirk.

"What good am I to our venerated Conclave if I don't aim to fulfill my purpose?" the warlord said. "My mission is still the mission of my predecessors, is it not? To destroy Coranthia."

Alcat frowned. "The timing is wrong. This was not part of our agreement."

"Another year of Rhynon is upon us. What benefit is there to waiting any longer?" said Tallen, the man seated to Orlen's left. "We tire of inconsequential skirmishes."

"Idleness leads to low morale," added Shira, one of two women present. "Many of our warriors grow restless and are ready to fight again."

Lebb raised his hand, inducing several laughs around him.

"Perhaps in your sheltered upbringing as an inert landlord, you're incapable of conceiving how our brothers and sisters have suffered," Tallen continued.

"Almost two decades have passed since our stalemate with the enemy," said Izven, one of the older war chiefs, markedly better groomed than the others. His clean-shaven face revealed deep wrinkles and a small cross-shaped scar below his mouth. "I speak for many when I reaffirm my intention to repay our invaders what is owed to them. I am resolved to see Coranthia fall in my time."

There were nods of approval all around. Alcat gritted his teeth.

"Their people fight among themselves," Shira said. "They know only how to count their money. But I suppose you'd know all about that, Ilarud."

Alcat's pride left him with little tolerance for such mockery. "You argue for war and dare to belittle me? What would you have your horde fight with? Should they sharpen their claws and wear their filthy rags? What is your army if not for my supply lines?"

Shira narrowed her hawkish blue-gray eyes, boring into Alcat's widened brown ones.

"Always boasting of your own success. And what value do your plantations have if their goods are unused?"

"What exactly is your problem, Ilarud?" Lebb snorted.

"You know damn well what my problem is!" Alcat belted out. "What is the point of attacking Elzamir? The swine will flock to their king, and he will unite his people behind him. And why did you not seek an audience with us beforehand? What good is conducting a preemptive strike with no momentum behind it?"

Shira replied icily, "You need not worry about that. All you need to focus on is keeping up production when the fighting begins."

Orlen, who had been listening with apparent disinterest, suddenly broke out in a throaty laugh. "Are all of you listening to this? Ilarud, you resemble a Coranthian more each day. You and the old men in Malegar have no business telling me how to conduct matters of war."

Alcat was beside himself with anger. "Say what you will, Orlen, but without the support of my brother and the rest of the Conclave, you will not have your war."

Orlen's smile transformed instantly into a snarl.

"You little worm!" he roared. "You come here and pester us while we offer tribute to Rhynon. We are preparing to lead our brothers and sisters into battle to take back our lands, and you threaten me with matters of *money*? Get out of my sight!"

Alcat was ready to protest, but Orlen had lost his composure. He yanked a knife from a chunk of meat in front of him and flicked it toward Alcat. The knife flew straight past his cheek with deadly accuracy; had its trajectory carried it several centimeters to the left, the knife would have pierced Alcat's left ear. Though unharmed, Alcat staggered backwards in surprise, almost tripping over his own cloak. The expression on his face caused Shira and Lebb to laugh loudly, while the others paid little attention.

He opened his mouth once again to speak but thought better of it and skulked off. Orlen stared after him with narrowed eyes as he limped away.

• • •

The five-story central fortress of Solterra-Volek stood on the eastern shore of Lake Navrek. Once the largest town east of the Great River, it had evolved into a large military complex, sufficient in size and sustenance to house over thirty percent of the Amelaren Army on a full-time basis. At the beginning of 987, it stood at nearly full capacity. Over the better part of two decades, the deployment of most warriors had been unnecessary, but the Amelaren war machine was preparing to awaken from its slumber.

The war room was located on the top floor of the fortress. As with the other rooms in the fortress, it was unremarkable in appearance, favoring utility over aestheticism. The ceiling stretched upward nearly twelve meters, while torches lined the walls, shaped from coarse, pallid ivean stone. Built into the back wall, directly opposite the entrance, was a fireplace, where a strong flame provided respite from the harsh winter weather during the later cycles of the year.

Orlen and his war chiefs sat in nine identical smooth, dark gray stone chairs around the circular table in the center of the room. The seating arrangement was as it had been the previous night. Orlen sat in the chair facing the door, with his back to the fire. Shira, Sol, Lebb, and Yura sat to his right in order. Zefrid sat opposite Orlen beside Xanos, Izven, and Tallen.

Helistos's sunlight reflected off Orlen's bald head, as it poured in from the three windows on the eastern wall. The warlord's expression was relaxed, as he pensively stroked his blond beard. The other war chiefs waited five reps for him to speak before he finally broke the silence.

"I expect the Coranthians to waste little time in launching an offense against our most obvious target. Tallen, you and the feigren will head to Ertel. There, you shall find a suitable opportunity to test her mettle in combat."

He ceased to stroke his beard before continuing. "Lure the enemy eastward and annihilate them!"

Tallen nodded hesitantly. Although only thirty-six, he no longer possessed a youthful mien. His face, while smooth and handsome, was tan, contrasting the streaks of gray and white swerving through his blond hair. In the early morning light, he appeared at once both wizened and ageless.

Across the table, Lebb was displeased with Orlen's orders and did a poor job hiding his disappointment. Everyone knew he preferred to fight alongside Tallen and was most effective in that capacity. Lebb himself itched to take point in the opening battles of the coming war and had trouble believing that the warlord would designate a young girl to play such a crucial role in the first battle.

"I trust that Tallen will manage to keep things under control," Orlen said, his voice even as he addressed the war chiefs once again as a whole. "I want the rest of you to ready your men for combat. We will not make the mistake of underestimating the enemy, as the Coranthians are sure to do to us. Which brings me to what I'm sure has been on everyone's minds: Aldova."

The name may well have been the sound of rusted iron scraping glass. Unpleasant looks were exchanged all around.

"I'm sure all of you are aware that without cutting off the head of the beast, our victory march into Corande is unlikely to occur anytime soon. I would like to ease your mind, at least momentarily. Shira, Zefrid, and I are drawing up a plan to deal with the abomination as we speak. I will inform you all of the details once it is complete."

Reactions around the table ranged from curiosity to skepticism. Orlen had no desire to say more at the moment. He motioned for the warlords to take their leave as he raised his hand. "You are dismissed."

The war chiefs immediately rose from their seats and began to file out of the room. Zefrid, the oldest of the war chiefs, remained behind to speak privately with Orlen. He was easily distinguishable from the others, favoring a worn tanned-hide robe to the heavy leather garbs donned by the other male war chiefs. He looked well beyond his years, and if he had ever seen battle, it was no longer apparent in his physique; his atrophied frame stood in stark contrast to other members of the War Council.

Orlen lifted a clay jug of poec mead from under the table and took a hearty swig. He offered some to Zefrid, who politely refused as he stared at Orlen through sunken eyes.

"How is she coming along?" Orlen asked the slouching old man.

"Her mental state can be a bit erratic at times," Zefrid said in a gravelly voice, "but I am confident she will make a worthy addition to your ranks." He cocked his head awkwardly to the side. "The results from the upcoming battle will speak for themselves."

Thoroughly enjoying his drink, Orlen wiped his mouth. "Good. I assume there is a reason you stayed behind?"

"There is. I wish to ask whether you have sensed any hesitation among the war chiefs regarding the onset of this war."

"Why would there be?" Orlen asked, somewhat affronted.

Zefrid cocked his head again. "Sacrificing Argiset will not sit well with some of the others. They will feel it opposes our warrior's code."

"They may feel that way," Orlen rubbed his cheek, "but our strength alone is no longer enough to overcome our enemy. At the very least, they must understand this."

"I agree, Warlord."

"And I'll not be obligated to answer to Ilarud or any of the rotting corpses in Malegar."

Orlen picked up the jug again and downed the remainder of its contents.

"You may leave now."

Zefrid nodded, then bowed deeply. He turned, slinked to the door, pulled it open with considerable effort, and exited, leaving Orlen alone in the war room.

Chapter 2

(987.1.33)

—1—

Upon his ascendancy, King Samsen immediately established an annual Coranthian celebratory tradition for all military academy graduates of noble birth. The young men and women were invited to galas throughout Inner Coranthia to celebrate their initiation into the proud ranks of the Coranthian Army. Over the past five years, the Corande Post maintained that a "concerted effort" was made to extend the practice to accommodate Outlander graduates. The most successful instantiation of this was the Cadets' Banquet, an event held for newly graduated unestated avets every year during the First Exile, at Stannis Manor in Corande. The venue was famed throughout the country as the original home of Creon Coranthis during his tenure as the magistrate of Corande, when the Coranthian capital was merely a remote Lynderan outpost on the banks of the Sarigan River.

Reznik Sylvera and Madeline Agilda strolled down one of the main streets in Audliné, the oldest and most populous district of the capital, where the two were merely a pair of faces among an assorted gallery of those making their way to the manor. The atmosphere along the road was especially vibrant. The more patriotic Audliné denizens popped in and out of their residences and establishments waving and hollering at the passing avets. These included many merchants and tradesmen, some of whom boldly solicited the avets with hand-out advertisement flyers for various shops and eateries within the district. Several military officials also took part in the procession, although they did not return the onlookers' good cheer. Unlike the fresh-faced graduates, they were forced to endure this event year after year at the behest of their superiors, and their well of enthusiasm had long since run dry.

Eighteen-year-olds Reznik and Madeline bore aged reflections of their childhood selves. Both wore their formal military uniforms: slacks, brown boots, white undershirt, and navy blue jackets with bronze trim. Matching bronze buttons on the jacket and small bronze pins in the shape of the royal crest affixed near the collars completed the ensemble. Reznik's blond mane was slicked back, while Madeline's cherry hair flowed just past her shoulders.

"How long do you think we'll have to stay?" Reznik complained, not for the first time that day. "You know I don't—"

"Will you stop already?" Madeline interjected. "We won't have to talk to the stiffs, as far as I know."

"I didn't think that such formalities were expected of an Outlander," Reznik said dourly.

Madeline punched him lightly on the shoulder.

"Oh, come on. We're all in the same boat. Try to enjoy yourself."

They approached the white stone wall, which enclosed the old manor, and they passed through the tall iron gate. The manor dwarfed anything that Reznik and Madeline had encountered in Jardis, though they had grown accustomed to more palatial architecture during their tenure at Tellisburg, and this old building failed to impress. It sported many over-sized windows and excessive lighting, as if compensating for the otherwise lack of grandeur projected by the actual structure. In terms of housing attributed to a high-ranking noble, it was utterly underwhelming. This was no surprise to anyone with basic knowledge of bureaucratic apportionment. The manor was now administered by the interior ministry, rather than by any specific lord.

Noise poured out the open front door of the manor as Reznik and Madeline walked past the arrays of bright white flower buds in the front gardens, lining the path to the entrance. A herald stood in the doorway, listening to a young woman with sandy hair and wearing thin, silver-rimmed spectacles. She was as tall as Madeline and wore a long velvet dress. As a military official approached, she stopped talking and retreated further into the main foyer.

A tall, gaunt herald raised his eyebrows in deference and smiled broadly as he greeted the official, matching his name to the guest list in his hands. Under normal circumstances, he would turn and announce arriving guests, but tonight he was merely acting as a gatekeeper. He motioned for the official to move past him and enter the main foyer, where the party was getting under way.

Spotting Reznik and Madeline, the herald immediately turned up his nose, staring down at them and clearing his throat haughtily. "Names, please?" he said in an unnecessarily loud voice.

Reznik narrowed his eyes. Madeline wrinkled her slender nose at him and then said to the herald, "Avets Agilda and Sylvera."

The herald casually ran his eyes over his list and wrinkled his nose. "Yes, avets Agilda and Sylvera. Go ahead."

He stepped stiffly aside. Without giving him another look, Reznik glided past him and into the foyer. Madeline gave the herald a quick, exasperated nod and followed.

A sea of uniforms swallowed the two as they entered. A look of perplexity fell over Reznik's face as he realized the party was far livelier than he had expected. Those on the floor were primarily graduates, although a few older men and women in uniform—veteran soldiers who had been invited to mingle with the new soldiers—were also present.

A group of estated bureaucrats from all the major cities of Coranthia sat around a long rectangular table set some distance behind the edge of an ornate wooden balcony overlooking the foyer. They were in the company of a small coterie of other noblemen and noblewomen invited by Minister Verinda to dilute the overwhelming ratio of commoners to nobles, and they had decided that there were worse ways to spend the evening than being treated to food and drink. To the right of the nobles' table, the military officials sat around their own table. They attended on behalf of the defense ministry. From their expressions, it was apparent that they found it difficult to enjoy the proceedings. A group of musicians sat in the corner of the balcony canvasing the air with a light background melody of nondescript ensemble pieces.

There were two large open doorways, one to the east, and the other at the rear of the foyer, leading to a ballroom, where a much larger crowd of soldiers mingled. A large stairway adjacent to the eastern doorway led to the second floor and the overhanging balcony. Finally, a smaller door on the west led to a more conventionally sized living room. Madeline peered into this room and pointed. "I see some of our classmates. Shall we go say hello?"

Reznik pressed his lips together with a clear lack of enthusiasm.

"I'd rather not. I'll just stay here."

She shrugged, having expected as much from him. She made no further attempt to coax him as she waded into the crowd.

"Try to have some fun, won't you?" she called over her shoulder.

Reznik watched as she disappeared into the living room. He looked around in disinterest. Although the party had just commenced, the veil of decorum had already begun to erode. As Reznik wandered aimlessly through the crowd, he noticed that quite a few avets were already drunk and others were equally intoxicated from the excitement of the atmosphere. He overheard various measures of frivolity and vulgarity in conversation and was loath to involve himself in the bawdy revelry.

His attention drifted to the overhanging balcony upstairs. It was an expanse at the top of the stairway within the foyer, forking into two hallways. A chest-high sheet of metal fencing spread across the top of the stairs, emphatically separating the social elites and officials from the ruckus below. Some of other privileged guests lounging upstairs stood and were shuffling listlessly. The nobles spoke to one another predominantly in Laestran, using their native Coranthian only for emphasis. Over the past century, Laestran had become the pervasive international common language. In recent decades, the nobility readily adopted it as a prestige dialect, perceiving it to be a mark of distinction that more clearly separated them from the lower classes. Although many merchants and craftsmen in major Coranthian cities were also fluent in Laestran, they used it only to conduct business with foreigners.

Three noblemen walked up to the railing and surveyed the crowd below. Two other women joined them, one wearing an opera mask, as if attending a performance, and the other carrying a sparkling glass of champagne. The noblemen promptly sprung forth a calculated stream of ridicule, each trying to outdo his companions in coming up with the most degrading remarks as possible about the party-going commoners, whispering them into the ears of the women and finding haughty fulfillment in their giggles of approval.

This went on for some time. Reznik lost interest and turned his attention to the living room. It was too crowded for him to make his way there without pushing through a cluster of avets. Standing on tiptoes, he conducted a cursory examination of the people in the living room, looking for Madeline, when he heard a voice to his left.

"And how are you doing tonight, madam?"

A sinewy, carnivorous-looking avet whom Reznik did not recognize craned his neck upward, projecting his voice to the women standing on the balcony above him. He was distinctly unshaven and his teeth spread in a crooked grin. His eyes were wild with impudence and the enabling effects of the ale in his hand.

"You certainly look ravishing tonight!"

The masked lady emitted a loud gasp too drawn out to indicate reflexive shock or outrage; the attention had piqued her interest and she baited for more.

"Hold your tongue, you filth!" one of the men upstairs shouted at the avet.

"Sir," the bushy avet continued, unfazed, "I don't approve of your slander. It's only fair to the ladies for us to present ourselves on our own terms. Don't you agree? Ladies, why don't you come down, and I'll show you what I'm all about!"

There was loud hooting all around him. The lady holding a flute of champagne let out a pinched scream as she retreated, while the masked lady's mouth ambiguously expressed disgust and intrigue simultaneously.

"Scoundrel!" roared the nobleman. The exchange began to attract a lot of attention. People above and below expected a momentous confrontation to break out at any moment. The men upstairs had collected at the railing and were staring down furiously at the avets. One ushered the two ladies away and out to the hallway.

The sandy-haired woman with the silver-rimmed spectacles trotted out onto the balcony and spoke quickly to the estated guests in a low voice. Suddenly, the noblemen turned away from the railing and returned to their seats at the table. Most still openly bore their anger but abandoned the encounter.

A pale bald man, wearing a pair of thick-rimmed glasses, appeared on the balcony and leaned over the railing. Reznik recognized his face, not from the first time the two had met over a decade ago, but from his more recent and intermittent visits to the academy, as was his duty as Minister of the Interior.

"Everyone, be respectful and orderly." Martin Stanton Verinda leaned over the railing and raised his arms. "Avets, I'll remind you that we are here to celebrate your deference, loyalty, and discipline as soldiers. Do you not want to leave your peers and fellow countrymen with such an affirmation?"

Reznik was unsurprised to see Verinda's prompt attempt to defuse the situation. A native of Kantor and approaching his sixtieth birthday, the minister had a well-earned reputation for expertly exercising diplomacy between commoners and nobles from his years of traversal throughout the country. This time, however, he was met with several derisive jeers from the audience below.

"It's our party," the bushy avet hollered, walking to the bottom of the stairs and planting one foot on the bottom step. "Let us have our fun!"

The sandy-haired woman marched down the stairs directly toward him.

"And who are you, darling?" he uttered with an unsavory grin.

"I am Minister Verinda's secretary, Asuna Lierra," she replied without blinking or slowing her pace. She descended the remaining steps and stood over the avet, glaring at him down the bridge of her nose through her glasses.

The avet's smile faltered; he seemed unsure of what to do.

"Well?" Lierra challenged. "You asked me to come down. Here I am."

He laughed uneasily. "Are you joking, missy?"

In response, Lierra put a hand on her hip while turning her left knee inward, exposing her leg tauntingly through the slit on the side of her dress.

"Here I am," she repeated. "What are you going to do about it, *boy?*"

The avet's smile disappeared. He backed away from the stairs, his face twisting uncomfortably. Beads of sweat oozed from his forehead.

"I thought so," Lierra said, enunciating so all could hear her. "Now conduct yourselves properly as Coranthian soldiers!"

The bushy avet shrugged, downed the rest of his drink and wobbled away in a haze of muted embarrassment. The secretary watched his stumbling retreat before she turned and made her way back up the stairs.

Reznik felt it neither wise nor desirable to remain among such crass company. He snaked through the crowd and entered the living room. Madeline was nowhere to be found. He walked over to the bar, planted himself on a stool, and ordered a cider from the bartender. The disgust he felt showed plainly on his face.

He sat alone at the bar in the living room for some time, nursing his cider. He lost track of the reps as he ignored the group of avets chatting behind him. Most of the furniture had been cleared to accommodate more people, with the exception of a pine-green embroidered couch and matching chairs placed at the western end of the room. This gave Reznik a clear view as he remained on the lookout for Madeline, but he still did not see her. Eventually, he got off his stool, abandoning his unfinished cider on the counter, and headed for the front door.

The foyer remained crowded but was not nearly as packed as when he had first arrived; most of the guests had moved into the ballroom. The mood among the remaining guests had lightened considerably; people carried on as if nothing had happened earlier. Reznik's eyes drifted around the room. It was then that he saw Madeline chatting with Lierra.

"Of course," he murmured to himself.

Curious to hear their conversation, he maneuvered through the crowd and tried to position himself as close to the pair as possible without alerting them to his presence.

"You put on quite a show earlier," he heard Madeline say with a mixture of amusement and admiration in her voice.

Lierra adjusted her glasses. "I'm disappointed in myself. This is the final event I will be planning as Lord Verinda's secretary. I had hoped to avoid any such inconveniences."

"Are you taking another job? There aren't really any better than the one you have now, are there, Miss Lierra?"

Lierra smiled warmly. "Please call me Asuna, and you're quite right, Madeline. For most people, it'd be unthinkable to move on to my new position from this one. I will be serving as the secretary for Magistrate Euliora of Calena."

Reznik could stay quiet no longer.

"That makes no sense to me. Why in Creon's name would you do that?" he blurted out, walking up to the two women from where he had been eavesdropping.

"Where are your manners?" Madeline exclaimed, frowning. Her green eyes bore down on Reznik.

He ignored her and walked up to Lierra.

"Sorry. My name is Reznik Sylvera. I am a classmate of Madeline's. Where are you from, if you don't mind my asking?"

Lierra offered him an interested half-smile.

"I don't mind at all. I'm from Calena. Does that make a little more sense, Avet Sylvera?"

Reznik narrowed his eyes, having noticed the fact that she chose not to address him as informally as she did Madeline and also that her response provided no clue as to the source of her unusual name, although her features were as Coranthian as those of anyone else in the room.

"Marginally, Miss Lierra," he replied. "I still don't see why you would demote yourself when you are already situated in the capital and working for the Cabinet."

Before Lierra could reply, someone called from behind Reznik. "There you are!"

He recognized the voice instantly. He turned to see Renard Renault, tanned and short-haired, breaking away from a crowd of late newcomers and pushing his way toward them.

Although Renard wore his uniform like his fellow graduates, his trim, buttons, and pin were silver, indicating his rank of vice captain. He had also chosen to embellish his outfit, as was his typical fashion, by wearing a white tunic with a puffed-up collar underneath his jacket and a dark blue cloak with generous silver embroidery over it.

"I like the outfit, Renard," Madeline said.

Turning to her, Renard gave a deep bow, bending almost to his knees.

"Maddy," he exhaled as he reverted upright and wagged a finger at Reznik, "has this useless fellow told you how wonderful you look tonight?"

"Renard, you ..." Madeline grinned. "Try not to break too many hearts tonight, will you?"

Renard laughed and clapped Reznik on the back, then extended his arm, exaggeratedly motioning toward the proceedings. "I'm sure you find all of this insufferable, Rez."

"Yes, and after your arrival, I must say I feel exactly as I did before."

"Bah, you're no fun! This is a party!" Renard pronounced cheerfully, glancing around. "What are we waiting for? I've got some catching up to do! Where are Glen and Douglas?"

"They couldn't make it," Reznik said. "They're already on their way to Aldova."

"What? What's the rush?"

Reznik shrugged. "I don't know. I'm not sure they knew before they headed out. But those were the orders."

"Is that so? I guess they wouldn't be much up for this anyway, even less than you are." Renard elbowed Reznik. "Come on, let's grab a drink."

Reznik glanced at Madeline and noticed that Asuna Lierra's attention was still on him and Madeline, despite Renard's flamboyant entrance.

"You boys have fun. I'll find you later." Madeline waved her hand and turned back to Lierra.

Reznik shrugged and allowed Renard to pull him back toward the bar.

—2—

The party carried on well into the night. The swarm of avets inside the manor gradually became more segregated, with most of the Tellisburg graduates occupying the ballroom, while those from Kendrall and Barrington remained in the foyer. Shortly after nine arc, some of the defense ministry officials approached Verinda, fervently thanking him with insincerity for inviting them to participate in such merrymaking before excusing themselves, stumbling in each other's way to leave, despite Verinda's appeal for them to stay. The noblemen continued to drink and idle upstairs on the balcony. The noblewomen had descended by means of an unseen stairway from the second floor into a parlor beyond the living room. Those in the living room could see the noblewomen through the edges of the door to the parlor, but the avets gathered in the living room were not the type to engage in foolhardiness and knew better than to disturb them.

Renard had spent some time with Reznik at the bar before moving to the couch, across the room, where the two matched each other, glass for glass, with a pilfered bottle of wine. Renard discussed his newly established lounge in Kantor—his own entrepreneurial foray into Kantorian nightlife, as he liked to call it—and incessantly implored Reznik to visit the establishment before finally forcing him to promise to do so in the near future. Several reps later, Renard returned to the bar, where he procured a glass of pontaerno, a cocktail of pontamelon juice and rum. Noticing light under the door to the parlor, he walked over and gently cracked it open. Peeking inside and listening to the noblewomen prattle to each other, he smiled to himself. He turned around and walked back to where Reznik still sat on the couch.

"Well, I'm off to save some beautiful ladies from the emptiness of their own conversation." He flapped his hand in the direction of the parlor with a mischievous grin.

Reznik shook his head. "Can't you ever give it a rest?"

"Why pass up a chance to have some fun? I assure you, they're as bored as we are."

When Reznik offered a knowing eye-roll, Renard shrugged and laughed good-naturedly.

"See you later, Rez."

Still holding his glass of pontaerno, Renard strutted up to the parlor door and slipped into the room nonchalantly.

"Ladies!" Reznik heard him say as he closed the door behind him.

Remaining where he was, Reznik began to feel a mixture of boredom and fatigue from the drinks he had with Renard and found himself nodding off. At some point, he closed his eyes. He was unsure how long he remained that way until a voice snapped him to attention.

"Avet Sylvera?"

Asuna Lierra sat across from him in a smaller leather chair, her hands folded neatly across her lap, occasionally moving to smooth the wrinkles of her dress.

"Look at you," Madeline remarked with amusement. Reznik started; she was sitting right next to him, but he had not seen her, having sunken into the couch, slightly slumped over. He quickly sat up straight.

"Where's Renard?" he asked.

"You should know better than to ask that," Madeline replied, "because I have no idea. He's up to his usual no good, I'm sure. Asuna here would like to pick up where we left off."

The piercing gaze of Lierra's brown eyes, her faint smile, her professional but striking profile, and the tone of her voice, which relayed no trace of reproach, despite Reznik's confrontational words earlier, made him somewhat uncomfortable and embarrassed.

"Miss Lierra, I apologize for my earlier brashness," he muttered.

Her smile grew slightly wider.

"That's quite all right. As you may have realized, I am rather interested in hearing your thoughts. I'd like you to offer them after I respond to your previous statement."

Reznik nodded. "Certainly."

"I care about my home, Avet Sylvera. I want to serve where I am most motivated. There is no doubt in my mind that I can do more in Calena than here in Corande. The experience I've acquired working for the ministry will be put to good use."

"I disagree," Reznik replied. "For an unestated to hold such a position in the Cabinet is no insignificant feat. Were you not resented by your estated colleagues?"

"Whether or not I was is irrelevant," Lierra said, adjusting her silver-rimmed glasses. "If you're implying that unpleasant treatment from others affects me, you need not worry."

"Actually, my point is that not taking advantage of every opportunity to be represented at the highest level of government is detrimental to all Coranthian commoners. Serving your hometown is certainly a commendable sentiment, but I find it ultimately short-sighted."

Madeline sat silently, content to watch the exchange.

Lierra's smile wavered. Her eyes drifted toward the doorway leading back to the foyer.

"By the way, how rude of me. I've already expressed this to Avet Agilda, but allow me to congratulate you on your graduation from Tellisburg."

Reznik was caught off guard.

"Thank you. Did she tell you that we attended Tellisburg?"

He glanced at Madeline, who shook her head.

"Asuna planned this banquet," she said. "She was in charge of the guest list. It's no surprise that she knows a bit about each of the attendees. When I introduced myself to her, she already knew who I was."

Reznik turned back to Lierra so as not to continue speaking as if she was not present.

"Tellisburg records are fully accessible within the Cabinet," said Lierra, her smile widening again. "If you don't mind, I would like to hear your opinion on a related matter."

"Oh?" He raised an eyebrow. "Go ahead."

"You were first in your class, yet you were not named the Cadet Officer as would usually be the case because of your pedigree. Does this upset you?"

She seemed to be searching Reznik's face carefully for a reaction.

"No. Why would it? The second-ranked cadet in my class had a comparable record."

"Of course, Renard Renault, who was here earlier. Correct? Do you not mind that the second-ranked cadet in your class will be rewarded with an automatic promotion to vice captain? Is it because the two of you are friends?"

Reznik blinked and jerked his head.

"Miss Lierra," he said with annoyance, "Renard deserves to be named Cadet Officer. The difference in our leadership abilities is not something that can be judged merely from a written evaluation. I find your words to be quite presumptuous."

"Come on, Reznik," Madeline urged. "Be a little more diplomatic, will you?"

"See, this is exactly what I mean," he snapped, taking her comment in stride. "Renard wouldn't be agitated as I am now."

"Very well, Avet Sylvera. But what if, hypothetically, you were clearly head and shoulders above your entire class in all respects? What then?"

"There isn't much of a point in discussing your proposed scenario," Madeline said, frowning. "By definition, the Cadet Officer is estated. It is a moot point. Even if Renard were not our classmate, the highest-ranked would have been estated, not Reznik."

Lierra's eyes flashed.

"That's it, that's exactly it," she said in a slightly raised voice. "That is the system, whether at the academies or in the Cabinet. And as far as I've come, as much as I've been able to do as the minister's secretary … I am unestated. I've reached my ceiling. In the end, I feel that it's best to accomplish what I can with the hand I'm dealt. For me, that means going back to Calena."

Her eyes drifted again toward the door leading into the foyer.

"Do you understand now, Avet Sylvera?"

Reznik did not reply immediately. The effects of the alcohol had not yet worn off; it took him a while to assemble the thoughts into the concise, coherent statement he wished to make. Suddenly, he rose to his feet. "Miss Lierra, it is true that we unestated are at a disadvantage," he said. "But that's hardly going to stop me. I suppose this is where we differ, and this may be why I am a soldier and you are not. Good evening to you."

With that, he trotted out of the room without as much as a glance back at Lierra or even Madeline, leaving the two women staring after him.

"I'm sorry if he offended you," Madeline said. "He can be rather brusque, even when he hasn't had anything to drink."

"Worry not. It was a fascinating conversation. I'm glad you encouraged me to return to it." Lierra laughed. "It's unfortunate, though. I had a response for him, but he never gave me the chance for it."

"Oh? I'd certainly like to hear it."

Lierra's amber eyes glowed faintly.

"Though your friend may be attuned to matters of class, Madeline, it seems he has neglected the issue of gender. You may very well be unestated and go a long way in the military. As a man, of course."

"There are female captains," Madeline rejoined. "And there's certainly no policy that prevents women from reaching a higher rank."

"Very true," Lierra agreed, pausing to adjust her glasses. "But is there any room in high society for a female colonel? Or even a captain? Are you aware of how female officers are treated by nobles? Especially by noblewomen?"

"I have to admit I never gave it much thought." Madeline frowned. "I don't have any plans to integrate myself with the nobility."

Lierra smirked triumphantly.

"Well, Madeline, I suppose this is where we differ, and this may be why you are a soldier and I am not."

Several ticks passed before Madeline burst out laughing.

"You are an impressive woman, Asuna."

"And you as well, Madeline. I'm certainly glad to have made your acquaintance."

"Likewise. I should probably follow Reznik now. I believe it is almost time for Minister Velmann's speech."

Lierra offered a cryptic smile as she and Madeline stood to face each other.

"Ah, the speech. Certainly, you won't want to miss that. I will be returning upstairs as well."

"Perhaps we can meet the next time I have business in Calena," Madeline said, extending her hand.

Lierra grasped it lightly and the two of them shook.

"I would like that very much."

—3—

"Excuse me! Excuse me, one and all, if you'd please…"

Minister Verinda's voice rang from the ballroom balcony, which wrapped all the way around, unlike in the foyer. There were no stairs in the ballroom; the two floors were completely separate from one another. In contrast to the beginning of the reception, where an assortment of nobles occupied the second floor of the foyer, Verinda now stood alone overlooking the ballroom.

The foyer was almost completely empty; all the graduates had packed into the ballroom in anticipation of the speech. With the addition of the late arrivals, the ballroom was not large enough to comfortably accommodate all of the guests, and they wound up standing at the edge of the assemblage, unable to move any closer.

"Well, what's all this about?" said Renard, coming up behind them. "I thought I was conveniently too late for all the speeches. Look at us, packed in like a bunch of hogs."

Madeline turned around. "Oh, there you are. Were you really planning to miss Minister Velmann's speech?"

Renard shrugged. "Only if everyone else hadn't cleared out for it. I don't really care to hear it. We've had enough graduation speeches, don't you think?"

Having finally quieted the crowd, Verinda continued. "Unfortunately, Minister Velmann is unable to attend today to make his traditional commencement address, but I do have the pleasure of introducing a guest of honor."

A thin-faced man with heavily graying shoulder-length blond hair and a neatly trimmed, triangular beard stepped out from behind him. His pale blue eyes stared into the crowd. It was none other than the king himself, and this evening he wore a white variant of the military officer trench coat, with crimson trim.

Murmurs rippled through the crowd as Minister Verinda moved aside to cede the spotlight. Everyone in the room recognized the uniform as the one Samsen had donned during the Coronation War; those who had never seen it personally knew of it by reputation.

Many of the avets burst into fervent applause. This went on for two full reps before Samsen raised his hands, and some semblance of order returned.

"Good evening, everyone," Samsen began. "I only have a few reps to spare, so I will keep my remarks brief. I am pleased to see you all. It is always exciting to see our patriotic spirit manifest in the young men and women of this country."

The king rattled off a string of statistics marking the number of soldiers who had graduated from each academy and made note of how the estated and unestated from all over Coranthia had gathered at the manor. Scattered applause rose from different sections of the crowd as Samsen mentioned each academy.

As this preface came to an end, the king raised his head and stared across the ballroom. Madeline craned her neck to follow his gaze. Many of the nobles, who were lounging upstairs in the foyer only moments before, entered when they realized who was speaking. They spread out along the balcony directly opposite Samsen and Verinda. Surprise and curiosity overtook their previously lackadaisical countenances. For some of the men, who had heard murmurings through the rumor mill earlier that afternoon, these sentiments gradually morphed into anxiety as Samsen continued his address.

After locking eyes with several members of his new audience, the king redirected his attention to those gathered below.

"Now, I want to highlight a very specific number, and that is fifty-seven. Fifty-seven of our countrymen and women stationed at Elsin Point. Before I make this news public through the Post, I would like to inform you, my fellow soldiers, that our outpost at Elsin was ambushed. Though not a single Coranthian remains to tell the tale, the carnage the Amelarens left behind clearly states their intentions."

A stunned silence fell across the room. Samsen scanned the ranks of his new soldiers, men and women, noble and commoner, all having spent the previous two or three years preparing for a moment such as this, though none having truly expected that it would come.

The king took a deep breath and continued. "I admit that the announcement is somewhat indelicate, but I have no intention of romanticizing such a tragedy. Nevertheless, I will attempt to articulate my feelings more appropriately.

"When I learned of the attack, I was immediately reminded of the events that led to the founding of our capital and the significance of this very building we now occupy—Stannis Manor, built by my grandfather Creon, the symbol of his proud foothold on this continent of Moriana.

"As all of us well know, there was no Coranthia at the time of this manor's construction. There was barely a Corande. There was only Lynderas. And it is my firm belief, as it was that of my grandfather, that Lynderas would have fallen to the Amelarens had Creon not transformed it into Coranthia. The barbarians would have overrun the Ath'ril people before crossing the Sarigan and besieging our forts. Even Tellisburg would not have withstood a relentless flood of warriors."

Samsen paused to clear his throat. He closed his eyes briefly and took a deep breath, summoning a recitation from within his memory.

"'I was not a crusader, nor was I a reluctant revolutionary. I was left with no choice but to take up a crown. The people required it of me,' so the Founder said. And so we secured the future of our people. And so we liberated the Outlands, liberated the region from incessant war and internal conflict among the natives. We welcomed to our civilization the Ath'ril and those Amelarens wise enough to realize the futility of their former way of life. And many years later, we finally secured our eastern borders. Western Moriana is now indisputably under Coranthian control.

"But after we have enjoyed peace for almost twenty years, the Amelarens have once again descended upon us with their brutality. They are incapable of coexisting even with each other; that we are not of their barbaric ilk makes us the target of their collective savagery. They regard our civilized, prosperous existence as only a blooming field waiting to be razed.

"And so I stand before you tonight to say that your country is in great need of your bravery and heroism. Everyone in this room has known that this day would eventually come. We must ensure once and for all that the Amelaren horde poses no threat to our survival. The only way we can accomplish this is to destroy them. We must go to war."

At his words, a feverish buzz swept through the crowd. Samsen held up his hands, commanding silence.

Renard leaned over and whispered to Reznik, "I guess that's why Glen and Douglas are already on their way to Aldova."

Reznik might not have even heard his friend. He stood rooted to the spot, eyes locked onto the king, fighting uprooted emotions and memories hidden behind a frozen mask of a countenance that belied his true internal state.

Samsen forged ahead. "Warlord Orlen has once again risen to threaten our lives and lands. Perhaps it was naive to think that an Amelaren warlord would accept defeat before death. Either way, make no mistake, he faces only those two options.

"Your upcoming mission is a righteous one. No test of strength will be more symbolically appropriate. I look out at you and see the future of our country. I have been through the inferno. I have seen the suffering the Amelarens bring upon our good people firsthand. So have many of your elders and countrymen. It is imperative that all Coranthians now stand in solidarity against this threat."

Out of the corner of her eye, Madeline saw Reznik unconsciously nod his head.

Samsen reached into his left breast pocket and pulled out a Coranox pin, the only piece missing from his ensemble. It was not the typically ornate crimson royal emblem but the crisp aeron military issue held by generals. Unconsciously and out of habit, Madeline reached to touch her neck, feeling the outline of her own Coranox hanging there. It was the pin that the king had given her on that day twelve years ago. Sebastian and Edith Sylvera attached it to a stainless steel chain, and she had worn it as a necklace ever since, keeping it on her person at all times.

"I have full confidence in our united strength and resolution. We must once again draw upon Creon's spirit if we are to answer this calling, not only as a means to our security but as a duty to the greater good. It is our destiny to reign as the supreme power of Moriana. I hereby pass the torch to you, my friends, countrymen, and successors. You shall be the first surge of these inexorable waves of history!"

With that, he stepped back. The room was completely quiet for what seemed like an eternity, although less than half a rep passed on the clock.

Standing beside the king, Verinda clapped emphatically.

"For Coranthia!" he hollered.

His words sparked a frenzy below.

"For Coranthia!" echoed many of the avets. A flood of applause and a roar of approval followed.

Although they remained silent, Reznik and Madeline joined in the applause. Renard, standing behind them, merely watched the scene unfold.

The cheering and clapping persisted for several reps as Samsen observed from above. Finally, the king turned to Verinda and warmly shook his head. After raising his aeron Coranox one more time, prompting another surge of applause, he withdrew, exiting through one of the doors on the second floor and disappearing from sight.

The clamor subsided; Verinda remained where he was for a while, waving and nodding encouragingly to the soldiers below, before announcing that he would return to the foyer shortly and that the party would continue.

Slowly, the mass of avets scattered. People were once again more evenly distributed between the two rooms. Reznik and Madeline hovered around the entrance to the living room, while Renard set off once again on his own to mingle. The merrymaking resumed, although the atmosphere was more subdued overall. Eventually, Verinda reappeared on the balcony above.

"I want to thank you all again for coming," he said, calling for the attention of those in the foyer. "Despite the terrible news of the attack and the anxiety I know most of you must feel regarding the days to come, we were graced by the presence of His Majesty, who has expressed, much more assuredly and eloquently than I can, that your courage will be celebrated long after we have finally brought lasting peace to this continent. This is what you, as soldiers, have trained for. Your deployment schedules will not be affected. You will still report to your station as you were originally informed during your graduation."

"Is that all, Minister?" someone shouted. "Is that all you have to say as you send us to our deaths?"

The partygoers began to pack into the foyer again with a renewed interest, sparked by yet another unexpected outburst. Reznik and Madeline pushed their way farther into the foyer and caught a glimpse of Verinda, who was currently attempting to stare down the man who had spoiled his parlance.

A short, ruddy-cheeked young avet took several steps up the stairs to be seen by all present. Reznik recognized him as one of his Tellisburg classmates, though did not know his name.

"I urge you to temper your tone, avet," Verinda said evenly.

"Like hell I will, old man!" he cried, pointing accusingly at Verinda. "You care not at all for us unestated. So we should just go fight the king's war for you? Or is it the nobles' war?"

"Hah! You tell 'em, Faber!" a husky female voice egged him on. Several others chimed in raucously. From the sounds of their voices, it was clear that they felt empowered by the refreshments and felt confident enough to speak out against Verinda, though certainly not against the king himself.

Avet Faber stared challengingly Verinda. "Well, Minister? Will His Majesty tend to our families and sustenance while we're dying for the sake of his personal glory out in the East?"

Verinda slammed his hand on one of the upstairs tables. "For your own good, avet, I think it is necessary to stop you before you do something that cannot be undone. Guards!"

Several members of the Royal Guard emerged from behind him and scrambled down the stairs. The metal sheeting had been removed, giving the soldiers a clear path to reach Avet Faber. The avet turned to run but was tackled and brought to the floor at the base of the stairs. The people closest to the scene drew back as the young man thrashed beneath the suppressive weight of the guards.

"What? Don't I have the right to speak? I've been listening all night. It's my turn now!" Faber spat, continuing to squirm. The guards, attempting to pin Faber's arms, finally lost patience and punched the protester in the stomach.

There came angry and confused shouting from those who witnessed the assault. Several avets hovered over the soldiers, while others retreated toward the exit. The guards hauled Avet Faber to his feet and attempted to drag him up the stairs.

"Unbelievable!" Madeline exclaimed.

"Taking me away? Where are you taking me?! Let me go!" Faber hollered, continuing to fight his captors as they ascended the stairs, practically carrying him off his feet.

"The avet is doing himself a great disservice with his outrageous remarks," Verinda declared. "I trust that his views do not reflect those of anyone else here and that any other rowdiness is merely a symptom of inebriation?"

He glared piercingly at the people below as the guards made their way past him with Faber in tow.

Madeline leaned in to speak to Reznik. "Well, what do you suppose Miss Lierra thought of that?"

Reznik stared at her quizzically.

"She caught your attention, didn't she, Rez? I saw you eyeing her earlier."

"Oh, please. You went to her first. You sure didn't waste any time working on her after that initial incident."

"Is that why you were being so difficult? She is an accomplished woman and worthy of acquaintance." She stared probingly into Reznik's eyes. "Someone like that would certainly share our path were she enlisted in the military."

"She is fairly sincere, I suppose," he conceded.

"I would have thought you'd be a little more accommodating, instead of throwing down your gauntlet with such little hesitation," Madeline returned.

Reznik frowned and turned away.

"Let's go. I've had enough."

He fell into line behind several other avets heading out the front door. Madeline followed him outside.

"Wait! Leaving me behind, are you?" cried Renard.

He ran up behind them, slightly short of breath.

"Where have you been?" Madeline asked in bewilderment.

Renard laughed. "I was … introducing myself, of course. I had to get rid of a clinger."

"Renard, your utter lack of scruples is inspiring."

"From what I've heard, I may have had more fun sticking with you guys," Renard said. "What do you think, Rez?"

"I think," Reznik said slowly, "that they won't be serving alcohol here next year."

Madeline shook her head disapprovingly.

Reznik frowned. "To think someone like Faber graduated from Tellisburg. He certainly made plain his wish to have lazed through his quota."

The three stood silently for a rep. They had gathered beside the main walkway just outside the manor.

Finally, Renard said, "I guess things are going to get much more interesting."

"Yes, it seems so," Reznik agreed.

To Madeline, her companions' reaction to what had transpired less than an arc ago seemed muted. The news had only barely begun to sink in for her. She was still shaken from the king's unexpected appearance.

"I guess it'll be a while before the three of us can get together again," Renard said. "How is it that I'm the odd man out, while everyone else got paired off into companies? Just my luck."

"I'm sure you'll find plenty of new people to drag around, Renard," Reznik replied.

Renard shrugged, looking uncharacteristically nonplussed.

"Come on, I'm sure we'll see each other. We'll all be at Aldova," Madeline said, reaching out and taking his hand. Renard squeezed it gently.

"You're right," he said, rocking back and forth on his feet. "Say hello to Edith for me, Rez. Oh, and you remember what we talked about, right?"

"Yes, Renard. I'll come visit as soon as time permits," Reznik said with a smile as he extended his hand.

Renard shook it firmly, grabbing Reznik's arm with his other hand. "Until next time!"

With a wave, he set out toward the gate, walking off into the chilly night.

Chapter 3

(987.1.38–39)

—1—

Garments lay in two distinct piles atop Reznik's bed. He stood pensively for several ticks before snatching a white shirt and moving it aside. Satisfied, he shoved the entire pile into a burlap sack on the floor, making no attempt to fold the clothing before doing so. His task complete, he stretched and slowly surveyed his room, committing the image to memory. After tomorrow, it would be cycles before he returned.

A plain pinewood bed lay in the back corner of Reznik's square room. A thick wool sheet was scrunched up against the wall on the inner half of the bed. Wool was a cheap and popular commodity throughout the Outlands, providing affordable and sufficient warmth during the winter. The bed itself was well-worn and seemed ready to collapse at any moment. A small square window was carved out of the wall opposite the bed. Normally, Reznik was able to see the houses to the south of his and sometimes the village square, on an exceptionally clear day, though today, the shutters were closed to keep out the unseasonable cold. In the corner next to the window stood a dresser on which Reznik kept two stacks of books. Seeing them reminded him of something he had neglected to pack. Reznik shuffled through the books before finding *Wildlife in the Dynan Midlands*. It was a purchase he had made half a cycle ago in Tellisburg, thinking it might prove to be a handy reference. He stuffed the book hastily into his sack as he scanned the room again.

A small wooden frame stood propped up on the nightstand next to his bed. He traced his finger around its edges. Affixed within the frame was a small photograph, one of Reznik's most prized possessions. It was also one of the few indulgences he kept from his friendship with Renard; it was almost unthinkable for commoners to afford photographs, but Renard and his father Gustaf insisted upon the gift. Nobody in Jardis, aside from Edith and Madeline, knew of its existence.

It was a portrait of the Sylvera family. Reznik never tired of looking at it; seeing himself sitting between his parents reminded him of a much different life. Until now, he had carried it with him wherever he went, keeping it stashed safely in the most secretive place he could find. Only briefly did he debate whether he should bring it to Aldova before he lifted it off the nightstand and placed it carefully inside his sack, ensconcing it between layers of clothes to ensure that it would not be damaged. Finally, he exited the room. Stopping in front of his mother's room, he cocked his ear to make sure that he had not woken her and was satisfied when he heard Edith breathing slowly in a deep sleep.

A fresh scent permeated the living room. He smiled faintly as he saw a bin of bread on the dining room table and made his way to the adjacent cupboard. He had planted a small knapsack on the counter to store food for the trip to Aldova. Inside the cupboard were large glass jars of reas jerky. He laid a cloth on the table and emptied one of the jars onto it. Next to the jerky, he placed two loaves of bread from the bin. Finally, he placed exactly three cubes of keepsalt between the loaves. He tied the cloth carefully and grabbed three apples from the bowl on the counter. He placed everything neatly into his knapsack.

Just then, a loud knock came from the front door. Reznik heard a faint rustling as Edith stirred in her room.

Reznik scrambled to answer the door and pulled it open to reveal a tall, impeccably dressed man in a gray cloak. His neatly combed black hair shimmered in the fading evening sun.

The man grinned. "It is rare to see you so off your guard."

"General Hagen," Reznik said after a few ticks, before remembering to salute.

Leland Hagen waved his hand. "No need to be so formal, Reznik. I am merely your former instructor."

"Pardon me for just a moment, please."

Reznik turned and hurried back into the house. A short time later, he emerged with two wooden chairs under his arms.

"I'm sorry, sir, but my mother is sleeping. I hope you don't mind talking out here. I'll get a fire started."

"That's quite all right. There's no rush," Leland said. He stepped aside, almost tripping over the small stone sundial on the lawn.

The display of uncharacteristic clumsiness by his teacher brought a smile to Reznik's face. He walked around to the side of the house and set the two chairs beside the firepit. When he noticed Leland glancing curiously at the sundial, he asked, "Is something the matter, sir?"

Leland moved to take a seat.

"Not at all. I just don't see many dialettes these days."

"Ah, I see. Yes, they are still common out here. I'll be back with some fuel."

Reznik retreated into the house again and returned with a copper can in one hand and two piping hot mugs in the other. He poured selim tree sap from the can onto the firewood lining the pit, then lit a match and dropped it in. The smoke caused Leland's chronic cough to surface.

"Oh, I'm sorry," Reznik said, immediately setting down the mugs.

Leland recovered quickly. He picked up one of the mugs and wrapped his hands around it.

"Don't worry about it."

"I hope you don't mind mint tea, sir," Reznik said.

"Not at all. Thank you." He took a sip and cleared his throat heartily. "With whiskey! Excellent."

Reznik sat down and took the other mug, holding it in his hand without drinking. A rep of silence passed as the chilliness of the evening air settled.

"What brings you to our village, General?" Reznik asked at last, raising his head.

"As I was unable to attend the festivities the other day, I absolutely had to pay a visit before you set out, especially given such a sudden and momentous occasion." Leland let out a small sigh. "We are at war again, after all these years. The collision between our destiny and that of the Amelarens can no longer be stayed."

They sat silently for several ticks before Leland, noticing Reznik's uncomfortable expression, smiled to soften his sober tone.

"I heard I missed quite the occasion at the banquet," he said slyly.

Reznik cleared his throat and ignored the comment. "Even so, Jardis is a long way from Kantor, sir. Is there something you require of me? How did you get here?"

"Suspicious already? Is it so wrong for a teacher to give his best student a proper farewell before he is shipped off to the front?"

"I am merely your former student, sir …"

Leland chuckled approvingly before breaking into another short fit of coughing.

"I had business in Calena. I rode over on horseback. She's tied to that post on the other side of your house. I hope you don't mind."

Fanning his cloak to remove wrinkles that had formed as he sat, he leaned back in his chair. He finished his drink with a final gulp and set the cup down in the grass beside him.

"You know, watching you and your class during the war games reminded me of my own time at the academy. Though you are not of nobility, I feel that you are quite similar to how I was." Leland smiled. "It certainly seemed like we were cut from the same block of wood."

Reznik shifted uncomfortably in his chair. He placed his cup down as well, although it was still full. His gaze drifted northward behind him. In the twilight, he could make out a few scattered farms, and the northern outpost stretched before them. The fields were all empty, though the winter-proof telgas grass was still vibrantly green. The only sounds Reznik could hear were the crackle of the fire, the low hum of wellers, and the occasional barking of dogs in the distance.

"How are your parents?"

Reznik's facial expression froze.

"My father… He fell ill recently and didn't pull through. He passed away during the last onyx cycle. My mother is taking it as well as she can, but she doesn't have as much energy these days. I …"

Leland frowned. "My matters of conversation seem to be quite unpleasant today. I apologize."

"It's fine. If may be direct, General, I assume there was another reason for your visit?"

The light from the firepit was dying down. Reznik reached to grab the can of sap and then refueled the fire. The sound of the wellers rose from a low hum to a loud buzz and then subsided. Most of the villagers detested the insects, but Reznik found their sounds to be relaxing. When he looked up, Leland was staring at him, his hands folded in his lap over a sheathed knife. The Coranox was painted around the slightly curved handle in a brilliant gold.

"Yes, I have something for you," he said, holding the knife out toward Reznik. "My graduation gift to you. This isn't standard issue for swordsmen, as you know, but it should be. It will serve you ably, I'm sure."

"Sir ..." Reznik took the weapon, his eyes widening.

"Well, you know I've always believed every soldier should carry a knife," Leland said.

"Yes, but this knife was on display in your office at Tellisburg."

Leland nodded. "I figure you'd put it to better use. The knife is given as a gift to generals. I think it deserves to be more than a conversation piece in my office."

Reznik tilted the knife slightly and held it up toward Rhynon, now visible in the dusky sky. The blade glowed softly.

"Is this aeron?"

The older man laughed. "Yes, it is. No reason not to give something that is both useful and aesthetically pleasing, right?"

"Thank you very much, sir," Reznik said graciously. He carefully pocketed the knife, not before examining it again in admiration. "How did you know to find me here? I never knew you visited Jardis."

"This is my first time here. A young man was kind enough to show me the way. Albert I think his name was."

"Albert Dunning." Reznik nodded. "He must have been quite excited to meet the great General Hagen."

"Quite the contrary. He didn't recognize me." The incredulous look on Reznik's face made Leland laugh again. "Actually, it is rather refreshing. There are few things I dread more than celebrity."

Reznik said, "It is difficult to avoid when you are in the public eye. Anonymity is rare, even in the Outlands. The word always spreads in some way."

"I don't disagree with you. It is unfortunate, isn't it?"

"Worth the nuisance to you, sir." Reznik's voice rang with veneration. "Is that not the case? You have continued to serve your country since your retirement from active duty."

Leland sighed.

"You give me too much credit. Though I suppose you are right. In fact, I came to bid you farewell not only because you are heading off to the front ... I will be leaving Coranthia for a while. I plan to travel overseas and can't say when I will return, so I figured I'd stop by to see you before heading to the harbor over in Lymria."

"Where will you go?" Reznik asked.

"The Empire. You could say I have some official business there, made more urgent by our recent declaration of war. So yes, I am still active. As active as I can be, in any case. There are ways in which I can contribute off the battlefield. And contribute I must, as now we are preparing to strike Orlen down for good."

Leland began to cough again. He slowly rose from his chair, brushing the dirt from his cloak. "I'd like to return to Calena as soon as possible. Thank you for the tea."

"Why not spend the night in the guest house?" Reznik asked, getting to his feet as well. "We can call upon the elder. He'll be happy to oblige you, I'm sure."

"No need. It will be a clear night. The road will be brightly lit. Good riding conditions. I should make good time in returning to the city."

Reznik was about to reply, though was distracted by the dull but distinct clatter of hooves coming from the north.

Dane Landsman, eldest son of the stabler and a member of the village watch, rode into sight at a gallop, slowing upon his approach. Reznik and Leland looked on curiously as the stablekeeper's son dismounted his horse, neglecting even to hitch it.

"I'm glad you're here," he said sternly as he ran up to Reznik. "We have a problem."

His thick lips, normally curled in a mischievous smirk, were drawn tightly together. His green eyes shifted nervously to the north and then back to Reznik.

"What is it?"

"We're about to be raided."

"What are you talking about?" Reznik demanded.

"I was doing my rounds and when I got to the north tower, my father alerted me of around twenty bandits emerging from the Kinnan Woods."

"Who's at the northern post?" Reznik asked.

"William and Stan. And my father, of course."

"How long do we have?"

"Ten or fifteen reps, at most."

Reznik thought for a moment as Dane shifted impatiently.

"Can you go into town and alert the elder?" Reznik said. "Get Madeline too."

"I was on my way to alert the elder when I saw you. I'll go on th—"

"That won't be necessary."

Both Reznik and Dane turned to look at Leland.

"Excuse me? And who are you?" Dane said.

Reznik cleared his throat. "Dane, this is one of my former instructors from Tellisburg."

A look of skepticism washed over Dane's broad face, but he nodded politely.

"My apologies, sir. I do not recognize you in civilian clothing. I'm Dane Landsman, one of the watch here."

The general laughed. "Not a problem, Dane. Please call me Leland."

"Well, Sir Leland, do you have some sort of plan?" Dane asked.

"About twenty of them and the six of us. We should be fine. No need to disturb the townsfolk. Furthermore, you might not be able to return in time with a large group."

Leland coughed softly into his hand and then nodded and turned his attention to Reznik.

"Grab your sword from the house and meet me by my horse. We will follow young Dane here to the north post."

Both Reznik and Dane opened their mouths to respond, but Leland instantly stopped them with one word. "Go."

Reznik bolted into his house, while Dane remounted his horse as soon as he could calm it down. Meanwhile, Leland strolled around to the other side of Reznik's house, where Milla, his beautiful brown zephyr, stood calmly, sniffing the ground. Milla was large for her breed, and there would be enough room for both Leland and Reznik to ride her.

Leland unhitched Milla from a large wooden stake that jutted out of the ground near the side of Reznik's house, and he mounted his horse. Just as he was getting settled, Reznik came running around the corner of the house, carrying a short sword around his waist.

"I had to leave a note in case my mother woke," Reznik said.

Leland nodded and helped Reznik onto the horse. "I see you're still carrying that letter opener," he remarked jovially, gesturing toward Reznik's sword. He steered Milla to join Dane on the road.

"That will change once I reach Aldova," Reznik responded stiffly. "Are you sure you're all right with this, sir?"

Leland did not respond, turning instead to Dane. "Onward."

Dane nodded and the three took off at a gallop, passing several farms and the Landsman's stables on the way to the northern watchtower. The Sylveras' house was near the northern edge of the village; they had soon arrived at their destination. They were greeted by two men, one older and one younger, and a boy two years younger than Reznik.

The older man said, "Son, is this your idea of reinforcements? Reznik and … I'm sorry, who are you?"

"My name is Leland. I was visiting Reznik when Dane here stopped by and informed us of the danger. Don't be upset with him. I told him we should return here as quickly as possible."

As Leland hopped off his horse and removed his cloak, the same look of skepticism Dane had shown earlier emerged on the face of the older man.

"Well, I'm Carl Landsman, Dane's father. This boy here is Stanley Alton. You'll excuse me if we don't have time for proper introductions."

He gestured toward the freckled, scarlet-haired teen standing next to him, who nodded and said nothing.

The third watchman, sporting a lanky figure and wild mustache, stepped forward.

"I'm William Cadrene, head watchman. I appreciate the help, Mr. Leland, but we can't face twenty men on our own."

"We'll be fine," Reznik said impatiently as he turned to Leland. "Right, General?"

Leland laughed. "I should have done my best to assert that, yes. Gentlemen, my full name is Leland Hagen. Perhaps you've heard it."

Carl Landsman's eyes grew wide. He took an unconscious step back. "*The* General Hagen, here in Jardis?" He turned to William. "If he is as he says, it will be the bandits who are outmatched."

"He is and they are. We really don't have time for this," Reznik insisted.

"Indeed," Leland said. "Let us exchange pleasantries later. What is the situation?"

Dane motioned toward the watchtower. "You should go see for yourself, Mr. … General."

Much like the southern post, the northern post of Jardis consisted of a single tower, having been mostly neglected over the years; only the eastern post bore any sort of reinforcement. Leland moved swiftly toward the ladder that led up the tower, and he scrambled to the top. He went into a short coughing fit before surveying the land with a pair of binoculars that he produced from his inside coat pocket. He stayed atop the tower for only half a rep before sliding back down.

"They seem to have broken into two groups of about eight each, but the groups aren't far apart, maybe a few meters at most. I think we should go meet them. We only have the one tower here. I presume none of us is carrying a bow?"

The others shook their heads.

"Then there's not much point in waiting for them to come to us. And they won't be expecting to see us charge them."

Leland looked at the five men who stood before him. "Are you each willing to face two of them?"

"Of course," Reznik said.

William stepped forward. "With all due respect, this isn't the first time we've faced bandits, sir. And we're well-trained."

Carl and Dane murmured their agreement and nodded.

Leland glanced at Reznik. "Thanks to your parents?"

Reznik permitted himself a small smile.

Stanley Alton tried to match the confidence he saw in everyone else, but the fear on his face was plain to see.

"I will take the western group with young Stanley here," Leland said, nodding reassuringly at the boy. "I want the rest of you to handle the eastern group."

Reznik frowned. "General, are you sure about this? Your condition—"

"Don't trust me, Reznik?" Leland interrupted, grinning and flashing a set of pearly white teeth. "In any case, the bandits might slow or stop when they see that we are coming for them. If they hesitate at all, charge immediately."

"Should we not attack them on horseback?" Dane asked.

Leland shook his head. "We could, but let's not. While it would give us a chance to trample them, the bandits could just as well take down the horses while we're on them. And you don't want to put the animals at risk to begin with."

"I see," Carl said. "You raise a good point."

Everyone nodded.

Leland took several ticks to look over the five men before motioning for them to move out. "Let's go."

—2—

The six men moved through the rolling fields to the north at an even pace. As they approached within twenty meters of the bandits, they could hear shouts of confusion from the enemy. When they reached within fifteen meters, the bandits began to slow.

"Hah, look at that," Dane whispered to his father beside him. "The general was right."

"He always is," Reznik said from ahead, without turning around.

Soon, the bandits came to a stop. Reznik heard one of them shout, "What is this?"

"Probably didn't expect to see such a small group," William muttered to no one in particular.

"That's our cue," Reznik said. "Go! Pick two and try to separate them from the group. Keep your swords close, and don't let them push you to the ground."

He pointed his sword forward. The four of them charged the group of eight invaders in front of them. Before the bandits could fully comprehend what was going on, Reznik's squad was upon them. Fueled by adrenaline and anger, Reznik thrust his short sword into the gut of one of the bandits, eliciting a scream of pain from the dirty, wiry man and bringing him to his knees. Using his foot, Reznik forced the bandit to slide off his sword and then brought the hilt down hard onto the man's head, rendering him unconscious and leaving him to bleed out.

"To your right, Reznik!" he heard William shout from behind him.

Reznik pivoted his feet just in time to raise his sword and deflect a blow from a small hatchet. His block caused his attacker—a plump man with glassy eyes and a stained beard—to lose his balance. Reznik took a step back and charged into the fat man, knocking the bandit to the ground. Without hesitation, Reznik plunged his sword straight through the bandit's throat. The man grabbed at the sword and tried to remove it, but Reznik held it firmly. The bandit gasped and gurgled as blood poured from both his mouth and the hole in his throat.

Though he never felt joy in taking a man's life, unlike with the first bandit, he had no choice but to stare into this terrible death mask. While Reznik was no stranger to such violence, the sight of the man's contorted, agonized face caused him to cringe.

"Father!" Dane's voice came from behind him.

Reznik quickly yanked his sword from the dead bandit and swiveled to see Dane lying on his back, several meters away. A tall, swarthy bandit prepared to swing a full-sized ax upon him. Dane feebly held up his own short sword with his right hand, as if he stood a chance to deflect the blow. Both Carl and William were too occupied with their own battles to come to Dane's aid.

Letting loose a wild scream, Reznik dove toward his companion and rammed his sword with all his might into the tall bandit's back. The man arched his body in pain. Reznik yanked the sword free and pierced the bandit again, this time lower and closer to the spine. The man let out a wail before crumpling to the ground. The ax fell from his hand and planted itself blade-down in the ground, only centimeters from Dane's face.

Dane remained frozen on the ground, wheezing and staring bewilderedly up at Reznik.

"Thank Creon," he choked out.

"Dane!" Carl Landsman shouted as he and William ran to them.

"I'm fine, Father," Dane said, as he scrambled to his feet. "What about you?"

"We're fine," Carl said, as he wrapped his arm protectively around Dane's shoulders. "The last two bandits ran off."

William stared past Reznik and mouthed slowly, "What in the hell?"

Still trying to catch his breath, Reznik grew aware of the total silence, perturbed only by occasional fits of harsh coughing. He turned to a bizarre sight. Four or five meters away, Leland had propped himself up with his sword as he coughed harshly into his free hand. Six corpses surrounded him in what was almost a perfect circle. Nearby, Stanley Alton sat on the ground propped on his hands. The teenager gaped at the general.

"I guess another two ran off," Carl said. "Look north."

Reznik briefly diverted his gaze to see four bandits running toward the woods at breakneck speed before returning his attention to Leland. As he approached the general, he could not help but notice that the bandits had been killed with almost inhuman precision. Some of the bodies suffered several deep cuts on their weapon-wielding arms, but each had a single stab to either the neck or heart. When he knelt next to his former instructor, Reznik noticed that not a speck of blood soiled Leland's clothing. The only blood he could see was on the general's black glove, which Leland was using to cover his mouth as he coughed.

"General!" Reznik said, putting his hand gingerly on Leland's shoulder.

"I'm fine. Never better," Leland managed to say, smiling despite his wheezing and watery eyes.

"Stan?" Reznik asked, looking at the young boy.

"I'm fine too," Stanley replied meekly.

Reznik gazed upon his former instructor with both concern and reverence.

"Would it be inappropriate for me to wish I had seen you in action?" he said.

Leland smiled wryly.

William approached them slowly, his eyes wide with admiration. "General Hagen. Thank you so much, sir. I've heard stories about how good you used to be, but—"

"Used to be?" Leland's eyes twinkled.

Everyone laughed awkwardly before the six of them began to make their way back to the watchtower.

—3—

It was now well into the night. Light from the Sylveras' house radiated through the open front door. Inside, Reznik's mother, Edith, moved about the kitchen as she prepared a late dinner. Reznik had just returned from reporting the incident to the elder with William and the Landsmans. Meanwhile, Leland had met Edith and politely declined to stay for dinner.

"Sir, are you sure we can't interest you in the guest house?"

Leland smiled warmly and shook his head.

"I really must be on my way to Calena, Reznik, but I appreciate the offer. Your mother is a wonderful woman."

"Yes, she is," Reznik agreed.

"You did well out there tonight," Leland said. "I knew I was right about you."

Reznik shrugged. "If you ask me, sir, Madeline and I have an advantage over the estated cadets. Most of the others at Tellisburg didn't grow up in a place where they had to fight and kill to defend themselves."

"An advantage it may be, though not a desirable one," Leland said gravely. "Such is the way of things these days."

Reznik nodded. Silence filled the air for half a rep. "Thank you again for the help tonight, General. I'm sure we could have handled it ourselves, but you ensured that we didn't have to disturb the villagers."

"Think nothing of it. Now that I'm no longer an instructor, it's good to get some practice once in a while. Have to stay sharp, you know. It's how I'm built."

Leland began to walk around the house to where Milla remained idle. Reznik followed him. The two men shook hands before Leland unhitched and mounted his horse.

"Will I see you again, sir?" Reznik asked as they walked slowly southeast.

"Oh, I'll be back," Leland said with a smile. "Count on it."

He cleared his throat and turned the horse to face Reznik directly. "Good luck out on the battlefield. I know you'll do our country proud."

Without another word, Leland snapped around and took off, galloping down the road.

—4—

Edith Sylvera sat across from her son, watching calmly as he downed a thick bowl of pork stew.

"I was rather surprised to wake up yesterday and see your note."

Reznik nodded. "I didn't want to worry you. Besides, General Hagen was with me."

"I see now why his name is held in such regard," Edith said. "He has lived up to his reputation. Not only from your account but how he handled himself when he visited us."

"Yes, I've said as much many times."

Edith watched her son eat with amusement, noting the nonchalance with which he spoke of such a revered man. After a rep had passed, she decided to change the subject and quipped, "Well, who knows when you'll get to eat like this again."

"Probably not for a while," Reznik replied between mouthfuls.

Edith began pacing, her eyes inspecting Reznik's luggage. His two sacks, bulging amorphously at the seams, lay on the floor, one slung haphazardly on top of the other.

"Why was I never able to get you to be tidy?" she wondered aloud. "You're a hopeless mess."

A soft knock came at the front door. Before answering it, Edith quickly tied back her disheveled hair, which she wore long as she progressed through middle age, and it was now a much brighter shade of brown. Madeline had arrived punctually and carried only one large knapsack in which she had encased all of her necessities. She wore a plain black cloak that would have been too big for her had it not been cut down to fit. It took Edith a moment to realize that the cloak was Harrison's; she had not seen it for many years.

"Morning," Madeline said brightly, with a polite but hesitant smile.

Beaming, Edith all but dragged her into the house.

"Look at this, Reznik. See? Nothing bloated, nothing to lug around, nothing she needs to keep tabs on during the caravan ride. Now how could you possibly need as much junk as you do?"

Reznik sighed. Having emptied his bowl, he moved to where his bags lay and began tying the drawstrings closed with great deliberation.

"Rez," Madeline said, "we still have to make our rounds. I told you I'd be here at three arc. Can't you hurry it up?"

"All right, I'm ready," Reznik said after several ticks. He gave one final pull on the string and stood.

"Forgive him, Maddy," Edith said with a smile. "He was up rather late last night. He has quite a story to share."

She grabbed her son by the shoulders. Tears welled in the corners of her eyes as she fussed with his collar.

"Mother ..." Reznik took her hand and gently pulled it away.

"Your father would be so proud of you, as I am," Edith said, a tremor in her voice. "I ... We will both be with you always. Promise me that you'll stay safe."

Reznik nodded.

Edith grabbed Madeline's hands. "Madeline, I only wish I could have done more for you."

Madeline felt a lump in her throat and began to tear up as well, but she fought the urge to cry. She shook her head and said, "You've done more than enough. The elder may have put a roof over my head for all those years, but my debt to your family can also never be repaid."

"You are family." Edith embraced Madeline tightly. The two women remained locked together for a moment.

"Do be mindful of your health while we are away," Reznik said after his mother had released Madeline.

"Of course."

"Say hello to Renard for me, if you see him." Edith walked to the door.

"We will," Madeline said, glancing at Reznik. "We'll be going now."

The young woman exited quickly, as Edith held the door for her. Reznik snatched up his bags and followed her, but when he reached the door, he dropped them and stooped to give Edith a kiss on the forehead. "Take care, Mother."

"I will. See you soon."

Again hoisting his bags, Reznik left the house. Madeline stared back at him from outside, motioning for him to follow. The two avets walked twenty paces before they turned around simultaneously. Edith watched them from the doorway. Madeline smiled and waved. Edith nodded in acknowledgment, made a shooing motion with her hand, which surprised neither of them, and slammed the door.

Reznik and Madeline made their way to the resting grounds—the small cemetery for the people of Jardis—a large fenced-in expanse of open land, northwest of the village square. With Helistos shining brightly above them, they wove through the headstones before coming to a large one, made of marble, straddling two burial plots and casting a long, forlorn shadow in the morning light. It stood out from the stones around it, and not only in size; Renard's father, Gustaf, had personally commissioned it, as he had commissioned Sebastian Sylvera's smaller and less ornate headstone as well, which was several plots away. Sebastian's gravesite, the dirt still fresh, having been preserved through the previous winter, was still an unfamiliar sight to the two.

Madeline stood for a long time, losing track of the reps, as she stared fixedly at the epitaph.

HARRISON & MAYA AGILDA
945.1.22–975.6.41
947.5.12–975.6.41
Beloved father and mother,
Son and daughter,
Neighbors and friends.
Cast into the sea together;
Graced with peaceful rest before rebirth.

Her eyes drifted slowly to a small tarnished piece of metal affixed to the stone below the epitaph. Gustaf Renault had been able to restore some of the shine to Harrison's locket and worked it into the stone's design.

They silently stood shoulder to shoulder. Each seemed to be waiting for the other to leave first. Finally, Madeline stirred and walked away and Reznik followed. They walked in silence toward the square as they passed the ruins of the old storehouse, which had not yet faded completely into the overgrowth. Out of habit, Madeline's gaze shifted to the mound of grass and debris. For her, it served as a constant reminder of how her life had changed that day over eleven years ago.

As the pair walked down the main road to the square, Reznik told Madeline of the events that transpired the previous night.

"I'm sorry the general didn't have time to stop and see you," he finished. "We were obviously occupied, and he seemed to be in a hurry."

Wide-eyed, Madeline said, "After such a story, you really think what I'd care most about is seeing the general?"

Reznik shrugged.

"Six men by himself? Maybe when he was younger … but now? I can't believe it."

"I can't either. Stan was the only person to witness it, I suppose, and even he was in disbelief."

Madeline shook her head. "I wish I had been there."

Reznik put his hand on her shoulder. "Sorry, we didn't have time to get you."

As they entered the village square and approached the elder's house, she pointed at his bags and asked, "What did you pack?"

"You wanted me to take care of the provisions, so I did," Reznik said matter-of-factly. "We have probably ten days' worth. More than enough for the caravan ride."

Elder Potts sat hunched over, in an old wooden rocker outside his house. Almost seventy years old and with deep wrinkles lining his face and spotty skin, he rarely strayed far from the square and appealed to the younger men and women of Jardis to handle whatever was required at the ends of the village. He was slow to move, though still alert and of sound mind.

He noticed the young avets approaching from afar. As they drew closer, he pronounced, "Ah, so it's time!"

The elder made no attempt to rise from the rocker.

Madeline said, "We already look forward to coming back, Elder."

"The two of you have done much already," the elder said, clasping his hands together. "I am sure you will make us all proud."

Madeline stepped up to him and placed her hands on top of his.

"We won't let you down, Elder," said Reznik.

"That much is clear from last night," Potts said. "Nor will we disappoint you. We'll manage without you, so there is no need to worry. William might not be as skilled as either of you, but he'll do a fine job."

"Yes," Madeline said. "And we know that Jardis will be safe in your care, as always."

She paused for a moment.

The elder waited patiently.

"Thank you. For everything."

"There's no need for that. I was blessed to be able to look after you all these years." The elder unwrapped her hands. "You still have to inspect the stockpile, don't you? Go on, get going."

Reznik and Madeline bade him farewell and continued onward. Soon, they could see the eastern outpost in the distance. It now consisted of two watchtowers connected by a bridge, instead of just one. Nearby was a wooden gate without any surrounding walls. Technically speaking, it was less a gate and more a waypoint for traveling caravans. Several years ago, the elder had imposed a more organized method of regulating travel to and from Jardis, enforced by the villagers and sentries. On the other side of the outpost stood a small shed, which had been hastily built after the destruction of the storehouse. The large shack that formerly housed the weapons stockpile had been converted to use for general storage, and all of the arms had been moved to this new shed where Reznik and Madeline were headed.

They were intercepted by William Cadrene and his small, white dog, Telly. Telly was one of several thenson in Jardis; the village used them as herding dogs to help with the management of its livestock.

"Good day, avets!" William said cheerfully.

Telly barked in greeting.

"How are you today, William?" Reznik asked.

"Well, I'm doing just fine, just fine. A bit sore from last night. Sometimes I wish I was still an unassuming goatherd."

"Give yourself more credit," Madeline said.

"Not too much more," William said with a laugh. "You missed a lot of excitement last night, Madeline."

"I heard. Everything worked out, didn't it?"

"Indeed, indeed."

William pointed toward the gates, where two wagons were parked. Two Jardisian militiamen chatted fervently with the drivers, offloading several nondescript wooden crates. Steps away, a group of commoners prepared to board the rear wagon. "They're leaving within the half arc. I suppose you don't want to be stuck here for another two days?"

"No, we wouldn't want that," Madeline agreed.

"Don't worry. We aren't letting them leave without you on board."

"Much appreciated, William," she said.

Telly whimpered. Madeline reached down to pet the dog.

"Did the shipment come in on time?" Reznik jerked his head in the direction of the shed.

"Arrived an arc after we reported to the elder," William confirmed, drawing a rusty key from his pocket. "I already checked it, but I know the elder wants your final word." He chuckled and moved to open the door. Light spilled into the shed, revealing a disarrayed collection of spears, rod-torches, and canisters of selim sap. Lying in the somewhat less cluttered central area were two large crates with blue streaks painted on their sides.

"Let me take your bags," William offered, eyeing their effects with amusement. "I'll load the caravan and stall the drivers. Then you can be right on your way, once you finish here."

"Thank you very much for your help," Reznik said, plopping his sacks down on the wooden floor. Madeline removed the knapsack from around her shoulder and handed it to William, thanking him as well.

William strapped Madeline's knapsack to his back and fumbled with Reznik's bags for a moment before finally snatching them with both hands. He marched out of the shed, arched over backwards, proceeding toward the gate with Telly at his heels, leaving Reznik and Madeline to inspect the weapons shipment.

Working quickly, Reznik and Madeline unlatched and opened each crate. Inside both was a stash of ten Noyle-grade crossbows, undoubtedly scrapped from military storage. The two thoroughly examined the caches and found that they were heavily worn but completely functional.

"Of course. We get whatever they throw out," Reznik muttered. "These things must be at least twenty years old. Older than we are."

"This will still help a lot, Rez," Madeline said firmly. "Longbows wouldn't be usable anyway. Our people might even find these easier to handle than spears." She frowned as she rechecked each crossbow in her crate, aiming down the small iron ring sight and recalibrating the springs.

Reznik watched as she worked. "They're fine. They all work."

When Madeline did not cease laboring, he sighed. "We don't have time to obsess over them. William can handle the rest. Carl, too."

He made sure the crossbows in his crate were securely nestled and dropped the lid, creating a loud bang, which caused her to start and look up as she fastened the latch.

"I know," she said. "I guess I'm a bit on edge." Having secured her crate, she clapped her hands together, dusting them off.

"No reason not to be. We'll be on the front lines and facing our first real battle before we know it."

Madeline's eyes widened. "You sure know how to comfort a girl."

"Sorry," Reznik said.

"It's a shame that Glen and Douglas aren't in our company. A couple of friendly faces would certainly ease my mind."

"Don't worry," Reznik said, hesitating slightly before adding, "you have me, don't you?"

Madeline smiled. "That's better. Come on, let's go."

She adjusted her father's cloak and exited the shed. Wordlessly, Reznik took one more look around before following her.

The two picked up their pace as they saw William wave from the gates. As they drew closer, they made out several other familiar faces, ones Reznik and Madeline had known their whole lives.

"Reznik! Madeline!" cried scarlet-haired Karen Alton, Stanley's older sister and daughter of John and Mary Alton. "You didn't think you could sneak away without saying goodbye to us, did you?"

"We were hoping to do just that," Reznik deadpanned.

"How terrible," Karen pouted, putting her hands on her curvy hips, but her face lit up as Madeline grabbed her by the shoulders and pulled her in for a hug.

"I heard my little brother was rather useless last night," she said to Reznik.

He shook his head. "He's still really young, and he didn't lose his head. I'm sure he'll make a fine addition to the watch."

Karen smirked at him, then decided to wrap Madeline in another embrace.

"How is the equipment?" William asked Reznik.

"Good," Reznik replied. "We'll leave it in your hands."

The head watchman nodded approvingly. Next to him stood Albert Dunning, a tall, tan, wispy young man of fifteen whose ruffled dark brown hair bobbed in the wind, and Franklin, his father, owner of the largest balis grain field in Jardis.

Franklin Dunning took a step toward them and thrust his hand forward, eyes trained firmly on Reznik. The two shook.

"Best of luck to you both. The girls are sick, so Sharon is at home looking after them."

"Thank you, Mr. Dunning," Reznik said. "Please give our best wishes to them."

Albert emerged from behind Franklin. Despite being as tall as Reznik, his ruddy face and lanky figure made him appear diminutive when the two stood together.

"I can't believe," he said, "that you two are off to fight for real, and so soon after your graduation." He looked back and forth between Reznik and Madeline and seemed to hold back from saying more. He finished with: "Stay safe."

"We will, Albert," Madeline said.

"Yes, please, please stay safe," Karen echoed, squeezing Madeline's hands tightly in hers.

"Give those Amelaren bastards as good as you've got, you hear?" Franklin offered, spurring everyone to laughter.

"It's time for us to go," said Reznik. "Thank you for seeing us off, everyone."

The caravan wagons were unbolted from their stations and tied to the horses. The drivers had already boarded, impatiently holding the reins and glancing scornfully at Reznik and Madeline as they walked briskly toward the rear wagon.

"Goodbye!" Karen called after them.

"Take care!" Franklin hollered as Reznik and Madeline climbed to the floor of the wagon, which had already begun to move.

The two waved. Atop the twin outpost towers in the distance, several militiamen also waved as the wagon picked up speed. The caravan traveled east down the road through the wide-open plains. After several reps, the travelers felt a noticeable increase in elevation as they entered the hill country that would span most of the way to Calena. The outline of Jardis receded into the distance.

Chapter 4

(987.1.46–47)

—1—

Lake Sanmoria spanned thirty-five kilometers along its longest axis from northwest to southeast and acted as the midpoint between the Alcones and Phoenicis, the continent's two major mountain ranges. It also ran roughly twenty-five kilometers orthogonally and, combined with the nearly impassable maze of ridges that lay to its south, formed a natural corridor between the two halves of the continent.

The name Sanmoria was bestowed by Cyril Coranthis, who eschewed the original Amelaren moniker in favor of one more properly reflective of its proximity to the centroid of Moriana. When the lake and its immediate surroundings finally fell completely under Coranthian control, King Samsen ordered the establishment of a massive fortress on the northeastern corner of Lake Sanmoria, near the mouth of the Invar River, as its first and best defense against the threat of an Amelaren invasion. After careful evaluation of all geographical, military, and financial factors, Samsen chose the site of the fortress and named it Aldova in honor of his predecessor Cyril. The fortress, fully completed in 978, overlooked a small strip of land to the north that was sandwiched between the lake and the Alcones, known as the Sanmorian Corridor. The Corridor stood as the only open route for an army to traverse. As a result, it became the single most important strategic position between the two countries and allowed Coranthia to thrive. The Amelarens were unable to pose any real threat against the fortress's defenses.

Aldova rose from the lake surface to a height of ten stories. Though it was not as tall as Castle Coranthis, it stretched almost eight hundred meters in both length and width, making it, by far, the largest known structure in all of Moriana. Its four sides had been erected with precision to face the cardinal directions. The overall design was conservative, lending both to simplicity and functionality; its only adornments were large blue Coranthian flags atop the roof, as well as several banners draped over the coarse gray alacore walls, parts of which were in slight disrepair.

Tall rectangular windows lined the eighth and tenth floors, where much of the projectile weaponry and ammunition were stored. By contrast, the windows on the first through seventh floors were small, permitting a minimal level of sunlight and ventilation, while there were no windows at all on the ninth floor. The ridged edges of the roof provided cover and enabled convenient deployment of ballistae and archers.

The southwestern corner of Aldova's exterior revealed three semi-cylindrical protrusions that ran from below the surface of the lake up to nearly the entire height of the fortress. The only other significant exterior feature of the main structure was the presence of three covered walkways, extending from the western and southern walls of the first, third, and fifth floors. These walkways were two hundred meters in length and connected the fortress to two identical and otherwise detached twelve-story towers, also built directly on the water to either side of the main structure.

The towers, known as Seras and Chari, were nondescript, aside from the top three floors. A massive metal cannon barrel protruded slightly from the northern side of Seras. Chari wielded a similar cannon, facing eastward. Both of these weapons, products of first-rate Norev technology, were capable of blasting large, high-velocity spherical bullets of water, capable of decimating entire army companies at a range of up to three kilometers, with a blast radius of half a kilometer. Once operational, Seras and Chari prevented the Amelarens from approaching Aldova, thus halting the enemy advance on Coranthia. This led to the end of the Coronation War in 971.

In the original instantiation of the towers, the cannons were restricted from exercising any flexibility in their aim. Once the ceasefire was in place, Samsen pushed for a redraft. He contracted the Norev guild's engineers to implement a swivel to the tops of the towers, granting them free, albeit slow, three-hundred-and-sixty-degree rotation. Vertical movement was also possible, though extremely limited; nevertheless, Samsen was satisfied with the results. Together, the fortress and two towers comprised a nexus of military might, unparalleled throughout Moriana, and no Amelaren force had again dared to venture into the range of Seras and Chari since they unleashed their fury upon Orlen's warriors more than fifteen years earlier.

Even Aldova's peripherals were imposing to those setting eyes on the complex for the first time. A long cobblestone bridge, known as the Crossway, linked the northwestern shore of Lake Sanmoria to the large gated archway of the fortress, level with its second floor. The bridge passed straight through the fortress to the other side, continuing until it met the northeastern shore. Almost thirteen hundred meters from end to end, it was wide enough to fit twenty columns of people, or up to seven medium-sized caravans at once. Its scope was designed out of necessity, for the bridge was the only dry route in or out of the fortress.

Despite having to wait over two arcs to gain entry into the fortress, Reznik and Madeline enjoyed every rep they spent outside on the bridge. Neither had seen a structure of such scale and wonder before, even though both had visited Corande on multiple occasions while attending Tellisburg. They passed the time admiring the architecture and landscape, frequently staring across the bridge to the solistone-covered lake, and before they knew it, they had moved to the front of the line and were pushed through the registration process. Once formalities were complete, they separated to find their respective rooms.

—2—

"Three-fifty-five one …" Reznik muttered to himself, carrying his belongings down one of the many unending hallways of Aldova's third floor.

He felt drained and was glad there was still time before the meeting with his company that evening. As he walked, he examined the waterways: large half-pipes that lined the halls and were built into the tops of the walls close to the ceiling, raised outer edges to prevent leakage. While there were small windows along the outer walls of the fortress, most of the lighting in the corridor was provided by the solistones floating down the waterways. Reznik was struck by the intricacies of the fortress's design.

Earlier, he had been in such a hurry to get in and through registration that he had not taken notice of Aldova's interior. Now, his preoccupation with these details caused him to bump into several avets as he shuffled along, inviting reactions of varying indifference.

After what seemed to be an interminable trek, he finally reached a door with its accompanying overhanging brass plate marked 355. The door was heavier than he expected, requiring him to push hard before he could fully open it. He stepped into what was now his new home and looked around. The entryway was large. Walls divided the area into six smaller sections, labeled one through six with three on either side of him. Each section had four top-and-bottom bunk beds, as well as a series of numbered drawers along the walls in correspondence with the numbering of the bunks. There were also two small desks in a section, each with its own solistone lamp. As Reznik walked to Section 1, located in the rear of the suite, he noticed that the room was mostly empty, though several avets occupied their bunks, most of whom were conversing with each other or reading. Only one avet looked up as Reznik passed by. Like Reznik and all other nonofficers, he wore the standard loose-fitting navy-colored military shirt and pants. The avet acknowledged Reznik with a slight nod, which he returned.

Reznik peeked through the door in Section 3 and saw a communal washroom, presumably intended for use among the sections on that side of the suite. The living quarters stood on the opposite end of the washroom. The washroom was lined with rows of crude shower heads, toilets, and sinks made of rusting metal. The shower heads were large bronze spigots protruding from the east wall with small drains in the floor below the heads. The north wall featured rusty, bucket-shaped toilets with circulating water flowing through their receptacles. An array of sinks ran along the western wall; each one had a spigot smaller than those used for the showers and was positioned to flow directly into a large connected basin mounted below. All of the utilities were connected to pipes that connected to a large, humming metal unit on the southern wall that processed waste before returning the water to the main supply. The washroom looked heavily used, though was not particularly dirty. When seeing the processor unit, Reznik hoped that it worked well.

Returning to Section 1, he saw that only one of the bottom beds was neatly made and unadorned by any personal effects. His new bunkmate had apparently claimed the top bed and likely also just arrived, for he was kneeling behind the bunk in the midst of unpacking. Upon hearing the newcomer enter, he looked up and rose to his feet. He took several steps toward Reznik, extending a fair-skinned hand.

"Good day to you, sir," he grinned, flashing pearly white teeth. "Liam Remington."

Reznik put down his bags and shook Liam's hand. "Reznik Sylvera. Are you a recent graduate?"

"I graduated from Kendrall last year. I'm afraid I don't recognize you."

"I attended Tellisburg. Graduated just this year."

"Ah, that's impressive, impressive indeed. I mean no offense, but I've not heard of your estate."

"Likely because it does not exist. I'm from Jardis. Northwest of Calena."

Liam arched a thin eyebrow. "Oh, I see. My apologies. I didn't mean to presume."

"No need to apologize." Reznik motioned to his luggage. "If you don't mind …"

Liam waved his hands deferentially. "No, of course not. Go right ahead. I need to finish up as well." He pointed to a stack of lavish leather bags stacked atop one another at the back of the room, making Reznik's luggage seem minuscule in comparison.

Nevertheless, as Reznik began to unpack in silence, Liam took it upon himself to provide a more thorough introduction; Reznik's lack of interest seemed only to encourage him more. Using many more words than were necessary, Liam conveyed his estated pedigree, albeit one of low rank, the location of his family's estate on the outskirts of Kantor, and his class rank of third at Kendrall Academy. He spoke enthusiastically of the healthy mix of nobles and commoners at Kendrall and, obviously, took great pride in his attendance there.

"If I might ask," Liam raised his eyebrows, "what was it like at Tellisburg?"

"What do you mean?" Reznik said.

Liam shook his head, shifting his perfectly molded wavy brown hair. "You know … Most of the students at Tellisburg are estated. Actually, you must have been there during Prince Adrian's stay, correct?"

Reznik shrugged. "It went as you'd expect it would for a commoner, but the tension wasn't always a bad thing. Studying at a military academy is not supposed to be a leisurely classroom experience."

"I see," Liam said. "That makes sense. I graduated three years ago, so I've been stationed at Aldova for a while, but I'm still not used to it. I've been on border patrols, but not since the Elsin Massacre—that's what they call it around here, by the way. I've some experience, though I must confess to a bout of nerves. I don't know what to expect now."

Liam shoved a stack of papers into one of the small drawers outfitting his desk.

"I was reassigned to the Upper 26th and had to move all my junk here, so that's why I have so much … well, you can excuse the mess, can't you?"

Reznik half-grunted in response. He was on his knees, pushing one of his sacks under the bed.

Liam watched him for several ticks and then remarked, "I can't say I ever expected to be deployed for an all-out war. I don't have much enthusiasm for it."

"Why is this unexpected?" Reznik asked. "Every Coranthian—especially ones who enlist—has been prepared for this inevitability. The Amelaren threat has always been there, at least for as long as I've been alive. And hopefully, we can eliminate it for good this time."

Liam cracked a small smile. "I understand, but you see, my father served in the Coronation War."

Reznik said nothing, waiting for Liam to continue.

"Of course, he told me the same thing. He always told me what a great honor it was to serve his country. I grew up hearing his stories. He was incredibly proud of his time in the military, but I could see a sadness and fear in his eyes that never left him."

Lost in thought, Liam's eyes glazed over briefly before lucidity returned. "Sorry, I don't want to bore you with this. Anyway, my father and others who have fought in a real war … What I've seen it do to them leaves a sour taste in my mouth. You're right though; we know what we signed up for."

The young men fell silent. Reznik was unsure of how to respond to the grim and off-putting observation. His thoughts drifted to the family portrait he had brought with him and placed securely in the drawer of the desk beside the bed. Memories of his own father came flooding back. After several ticks, Reznik returned to sorting his belongings. Liam had already resumed unpacking and said nothing more.

A while later, their attention was drawn to the sound of seven loud rings from the hallway outside their suite. The source was one of several bells drawn up on each floor, all of which were controlled from a single rope located somewhere along the hallway. A maintenance officer pulled the rope every arc to signal the time.

"Time for the meeting, is it?" Liam said, watching Reznik empty the remaining contents of his backpack onto his bed.

"Shall we be going, sir?" Reznik said.

Liam slammed the drawers on his desk shut. "Yes, let us go. And please don't address me as 'sir.' Rank is the only distinction that matters here, and I am not your superior."

"Very well then."

They left their quarters. As nighttime had just set in, additional solistone lanterns had been activated to illuminate the stairwells. Reznik and Liam entered the one closest to their room and began their climb to the sixth floor. They exited to a hallway that was wider than the one on the fourth floor, though, otherwise, the layout appeared almost identical. Reznik made a comment about this as he followed Liam.

"Well," Liam said, "the sixth floor is primarily captains' and vice captains' quarters, so it's no surprise, really. Though there are a few meeting rooms and small auditoriums."

Reznik thought of Renard and wondered which of the rooms he was in. He noticed several soldiers who stood at attention, eyeing him and other avets as they passed by. When one of them caught Reznik staring curiously at him, he glowered back.

"Have you already met our captain?" Reznik asked.

"I have. You won't believe who it is." Liam paused for effect. "Minister Havora's son."

"Really?" Reznik said with interest.

Having noticed the exchange of glances between Reznik and the other soldier, Liam lowered his voice. "Anyway, normally we wouldn't be allowed up here without proper clearance. Those guards would stop you immediately at the stairwell. Floors six through nine are typically restricted to officers and special personnel."

"You seem to know your way around," Reznik said with a hint of approval. "How long have you been here again?"

"Not long, but I knew a bit about Aldova before I arrived here. My father was stationed here toward the end of the Coronation War, when the fortress was first functional."

There was unmistakable pride in Liam's voice.

"To be honest," he continued, "both my father and I are rather fond of engineering. It could never be more than a hobby for us, but Aldova has much to be excited about."

"I can imagine," Reznik said.

Liam's eyes shone. "Sylvera, when you were on the bridge, did you notice the large pipes running along the south side of the fortress and down into the lake?"

Reznik nodded. "Rather hard to miss."

"Those pipes pump up water from the lake to Aldova's heart on the ninth floor."

Reznik raised his eyebrows. "The heart?"

"That's what they call the water filtration and distribution system used to pump the water you see lining the halls throughout."

"Is that you, Liam?" A woman's voice rang out from ahead of them.

Liam's concentration broke, and he stared straight ahead. "Bethany?"

Reznik could make out two female figures standing ten or fifteen paces away, though it was difficult to discern their faces in the hallway light. From the outline of the figures, he thought one of them was likely Madeline.

"So you've been assigned to the Upper 26th as well?" Liam asked.

"I have," Bethany said. Reznik could now make out her features and saw that she was noticeably older than many of the avets he had seen up to that point. He would not have been surprised to learn she was over thirty. Bethany was rather tall for a woman, though not quite at the eye level of Reznik or Liam. She also carried the unmistakable air of someone who spoke confidently to those less experienced, though it was apparent that she was on familiar terms with Liam.

"We'll all be in good hands, then," Liam said. He gestured to the other woman. "And this is?"

"My new bunkmate, Avet Madeline Agilda."

"Pleased to meet you … and Avet Sylvera," she said, breaking out into laughter.

Liam shifted his gaze between Reznik and Madeline. "We all know each other then?" He held his hand out to Madeline. "Liam Remington."

Madeline shook his hand and introduced herself properly. She turned to Reznik and said, "This is Bethany Lane."

Reznik nodded at Bethany.

"Not a talkative one, is he?" Bethany remarked, brushing aside strands of long, wavy blond hair.

The hall was mostly empty as the four continued on. Eventually, they reached a door of room 626. Liam led them in, and they made their way to a large open doorway at the back of the room. They ascended a small flight of stairs into a packed auditorium. Built to hold two hundred people, it was filled to about three-quarters capacity with avets. Rows of chairs were arranged on offset rings of platforms, allowing each avet an unobstructed view of a large podium that was affixed at the center of the room, a small table off to its side. A collection of solistone lanterns shone down from the ceiling.

The four took the first open seats they could find and settled in as they waited for the meeting to start. Standing at the podium was a tall, thin man who looked to be in his forties, accompanied by a spectacled young man of around Reznik's and Madeline's age who had short blond hair. Both men wore matching navy blue trench coats with silver trim and buttons. This uniform was typical formal attire for captains and vice captains and rarely worn into battle. The two men spoke to each other in low voices, while the room buzzed with chatter among the avets.

"That's a very young vice captain," Madeline said, pointing as inconspicuously as she could to the younger man.

"No, no. That's the captain," Bethany said. "Nash Havora."

"He's younger than I am," Liam said, a hint of amusement in his voice, "and already a captain."

"He must have graduated at a very early age," Reznik said.

"Long before any of us enrolled, I'm sure," Liam said. "I think he entered Tellisburg when he was twelve."

Bethany smiled faintly. "Pretty much what you'd expect, given his status."

Madeline's eyes drifted across the room. "This is the entire upper platoon, then? Most of these avets can't have graduated that long ago."

"You're a lot of fresh faces, that's for sure," Bethany agreed with a chuckle.

Three reps later, Captain Nash Havora took a seat behind a table next to the podium, while the older man stepped up to it. Even from the outer edge of the room, the wrinkles and scars stood out on his face. His midlength hair was jet black on top but mostly grayed at the ends. His hardened look easily distinguished him as a seasoned veteran. He produced a gavel, which he pounded on the podium, immediately silencing the room. A short, pudgy soldier with shortly cropped brown hair and a plain navy blue uniform entered through a side door and made his way to the table next to the podium. He took a seat beside the captain and dropped a stack of papers onto the table.

The man with the gavel began to speak, his voice resounding throughout the auditorium.

"Avets, let us begin. For those of you who don't know, I am Vice Captain Parsons. With me is Captain Havora. We shall preside over the orientation and partition of the Upper 26th. If you are not a member of the platoon, please leave at once and redirect to your assigned meeting place."

He paused and looked around. Seeing that none of the avets moved from their seats, he said, "Good. Now, as you know, the captain oversees the upper platoon directly, so you will report to him. Nevertheless, if I issue a direct order in his stead, you are to obey it without question. Is that understood?"

"Yes, sir!" the avets chorused.

Quincy Parsons stepped from behind the podium and began to pace back and forth in front of it. "The platoon will be split into seventeen squads, and within each squad, a sergeant will be appointed as lead. Most squads in the 26th are based around collective mobilization. Of course, there will be several specialized squads. Aranow, Colonel Gavere's adjutant here, has the assignments."

He stopped pacing and turned in place, addressing the avets in each direction.

"He will now organize you by your squads. Each squad is to group together in its designated area. Bunkmates are automatically assigned to the same squad, so if you're not sure which group you belong to, look for your bunkmate. You may all stand."

On cue, the soldiers rose from their seats and awaited the squad announcements. The seated soldier, Aaron Aranow, snatched up his papers and made his way to the podium. He spoke quickly but clearly and went through the entire roster within ten reps. After a shuffling of bodies, Reznik and Madeline found themselves assigned to the 9th Squad. This meant that Liam and Bethany were also with them.

Parsons stood behind the podium again. He politely motioned for Aranow to leave, and the adjutant exited through the side door in a hurry.

"That will be all for now. Sergeant appointments will be made squad by squad. We are to set out in two days. General Leynitz will lead the offensive, along with colonels Gavere and Dyers. Colonel Gavere will be our direct superior. He will introduce himself to you before we set out." He paused to survey the room. "We will be striking preemptively and with great ferocity. Be prepared and well rested. The captain and I will now have a few words with each squad individually. Please remain seated until your squad is called."

Madeline gave Reznik a nudge and whispered, "The captain didn't say a single word."

When the time came for the 9th Squad to step forward, nine of the squad members lined up in front of the table where the captain and Parsons sat.

Reznik, Madeline, Liam, and Bethany fell in line next to a tall young man with long, messy black hair and several scars across his throat. Liam appeared to recognize the man and gave a nod, to which the man nodded vigorously before straightening up and staring forward.

Nash Havora remained seated, examining each of them in turn. When his bright blue eyes fell on Bethany, he finally spoke in a soft voice. "Avet Lane."

Bethany stepped forward and saluted. "Yes, sir."

"You are the senior member of this squad and a veteran of the Coronation War. I have no doubt that the other avets will rely on your experience. I chose you specifically to be part of a squad that I have singled out for … for … I expect much from you all. The assessments from your respective academies are among the best that our company has to offer. All of you have extremely high-scoring training records.

"Avet Remington." Nash paused to clear his throat. He looked uncomfortable, and when he resumed his speech, his words tumbled out of his mouth rapidly and a bead of sweat ran from his short blond hair across his right temple and down his fair-skinned cheek. He leaned forward as he spoke, his hands gripping the podium tightly. "You will lead this squad as sergeant. Avet Lane, I trust that you will ably assist him and your other squad members in times to come."

"Of course, sir," Bethany responded without a moment's hesitation.

Reznik's eyes darted between Liam, Bethany, Nash, and Parsons. Madeline noticed this and knew exactly what he was thinking. She, too, was puzzled at the choice of sergeant.

Nash reached into his pocket and pulled out a small object. Walking around to Liam, he extended an open palm. Resting in it was a bronze sergeant's pin, similar to the ones used on the collars of military dress uniforms, though much larger in size. Liam hesitantly reached out and took it in his left hand, withdrawing it quickly. With his right, he saluted formally. Nash returned the salute.

"Thank you, sir," Liam said graciously.

Nash nodded. "You are all dismissed."

The entire squad saluted Nash and Parsons before dispersing. Without waiting for anyone else, Reznik turned and marched up the aisle and out the door. Madeline stared curiously after him.

—3—

Madeline arose the following morning to find Bethany shaking her shoulder.

"It's time to go."

She yawned and rolled out of bed. It was still a day away from deployment, and she had hoped to get a chance to rest after the long journey, but their new sergeant had other plans. Liam wanted the squad to meet for an equipment check before most of the other squads woke. The equipment rooms on the second floor were divided by company and platoon. Since equipment checks were mandatory, Liam did not want his squad's executed when it was too crowded.

Once Madeline finished dressing, she and Bethany made their way to the second floor. Their platoon's equipment room contained armor and weapons that lined the walls, while various bags and accessories were placed on and under benches. Wooden dividers separated the equipment sets, providing each soldier with his or her own personal equipment space, labeled with a brass nameplate.

At the back of the room, Madeline and Bethany saw several soldiers chatting and checking their equipment. Madeline did not recognize them and assumed they must be from another squad.

"There," Bethany pointed.

Madeline turned her attention to where several members of the squad stood. Reznik was with them; it took a few ticks before he recognized the people walking toward him as Madeline and Bethany; he waved once he did.

The two women greeted him as they approached and proceeded to find their respective spaces and began going through their equipment.

"Where is our sergeant?" Bethany asked.

Reznik frowned.

"No sign of him yet. He was gone when I woke."

Next to Reznik stood a young man and woman, both blue-eyed and exceptionally tan for Coranthians. They appeared to be twins. Slightly farther away from them, a plain young woman with short, faded black hair was searching through a large dark green bag.

The male twin spoke. "He arrived quite early, as my sister and I did. Then he left to gather the rest of you."

His accent clearly indicated he was from a small Outlands town in the north.

Bethany nodded. "He should be here shortly then."

The female twin turned to address Madeline and Bethany in the adjacent spaces.

"By the way, I'm Amy Trenton. This is my brother, Alphonse."

"Pleased to meet you," Alphonse said with a wave. The pair oozed enthusiasm. Madeline and Bethany returned with their own introductions.

"So, where are you two from?" Madeline asked, removing a gladius from the wall.

"Warrenhill," Amy said, brushing her long black hair casually out of her eyes.

"Ah. My friend and I are from Jardis, actually," Madeline said. She pointed to Reznik, who gave no indication that he had he heard his name being spoken.

"I have to say, you two look rather young to be in the military," she continued.

The twins laughed.

"We get that a lot, but we're eighteen," Alphonse said. "Pa used to run our farm, but he got in an accident and can't work anymore, so …"

"I'm sorry to hear that," Madeline said, feeling a sorrowful twinge as an image of her own father flashed through her head.

"You meet any of our other squadmates yet?" Amy asked. "Besides your friend, that is. And Avet Lane, I guess."

"Please, call me Bethany."

"I met the sergeant briefly," Madeline responded.

Her gaze drifted toward the woman with the short black hair. Madeline decided to walk over. It was apparent from the contents of the woman's large bag, as well as the small red heart sewn onto its side, that the fair-skinned young woman was the squad's medic.

"Hi, I'm Madeline. Nice to meet you."

The young woman nodded. "Patrice Konith." She resumed going through her bag and said nothing more.

Madeline smiled, causing Patrice to blush.

"She doesn't say much," Reznik said from behind her.

Madeline turned around and grinned. "Well, then apparently you two have a lot in common."

"Anyway," Alphonse said, "we ran into the sergeant last night. He doesn't seem like such a bad guy. We were both wondering why he was made sergeant instead of you, Miss Bethany. Still, it doesn't seem right to hold it against him."

Amy began to add, "Sergeant Remington, he—"

"I what?" came Liam's voice, startling her. The group turned to see their sergeant with a short, ponytailed man and the tall man with the scarred throat. Counting quickly, Reznik noticed that one squad member was not with them.

"So what were we talking about?" Liam asked, appearing somewhat flustered.

"My sister here," Alphonse said with a smirk, "was telling us what a wonderful person you are, Sergeant."

The look of fear on Amy's face elicited chuckles from Madeline and Bethany. Liam took it in stride and smiled warmly.

"I don't think everyone has been properly introduced. This is Philip Dyson." Liam gestured at the scarred man beside him, who gave a slight nod but said nothing.

"Please don't judge his silence. He cannot speak. He is not being rude."

Amy and Alphonse exchanged curious looks.

"And this," Liam gestured to the shorter man, "is Josef Reinbach."

"It is my great pleasure to meet everyone," Josef said in a thick Doromalian accent.

Josef appeared a little older than the others, and Madeline would have found him quite attractive if not for his below-average height. He sported a thin build and a sharply handsome face with pale skin and dark eyes. His hair fell past his shoulders in a thick, dark brown ponytail. His accent was difficult to understand. It was not uncommon for Doromalian families to move to Coranthia and serve in the army or have their children serve, though Madeline and Reznik had little exposure to foreigners at Tellisburg. Most Doromalian recruits attended either of the country's other two military academies.

With introductions out of the way, the members of the 9th Squad resumed attending to their equipment, making sure everything was there and in acceptable condition. After going through his own equipment, Liam assisted the other squad members.

When Liam checked on Reznik, the latter spoke tersely. Liam was not oblivious to the tension, but decided not to push the matter. For his part, Reznik was bothered by Liam's inexperience. The sergeant had originally called the group meeting as a team exercise, and Reznik could tell that Liam was at a loss as to what to do.

"Sergeant Remington?" Alphonse asked when Liam approached.

"Yes?"

"I heard you know a lot about this place. I was wondering why all the main facilities are on the second floor and not the first."

"Oh, you want to know what's on the first floor?" Bethany said, grinning mischievously at Alphonse. "It's a prison."

Alphonse's eyes lit up. "Prison?"

"Yes," Liam said, shaking his head at Bethany. "That's where they keep prisoners of war. It's not like you'd be able to get in anyway. It's only accessible from the stairs on the Crossway. I'd imagine you'd have more luck breaking into Castle Coranthis."

"Interesting. What happens to the prisoners?" Alphonse asked.

"I don't know for certain. Only high-ranking officers and prison staff really do. I …" Liam seemed vexed. "Let's not talk about this anymore. Is your equipment in good order?"

"Yes, sir."

Liam continued to converse with Alphonse about more casual topics. Given his urban upbringing, he was particularly interested in the lifestyle of a commoner in the Outlands.

"I can't help but notice we have a squad member missing," Bethany commented after several reps.

The flustered look returned to Liam's face. "Yes, well … Avet Marcole will not be joining us this morning."

Bethany raised her eyebrow. "I see."

"He's a real ass," Alphonse chimed in.

"What?" Liam said as everyone turned to look at Alphonse.

"Cyrus Marcole. He's my bunkmate. A real ass, and he keeps to himself most of the time. Haven't talked to him, but I don't want to either. Maybe he's permanently depressed about that ugly scar on his face."

Liam rubbed the back of his neck. "He does seem to have a rather unaccommodating demeanor, but there's no need for you to reciprocate his negativity, Avet Trenton."

Alphonse looked down at the ground, shrugging embarrassedly.

After half an arc, the equipment check was completed. Liam announced his plans to eat dinner in the main mess hall on the second floor at seven arc and invited everyone to join him. The squad dispersed, and its members went their separate ways. Reznik waited in the hallway for

Madeline to catch up with him. She had stayed behind to get in a few words with Bethany and the twins.

"They seem like a decent group," Madeline said, as she strolled up alongside Reznik.

Reznik nodded. "I'm a bit concerned about our shy medic. Does she seem like the type who can handle the stress of medical emergencies?"

Madeline laughed. "She's probably just nervous. After all, we're still strangers."

"And there's also the fact that we have a mute, a loner, and an inexperienced sergeant," Reznik continued.

Madeline frowned. "You're being too hard on Sergeant Remington."

"What?"

"You were giving him the cold shoulder. Did you think you were being subtle?"

"No, not really," Reznik said sourly. "I haven't been entirely outgoing with him either."

"As opposed to how you usually are," Madeline observed.

Reznik let out a short laugh. "Right."

"Did you manage to see Glen or Douglas yesterday? I looked as I walked around but never ran into them."

"No, I didn't really remember to ..." Reznik trailed off.

With that, Madeline understood that Reznik was probably just as anxious as she was about the upcoming battle, as was everyone else in the squad. Seeing the worry seep through the cracks of Reznik's stony countenance comforted her. She knew that she would not be alone in facing their upcoming ordeal.

Turning to Reznik, she reached out and impulsively pulled his ear, causing him to start.

"Come on, let's get some breakfast," she said cheerfully, giving him a warm smile.

Reznik stared at her in surprise, but the muscles in his face relaxed. His lips twitched, not fully forming a smile, though drawn less tightly nonetheless. "Might as well. Let's go."

She gave him a playful shove as the two of them continued on to the mess hall.

Chapter 5

(987.1.50)

General Marsell Leynitz scanned the ranks of soldiers lined up beyond the eastern entrance to the Aldova Bridge. At thirty-eight years old, he was the younger of the two active Coranthian generals, while equal in every other way. Impressively perched atop his majestic white durion, Silvermane, he trotted from one end of the formation to the other, inspecting the Coranthian forces with his dark brown eyes. He wore heavy steel armor with ornate gold trimming. Affixed to his chest plate, an aeron general's Coranox reflected the sunlight, which was pouring down overhead. His majestic gold-trimmed blue cape flowed in the breeze. He carried his open-faced helmet, no less adorned than his armor, under his arm.

Leynitz was the portrait of a consummate Coranthian elite, a count and the recent inheritor of a prominent Lynderan estate of stellar repute. Though short, he was handsome, well-built, and projected effortlessly when he spoke. Uncommon among Coranthian men, his black pompadour shone, matching in color an impressive handlebar mustache that added to his distinguished appearance. One of the youngest to ever ascend to generalship, he was doted on by Samsen and the Assembly, in equal measure. Many of the estated saw him as the current military standard-bearer. He had, with great rigor and efficiency, scouted the Amelaren side of the Corridor immediately after the Elsin Massacre and, with the approval of Samsen and Minister Velmann, developed a robust mobilization protocol in far less time than anyone thought possible. Along with the senior general, Leopold San Mortigan, who presided over the defenses at Aldova, Leynitz had been tasked with mounting a preemptive offensive designed, primarily, to make a statement about Coranthian might. Using the intelligence he gathered, he chose to expand the initial plan and shape it into a full offensive campaign.

Ten companies in all, just over one-quarter of the entire army, fanned out before him: fully armed, statuesque, and ready to march at first call. They would be led by colonels Gavere and Dyers, directly commanding the 5th and 7th companies, respectively. The colonels, captains, and vice captains led their respective companies and platoons atop their steeds at the edges of the formation. All awaited the general's address.

Twenty surveyors sent by the Assembly to observe the proceedings and battles stood to the side. Unlike the soldiers, who wore the necessary armor over their standard military uniforms, the surveyors wore relatively light armor underneath dark gray robes. The group's leader, Nelhart, reported directly to Sebastian Eurich, First Chair of the Assembly of Lords. Leynitz was less than pleased that the Assembly felt it necessary to send them. Having to accommodate the surveyors while running an efficient campaign was a loathsome inconvenience. He had no love for Eurich either, though ultimately he was resigned to the situation. He sought to make the most of an opportunity to make a positive impression on the First Chair and, by extension, the Assembly as a whole. Above all else, Leynitz served the king as a soldier, though he was also implicitly involved in Coranthia's political vortex as a general. Keenly aware that his ability was judged as a reflection of the king, he accepted the incommodious fact that such bureaucratic lackeys and lesser men, including this Nelhart, were pivotal to the balance of power between sovereign and aristocracy. It served only to more strongly fuel his eagerness to make the upcoming operation a success. Before that, however, he had to impart a few words to his troops.

Leynitz motioned toward the soldiers who stood before him. "Behold our strength." He retracted his hand and clenched it into a fist. "They will fall easily under our might."

As he spoke, he turned Silvermane around and directed him to the central columns of the formation, where his direct command, the 3rd Company, stood at attention. Leynitz reined in his horse and slowly turned his head, making eye contact with as many of his soldiers as he could. He glanced at his second, Colonel Radley Lariban, watching him intently from atop his zephyr, Vermilion, named, quite apparently, for its color.

"Despite the ill-bred nature of our enemies, they had the presence of mind to erect a base and several small outposts on Argiset Plateau during their occupation. Argiset is critical to our current and future offensives against them. We shall take it with extreme prejudice. *But*," he enunciated, wagging a finger, "we will not raze their structures. Instead, we shall occupy and fortify them ourselves. It will be a forceful message that even brutes like them will understand."

Colonel Dyers let out a guffaw that he quickly muffled.

"Unfortunately, this means we cannot afford to escort the Engineering Company. We must rely on our initiative if we are to minimize losses. In two days, we will overrun the plateau and sweep it clean of any Amelaren presence. I will direct you to make use of your utility training and lay structural foundations for the engineers. They will depart precisely three arcs from now and reach Argiset on the night of the second after we have secured the plateau."

Leynitz dug the heels of his boots softly into Silvermane's side, directing the horse toward the road that led into the highlands, from whence he could view the entire deployment. He turned Silvermane to face the soldiers.

"There shall be only one night's rest at Argiset. Ertel Ridge must fall shortly thereafter. I acknowledge the unease with which some of you may regard this second phase of operation, but make no mistake, we shall succeed. We will blitz their feeble garrison and show them the might of the Coranthian Army!"

"Yes, sir!" chanted the soldiers in unison.

"After we demolish their forces at Ertel, we will fortify the base there and defend it until construction at Argiset is completed, which will serve to supply us in our fight against the Amelarens. The rest of the army's companies will join us at Ertel, bringing fresh supplies. Then, we shall march deep into the heart of Amelares, avenging our fallen brothers and sisters at Elsin. Never again will they be allowed to threaten our homelands with such cowardly atrocities!"

The soldiers roared in agreement. Several even raised their weapons high into the air.

Leynitz briefly basked in the cheers before motioning for silence. "We will depart within the arc," he said once it was mostly quiet. "Your captains will brief you further. That will be all."

Snapping his reins, he veered his horse northward. The 3rd Company moved forward and fell neatly into step behind him. Riding alongside the 3rd, Lariban caught up to the general and joined him at the front of the formation.

Standing near the southern end of the array, the 26th Company turned its attention to their young captain, Nash Havora, who was steadying his horse while talking in a low voice to Vice Captain Parsons. Several rows deep within the formation, Madeline was unable to hear anything they said over the discordant pockets of conversation that had broken out among the soldiers around her.

"A fine speech," Josef said. He spoke to no one in particular, bobbing his head up and down, his ponytailed hair oscillating in rhythm. He leaned against his lance, firmly planted into the ground.

Patrice glanced around impatiently. She caught Josef's eye and asked quietly, "I wonder what the captain will say?"

Josef shrugged, but Patrice did not have to wait long to find out. Nash broke from his huddle with Parsons, petting the dark mane on his large tan durion, Alma. Then, he gave her a firm pat and trotted forward to address his command.

"Attention!" Nash pronounced. He snapped his left arm straight into the air to command attention and then quickly lowered it to adjust his glasses. "The 26th will assault the fortification at Argiset from the northwest along with the 5th, 28th, 17th, and 35th. Stay in formation and follow my orders and those of the vice captain. Any contingent orders from Colonel Gavere will go through me, unless he speaks directly to us, so you are to obey only our instructions."

He paused to clear his throat. When he resumed, his voice was noticeably less intense. "I know … I know that most of you will be tested in battle for the first time … But our victory is assured! Let's all make it through this. Sergeants, prepare your squads to move out!"

Nash paused to wipe the drops of sweat rolling down his forehead. He remained still for several ticks as he looked out at his company before turning Alma around and heading back to the head of the formation where he had remained for Leynitz's speech.

Standing one row ahead of Madeline, Reznik turned around, an incredulous expression plastered across his face. She shrugged in return.

Avet Cyrus Marcole snickered from two rows behind her. His slicked-back black hair shone in the morning sun. A tan man with hazel eyes, he had a long, prominent scar across the bridge of his nose that started on the left side of his forehead and ran halfway down his right cheek. This morning was the first time he had made himself present to the rest of his squad, much to Liam's chagrin. Everyone but Cyrus—including an unenthusiastic Reznik—had attended dinner with Liam the previous evening.

"Another fine speech," Josef said, nodding once again, though speaking in a wholly different tone.

Not moving to face his squad, Liam said sternly, "I daresay have some respect, avets."

Bethany glanced at Liam and then turned around and said smoothly, though firmly, "This will be the captain's first real battle as well. He may have had his position for some time, but patrol duty does little to prepare you for real combat. He is likely suffering from the same nerves as many of you, so give it a rest and stand ready."

Josef straightened and said no more. Cyrus mumbled something to himself and then fell silent as well.

Reznik snuck a glance back at Madeline and gestured toward Bethany with an expectant look on his face. She shook her head and made a twirling motion with her finger, indicating that he should revert to proper stance. Reznik gave a shoulder shrug and obliged.

Ten reps later, Leynitz returned on his steed, though not accompanied by the 3rd Company. After brief exchanges with both colonels at the head of the formation, he jerked upward and yanked on his reins. Silvermane whinnied harshly and kicked up a cloud of dust. Leynitz brandished his sword and pointed it eastward.

"My fellow countrymen," he shouted, "it is time to set forth on our righteous campaign. I look forward to seeing all of you stand tall atop Argiset in two days. Move out!"

"Yes, My Lord!" the collective before him intoned. Leynitz raised his sword high in the air as a horn sounded to the north.

"Forward!" Gavere and Dyers shouted.

The collective of Coranthian men and women commenced its march into Amelaren lands. The forceful rhythm of boots on soil resounded through the cold morning air, tolling the onset of war anew.

Chapter 6

(987.2.02)

—1—

Traveling fifty kilometers eastward over six arcs, the army, which numbered almost thirty-eight hundred in all, took respite atop a lightly wooded and easily defensible hill southeast of Pyrean Valley. The more direct route to Argiset was through the valley, but the narrow paths through the winding cliffs were not conducive to the movement of a large force. Even then, the detour required the navigation of several ridges, during which the need for caution slowed progression for more than an arc. Nevertheless, the troops remained on schedule. Forward scouts from Delmond Cleft, one of two forward bases flanking Aldova, had already been dispatched to the designated campsite to set up for the night. The Coranthian forces arrived just before midnight. Leynitz brought up the rear and declared that they would resume the march not long after dawn, which allowed for slightly over three arcs worth of rest. Night-watch shifts were established; most of the soldiers fell asleep quickly after having endured a long day's journey.

The sun had just begun to peek over the horizon when Gavere and Dyers were summoned by Leynitz. They found him outside the tent, dressed in his officer's coat, his aeron Coranox glistening from his left breast pocket. He held an apple in one hand and was feeding Silvermane. Occasionally, he paused to take a swig of brandy from the small flask in his other hand; it was a sight that was familiar to his closest subordinates.

"We should make good time," Leynitz said, tossing the apple core aside and, absentmindedly, patting his steed. "Gavere, I want your troops to lead the charge."

Armand Gavere, heavyset and powerfully built, spoke in a deep voice that projected gravitas. "I would be honored, My Lord."

"I want this to be a tad unconventional," Leynitz continued. "If old man Mortigan were here, his plan would involve some sort of systematic rout, but I wish to capitalize on our initiative. We have to take the fight to them and do it quickly, without overemphasis on procedure. Gavere, you need to flood their ranks and scatter them as quickly as possible. Get a foothold inside their outpost and then defend from within. Dyers will provide external reinforcement. We'll save time this way."

Gavere nodded, stroking his short, neatly trimmed beard.

Theodore Dyers stepped forward. He was an impish man with the face of a bulldog; people found him hard to approach; his levelheaded nature and rationality, and not his charisma, were what ultimately qualified him as a colonel.

"I don't mean to question your judgment, sir, but wouldn't that incur heavier losses than if we marched in formation?"

"Perhaps," Leynitz responded at once, as if he had already anticipated that Dyers would say something to that effect, "but the likeliness of similar losses would be quite high if we gave the Amelarens the time to mobilize. These next few arcs will be critical. If we are to facilitate the construction of our forward base while maintaining the momentum of this offensive all the way to Ertel, there is no better option."

"Very well, My Lord," said Dyers.

They all stood silently for several ticks until Gavere spoke. "Do you really think this will work, sir?"

"Yes." Leynitz took a large swig and looked solemnly at Dyers. "I'm sure you have your doubts as well, Theodore, but this is our one chance to surprise them with the swiftness of our attack. If we miss this opportunity, we may find it significantly more difficult to take the mountain base later. It *must* work. Any other questions?"

When neither colonel spoke, Leynitz said, "Then let's move out. May Creon be with us today, gentlemen. I will see you both after our victory."

The two colonels saluted Leynitz before mounting their horses and rode back to their respective battalions.

Most of the captains had already rounded up their troops and were ready to head out. After a cursory examination of the formation, Gavere led the 5th Company forward. The other companies under his command followed closely behind. Shortly afterward, Dyers set out with the second wave. Leynitz's 3rd brought up the rear.

By four arc, Gavere's five companies—the 5th, 26th, 28th, 17th, and 35th—had reached the outskirts of the Amelaren perimeter at Argiset Plateau. The colonel climbed to the top of a small, thicketed hill and surveyed the defenses with a team of scouts from the 5th. A kilometer away, a small fort stood as the nexus of the Amelaren base, with many small, flimsy watchtowers radiating outward from its position. Haphazardly erected sandbags littered the bases of the towers. Gavere took all of this in and ordered the scouts to estimate how many defenders could be seen from their perch. After reaching a consensus, he descended to the bottom of the hill, where his captains awaited his orders on horseback.

"Given the number and size of their towers, it is reasonable to assume that two-thirds of their numbers are inside the fort," Gavere told them. "Going by the scouts' count, there are about three-fifty outside the fort … probably about eight hundred in all."

Captain Gregory Valteau of the 35th Company asked whether that fell within the expected range.

"There are likely more than were anticipated," Gavere replied. "The estimate is conservative, as we cannot see inside the fort. It is of little import. We overwhelm them in numbers. Let us not waste any more time."

Gavere raised his hand and motioned for the captains to return to their respective companies. Nash, who stood slightly apart from the other captains, trotted slowly back to where the 26th stood. He felt his stomach knot as he relayed Gavere's orders to Parsons.

"Anytime now," Nash muttered. "Are the soldiers prepared?"

"They are simply awaiting the command, Captain," Parsons said, donning his helmet and readying his lance. "Perhaps you should line up as well, sir."

Nash nodded and gave Alma a slight nudge with his boot. He waded through the ranks of his command to join the 1st Squad at the rear of the formation. He was one of the few captains who did not lead from the front, as he was also a medic. Once he reached his position, he steadied Alma to a halt, removed his glasses and placed them in the pouch he wore on his belt.

As Nash passed Madeline on his way back, she caught the anxious look on his face, which did little to relieve her rising pulse. She was struck by the changes in most of her squadmates. Tension oozed out of most everyone around her, as all were acutely aware that the battle would begin at any moment. Straining to suppress her nerves while maintaining stance, Amy repeatedly clenched and unclenched her fist to relieve the rigidity in her arm, but her other hand virtually strangled the gladius it held. Cyrus bobbed his head up and down faintly, his sword and shield up, ready to fight. Reznik was still, his eyes locked straight ahead, frozen in concentration. His weapons were lowered but held firmly. Only Liam, standing fully upright at the front of the 9th Squad's two-column formation, Bethany, whose dark green eyes were closed as she took measured, tranquil breaths, and Josef, who was scraping dirt from his lance with his fingernails, seemed relatively at ease.

The sounding of a trumpet by Aranow, Gavere's adjutant, came as a surprise to Madeline, as she expected a more conventional vocal cue from the colonel. She realized the faultiness of her reasoning; there was no need for subtlety. The Coranthians would rush headlong into the Amelaren position. She was only partly conscious of moving with the rest of the troops as they circled the hills behind. Weapons were drawn and shields were raised—they marched up the hill and out onto the plateau. The Amelarens came into view.

From their perspective, the Amelarens saw plainly that the enemy made no attempt to disguise their numbers or intentions. Lookouts atop the watchtowers shouted urgently. With only half a kilometer between the Coranthians and the fort, there was not much time before the two forces would clash. The Amelaren warriors immediately stirred and assumed defensive positions. Others emerged from within the central fort.

Amelaren military structure vastly differed from that of the Coranthians. Unlike the Coranthian Army, which was divided into squads, platoons, and companies, Amelaren warriors fell under the direct command of one of the war chiefs or the warlord himself, Orlen. The forces of each war chief typically numbered up to four thousand warriors, sometimes even more. Each war chief's command was wholly independent, barring any direct commands from the warlord. Some war chiefs preferred to divide their forces into smaller platoons led by chiefs and lesser chiefs, known as elbars and ilbars, respectively. Such was the case with the Amelaren fortification on Argiset. War Chief Tallen had given the commander at Argiset a young elbar named Rengvir, two ilbars, and the equivalent of two companies in the Coranthian Army for defense. Rengvir grew thoroughly agitated, having been reassured several days earlier that reinforcements from Ertel Ridge were on their way and that Argiset would be properly fortified before the Coranthians attacked. Reflecting on the message he had sent to War Chief Tallen, in which he swore an oath to defend Argiset to the death, he realized that he was soon likely to fulfill that oath. Upon being asked by his ilbar for orders, he offered nothing of value, simply telling him to prepare for battle and that the warriors must cut down the Coranthian maggots at all costs. Before long, his blood had completely boiled over. Facing impending catastrophe as the Coranthians advanced on the fort, he knew, nevertheless, that as an elbar, he would be irreparably shamed were he to renege on his word and flee. Thus, his frenzy grew without bound as the Coranthian ranks steadily advanced toward him.

All of the warriors wore garbs or armor painted in the color of their war chief; Tallen's warriors donned onyx, which made it easy for Gavere—who rode alone at the head of the Coranthian formation—to track their movements. Noting their imprecision, he bellowed in a rumbling bass, "They are in disarray. Hold the line!"

The captains and most of the soldiers on the front ranks shouted their acknowledgment.

Perched atop a horse he had named after his former wife, Gavere leaned over the animal's ear and whispered, "Monica, you whore. You better not fail me today when I need you most!"

Monica whinnied in acknowledgment and Gavere let loose a throaty laugh.

The gradual but inexorable advance on the fort instilled a pronounced dread in the Amelarens, just as Gavere had intended. Seeing that they had no plans to retreat, and in light of Leynitz's earlier words regarding the emphasis of overrunning the fort, he wanted to strike as severe a psychological blow as possible before any actual fighting began. His expectations crumbled when one of the Amelarens, ostensibly the commander, yelled incoherently and then broke from his position just in front of the entrance to the fort. Rengvir charged toward them at breakneck speed. Gavere quickly considered that perhaps the man, who appeared to blatantly disregard his own life, had snapped within. Within ticks, a number of the Amelarens let out raucous war cries and had followed their commander's lead. Here was a group of warriors given to desperation and heading straight for the Coranthians. Gavere, who had tried to minimize potential chaos, knew now that it would be inevitable.

Maintaining his forward pace as the Amelarens came on quickly, Gavere was about to repeat his instructions to steady the line when he noticed Amelaren bowmen atop the watchtowers and roof of the fort, their bows notched with arrows and ready to fire. Though they were few in number, Gavere changed his mind, seeing no further need to preserve any pretense.

As he saw more Amelarens stream out of the fort, he hollered, "Full assault!"

The sounds of pounding metal and war cries filled the air as the Coranthians hurtled down the gentle slope of the plateau toward the oncoming Amelarens.

"Fan out!" Parsons cried from atop his horse, Castor. The lower 26th followed his lead. "Break formation and surround them! Make for the fort as soon as they're neutralized!"

Taking the cue, Nash issued a similar order to his own platoon.

From the watchtowers and behind the makeshift sandbag walls, the archers fired rapidly and methodically. Several Coranthians in the front ranks were struck by arrows. Others fell, as some of the Amelarens produced hand axes and hurled them with all their might at the soldiers before them. This did little to stop the Coranthian advance, and the most forward Amelarens were soon met with and mowed down by dozens of soldiers. The leather armor worn by most of the Amelarens did not hold up well against Coranthian weaponry. Some of the more alert warriors—including the elbar, who came to his senses momentarily—quickly reversed their direction, attempting to lead the Coranthians closer to the fort to allow their bowmen on the towers clear shots.

Madeline could see the fort more distinctly as the Coranthians spread out. She felt the adrenaline surge within her. Screams and clashes of weapons rang in her ears. The Coranthians broke through the outermost ring of sandbags, cutting through any Amelaren defenders who stood in their way. She had still not raised her gladius against anyone but knew that it was only a matter of time. Arrows rained down on them as they pressed forward, and the majority of the Amelaren defenders stood ready near the fort. Just ahead of her, Bethany, who had been firing her crossbow as efficiently as possible while keeping pace with the rush, finally pulled out her combat knife. Reznik, who was level with Madeline, caught her eye and gave her a firm nod. Madeline took a deep breath and exhaled slowly.

"Squad, listen up!" Liam shouted. "Stick together, even if they separate us from the rest of the platoon!"

From behind, Madeline heard Nash yelling for the troops to hold formation.

The Coranthians breached ring after ring of sandbags and swarmed the outer watchtowers. As Parsons approached one tower closest to him, an archer, who had been firing ceaselessly at them, abruptly laid down his weapon and waved his arms in the air, shouting his surrender. Parsons saw him and, in one swift motion, took out a throwing knife and hit him in the leg. The archer cried out, mostly in surprise, dropping his bow and grabbing at the steel that was lodged in his leg. Before he could recover, another Amelaren shoved him over the side of the tower to the ground. The new Amelaren picked up the bow and began firing into the ocean of Coranthian soldiers.

The scene fell into further disarray. The Coranthian blitz slowed as they met fiercer resistance. They attempted to surround and overwhelm the enemy, but the Amelarens maneuvered to use the Coranthians' own movements against them. As a result, the Coranthians ran into one another, sometimes tripping each other, allowing the Amelarens to take advantage of the confusion and indiscriminately attacking anyone they came across, driven by various degrees of instinct, bloodlust, and desperation.

Suddenly, the line split wide open in front of Madeline. A group of around forty Amelaren warriors engaged the 26th Company in direct combat. Coranthian soldiers scattered as Madeline lost sight of her squadmates in a haze of wood and steel. For a tick, she thought she heard Reznik calling her. An ear-splitting wail rattled her to the bone. When she regained focus, she saw the body of a young Coranthian, whom she did not recognize, sprawled awkwardly on the ground, his broken face masked in blood. The Amelaren warrior who had bested him stood before her, staring into her eyes. Madeline was jarred to find that the warrior was a young woman of similar age. She had little time to process this before the woman let out a high-pitched cry and ran at her, gripping a battle-ax with both hands.

Fragments of memories from her training and conditioning at Tellisburg, seemingly eons ago, flashed instantly through Madeline's mind. She felt not fully in control of her body. Everything around her slowed as the Amelaren, who held her ax high in the air, suddenly swung her arms to the side and prepared to slash at Madeline horizontally, trying to catch her off guard. Her heart pounding, Madeline squeezed the gladius in her right hand and ducked precisely as the ax sliced just above her head. In one swift motion, she thrust upward with the sword, stabbing the Amelaren through the chest. The woman's eyes bulged as she tumbled backwards, letting out a harsh and terrible gasp. Frantically, Madeline yanked out her combat knife and lunged again, even though the Amelaren no longer resisted. Putting all of her weight behind the knife, Madeline pushed the Amelaren. She found herself sprawled on top of her enemy, whose glazed eyes bore into hers. The woman's face, seized with terror and despair, relaxed as her head rolled off to the side, the life having left her body. Yanking the knife out from what was now a corpse, Madeline felt lightheaded. It seemed to her that she was staring into a mirror, although the woman looked nothing like her.

Another Amelaren, a stocky man with long, wild hair, bore down on her. Her thoughts still scrambled, instinct alone propelled her as she pulled the gladius from the chest of the fallen woman and swung her legs around, tripping her new attacker, who appeared to have tried to stomp on her head. She sprung on top of the other Amelaren and brought her sword downward into his stomach and then immediately jumped back and watched as the man convulsed on the ground, fully incapacitated and doomed to expire.

Her thoughts finally regained focus. *Stay with the troops. Take the fort.*

She tripped over a rock and crawled back to reclaim her sword. Standing up, she quickly turned around and glanced at the body of the Amelaren woman. Her second victim bore little impact, but she could not resist one last look at the first, wondering who she might have been were she a Coranthian.

Think about this later, her mind said sternly.

Madeline turned and ran northward.

She had lost all sense of time, but eventually managed to find the 9th Squad. They had dispersed into smaller groups and followed the front-rank Coranthians, who continued to push toward the fort. Amy, Alphonse, and Cyrus had fallen behind, caught in the midst of an encounter with two much larger Amelarens. One charged Amy, who nimbly evaded several attacks but either did not want to retaliate or lacked the presence of mind to do so. As she struggled to anticipate the Amelaren's next move, Alphonse crept behind and drove one of his javelins into the Amelaren's back. The warrior bellowed, more out of surprise than pain, and toppled over. A few ticks later, the Amelaren scurried to his feet and took off, javelin still in his back. There was a wild look in Alphonse's eyes, and his lips twitched involuntarily. He pulled out another javelin, but the Amelaren was already too far away to hit. Alphonse calmed himself and sighed. A mechanical grin spread across his face as he dropped his weapon and helped his sister to her feet.

Meanwhile, Cyrus was left to contend with the other Amelaren, who flailed at him with a pair of hand axes. Cyrus parried the blows, but one of the axes glanced off his sword and rang against his helmet, jarring it loose. Cyrus held his sword out in front of him, uninjured though dazed. Seeing the opening, the Amelaren roared and swung again. Cyrus reeled, his momentum carrying him backwards as the Amelaren lunged. Somehow, he swung his body around and rocked forward, sticking out the point of his blade and connecting with the side of the Amelaren's neck. As the burly man collapsed into an untidy heap, Cyrus's knees buckled, and he dropped to the ground, clutching and shaking his head, still ringing from the earlier blow.

"You all right?" came the sound of a voice from someone standing over him.

Cyrus said something unintelligible.

Madeline bent down, grabbed his shoulders and shook him hard. "Hey! Snap out of it!"

She shook him again and again.

Finally, he grabbed her hand and pushed it away. He squinted up at her and then swiveled his head around, observing the incessant clamor and bloodshed.

"I … Thanks." Shakily, he got to his feet as Amy and Alphonse came behind Madeline.

"Let's stay close until we can rejoin the others," she said.

No sooner had she finished her sentence than a trumpet blared to the north. All of them turned toward the fort, where the Coranthian flag-bearer wildly waved his standard from the rooftop. Bodies littered the outside of the fort, most of them Amelaren. All of the inner towers had been claimed by Coranthian soldiers. While some of the Amelarens paid no heed and continued to fight, a few began to lay down their arms. The imposing figure of Colonel Gavere materialized next to the flag-bearer. His voice reverberated across the plateau.

"Enemies of Coranthia!" he boomed. "Throw down your weapons if you wish to live! Do not throw away your lives."

Another soldier appeared on the roof, dragging a body behind him. Gavere reached down and yanked a heavy wooden necklace from the corpse's neck. This was the symbol of an elbar, a token carved with the Mark of Orlen on a thick, metal chain and decorated with a coat of garish crimson war paint. Grasping Rengvir's necklace tightly, he raised his hand and waved it vigorously, so all in the vicinity could see.

One by one, the surviving Amelaren defenders responded. While some threw down their arms, most resumed fighting even more fever-ishly, catching some of the Coranthians by surprise. Naturally, Coranthian soldiers fully expected a complete surrender from the Amelarens upon verifying the death of their commander, reflecting their own predispo-sitions. As a result, the indignant Amelarens managed to register several more casualties. In the end, however, they were ruthlessly cut down, mainly by the members of the detachments led by Colonel Dyers, who had joined the fray by cleaning up pockets of resistance on the outskirts, as was according to plan.

Gavere surveyed the scene as the sounds of battle subsided. When he was satisfied, he proclaimed, "This battle is over! Argiset is ours!"

A roaring cheer rose from the Coranthian men and women left standing. The opening battle of the war had lasted slightly over half an arc.

—2—

Leynitz arrived with the 3rd Company one arc after Gavere had called for the Amelarens' surrender. The general rode with fervor across the plateau and through the remnants of the base that was now under his control, holding his head high. Trailed by Lariban and a cadre of scouts, he inspected the perimeter of the fort and called for Gavere and Dyers to join him after he had circled the structure five times.

"I should have expected this … this *shack*," he uttered disdainfully. "This won't do at all. Its foundation appears weak. We'd do better to start from scratch and use this as an auxiliary station."

"I presume we will build westward, then?" Dyers asked.

"Toward the Pyrean entrance, yes," Leynitz said. "The engineers will start tomorrow morning. The 39th is to remain here and await reinforcements. We will lead the rest to Ertel in the morning."

Around them, Coranthian soldiers cleared bodies from the vicinity of the fort. Those of their fellow countrymen were collected and set delicately aside, while the Amelaren corpses were hastily piled onto carts that the 3rd Company had brought along, and they were carried off to the east. Leynitz rested his eyes on the few surviving Amelarens who were bound and tied together, lined up against the outer sandbags.

"What do you suggest we do with the prisoners, sir? We can't let them stay and gain any knowledge of our layout."

"I agree," Gavere said, "but we cannot afford to dedicate an escort back to Aldova. We should just slaughter them all."

Leynitz cast a disapproving look in his direction.

"That joke is in rather poor taste, Armand."

The colonel's grin promptly vanished. "Apologies, sir."

"There aren't many," Leynitz said. "I was right to assume that most would not surrender. Call Captain Shelton over."

Jane Shelton, the veteran leader of the 39th Company and one of the few female captains, appeared shortly after Dyers summoned her.

"Captain, you will keep watch over the prisoners once we are gone. They are not to be let out for any reason. I will leave the size of the guard to you, but you must not allow a single Amelaren to bear witness to our construction efforts."

"Yes, My Lord. Shall I herd them into the fort now?"

"No. I will oversee the prisoners personally tonight."

"Very well, sir." Captain Shelton saluted and took her leave.

While the army awaited the arrival of the engineers from Aldova, Gavere led an impromptu memorial for the fallen Coranthians, who numbered close to one hundred. Excluding Leynitz and several of his aides, who corralled the Amelaren prisoners into the fort, everyone was in attendance. Upon its conclusion, the troops began to set up campfires and tents in preparation to spend the night.

The sun descended slowly toward the horizon, and soldiers from different details began to mingle. The buzz of conversation filled the air as men and women helped each other with their tents. Occasionally there came sounds of compacted flutes and harmonicas as soldiers, who took on the additional burden of carrying their instruments to the front, eagerly indulged in playing music to inaugurate their respite. A large convention of scouts mixed with a smaller cadre of other soldiers broke into parties and set off to the northwest and southwest in search of forage or small game, eager to indulge in a feast before the onset of their next battle. Concurrently, a lone scout approached from the west and informed Leynitz that the engineers had arrived. Ten reps later, a group of men appeared on the same path that the army had taken and streamed into the camp.

—3—

Reznik and Liam established a campsite slightly west of the fort. After he finished pounding down the last stake of their tent, Liam immediately began to construct a crude dialette with stones and whatever other suitable debris he could find around him.

Reznik watched impassively as Liam worked and sensed that the sergeant wanted to say something to him. As predicted, Liam stood and turned to face Reznik upon completing the dialette.

"I may not have known you for long, but I can already tell you are one who usually speaks his mind." Liam shifted his weight from foot to foot; he was clearly uncomfortable with the confrontation. "If you have a problem with me, just say it. It was the captain's choice to make me sergeant, not mine."

"I understand that," Reznik said reluctantly. He seemed not to want to continue. He scanned Liam's face.

"Do you?" Liam wondered aloud, staring straight into Reznik's eyes. After several awkward ticks, he smiled faintly and shrugged. "Well, that's good to hear. There's no reason we shouldn't get along then, right?"

Reznik merely nodded.

Wiping the dirt from his hands on his uniform, Liam told Reznik that he was going to help some of the other squads set up, given that they had already finished their own. He asked Reznik to join him, but Reznik declined, citing sore feet and fatigue. After finding and recruiting Philip to help, Liam absconded while Reznik started a fire.

When Reznik saw that Liam was no longer around, he sat down on a log brought to him by a designated supplier from Leynitz's vanguard. He proceeded to clean his blade, wiping it and running it through the flames. Next, he went through his armor and boots, checking for cracks, tears, and other infirmities. When he finished, he looked around. He could see Amy napping inside her tent. Cyrus, huddled over his own campfire, nursed a bruised shoulder. His other squadmates were nowhere in sight. Reznik considered this for a moment before abruptly getting up and walking away.

He weaved through the mass of campsites and stopped occasionally to observe his surroundings. Reaching a cluster of tents about two hundred meters to the east of the fort, his face lit up in recognition. He quickened his pace, and before long, he stood before two familiar figures. One, a tall and thin but fit male with short, wavy brown hair and tanned skin, gave a cheerful shout upon sighting him.

"Not a speck of dirt on you," Reznik observed, gesturing to the other man's spotless outfit.

"Good to see you too," Glen Emerett said sarcastically, tugging absently at his scout's uniform and smoothing its creases. Seeing that Reznik was alone, he craned his neck. "Where's Madeline?"

Hearing this, the short young man seated next to Glen stood up. Douglas Drake was rather heavyset but got to his feet in a flash. Waiting anxiously for a reply from Reznik, he adjusted his spectacles and scratched his matted brown hair.

Reznik raised his hand. "She's fine, though I don't know where she is. My entire squad is nowhere to be found. I think most of them may have gone hunting."

Glen raised his eyebrows.

"And why aren't you off with the hunters?" Reznik asked him.

"It's dark. Wild animals. I'm tired. I think it's an unnecessary risk for a bit of gluttony."

"Your culinary standards are quite a bit lower than those of many here," Reznik remarked with amusement. "It's about the celebration, Glen. It's a good way to mark such a decisive victory. Not that I disagree with you, though. I don't care either."

Noticing that Douglas—looking uncharacteristically gloomier and paler than usual—sat back down several paces away from the two of them, Reznik made eye contact with Glen and gestured inquisitively toward Douglas. Glen motioned for him to step out of earshot.

"I can't say I'm surprised," Reznik said in a low voice, as they walked randomly around the camps of other squads.

"One of our squadmates, Wheeler, had his arm partly severed," Glen said. "He ran around looking for a medic when the Amelaren returned. The bastard actually grabbed his arm and ripped the rest of it clean off. Then he picked up it and pried Wheeler's own sword loose from its grip to run him through with it."

Glen shook his head in disgust. "It happened right in front of us. He came straight at Douglas after that."

"What happened?"

"He froze."

Reznik hung on to that for a moment and then prodded. "So …?"

"Well, we're fine, aren't we? Disaster averted." Glen kicked up a patch of dirt from the ground.

"Some of us were like that our first time, Glen. He isn't the only one here afflicted. How many of these Lynderans have never seen so much as a fistfight on the street?"

"You know, I have noticed that. Is it a good thing that we're apparently so well-adjusted compared to non-Outlanders?"

"It's not good or bad," Reznik said. "Just the way it is. Still, I hope he snaps out of it soon."

Glen looked back up. "He'll get used to it eventually."

"I'm worried about a lack of focus during the upcoming battle. We'll all need our wits about us," Reznik said.

A faint clamor caught their attention. Several hunting parties had returned from the shadows to the north and west and converged on Colonel Dyers, who stood north of the fort by the largest campfire and waved them toward him.

"There they are," Reznik said. "They're going to divide it up for only our most distinguished comrades, I'd imagine."

"I'd imagine so," echoed a new voice. "Come on, I'll go grab some for us."

Reznik turned to see Renard standing where Glen had been ticks ago. His best friend's unblemished uniform hung loosely. Renard did not carry his lance, undoubtedly having dropped it off at the first opportunity. As usual, he stood in marked contrast to his surroundings by appearing completely at ease. "Never heard me coming, eh? I knew I should have been a scout."

Glen had returned to his campsite, where he attempted, with minimal success, to engage Douglas in conversation. Reznik and Renard looked on.

"Sorry for eavesdropping," Renard said, "but I think Douglas needs some company, so let's all have dinner together. Where's Madeline?" As Reznik pointed toward the hunting parties with a shrug, Renard continued smoothly, "No matter, we'll find her after we get our hands on some … whatever they have."

Reznik's gaze lingered on Glen and Douglas. In turn, Renard studied Reznik and found something unfamiliar in the piercing eyes, stiff pose, and distinct but inscrutable expression, though he could not place it. Leaving his former classmates as they were, he hustled to where Dyers judiciously directed the apportionment of spoils from the hunting expedition, resolving to employ his charm on the colonel and procure an ample feast for his friends.

—4—

Renard returned to the campsite carrying a wooden board, atop which lay a small piglet. Looped around each forearm was a thick string tied to small knapsacks containing berries and melons.

"Well, boys! I've got quite a meal for us tonight," Renard said, dropping the spoils. "What? You haven't even started a fire yet? You're all useless!"

Reznik had rejoined Glen and Douglas; they sat together, with Reznik slightly apart from the other two.

"Thanks for the food, Renard." Douglas said sheepishly.

"Don't mention it. Why don't you come with me to get a spit so we can keep our dinner warm?"

"Sure," Douglas said, standing and brushing some soot from his pants.

As the two headed back toward the crowd, dividing the spoils from the hunting expedition, Renard leaned over to Douglas once they were out of earshot and asked, "Doing okay?"

Douglas nodded. "It'll just take some getting used to. I'm still green."

"Aren't we all?" Renard laughed. "This is also my first real campaign, you know?"

Douglas smiled. "You wouldn't think it."

They entered the crowd surrounding the spoils, where, near the food itself, several spits were set up to be distributed to the different company. Renard caught Dyers' eye and nodded as he and Douglas lifted one of the spits.

"Up it goes," Renard said, grunting as he held one end, while Douglas took the other.

They made their way back to where Reznik and Glen had managed to light a fire.

"Great!" Renard exclaimed. The four of them worked to skewer the piglet and mount it onto the spit, which they moved into place, roasting the piglet over the fire. They ate fruit while they waited for the meat to cook.

"How's the family, Douglas?" Renard asked, breaking the silence.

Douglas shrugged sullenly.

"You know how it is. Nothing I do will ever be enough for them."

Renard shook his head. "Sorry, that was stupid of me. Just making small talk. You don't have to say more."

Douglas sighed and picked at his hair.

"And yours, Glen?" Renard said looking toward his friend. "It feels like it's been forever since we last saw each other."

"It has," Glen said. "Sorry, I wanted to catch you in Corande, but they shipped me over early. Shame, I heard I missed quite a party."

Renard laughed heartily. "That you did."

"My folks are fine, though," Glen said as he bit into an apple. "They are a bit upset I had to leave when I did. Well, at the same time, I think they're glad to be rid of me." He stared into the distance.

"For Creon's sake!" Renard shouted. "You're all quite depressing! No wonder you're such good friends."

"Don't be an ass," Glen said.

"Now, now. Watch your tone when addressing a superior officer."

The four of them broke into laughter.

"And how's that working out for you?" Reznik asked, poking the fire.

Renard cocked his head slightly. "Oh, it's not bad. I get the respect I've always deserved."

"The respect you've always thought you deserved," Reznik corrected.

"There is a serious amount of work, though." Renard's grin faded. "I don't think I've ever had to try so hard in my life. And I'm privy to certain things that I'd rather not be privy to. It's all useless politics."

"Never had to try so hard in your life?" Reznik repeated. "That's not really saying much, is it? The only thing you've ever tried hard to do is to set the bar as low as possible."

Renard shrugged, feigning innocence, but his grin returned.

"So, nice little reunion we are having, huh? If only Madeline were here, then it'd be perfect!"

"And the prince," Glen added.

At the mention of Prince Adrian, Reznik's fist tightened slightly. "No."

"Aw, but you two got along so well," Renard teased.

"You needn't remind me," Reznik said.

Renard leaned forward. "What was it he put in your clothes? Itching powder?"

A voice from the darkness startled the group. "Lord Renault? Or should I say Vice Captain Renault? Is that you?"

Liam stepped into the light of the campfire.

Recognition dawned on Renard's face. "Liam Remington! It's quite a small world. Come join us!"

Renard moved aside so Liam could get through and sit across from him. Liam seated himself next to Reznik, who shifted uneasily.

"You'll call me Renard, just like they do," Renard grinned, gesturing to Reznik and the other two young men, whom Liam did not recognize.

"Oh? You know them?"

"My friends from Tellisburg. Well, I've known this one here much longer."

Renard pointed casually to Reznik, who shrugged and said, "Hello, Sergeant."

"Ah …" Now it was Liam's turn to fidget.

"Sergeant, is it? Are you two on the same squad?" Renard asked.

Liam nodded and straightened.

"Yes, I'm the squad leader."

Renard threw Reznik a glance and said, "I see. That's good, that's very good." He burst out laughing. "Your squad isn't giving you too much trouble, I hope?"

Liam smiled. "No, my squadmates are very reliable. They performed quite admirably in today's battle."

Renard nodded, though he appeared distracted by something. Switching topics, he began to discuss the upcoming yugo season with Liam. They fervently lamented the fact it had been ten years since Kantor's team last won the championship. After the conversation gave way to dismayed silence, Renard told Liam that he had coaxed access to some spoils of the hunt, and he admitted, bashfully, while he could have taken less than he was offered by Dyers, he was unable to resist.

"Just as well that you showed up. It gives me an idea. Let's split this extra food with your squad when they get back. We'll supplement the good stuff with some of our rations. This way, people won't hate us too much."

Liam smiled.

"That's very kind of you, Renard," he said. "The rest of my squad has returned already, and we were about to set up to eat, but Avet Agilda insisted we find Avet Sylvera before we started. I told her I'd look for him. Seems I found a small feast as well!"

Renard chuckled. "We'll join you. We can carry this stuff over to your squad's camp."

Liam nodded.

The five young men carried the spit and food supplies back to the camp. By the time they arrived, the rest of the squad had settled around the campfire, preparing to break out their rations. Some of them exclaimed when they saw Reznik and the others carrying the piglet. Madeline, who had been talking to Patrice Konith, jumped up and hurried to greet Renard and the other young men. As Madeline continued to chat with her friends, Liam sat next to Philip and stretched his tired legs.

Reznik moved to set the piglet on the spit. Josef and Bethany moved to help him, as Glen and Douglas settled themselves on the grass, slightly away from the rest of the group.

Renard looked around, the familiar smirk plastered over his face. "So, let's get introductions out of the way, shall we? I'm starved."

As the members of the 9th Squad began the meal by breaking out small portions of their rations, Renard settled in and made their acquaintances. Almost everyone already knew who Renard was and reacted accordingly. For his part, Renard sized up the members of the squad as he was introduced to each in turn. He had always found that he could conveniently discern much about a person simply by observing his or her eating habits.

A notable exception was Cyrus Marcole, who denied having heard of Renard and made no attempt to ingratiate himself to the visitor. This did not surprise Madeline in the slightest; nevertheless, she found it curious that he chose to sit with the rest of them. Amy and Alphonse did not know of Renard either, though they regarded him with interest. Amy, in particular, had a look of wonderment in her eyes, one that Madeline knew all too well and had seen all too often in the eyes of innumerable young girls meeting Renard for the first time. What struck a chord with Madeline was the fact that Liam and Renard knew each other; she had not known that Liam was from Kantor. Furthermore, Renard knew Philip as well.

"And Dyson is also here," he acknowledged with a nod as the two of them shook hands.

Madeline took it upon herself to introduce Glen Emerett and Douglas Drake as friends of hers from Tellisburg, noting that they, along with her, Reznik, and Renard, had attended academy together. Knowing that Douglas would prefer not to stand out among a group in which the majority was unestated, she used his occasional alias of only his first and middle names, "Douglas Stover."

Reznik continued to roast the piglet, assisted in turn by Josef. When it was ready, Renard called upon Liam to arrange the distribution of fruit and meat. Liam complied, making sure to give Glen and Douglas portions equal to those of his squadmates and offering Renard the largest portion, which the vice captain immediately refused. Liam insisted but to no avail, and ended up spreading the rest evenly across several other servings. He and his squadmates thanked Renard for the food, but Renard insisted they not venerate him in the slightest and claimed that he did not want to "draw unnecessary attention," which elicited a rude guffaw from Madeline. To the surprise of most, Renard ceased talking once he began to eat, giving the food his full attention. Slowly, the members of the 9th Squad resumed chatting as they enjoyed their meals.

"I'm glad for this," Josef said to Bethany, "but also thoroughly exhausted. I'll be going to sleep shortly after dinner."

"We'll all need the rest," Bethany agreed.

"There may not be much fighting while trekking through the canyons," Liam said, "but we need to be on high alert the whole time."

Reznik noticed how far away Glen and Douglas sat. The two ate in silence, though listened attentively to the conversation. Behind them, a pair of young women paced around a nearby campfire. They were hard to make out in the dark; Reznik thought they looked distinctly alike and guessed they were siblings. The only discernable difference between them was that they carried different weapons.

"There they are. Those are the two I told you about earlier," Patrice said from across the campfire, nudging Madeline and pointing in the same direction.

"I've never heard of co-captains," Madeline said. "Are they actually of the same rank?"

Bethany leaned in toward them. "Jasmine, the one with the ax, is officially captain of the 28th based on her performance record, but she refuses to be treated as superior to Rosalina, so within their command, they are of equal status."

"They are really quite pretty," Josef remarked.

Everyone turned to stare at him. There was a moment of silence before Renard burst out laughing.

"Were they both born in the second cycle?" Amy said, pulling her gaze away from Josef.

"You mean because of their names?" Liam said. "They're twins, aren't they?"

"The real question is *which* second cycle?" Alphonse wondered.

Bethany smiled. "I grew up with them, but even I forget, and they'll never tell you. It's their own inside joke."

"How do you know them?" Patrice asked. "Did they fight in the Coronation War as well?"

"No, they were too young ... but we're all from Densley."

"You're also Lynderan, then?" Josef asked.

"That's right." Bethany looked around slowly. "I think I'm the only unestated Lynderan here."

Everyone exchanged glances. Reznik, Madeline, Renard, and Glen stared knowingly at Douglas, who shrugged.

"What about you, Marcole?" Alphonse said.

Cyrus frowned, clearly displeased at having drawn attention.

"Calena," he said curtly.

"I guess it does, then," Bethany said.

"Bethany knows many people," Liam remarked approvingly. "She fought alongside my father seventeen years ago."

He stood up.

"Anyway, Renard, I must thank you again for the wonderful meal. Now I'll check our inventory before we turn in for the night." He walked away from the fire and began to inspect the piles of gear stacked beside each of the squad tents. Philip gave Renard a slight bow and followed Liam.

"Avet Lane," Reznik blurted out once Liam was out of earshot, "you should have been named sergeant."

This drew the attention of all present.

Bethany smiled and shook her head without missing a beat. "No, I'm not much for leading. The captain made the right choice. Besides, Liam is doing well. I know him, and I know that he'll continue to do well."

Reznik frowned. "Perhaps. Regardless, I wanted to hear your opinion on the matter."

Madeline looked at Reznik in surprise.

"I've served a long time," Bethany said with a smile. "If I had wanted to be sergeant, don't you think I'd be one by now?"

Renard stared at Bethany for a moment with a glint in his eyes. He put down his bowl and clapped Reznik on the back. "On that note, I have to return to my own camp. I'm sure my company would be jealous if they found out I was here, although I saw that our captain had secured quite a feast for them. Maybe they haven't even noticed I've gone." He laughed. "I hope I haven't imposed on you for too long."

"Not at all!" Amy blurted out, breaking her silence. Cyrus, who sat nearby, stared at her incredulously before bursting into harsh, mocking laughter.

"It was a pleasure meeting you all." Renard smiled, though instead of turning to leave, he walked slowly to Bethany.

Madeline's eyes widened. "Here we go," she groaned.

"Miss Lane," Renard crooned, "I am terribly sorry that we do not have more time to become acquainted. All I have learned is that your charms and reason are irresistible, even to this stubborn friend of mine." He pointed theatrically at Reznik before continuing. "I expect all of you to treat my lady here with the utmost deference and respect."

He bowed deeply to her and extended his hand.

"Well, well! But this is hardly fitting of a vice captain!" Bethany exclaimed, blushing deeply, clearly delighted. She gave him her hand, which he clasped with both of his.

Amy Trenton's eyes widened as her expression morphed into naïve envy and disappointment.

"You really have no self-control, you know that?" Reznik said disapprovingly.

"Go on, get out of here," Madeline shouted, waving her hands to drive him away.

With a flawless smile, Renard released Bethany's hand and sauntered away, giving Reznik one last clap on the back as he passed. He paused briefly to bid farewell to Glen and Douglas. Reznik broke into a heartfelt grin when he saw that Douglas seemed to have come out of his languor and had thoroughly enjoyed Renard's display. It was a sight familiar to Reznik; Renard was always willing to act inappropriately to lighten the mood and bring out the best in others.

Glen nodded with satisfaction as he shook Renard's hand and rose to his feet. He addressed the members of the 9th Squad in a subdued voice, while echoing Renard's words in professing his thanks for the meal and offered his best wishes to all of them for the upcoming battle. Meanwhile, Reznik walked over to Douglas and the two conversed briefly.

Madeline was glad to see that Douglas had reverted at least partially to his more animated self and wished to see them off, but for some reason, she felt it better not to circle the campfire to join her friends on the other side while the rest of her squadmates watched. She was worried this might reflect negatively on her and Reznik, especially given their acquaintance with Renard. She did not want to feel alienated, nor did she want to impart such feelings to her squadmates, so she remained seated beside Bethany and Patrice, content to wave goodbye to Glen and Douglas as they left.

—5—

From his tent, Liam looked on as the members of his squad sat and conversed around the campfire. The festivities receded soon after Renard left. After chatting for a while longer, Amy and Alphonse retired to their respective tents for the night. As Madeline cleaned up around the campfire, she caught Cyrus staring at her. He broke eye contact immediately and left for his tent. Though Reznik noticed this, he exhibited no visible reaction. He joined Madeline in cleaning. The two remained mostly silent.

Liam kept his eyes firmly locked on Reznik as the avet helped Madeline. The evening's earlier attempt to clear the tension with Reznik had not gone entirely according to plan, but Liam hoped he had made some progress with his hostile squadmate. It was imperative for him to clear the air as best as he could. He hated to see people ill-disposed toward him.

Throughout it all, Josef sat in front of the fire, reading his field manual, occasionally jotting notes in the margins. Eventually, he was alone in front of the fire. Other campfires slowly extinguished across the plateau. Rodtorches were lit and erected atop the fort and up in the watchtowers, as the 39th Company, designated to stay and wait for reinforcement from Aldova after the rest of the force left the next day, took up their positions for the night watch.

Liam decided to take advantage of the opportunity to have a one-on-one with someone from his squad. He quietly exited his tent and sat next to Josef by the fire.

"How are you, Avet Reinbach?" he asked.

"Me?" Josef was visibly surprised by the sudden appearance of his sergeant.

"I haven't seen you move from this spot all night. I thought you were going to sleep right after dinner?"

"Ah, yes. I am tired, definitely, but I got caught up in my reading. And please, just call me Josef."

"That's good, that's good," Liam said, rubbing his hands together and reaching for the fire.

"That vice captain. Renault, was it? He acts quite comfortably around commoners. I would not have expected that from a fellow estated. Although I must confess that I am still adjusting to Coranthian social norms."

Liam laughed. "Are you saying I'm uncomfortable around commoners, Josef?"

"No, of course not, sir," Josef said, apparently oblivious to Liam's jest. "Rather, he doesn't really behave like a noble."

"I know what you meant," Liam said. "He's always been like that, though he's an exception. He may be estated, but he is at the lower end of the hierarchy, and his father never really cared to obtain a higher standing. I think he and his family are simply comfortable where they are."

"And that's not common here?" Josef asked.

"No, most estated make it their life goal to climb higher. In a way, I envy him."

Josef raised an eyebrow and reached back to adjust his dark brown ponytail. "How so?"

"Less pressure. He has the perks of being an estated, while at the same time he can be himself."

Renard was only a casual acquaintance, but Liam was familiar enough with him to know that the two of them grew up with similar means. Despite that, their family fortunes had diverged drastically. Liam became pensive as he reflected on how he was following in the footsteps of his father, who ultimately had little to show for his military service, and wondered how well he would be able to bear the burden of his family name.

Josef chuckled. "He does seem to rather enjoy life."

"Well, don't let his demeanor fool you. He's an extremely capable individual when he's motivated. I'm sure he'll be a fine officer …"

Liam stared at Josef who shifted uncomfortably.

"Yes, sir?"

"Tell me, do you think I should be sergeant? I'm not sure I'm doing such a great job as a leader. Everyone seems to be pulling in a different direction."

"Ah, speaking for myself, I think you are doing just fine. We are all inexperienced, but I think we will come together, though it may be through force."

"You're referring to a trial by fire?" Liam asked, somewhat skeptically.

"Perhaps," Josef rubbed his nose. "At the very least, it seems you have reached an understanding with our Tellisburg friend."

"Reznik Sylvera, you mean?" Liam was pleased to hear that Josef perceived at least a partial deflation of the tension between him and Reznik.

"From what I saw during the battle today, he is very serious, perhaps overly so, but he is also very good."

"Indeed," Liam agreed.

"Ah, and as are you, sir. You have my vote of confidence. I have not yet had reason to doubt your capabilities."

Liam nodded. "Thanks."

Josef resumed scribbling in his manual. Liam watched the avet in silent contemplation. The Doromalian was certainly eccentric, though not a bad conversationalist.

"Do you have anyone waiting back home?"

"Hmm?" Josef looked up.

"A family."

"I do. I'm married."

Liam raised an eyebrow and said, "She must miss you."

"Yes, and I miss her very much. Maybe next time I'm on leave long enough to go to Lymria, I'll get to see her. I can, at least, write letters." Josef cocked his head.

"I see."

"How about yourself, sir?"

Liam stared off into the darkness and closed his eyes as he spoke. An image of a woman came flooding into his mind. He thought of her raven hair and deep brown eyes. "I have a girl back in Kantor, Anne. I was on border patrol for a while before coming to Aldova, so I haven't seen her in quite some time."

"It's difficult to think about sometimes," Josef said. "Many soldiers must deal with similar situations."

Liam opened his eyes with some effort. Giving in to his fatigue, he rose to his feet.

"Well, good night, Josef. I'll be retiring now."

"Good night, Sergeant." Josef said.

With a nod, Liam departed for his tent.

After several reps, Josef closed his manual and laid it beside him. He rose from his seat and picked up the bucket beside the pit, upending it to unleash a stream of dirt that extinguished the fire. He felt around where he sat to retrieve his manual and then used the dim light pulsing from the few remaining fires to make his way to the tent he shared with Alphonse.

As the remaining campsites went dark, the long day finally came to an end.

Chapter 7

(987.2.05)

The army marched deep into the eastern Ghend Highlands, forty kilometers away from the Coranthian encampment at Argiset. The sun was out in full force but could not be seen over the sheer granite walls that were lining either side of Ertel Gorge, through which the troops were moving. The contrast between the sparkling clarity above them and the long shadows cast by the walls made for poor visibility. The gorge itself was barren; only the occasional shrub or small tree protruding from surrounding ridges decorated the scenery. The passage also acted as a wind tunnel; a light breeze blew against the troops, at first capricious but gradually strengthening as the army moved farther east.

Eventually, the path narrowed to the point where two companies could not move alongside each other; the lower platoons lined up to the north of their respective upper platoons and the ensemble of companies advanced in this fashion, spaced approximately two hundred meters apart from one another. The group of surveyors, save for two who remained at Argiset, followed Nelhart and marched along with Leynitz's company at the formation's rear.

Marching among the 26th Company in the middle of the procession, Liam stared at the armored backs of his fellow soldiers as he plodded on. Occasionally, he cast a glance behind to check on his squadmates. The 9th Squad was positioned toward the middle of the platoon's configuration.

Nash had organized the squads so that those with more experience were near the front of the formation. Liam was unnerved by how close to the front of the company his squad was.

Nash led the formation during this part of the trek, trotting along on his steed. He wore a standard military uniform with armoring underneath and a lightweight open-faced helmet. The outfit was identical to that worn by nonofficers, and his glasses were once again tucked safely in his bag. A heavily armored Parsons rode parallel to him. Officers' coats and capes were not worn when there was risk of battle; the steeds and the officers' pins affixed to the left breast of uniforms and armor identified officers in the field.

Occasionally, messengers galloped to or from Leynitz's position, tersely relaying information from either the general or one of the colonels, and moving on to the next company without a tick wasted. Other than that, the clanking of metal, the sparring rhythms of boots and hooves on rock and dirt were all that could be heard.

As she carried forward, Madeline tried not to let her mind wander, but the monotony strained her efforts, and before she knew it, she was watching a large bird circle far overhead. Though its features were difficult to discern from such a distance, she surmised it was a condor. Despite the fact that she had never actually seen one, she knew from peeking at Reznik's copy of *Wildlife in the Dynan Midlands* that the highlands were home to various condors. Inevitably, it dawned on her how far away she was from home and how much had changed in so little time. Her thoughts shifted to her parents; every time she thought of them, she made a conscious effort to conjure as many details involving them as she could. She traced through her uniform the outline of the Coranox she wore around her neck.

She thought of her mother, and abruptly, the horrific image of her sprawled, unmoving body loomed over her. Just as suddenly, she flashed back to several days before. Her mind laid out before her the dead Amelaren soldier—no, not only a soldier, but a young woman whose life had been extinguished at Madeline's own hand—next to her mother. She shuddered violently.

A hand fell on her shoulder, its firm grip steadying her and snapping her back. The steady tune of soldiers and horses drumming through the gorge faded back in. She turned her head and saw Reznik staring at her. She felt his penetrating gaze, the one that always made her feel that he knew exactly what she was thinking, even when it was unlikely. She had not spoken to him about Argiset and realized she knew just as little about his first real battle experience as he knew about hers.

She looked around. Nobody else paid them any attention. She felt Reznik's grip loosen and his hand slide away. She turned back toward him; he still looked at her, but the expression on his face had reverted to its usual neutral blankness.

After several ticks of silence, his eyes drifted away, and he pointed forward. "Look," he said, "the canyon walls widen up ahead. That's most likely where the junction is."

Madeline turned and squinted. "I can't see a thing," she declared.

Hearing them, Liam turned around. "I'm positive that the 17th should be nearing the junction by now. It shouldn't be much farther. I think it's just hard to make out from here."

"Yes," Josef grumbled in agreement from behind them, "rock everywhere."

Liam and Reznik were proven correct when, fifteen reps later, the walls began to widen. Madeline recalled that someone, possibly Reznik, had told her that the mapping of the area was tenuous at best, and it had been more than five years since any Coranthian documented the area firsthand. Nevertheless, according to their intelligence, the troops would soon arrive at a three-way junction with a north-south split. Down the northern path was Ertel Ridge, formerly a collection of small Amelaren lookouts built on a slope not as steep as its name implied, now purportedly a larger fortification installed within the rocks themselves. The southern path was allegedly blocked by a large landslide partway down the corridor. The conquest of Ertel Ridge was of great strategic importance and would cede complete control of the main corridor into enemy lands to the Coranthians. The northern corridor was the most direct route to the Amelarens' main military fortress and capital, while the southern route led to the vast Amelaren plantations.

Suddenly, Patrice tilted her head and said nervously, "What is that? I think I hear something ahead."

Madeline listened intently. At first, she heard nothing except a low rumble, but as they pressed on, the rumble morphed into the distinct sound of clashing metal.

"Sounds like fighting," Bethany remarked dryly, staring straight ahead as she spoke. The rest of the squad remained silent. Murmurs soon swept through the entirety of the 26th, as it became clear to everyone that a battle was raging ahead.

A horse's gallop grew louder and a messenger soon appeared, racing toward them. He stopped for only a few ticks to impart some words to Nash before proceeding to the next company behind them. Madeline turned her head to follow him as he raced past. Her focus shifted to Patrice and the Trenton siblings. All three were tensed, though she noticed that Alphonse appeared to be excited rather than nervous. Josef caught her eye and gave her a brief, calm smile. He appeared rather relaxed, all things considered. As she spun back around, she almost ran into Liam. The soldiers had come to a halt.

"Troops!" Nash said loudly but in a strained voice. He spun his horse to address his company and cleared his throat before continuing. "The Amelarens have laid an ambush ahead. The southern path is not blocked as we had previously thought. The enemy is attacking from both directions. The 5th, 17th, and 35th are currently engaging them. Unfortunately, poor visibility is preventing an accurate estimate of enemy numbers."

He paused to clear his throat again, trying unsuccessfully to hide his unease as the sounds of battle grew louder. "Colonel Gavere is handling the enemy attack quite capably, I'm certain, but we shall prepare to join in should it be necessary."

With his entire command hanging on his words, he struggled to come up with an eloquent finish and managed only to hastily add, "Just follow your sergeants, and we should be fine," before turning around and waving meekly to restart the march as he spurred Alma to resume trotting.

Liam shook his head faintly. Behind them, Reznik gave Madeline a knowing look, to which she tried to respond with a shrug, but even she was rendered incredulous by their captain's lack of eloquence. On Reznik's other side, Cyrus stood with his hands balled into fists. His face was pale, and his entire body trembled.

"Stay alert, everyone," Liam said as firmly as he could without turning around.

Alphonse whispered excitedly to his sister, "Finally, some action! We didn't get much of it last time." He gripped his javelin tightly and waved it in an exaggerated manner.

Amy frowned at him.

Next to them, Josef said, "Alphonse. You sound like many young men of the Empire. They love their wars. Maybe not so much as the Amelarens, but they do get caught up in the bloodlust and spirit of battle. They are quite mistaken, I think. There is little glory in taking lives, no matter how justified."

Amy nodded in agreement as Alphonse fell silent.

As the 26th crept farther eastward, distant screams and other sounds of battle could be heard. Because Nash had temporarily halted the advance of the company and slowed its pace, the distance between the 26th and the 28th, which was lined up ahead, began to lengthen, while the 32nd was catching up from behind. A disheveled and frantic messenger arrived and beckoned to Nash, who rode to the southern side of the formation. The messenger spoke quickly and urgently, though with appropriate precision. Nash glanced uneasily from side to side as the messenger spoke. He reached into his bag and slipped something into the messenger's hand. Nash did this adroitly and unnoticeably. The messenger gave him an uncertain glance before nodding and spurring his horse. As he sped past the 26th, most of the troops took notice of his torn uniform, which was coated in dirt, as blood seeped through his right sleeve. Most strikingly, a broken arrow protruded from his shoulder.

Nash rode to Parsons, and the two conversed in low tones. The captain produced a handkerchief from his left breast pocket and mopped his forehead as he spoke. After they were finished, Nash and Parsons separated. They stopped their horses and turned around.

"Listen up, soldiers," Parsons said in a firm but matter-of-fact voice. "The 17th and 35th have been routed, and the 5th took heavy losses. The survivors are currently regrouping with the 28th. They are attempting to hold back the enemy ahead. Should they fail, that task will fall to us, and I expect nothing less than the best from all of you. If the Amelarens do not break our formation, they shall not overcome our formidable defense." As he spoke, another messenger whizzed past, this time from behind, carrying an order from Leynitz.

Nash expected a strong verbal reaction from his troops, but to his surprise, hardly a word was uttered. Instead, he watched as the 26th collectively steeled itself in preparation for battle. He saw Parsons regarding him expectantly and nodded. Together, they turned and began slowly advancing. As the two platoons fell in line behind them, the wind began to kick up a large amount of dirt into the air, further decreasing visibility. Nash kept a careful rein on Alma, not wishing to move too quickly. He had no desire to rush into battle.

Liam looked back at his squad and offered a nervous grin, eliciting nervous chuckles from Alphonse and Patrice. He was pleased to have deflated the tension, however infinitesimally, though deep down he was terrified. He was deeply concerned with the clear miscalculation by the general and knew that an ambush by the Amelarens in such a vulnerable location was not good. He wondered how much of the Coranthian initiative had been blunted. Of course, there was nothing to be done about the situation. All that mattered was making it through the battle alive. He took a deep breath and calmly drew his sword, holding it ready. Several others followed his lead.

The 26th continued to crawl forward. After several reps, a single man came charging toward them along the southern wall. Nash's heart pounded fiercely, but subsided somewhat when he recognized the man as Colonel Gavere. He blazed past them, and around ten reps later, returned heading up a small unit of ten men. The colonel rode to Nash and placed his hand on the young captain's shoulder, whispering something to him before turning to the whole company. He raised his ax above his head proudly and authoritatively and then abruptly and wordlessly whirled around and rode into the east.

Having regained some of his composure, Nash addressed his command. "Attention! General Leynitz has ordered a full retreat. The company behind us has already begun to withdraw. We will regroup and consider another plan of attack. Colonel Gavere has ridden ahead to pass the orders to the 28th and assist with the retreat."

Without a moment's hesitation, Nash began to ride westward. A look of relief washed over his face, and several soldiers stared at him with uncertainty. The soldiers of the 26th underwent a collective about-face and marched west, with Nash and Parsons now leading from the rear of the 26th's formation.

"We're just going to leave them there?" Amy asked worriedly.

"We can and we will," Liam said resolutely. "We will listen to the captain and retreat while we still have time."

Madeline and Reznik stared at each other. He knew she was thinking about Glen and Douglas.

"They'll be fine," Reznik said.

She nodded.

Liam overheard them and immediately felt a pang of guilt. He had forgotten that their friends were part of the 28th.

"The Curtlands lead the 28th," Bethany said confidently. "I know of no better captains with us today. They will pull themselves out without question."

Despite the concerted effort made by the 26th to withdraw expediently, the battle soon caught up to them; the ranks of the 28th had significantly thinned, and some of its soldiers were pulling back to catch up with the 26th. The members of the 9th Squad, among the closest to what was the rear of the now-reversed formation, stopped in their tracks to consider this new development. Parsons, who had lingered behind everyone else, rode farther east to meet the soldiers from the 28th.

Suddenly, Madeline saw one of the Curtland sisters emerge from the shadows and ride up to Parsons. With her thoughts scrambled, she could not make out which twin she was. Parsons pointed toward the east, and the Curtland sister nodded. He called out to Nash, though his words were meant for all to hear.

"Captain! The 28th requires assistance. The lower platoon will fan out and make a stand here to reinforce incoming retreating soldiers."

Nash gaped back at him and then turned his head to look at the lower 26th. He barely managed to say, "Do as the vice captain instructs."

Slowly, the lower 26th took up positions across the gorge. Many of the soldiers were uncertain and afraid, and it showed plainly on their faces, though ultimately, they were all committed to their duty. Once Parsons was satisfied with the formation, he began to lead his troops east. A cloud crept ominously toward them, and as Parsons rode forward, he realized that it was not just a cloud of dirt but one of smoke as well.

"Be ready for smoke bombs," he shouted, raising his lance and shield. "Onward!"

Madeline watched as Parsons and his platoon vanished into the cloud. She turned back and saw that Nash had moved to the front of the retreat. She also realized that the Coranthian troops scarcely moved. The passage, once again narrowing as they retraced their steps, definitely hampered their progression. Madeline heard voices rising from the east. They grew louder; the fight would be upon them before long. If this was the Amelaren plan, she thought, it was a good one. The Coranthian command had gravely underestimated its supposedly savage and brazen opponent.

After several reps had passed, a harsh whinny blared as a horse broke through the ranks of the 26th, knocking aside several soldiers as it galloped west. It moved unsteadily, bleeding from a cut on its left ear. Nash watched as it raced past. He recognized the black durion, Castor. Nash's second-in-command was not on the horse.

"Parsons …"

His face was white with dread as he halted and sat frozen atop Alma. Many of the soldiers were unnerved by the sight of their captain's loss of composure.

Meanwhile, the fighting came into plain view. Members of the lower 26th and 28th tried to hold a pack of Amelarens at bay but were being continually driven back toward the Upper 26th. Screams of agony mixed with the clangs of weapons as soldiers continued to fall. Despite the collapse of the Coranthian front lines, the Amelarens did not seem to significantly outnumber them. With Parsons missing and Nash effectively incapacitated, Liam felt that as a sergeant, he had to intervene. He tried to estimate the size of the Amelaren force that was visible from where he stood and thought five hundred to be a conservative estimate. That was hardly an overwhelming force in numbers, though the Amelarens had positioning and momentum in their favor. Scanning the ranks of those fighting, Liam's heart sank as he realized that Parsons was indeed nowhere to be seen. He could make out the Curtland twins, who appeared to have taken over the combined forces of the lower 26th and 28th. He decided that he would muster his squad and as many others as he could to rally.

Raising his sword, Liam cried, "We will stay and fight! We have to support our countrymen as best as we can! I know we—"

Before he could finish his sentence, a volley of arrows emerged from the cloud of dirt and smoke and rained down on them. Several soldiers were hit. One arrow struck Liam in the back of the neck. It pierced almost completely through, severing his jugular. Blood spurted from the wound and from Liam's mouth as he grabbed frantically at the arrow, choking on his words. Amy let out a scream as Liam fell onto his knees. With the exception of Philip, who ran toward Liam, the entire squad froze, standing aghast as their sergeant crumpled to the ground.

Philip caught Liam before he could completely topple over and laid him gently on the ground, his eyes wide with terror. Liam reached out blankly with his hand. Philip grabbed it and clutched firmly as Liam began to lose consciousness.

Liam's final thoughts were filled with sadness. This was not what he had envisioned his life to be, not how he had wanted it to end. He felt that he had disgraced his father and his family's name. An image of the girl with whom he had only recently begun a relationship, and would not have the chance to know more intimately, flashed before his eyes. Within a rep, he had gasped his last breath.

Philip realized that his friend was no more and released his hand. He sat heavily on the ground and stared blankly at Liam's body. Cyrus looked away, while Amy and Alphonse stood rooted to the spot in horror. Patrice's training kicked in. She knelt next to Philip to examine Liam, but as she fumbled with her bag, she released the sobs she had tried to suppress, knowing there was nothing she could do. She reached out with her hand and closed Liam's eyes, which were locked in a lifeless stare, and began to bandage his neck wound anyway in an attempt to stop the bleeding, appearing not wholly cognizant of her actions.

"The arrows stopped?" Josef asked nervously, addressing Bethany, but she did not and perhaps could not answer and simply shook her head. She brought a hand to her face and covered her eyes.

Madeline felt everything spin around her. The Amelarens were practically on top of them, and the number of Coranthians standing dwindled, yet the Upper 26th was completely incapacitated despite the imminent danger. Nash sat atop Alma as if he were a statue. Gavere was nowhere to be seen. The sight of Liam's corpse seemed entirely too surreal to her. He had been speaking to her, to the whole squad, reassuring them and directing them just a few reps ago. She searched for Reznik and saw him staring grimly at Nash. She wanted to say something to him but was at a loss.

When she looked to him again, he was no longer there. Gazing around, she spotted him standing beside Nash's horse. He spoke to the captain, who initially regarded him as if he did not understand what was being said. Suddenly, Nash nodded and dismounted. Without any hesitation, Reznik climbed on, provoking a stir among the soldiers of the 26th.

Reznik drew and raised his sword. "Listen!" he shouted clearly and purposefully. "We need to buy some time for the 21st and the rest of the companies behind us to pull back. And we must aid our comrades in the lower platoon. Leaving them to fend for themselves is unacceptable. Those of you who are not comfortable with this, join the retreat. But I will not turn back. The soldiers ahead are doing their best to show off the resiliency of the Coranthian Army and I plan to join them in doing so."

The Upper 26th was confused by this outburst from an avet who had commandeered the captain's horse. Many of them looked to Nash for a response.

Seeing this, Reznik added, "I shall stay and fight! Captain, what do you say?"

Nash turned to regard his soldiers. The sea of faces hinged on his every word. "Listen to Avet Sylvera," he said, though his voice did not project well, now that he was off his steed. "To those who are willing and able, the lower platoon is in need of your services."

After a moment's pause, some of the soldiers stirred and sheathed their weapons and resumed heading west. Others looked uncertain but held their ground. Cyrus saw Philip join the retreat, carrying Liam's body on his back.

"Hey!" Cyrus barked.

Philip's normally gentle brown eyes glared wrathfully at him, and he kept walking. Soon, he was out of sight, helped along by several other soldiers who also decided to leave.

All in all, well over three-quarters of the platoon remained. There were even a few cheers as they tried to rally their spirits. Reznik addressed the remaining soldiers.

"We will form a wall at the front lines and advance until we meet with the others, absorbing the lower platoon and anyone else left. After that, we'll retreat, while maintaining formation. We must hold formation at all costs! That will be the key to our survival."

He spoke with the sternness and confidence of a colonel. Madeline felt a twinge of hope and pride swell within her, in spite of the grim circumstances.

Josef sighed. "I guess this is better than waiting to die."

"That may still happen," Cyrus said with a grimace.

"Well, you're still here, aren't you?" Patrice said, struggling to calm down.

Reznik pulled gingerly on Alma's reins and trotted past the 9th Squad to the front of the formation, with Nash following on foot. He ordered the rearrangement of soldiers into six rows, each row, except the last one, spanning the width of the passage. The front two rows were comprised entirely of those with shields.

"Why the hell should we listen to you?" one of the soldiers shouted. "What estate are you from?"

Reznik blinked rapidly and let out an incredulous, humorless laugh.

"Do you have a better idea, *sir*?" he asked, jumping off the horse to fall in with the front row. He said to Nash, "Thank you, Captain. I apologize for taking your horse."

Nash nodded. "Avet Sylvera's plan is sound," he said to the soldiers who were lined up in front of him. "We will proceed with it. Forward, troops!"

"Forward!" Reznik echoed.

The wall of soldiers began to advance. Although the battle had been within his sights from the beginning, Reznik could not easily follow its details. Before long, the gap was only one hundred meters. Coranthians and Amelarens alike paused to consider the arrival of the Upper 26th. Most of the Amelarens withdrew to reorganize, granting their opponents temporary respite. Reznik saw that many of the remaining Coranthians had grouped into a staggered formation to hold off the Amelaren force bearing down on them. He recognized the twin captains of the 28th from their armor and was able to make out Glen and Douglas who were standing just behind them as the Upper 26th approached.

Before the two Coranthian units could merge, the Amelarens returned, charging hard into the group led by the Curtlands. Although he was a scout, Glen fought up front with the more heavily armored soldiers. He wielded two gladii just as well as they could a sword and shield. An Amelaren heavy axman took a swing at him. The weight of the blow knocked him back, but Glen recovered immediately and slashed the warrior's right leg, slicing through to the bone. The injured Amelaren screamed and fell over and was quickly pushed aside by his comrades as a new fighter took his place. Meanwhile, Douglas held his own with a lance and shield, though he was almost completely spent after having fought for so long already. Still, he pressed on, fueled purely by adrenaline.

"Glen! Douglas! Glad to see you!" Reznik said. The Amelarens were temporarily beaten back, and the Curtlands, upon noticing the arrival of backup, shifted their formation to fold into that of the advancing soldiers of the Upper 26th, who advanced to relieve their winded compatriots.

Glen did not turn around, for his attention was trained on a group of oncoming Amelarens. He dodged a wild swipe of the warrior's sword and rammed into the Amelaren, causing him to stumble backwards and trip two others.

"Come, get behind the line," Reznik said.

"They charged right through after they jumped on the 17th, 35th, and 5th," Glen said, coughing slightly as he waved at lingering tendrils of smoke. "Practically wiped them out, using only smoke bombs and grenades. They haven't thrown any since. I think they used them all during the ambush, but watch out."

"Thank you for coming," Douglas huffed. "I thought … we thought, after Colonel Gavere's orders …"

"Thank us later," Reznik snapped. "Keep your shield up!"

He strode forward to meet another warrior, blocking two successive attacks before jabbing his sword into the enemy's chest. Blood gushed from the wound, some of it spattering onto Reznik's armor and shield. To either side of him were Josef and Cyrus. To their right, Alphonse waded enthusiastically into the mass of clashing flesh and metal, swinging his javelin in a frenzy.

"Medics in the back!" Reznik shouted to those retreating past him through the formation. Glen, noticing Douglas's winded state, tapped him on the shoulder and indicated that they should withdraw temporarily to catch their breath. Panting, Douglas nodded, and the two went on their way.

Reznik got his first direct glimpse of the Curtlands. Though they wore partial face helmets, he could tell they were significantly older than he, though younger than Bethany. Both had tanned skin, thin lips, and dark brown eyes. Both were fighting for their lives and the lives of their subordinates in the 28th.

After smashing through a swarm of Amelarens with her one-handed ax and shield, Jasmine finally stopped to address Reznik after watching him for some time from her periphery.

"Disobeying orders, are you?" she said after relieving an Amelaren of an arm and a leg. "Who are you anyway? Where's Captain Havora?"

"Avet Sylvera. I am acting as the captain's proxy on the front lines," Reznik said, blinking hard. His eyes had grown irritated from smoke and dirt.

"Avet? What—" Jasmine began, her eyes widening. She turned toward him, leaving her blind side vulnerable.

"Jasmine, focus!" Rosalina Curtland said. She fitted a bolt to her crossbow and fired, splitting open the skull of a warrior approaching her sister from behind. The fact that she was fighting up front with light armor, a crossbow, and a knife was not lost on Reznik; he was duly impressed by both women.

"Captain, please retreat," he said to Jasmine. "We'll buy you some time."

"Retreat?" Jasmine roared. "The hell I will! Since when do you get to tell me what to do? My sister and I lead our troops, so we lead the fighting. We're going to hold off these bastards. I don't know what the hell Captain Havora is doing, but you'll follow *our* orders. Understand?"

Reznik nodded. "Where's Colonel Gavere?" he asked.

Jasmine shook her head. "I don't know. Fall in beside me, Avet."

"Yes, Captain," Reznik said, with no small measure of relief.

Jasmine took command at the front of the wall, while Rosalina moved back several rows to issue commands from the middle of the formation. Slowly, the collective of soldiers retreated west. The Coranthians held the Amelarens with relatively little trouble, which seemed to take some of the warriors by surprise. Now that the soldiers had recovered both in terms of numbers and organization, the Amelarens were unable to break through their defenses. The Coranthians, their spirits somewhat renewed, pulled together, improving their performance. Soldiers stepped forward to fortify the wall whenever anyone in front fell or was forced to retreat with a grievous injury. The formation loosened further behind the front lines, enabling medics to shuttle injured soldiers to safety before working on them. The Amelarens launched volleys of arrows toward the rear of Coranthian formation, but the strong wind greatly reduced their accuracy. The retreat progressed relatively smoothly; after twenty reps, a messenger arrived from the west and spoke to both Nash and Rosalina, informing them that all of the companies behind the 26th had moved farther out. After this information was relayed to Jasmine, she issued an order for everyone to hasten the retreat. Roughly forty reps after the Upper 26th joined the battle, the two sides exchanged what seemed to be parting shots from bows and crossbows. While the Amelarens kept pace with the retreating Coranthians, they maintained a deliberate distance and ceased to attack.

"This is odd," Josef muttered.

Reznik looked around and accounted for the remainder of the 9th Squad with the exception of Philip, who had carried Liam's body back to the main force. Among the frontliners, Josef did not appear tired in the least, as he stood at attention and peered intently at the Amelarens. Cyrus and Alphonse were worn but uninjured. Reznik himself had suffered only an insignificant cut on his hand but remained tense.

"You're right, Reinbach," Reznik agreed. "There's too little resistance."

"Don't let your guard down until we back out of this passage," Jasmine said. "They shouldn't follow us once we make it out of here."

Only two kilometers separated the 26th and 28th from the entrance to the gorge, where the rest of the main force awaited them. As the Coranthian force continued westward, the walls began to widen. To cover the entire width of the passage, the formation would have to spread out. Rosalina realized immediately what was happening and charged to the front, her crossbow at the ready. Madeline, Bethany, and Amy followed her lead.

Jasmine understood as well. "Reinforce the front! Get more soldiers up here now!" she shouted.

A roar went up on the Amelaren side as the steadily advancing warriors broke into a run toward the Coranthians. A man clad in studded onyx leather armor emerged from the center of the wave. Streaks of blood covered him from head to toe, most notably staining his blond and silver hair. Jasmine's eyes were drawn to the man's weapon, which dwarfed the size of any Coranthian blade. It took only a tick for her to recognize him as War Chief Tallen, carrying a massive broadsword that cast a long shadow of death over its inevitable victims. Though Jasmine was not well versed in Amelaren dialects, when he yelled and pointed that sword at her, she needed no translation: He was coming for her.

Once again, the Amelarens ran to engage the retreating Coranthians. Their vigor renewed, they fought savagely and relentlessly. The Coranthian formation buckled as the front line had been insufficiently reinforced. Tallen and the warriors around him hacked their way through several groups of soldiers. Reznik knew the situation was dire. Tallen locked into combat with a small group of shield-bearing soldiers who had separated from the rest of the formation and were trying to withstand the war chief's onslaught. Although Tallen had yet to break through, he had not tired; on the contrary, he seemed to be enjoying himself immensely. His face flushed as if with fever, he wound his broadsword and swung at his targets with all his might. The soldiers, who merely tried to brace themselves against the hit, were knocked to the ground. Several warriors jumped from out behind Tallen and descended upon the fallen avets, brutally hammering them to death and relishing the terrible screams of the writhing soldiers.

Most Coranthians were exhausted. Those without shields moved up to support their fellow soldiers, though many were unprepared to handle the ferocity of the enemy's attacks. Before long, the line had collapsed. The Amelarens surged forward and tore into the Coranthian ranks. The passage entrance was now no more than one kilometer to the west; some of the soldiers decided simply to turn and run. Bodies fell quickly and unceremoniously. Swirling winds filled the air with the stench of blood and sweat.

Madeline and Amy scrambled to keep their wits about themselves as they fell back to the middle of the now-broken formation. Even some of the medics had been caught in the fighting, and without much protection, they fell to the blows of bloodthirsty warriors. Madeline looked around once or twice for Patrice, but did not catch sight of her. After trading blows with an Amelaren warrior, she feinted and caught her opponent off balance and then planted her gladius into the woman's chest. The exchange was similar to the one that had taken place at Argiset, though this time, she could not afford a moment to reflect. Even a tick's lapse in concentration would be fatal. She panicked as she realized she was unable to pull out her sword. She finally raised a leg to kick the body back, releasing the gladius. She fell on her backside and looked up just in time to see an Amelaren bring his sword down on her. She narrowly managed to roll out of the way and then jumped to her feet and continued to fight.

Meanwhile, Glen, having returned to the fray, single-handedly engaged two ax-wielding Amelarens. He managed to dispatch them both after a brief struggle, but did not see Tallen barreling toward him until the war chief was almost on top of him. Instinctively, Glen raised his swords in front of him to block the blow, but Tallen's swing knocked him to the ground. Glen struggled to rise and was suddenly pushed back down. He heard a large clang and looked up to see that Reznik had blocked Tallen with his shield. Tallen shouted in surprise and staggered. Jutting from a notch in his armor, near his upper thigh, was a knife with a gold Coranox painted on its hilt. Tallen grabbed it, yanked it out, and hurled it blindly back at them. It struck the dirt several paces away from Glen, who scrambled to his feet.

"You!" a seething Tallen yelled in Laestran. Lifting his sword, he prepared to rush Reznik.

"Glen, go!" Reznik shouted.

Glen bent down and picked up Reznik's knife before retreating to help the rest of the unit, leaving Reznik to face Tallen.

Reznik winced. Tallen's sword had struck his shield, causing the armor to dig into his skin. He felt warm blood seeping through the joints of his shoulder plating, which was damaged. His shield had crumpled and would not withstand a second blow. He tossed it aside. Tallen charged him, prepared to swing. Reznik fought the impulse to throw a parry and stepped aside instead, avoiding the sword's downward arc. He felt confident that he could evade Tallen's swings, though was surprised when his attempt to counter was met with the large blade of Tallen's sword. The war chief handled his large weapon exceptionally well and was able to deflect the swing easily.

Reznik soon found he had crept far enough back that he had reached the gorge's western entrance. He was fatigued after trading many attacks with Tallen and knew it was only a matter of time before he would no longer be able to keep up. Out of the corner of his eye, he saw Jasmine shout something in his direction and turn to run for the opening with the remaining Coranthian soldiers. He reversed the grip on his sword and launched it with all his strength at Tallen. At the same time, he remembered the tactic Glen had used earlier and rushed straight at the Amelaren. Tallen raised his weapon and swatted away Reznik's sword but could not recover before Reznik slammed into him, causing him to lose his balance. Reznik turned to run, though had not stopped Tallen completely. From his knees, the Amelaren war chief swung wildly with his sword. The blade sliced through the back of Reznik's armor, causing him to stumble and arch in pain, but he was quickly on his feet again, running as hard as he could.

Tallen got back up and pursued the remaining Coranthians to the edge of the entrance and then stopped and darted behind a rock as a hail of crossbow bolts flew into the passageway, killing a number of Amelarens behind him. After remaining in cover for several ticks, he peeked out at the retreating Coranthians. A look of satisfaction crept across his face as he turned toward the other warriors and called out for them to withdraw to the east.

Madeline was safely behind the Coranthian line, having escaped the passage together with Douglas. Leaving him to catch his breath, she looked for her squadmates and for Reznik in particular, though found no one. Suddenly, she heard a piercing scream and recognized Amy Trenton's voice. Pushing her way through to the back of the Coranthian formation, Madeline emerged upon a large area that had been cleared to dress and treat the wounded who were strewn across blankets on the ground. Medics tinkered with their supplies as they tended to injured soldiers. Madeline saw Amy speaking frantically to a middle-aged medic with dense, knitted eyebrows and an impatient expression on his face. She grabbed his sleeve, causing him to flinch and pull away. He barked something at her and walked away hastily. As he left, Madeline was able to see behind him, where Alphonse lay thrashing and groaning. The blanket was soaked with blood. The lower half of Alphonse's left arm was missing. The young man mumbled hoarsely to his sister, having already expended his voice from screaming in pain. Patrice was by his side working furiously to stop the bleeding.

Madeline was so focused on Alphonse, as she walked up to where he lay, that she did not notice Nash, who approached from her right and immediately began to prepare a tourniquet with Patrice.

"Captain, help!" Amy gasped. "Please, help him."

"He'll be fine," Nash said. "Everything will be fine."

As he worked, Nash repeated these words several times to calm Amy. Occasionally, he raised his arm to wipe the sweat from his forehead and push up his glasses.

Madeline had been thoroughly disappointed with Nash, perceiving him to be a coward and a poor captain after his display while he was in command. When Reznik took control of the Upper 26th, it served only to further her sentiment. On the other hand, it was hard for her to deny that he was an excellent medic. He worked quickly and calmly and took the time to offer reassurance to those who needed it, which made her less disdainful of him. Nash seemed the type of person who got along well with and earned the respect of everyone off the battlefield. He and Patrice worked together without missing a beat.

"For Creon's sake," Madeline heard someone exclaim in a distressed voice, "is he going to make it?" Faintly, she realized the words had come from her own mouth.

"We need to stop the bleeding," Nash replied without turning his head.

Nash reached into his bag and pulled out a thin wooden stick that was wrapped in a clean white cloth.

"Get him to bite down on this."

Patrice looked up and said, "Amy, hold his head and grab his shoulder. Madeline, take the other shoulder."

Madeline did as she was told. Amy whispered into Alphonse's ear, urging him to relax and clamp down on the stick as Patrice brought it to his mouth.

Meanwhile, Nash opened a small pouch on his belt and produced five small vials of dark blue liquid.

"What's that?" Amy asked nervously.

"We have to cauterize the wound immediately," Nash said. "Hold him still."

The three women held Alphonse tightly as Nash popped open three of the vials and poured the contents onto the wound, which began to smoke and sizzle. Alphonse let out a howl, his eyes rolling into the back of his head, and he passed out. Nash checked him quickly, before removing the stick between his teeth.

"What was that? What did you do?" Amy cried, nearing hysterics.

"He's unconscious from the pain, that's all. We should have neutralized any possibility of infection." Nash returned the vials to his pouch and began to wrap the tourniquet around the stump.

"I've never seen that type of cauterizing agent before!" Madeline said.

Nash finished bandaging and stood up. "It's my own concoction," he said as he wiped his glasses.

Patrice's eyebrows shot up, but she said nothing.

"I've done about all I can. Avet Konith, please look after him."

"Yes, sir," Patrice said. Casting a glance at Amy, she added, "He will pull through."

"Th-thank you," Amy stammered. "I apologize for snapping. I was ... I was ..." She broke down, unable to finish.

Nash smiled, but his voice was strained. "Take care of your brother, Avet Trenton."

He turned to walk away. Impressed that he remembered their names, Madeline ran after him.

"Captain, what you used on him ... What was that?"

He frowned. "Yes, well ... That's not important right now. His life is no longer in danger. That's what matters."

"My apologies," Madeline said, sensing his reluctance to elaborate. She fumbled for a proper transition into what was really on her mind and then gave up and asked point-blank. "Have you seen Avet Sylvera, sir?"

Nash appeared relieved to change the subject. "Yes, of course. I saw him come in with Captain Curtland." He pointed north. "He should be over there, with the 28th."

Madeline thanked Nash and left in that direction. On her way, she spotted Cyrus and Josef who were helping escort the wounded to the medics. She also recognized some soldiers from the 28th and saw Douglas resting on a patch of grass, oblivious to his surroundings and thoroughly spent.

When she finally managed to locate Reznik, he was helping Glen carry an injured and unconscious woman toward the medical area. Falling in step with them, she took one of the woman's legs. The three avets carried the woman to an open blanket and laid her down. When Madeline and Glen stood up, Reznik did not follow suit. Instead, he doubled over on his knees, breathing heavily, which exposed the tear in his armor and the gash across his lower back. His wound bled profusely.

"What?" Madeline cried out. "Why didn't you ... What were you thinking?"

"I'm fine," Reznik muttered. "It's not too bad."

Glen, who had started to walk away, peered over his shoulder. His eyes widened, and he rushed back to help his friend.

"Really, you're making too much of it," Reznik said. "I'm just ..."

"You're a fool," Madeline said, feeling a lump rise in her throat. "A damn stubborn fool."

Reznik made to reply but managed only to choke out a weak cough.

Madeline slung Reznik's arm across her shoulders. Glen grabbed his other arm. The two carried him off in search of a medic.

Chapter 8

(987.2.12–30)

—1—

Reznik slowly opened his eyes. The blinding light made it difficult for him to focus on the blurry shapes dancing before him. He lay in bed, unable to remember how he got there. Finding his neck nearly completely stiff, he attempted to sit up but was ambushed by the searing pain in his lower back and left shoulder. He pushed his pillow clumsily aside, using his good arm, and propped himself against the wall behind him. His trunk was wrapped almost entirely in bandages. He allowed his head to tilt lightly against the wall, breathing deeply and trying to distance himself from the pain.

"Awake?" came a familiar voice.

Reznik rolled his head to the right and saw Amy Trenton hunched over on a steel chair beside another bed. Finally able to inspect his surroundings, Reznik recognized the room as part of the medical bay at Aldova.

"Wait, don't move, I'll get the doctor," Amy said, springing to her feet. She marched past Reznik and out of sight.

Reznik could now clearly see it was Alphonse who lay on the bed next to his. He was struck by the sight of Alphonse's left arm, or rather its absence, which triggered a flood of memories: the retreat through the Ghend Highlands, the confrontation with an Amelaren commander, and his subsequent injury during his attempted flight. All of this overwhelmed him and he grew lightheaded. He put his right hand against his forehead, hoping to quell the dizziness. After his thoughts had cleared somewhat, he found himself staring at Alphonse's tightly bound stump where his arm used to be.

"They got me pretty good," escaped from Alphonse's lips, causing Reznik to start. Somehow he had not noticed Alphonse was awake and had been staring straight at him.

"Oh … looks like it," Reznik managed awkwardly. He immediately regretted his words.

Alphonse laughed weakly. "I was surrounded. I don't know what I could've done. Don't really remember what happened afterward. Someone got me out of there. I think it may have been one of those Curtland captains. Can't say the same about my arm though."

Reznik shook his head and redirected his eyes toward the stone ceiling. "I'm sorry. I don't know what to say."

"I can go home now, I suppose. They'll send me back with a medal and a nice pension. At least the farm will hold for a while." With some effort, he returned his head to a neutral position. "Sis says they're going to write up how brave I was and all that, so I'll have a letter to show my folks. What a story, huh?"

"You were brave," Reznik replied. "You stood and fought all the way through the retreat, even though we were being routed."

"What does it matter?" Alphonse spoke in a low voice, raspy with agitation. He closed his eyes, trying to fight back the tears that had already begun to pour down his cheeks. "How am I supposed to go home like this and look my pa in the eye and tell him I left my sis to fight by herself?"

Reznik could not find the words to comfort him. He turned away again, gazing across the room at another bed. His left view was obscured by a melancholy gray curtain that was partially drawn. The curtain, fastened to the wall by a hook, wrapped almost completely around the end of the bed. A young female avet, whom Reznik did not recognize, was sleeping there. Blood-soaked bandages were wrapped around her neck and forehead. Reznik felt queasy and closed his eyes. He gradually lowered himself again. Rest seemed the best recourse for the intermittent pain.

He did not know how long he lay there; he could not fall asleep. After some time, he heard two voices he did not recognize, one male and one female; the male was especially throaty but clear and authoritative. They stopped talking; there followed the sound of approaching footsteps. Reznik tried in vain to ignore the noise and to will himself to sleep.

Suddenly, he felt the cool moistness of a towel scrubbing his cheeks. His eyes snapped open.

"How are you feeling, Avet Sylvera?"

A tall, wiry man, whose appearance did not match his deep voice, sat in a small wooden chair and took notes on a pad. He looked to be in his forties. His long gray hair tangled in the collar of his brown overcoat. Over his right breast pocket was a patch; embroidered onto it, above a shield-framed dark green Coranox, was the man's name.

"Terrence Halstead," Reznik recited.

"That's Dr. Halstead. Glad to see you're up. Your recovery has been surprisingly swift."

Meanwhile, on the other side of the bed, a short and pudgy blond nurse bent over him, dabbing his face with the towel. Occasionally, she dunked the towel into a metal pan filled with water. There was a bar of soap on a small dish next to the pan, though it remained untouched for the time being. The nurse withdrew the towel when the doctor, looking up from his notes, gestured for her to remove Reznik's bandages. She took hold of him and gently leaned him forward. Slowly and methodically, the nurse unwrapped the dressings that covered Reznik's chest, dumping them unceremoniously into a small bucket that lay at her feet. There were some puslike stains on the bandages but not much blood.

"How long have I been here? What day is it?" Reznik asked Halstead.

"Only a day. It's the twelfth," the nurse replied after the doctor gave her a glance to defer the question. "You were held at Argiset camp for two days. The on-site clinic refused to move you until the infection was contained."

Halstead rummaged through a large leather bag of medical supplies that lay on the floor and withdrew from it a jar of red-brown ointment. He handed it to the nurse who unscrewed it and grabbed a handful of its contents. She began to spread it around Reznik's lower back, causing him to wince from its sting.

"That's it?" Reznik said. "An infected cut? I was sure my injuries were much more severe."

"You were fortunate," the doctor said, allowing himself a small smile. "Aside from the infection, you had some bruised ribs and a dislocated shoulder. The fever was the worst of it all. That's why we've kept you here this long."

"Did you not fix my shoulder?" Reznik said. "It feels as though it's about to fall off."

Halstead frowned. "It's fine. You should be glad there wasn't an infection there as well."

Soon, the nurse had finished applying the ointment and covered Reznik in fresh bandages. After she finished, she washed her hands in the pan.

"You'll be back on your feet in a few days," Halstead said curtly, hauling the medical bag over his shoulder. "You should get some more rest. I'll have Elena here check on you from time to time."

With that, he took his leave. The nurse gave Reznik a reassuring smile as she helped him lie back down. Elena removed the pan and bucket and disappeared briefly before returning with a tall glass of water and setting it down on the table.

"Ring if you need anything," she said, placing a small bronze bell beside his water. "Try to get some sleep for now. I'll be back later."

Reznik watched as she left. He glanced to his right; Alphonse faced away from him. With considerable effort, he reached for the glass of water and, without rising, tried to sip it.

"Great," Reznik muttered. He returned the glass to the table and settled back on his bed.

The room grew quiet beyond the occasional rustling of blankets. Reznik grew drowsy and finally drifted to sleep. When he came to, two familiar faces greeted him.

"You're wrapped like a cheap present," Madeline giggled.

"Do you feel as comfortable as you look?" Glen chimed in with a grin. He stood behind Madeline, who sat on one of the many rickety stools lying around the medical bay.

"And a good day to you both," Reznik said. "I'll be fine, or so I've been told."

Madeline crawled her hand along the side of the bed to take his, attempting to be inconspicuous, but Glen caught sight of the movement.

Reznik's eyes darted toward Alphonse's bed, though it was hard to see over his bedside table that had on it a bowl of porridge, a small chunk of bread, and his glass of water, now refilled.

"So what happened?" he asked after a rep of silence, turning back to his friends. "At the gorge, I mean."

"We lost a lot of soldiers. Surely you didn't forget …" Madeline's expression sobered as she released his hand.

Reznik thought of Liam. "No, I remember that part," he said, shaking his head. "What happened after we made it out? I must have been given a durion tranquilizer as a painkiller. The next few days were a blur."

"We set up positions at the entrance to the gorge that night," Glen said, "and fell back to Argiset the next day. You and most of the wounded stayed for medical attention, but about half of us marched straight back here."

Madeline studied Reznik's reaction as he processed the information.

"I remember … the vice captain. I suppose he never made it back?"

Glen nodded somberly.

"And Colonel Gavere?"

"We have a new colonel."

Madeline could not be sure whether the strained expression on Reznik's face was due to fatigue or distress.

"Come on, Glen," she said, standing up, "let's leave him so he can rest."

"I'm fine," Reznik said, but Madeline was already dragging Glen away.

After they had gone, Reznik remained as he was before reaching over to the table with both hands and taking the tray of food. He balanced it on his lap as best as he could. He had picked up the spoon on the tray and had begun to poke at the porridge when he heard someone speak his name.

Glen wore a sheepish expression as he pulled up alongside the bed.

"Listen, I wanted to … I want to thank you for saving my life. You were injured on my account. I owe you."

"Don't be like that. You owe me nothing. You would do the same for me."

Glen glanced over his shoulder to make sure that no one was paying attention and then reached into his waist pack. Reznik's eyes widened as Glen produced an aeron knife with a gold Coranox painted on the hilt.

"How were you able to retrieve this?"

"The Amelaren you were fighting didn't appreciate the souvenir, I suppose." Glen grinned. "Threw it right back at my feet."

Reznik dropped the spoon and took the knife from Glen's outstretched hand. He turned it over, tracing the Coranthian crest around the handle, examining it closely. The knife was in immaculate condition.

"I cleaned it for you," Glen said. "Where did you get this anyway? It looks like the one General Hagen had in his office at the academy."

Reznik laughed softly. "It is the one from his office. He gave it to me as a graduation gift."

Glen nodded knowingly. "He always did favor you."

A momentary silence followed.

"Anyway, I should go," said Glen. "Eat something." He gestured toward the bowl in Reznik's lap and turned to leave.

Reznik watched him go and then put the knife down on the bedside table, trying not to turn his body. Returning his attention to the food in front of him, he picked up the spoon once more and swirled it around the porridge before raising a mouthful to his lips and downing it gingerly. The texture was rough and sludgy.

"Disgusting," he concluded aloud.

—2—

The next several days passed in similar fashion. He slept soundly, though irregularly, and ate adequately, but reluctantly. Renard never visited. A concerned Douglas dropped by, immensely relieved to hear that Reznik's injury was not serious. Several other soldiers from the 26th passed through and offered their greetings to both him and Alphonse. They gushed over how Reznik had taken control of the company and led them to safety during the Ertel debacle. While Reznik accommodated them, he often asked Alphonse whether the traffic bothered him. Alphonse would reply that it was of no inconvenience to him and that Reznik deserved the praise that he got, but Reznik persisted in asking the habitual question, as if looking for a reason to send the visitors away.

Amy remained in the room with Alphonse more often than not, doing her best to entertain her brother and keep up his spirits. On more than one occasion, she slept in a chair that she pilfered from outside the medical bay. Whenever Alphonse was alone and seemingly on the brink of depression, Amy would show up as if on cue and turn him around in short order. Reznik was keenly aware of her presence and their interactions, although he made sure not to eavesdrop or let his gaze linger on them for long.

After spending three more listless days in the medical bay at the insistence of Dr. Halstead, Reznik's fever finally subsided sufficiently for release.

• • •

After Reznik checked out of the medical bay, he made his way back to his quarters. It seemed a long time since he had traversed the quiet, solistone-lit hallways. He carried a small, burlap sack of bandages and ointment that he had been forced to take with him. When he reached room 355, he hesitated before opening the door. The fore of the room was empty, aside from one soldier lounging on the lower bunk inside his section. He looked up briefly and nodded to Reznik, who returned in kind, though they did not know each other.

Reznik continued on to Section 1. He expected to find the bunk above his empty, but instead he found Josef Reinbach sitting with his back against the wall, busily writing in a little booklet he always carried, munching on a bolve, a popular Coranthian snack made of baked yoa and oat. He was so thoroughly absorbed in his writing that he did not seem to notice Reznik.

"Hello, Reinbach."

Josef's head whipped around, his face momentarily blank, and then it lit up in recognition. "Ah, Sylvera! Good to see you up and about."

"What are you doing here?"

"Business as usual, yes?" Josef dropped his pen and put his booklet to the side. "They moved us around the other day when the company was reorganized."

"Reorganized?" Reznik raised his eyebrows, his gaze still on Josef as he set his bag on the lower bunk.

"Well, you know, four of our companies took a beating out there. I believe the 28th absorbed most of what remained of the 17th and 35th. So they shifted bunk assignments. For some reason, they split up me and Dyson. Beyond that, I don't know much. It's been a real mess around here. I don't think the higher-ups know what they are doing."

Reznik laid down gently on his still-tender back and stared up at the bunk that used to be Liam's. Suddenly, Josef's head crept over the side of the bed as he stared down at Reznik, his eyes owlish yet slightly vacant.

"Oh yes, I almost forgot. The captain just got back the other day. He asked me to relay his request for your immediate presence in his office upon your release from the medical ward."

"The captain? I wasn't aware that he left."

"He returned from Corande this morning."

Reznik awaited an explanation of Nash's trip, but it did not come. "Thank you," he said. "I'll be on my way shortly then."

Josef cocked his head indifferently and retracted from view.

Reznik did not stir immediately and remained as he was for several reps. His gaze wandered and settled on his family portrait on the desk nearby. Thoughts of home came to him and provided a modicum of comfort.

Occasionally there came the sound of scribbling from above, sometimes accompanied by a drumming noise as Josef rapped his fingers on the pages, one of his many odd tics. Finally, Reznik grew annoyed and rose carefully from the bed.

"You know," Josef said without looking up, "I've been meaning to ask you about your name."

Reznik stared at Josef. "What about it?"

"It's Doromalian, no? I am just curious," Josef stopped writing and his brown eyes locked with Reznik's blue ones.

Reznik shrugged. "Doromalian names aren't all that rare, even in the Outlands. Our colonial roots still run deep."

Josef seemed disappointed that Reznik did not appear inclined to elaborate. "Ah, I was just curious whether you were named after *that* Reznik."

"What are you talking about?"

"The famous Doromal, Reznikov."

Reznik shook his head. "No, not that I know of."

"He was an interesting man. If we have time, at some point, I would like to share the story with you. I suppose Coranthians are mostly unfamiliar with it these days. But now, I am busy, and you should not keep our captain waiting."

Josef returned to his manual as if their exchange had never taken place. Perplexed, Reznik left the room.

On his way up to the seventh floor, where captains and vice captains held office, Reznik could not help but notice that Aldova was much more chaotic than it had been over the previous days. During his stay in the medical bay, he had been allowed to wander the hallways for exercise. Now he saw reinforcements and military officials streamed in from Corande to make up for the displacement of the troops that were in the process of fortifying the Coranthian position at Argiset. General Leopold San Mortigan, the man in charge of Aldova's defense, expertly arranged the coming and going of the fortress's charge. Despite the fact that the dust had barely settled from the opening salvo of the war, Mortigan and Leynitz were already planning several steps ahead, as was expected of them. Yet despite the action being taken, an unease hung in the air. It had been a long time since Coranthia had experienced a military loss to this degree.

As Reznik steadily climbed the stairs, he wondered how this meeting with Nash fit into the grand scheme. It also occurred to him that Nash might simply wish to reprimand him for his actions during the retreat from Ertel, though he had a hard time picturing Nash summoning the assertiveness to do so.

Upon his arrival at the seventh floor, two male guards by the stairwell asked for his identification and purpose of visit. He had not ascended past the sixth floor since the initial company meeting upon first arrival at Aldova. He recalled Liam's words to him about the upper floors being well guarded. After presenting his military identification card, he was allowed past the guards, who directed him to Nash's office. He stopped when he saw the large wooden door with the mounted brass plate showing Nash's name and rank.

Reznik knocked on the door, feeling a slight twinge in his back as he did so. When no reply came, Reznik knocked harder. Again there was nothing. He grabbed the handle and cracked open the door. The room was dimly lit with solistone lamps—not enough light to indicate that anyone was there. Reznik stood for a moment, planning when to come back, before a loud crash came from the next door down. Curious, he walked over and saw that the door was marked with Parsons' name, apparently not having been turned over yet. Just as he did with Nash's door, Reznik opened it, just enough to peek inside, where he saw Nash sprawled awkwardly on the floor, surrounded by a scattering of books. Nash scrambled to his feet and began to collect the fallen books, muttering unintelligibly. A collapsed ladder-stool lay next to him. Judging by its position, it had been leaning against a line of tall bookshelves against the back wall. A small smile formed at the corners of Reznik's lips. After a few ticks, he pushed the door open wider, knocking to make his presence known.

Nash plopped the stack of books onto Parsons' large wooden desk and adjusted his glasses.

"Hello, Avet Sylvera. Glad you're back with us."

"Captain."

"Take a seat."

There was no chair in front of the desk. Reznik looked around for one. Nash pointed to the high-backed chair behind the desk and said, "Over there. It makes no difference. I need to take down the rest of these books."

Hesitantly, Reznik walked around the desk and sat. He fidgeted uncomfortably for several ticks. His eyes were drawn to Parsons' desk. The surface of the desk was empty, aside from a transceiver and a small solistone lamp. A small chill ran down Reznik's back as he contemplated how, just a few days earlier, the now-empty desk was likely covered in papers and Parsons' office decorations. The room belonged to a ghost.

Reznik's thoughts were interrupted when he heard Nash refit the ladder-stool against the bookshelves. Reznik watched as Nash nervously climbed atop it and strained to reach the top of the shelf to grab two more books.

"I wasn't expecting you to be discharged for another day or two. I thought I'd clear out the vice captain's belongings." Nash stepped back down with the books tucked under his arm. Reznik noticed two wooden crates filled with various personal effects lying close to the desk. He wondered why someone of Nash's status would bother with such a task.

"I was released early."

"So you were."

"They kept me for too long as it was," Reznik remarked.

"It is fortunate that you escaped grievous injury. I wish the vice captain had been as fortunate."

Reznik remained silent. He was uncertain how to respond to the remark.

Having cleared out the lower shelf, Nash carried the entire stack of books to the desk and dropped it. He stared at Reznik, who cast his eyes sideways.

"The vice captain and I were not particularly friendly with one another, you know," Nash said with a trace of indignation, indicating that he was building up to a point, "but I had a great deal of respect for him. They could have stuck me with far worse, Sylvera."

Reznik caught the odd choice of words.

"What do you mean, sir?" he asked, returning his gaze to meet Nash's blue eyes.

Nash squinted at him curiously. "There is no need to feign ignorance. Parsons' appointment as my vice captain was neither by chance nor choice. It was painfully obvious that he was far more capable than I. Certain parties in the Assembly believed I required monitoring in addition to good help. Parsons was capable, and he kept an eye on me for them. He made no attempt to hide the duality of his task, so I was not reproachful. He was never anything less than respectful and professional."

"I was not aware of this," Reznik said. He was surprised, though felt he should not be.

"I never wanted to be a captain or hold any extended tenure in the military. I did not take up the office for my own sake. There is nothing rewarding about being a pawn in the Assembly's game."

Nash sighed, leaning against the edge of the table and cocking his head.

"Anyway, I did not call you here to discuss the Assembly. The first thing I need is to assign a replacement for Parsons. I told the Assembly that I should be allowed to choose my own vice captain and the general agreed, so I shall. I need someone I can trust to get the job done. How about it, Sylvera? What do you think? Are you up to the task?"

Nash's abrupt words left Reznik speechless.

"Well? You don't have much experience, but I know for certain that you are more than capable. I saw your ability with my own eyes."

Nash brushed some splinters from his uniform and gestured to a side door that connected with his own office, prompting Reznik's gaze to follow his hand. Reznik had noticed it briefly upon entering and wondered if all adjacent offices for captains and their vice captains were connected in the same way.

"Let us continue this conversation in my office," Nash said. "I have some paperwork that you'll need to fill out."

Without waiting for a response, he turned off the solistone lamps and walked over to his office. Still at a loss, Reznik managed to lift himself from the chair and follow Nash into the next room. Nash walked around his desk, easing himself into a grand blue velvet chair with decorative gold trim and motioned for Reznik to sit across from him before he leaned back. Reznik was struck by how at ease Nash seemed in his office, in stark contrast to how he conducted himself as a captain on the battlefield. The irony of Nash's relaxed state compared to Reznik's own discomfort was not lost on him.

"Don't be so stiff." Nash pointed again to the empty chair facing his desk. "And no more *sir*. It's just the two of us. Speak freely. You're going to be a vice captain now."

Reznik took his seat and looked around the room. Nash's office was significantly larger, though similar to Parsons' in many ways. Both rooms had matching desks and bookshelves, though the chairs in this one were more ornate. Along the back wall, beside the bookshelves, stood a tall wooden cabinet with glass panels. Nash had liberally decorated his office. Paintings of Nash, Minister Havora, and even the king embellished the southern wall. A banner adorned with the Coranox hung beside the front door. Beneath the banner was a tabletop map covered with miniature figures, war pawns, and did not appear to have seen any use in some time.

"This is very sudden, Captain," Reznik said. "I was certain I'd be punished for my actions."

"It is rarely appropriate for an avet to assume command in any situation," Nash said with a nod, adjusting his spectacles, "but what you did was necessary and decisive."

"But I'm not even a sergeant."

Nash produced a document consisting of several sheets of paper bound together and placed them on the desk. "I had this drawn up for you. All you need to do is sign, and your promotion will be effective immediately."

Reznik did not move. After a rep, Nash reached out with a quizzical look, as if to withdraw the papers.

"Did I misjudge you? So you refuse then?"

"No, I accept, Captain. I'm honored …" He snatched the document from under Nash's creeping hand, bolted up from his chair, and saluted. Reznik wondered if he was the one who had misjudged Nash.

Nash returned the salute without standing, chuckling, "Again, I must insist that you drop the formalities."

Reznik had already reached for the fountain pen that lay on the desk. He signed quickly and smoothly on the last page of the document.

"That's that, then," Nash said, rubbing his hands in satisfaction.

Before he could continue, there came a knock at the door.

Nash frowned. "I am not expecting anyone," he said loudly.

The door flew open. Reznik glanced over his shoulder. When he saw who stood in the doorway, his eyebrows knitted with displeasure.

Nash bolted from his seat to salute. "Your Highness, welcome back."

Prince Adrian Coranthis strode into the room, extending his hand. Nash hastened from behind his desk to meet him.

"Good to see you, Havora," said Adrian. The two shook hands vigorously.

"How quickly you have returned. You must have departed shortly after I did, Your Highness."

Adrian brushed aside several loose strands of hair. "The trip seems to grow longer each time I am forced to make it."

He stopped in his tracks when he saw Reznik. His mouth contorted; all he managed was a simple, "Oh."

Trying his best to be discreet, Nash motioned to Reznik for him to stand and pay his respects, but Reznik remained with his back turned to Adrian, peered over his shoulder, and said simply, "Your Highness."

"Sylvera," Adrian returned disdainfully.

Nash looked back and forth between the two. "So you have met," he said, uncertain what to make of their casual regard for one another. Then: "Ah, you two must know each other from Tellisburg."

"Well, it's a small world, isn't it?" Adrian said with a humorless smile, and without waiting for an answer, he walked up to the desk and dropped himself into the chair next to Reznik. "Nash, I suppose you've had the misfortune to take this avet under your charge."

"Actually, he just promoted me to vice captain," Reznik said evenly, finally turning to face the prince.

Adrian glanced in disbelief at Nash, who had retaken his seat behind the desk and was busy wiping off his glasses. He looked as uncomfortable as Reznik had ever seen him.

"Tell me," Reznik went on, "how have you been enjoying your vacation at Aldova, your Highness?"

The prince reddened and laughed spitefully. Refusing to look at Reznik, he continued to address Nash. "Has he sweet-talked you into letting him replace Parsons? Surely you must have a gaggle of better choices, more experienced and less difficult to manage." His eyes darted fleetingly in Reznik's direction.

"I see you two are well-acquainted," Nash said hesitantly, "but, please, both of you, refrain from such rabble in this office. It's unnecessary." Though his words were clumsy, Nash was now more curious than anxious. Adrian treated Reznik's words, coming from someone so far removed from the prince in status, not as a capital offense but merely as an irritant.

"Soft as usual, Havora," Adrian chuckled, not unkindly. "Well, you're getting there, I suppose. But don't let people walk all over you." Again he threw a sidelong glance at Reznik. There was no longer any venom in his eyes, merely annoyance.

Nash picked up on it and said, "I presume you wanted to speak to me about something, Prince." To Reznik he remarked, "In any case, that is all for now. We will need to meet with the new colonel, but that can be done another day."

"Yes, sir." Reznik stood and added, with a slight drawl that barely masked the mockery in his voice, "I will take my leave now, Your Highness."

Adrian rolled his eyes and waved his hand, as if to chase away a fly, but as Reznik marched to the door and made his exit, the prince looked over his shoulder in the same manner that Reznik had done when he had entered. A contemplative look flashed across his face.

—3—

The next two turns were incredibly busy for Reznik. He and Nash met with their new colonel: the veteran captain of the 27th Company, Hector Osterfeld. Though Reznik found him intimidating, Osterfeld did not seem to care much about what Nash had to say regarding his selection of a vice captain and hurried the paperwork through, confirming Reznik's appointment in short order. The next day, Nash called together the 26th Company to formally introduce Reznik as his new second-in-command. Despite their unilateral surprise at the news, the 26th, composed primarily of commoners, many of them Outlanders, was generally supportive and enthusiastic. That night and over the next few days, Reznik dealt with a wave of awkward social calls; his visitors ranged from various members of the 26th with whom Reznik had not been previously acquainted, eager to establish favor with their new vice captain, to familiar faces like Madeline, Glen, Douglas, and even the Curtlands, offering their congratulations and well wishes. Throughout it all, Reznik had little time to relax or be alone, and he was generally fatigued.

• • •

Reznik made his way down the stairs to the second floor and over to the exit. His back felt much better after several more days of slow rehabilitation. Outside, it was overcast, though warm. He walked forty meters out on the bridge and then leaned against the northern wall, which rose just above his midsection. Staring at the majestic Alcone Mountains, he breathed deeply, ignoring the few others along the bridge. A pleasant breeze wisped against him, carrying with it the fresh smell of the lake and the mountains beyond.

"Well, this is a rare sight," came a familiar voice. "You've never been one to stop and take in the scenery."

Renard had come up next to him, his hands folded behind his back, staring at him with an impish grin.

Reznik nodded in greeting. "You've been busy."

"It's been a mess. I'm one of the lucky ones who had to pull double time, slogging through a morass of paperwork, covering for the people who will return to Corande to answer for what happened at Ertel."

"How many are being questioned?"

"Obviously too many. The Assembly is at its most efficient when seeking a scapegoat. Meanwhile, it puts a wrench in the cogs here. Of course, that ends up being more reason for them to blame us."

"Dumb," Reznik said, shaking his head.

"Yes, although, they seem to be having difficulty finding someone to finger for this mess. Almost everyone the Assembly might blame is untouchable or dead. What a shame, right? And they probably won't give General Leynitz too much grief. They rather like him, you know?"

Renard rubbed his chin thoughtfully.

"Sorry about not visiting. I just came from your room. The person who was there ... He wasn't much help. A bit odd, that fellow."

"He is peculiar, isn't he?"

"So while I was wondering when I'd ever be able to catch you, I came out for a bit of air. Imagine my luck." Renard was about to continue when he noticed the silver pin on Reznik's uniform. "Whoa there, Rez. I suppose congratulations are in order. You're the new vice captain, huh? That's great!"

"Thanks."

"Not wearing your officer's coat?" Renard asked.

Reznik shrugged. "Look who's talking."

Renard smiled and clapped Reznik lightly on the shoulder as he moved forward to lean against the wall. Reznik looked for the same pin on Renard's uniform and was surprised to see that it had been replaced with one that was also silver but shield-framed and larger than his own.

"I see you were promoted as well," Reznik remarked. "No wonder they've been running you around."

"Promoted, yes, but not in the way I wanted. Captain Falorann rode ahead with Colonel Gavere at the gorge." Renard shook his head. His smile became wry. "Truth be told, I'm really not sure how I feel. The higher up I go, the more I'm forced to abide by some stiff protocol. You know I'm not big on that."

"If you don't want it, I'll take it," Reznik deadpanned.

Renard chuckled. "So why are you still holed up in that bunk? Shouldn't you have been assigned your own room?"

"I turned it down," Reznik said in the same flat tone.

Renard considered this for a moment and then laughed again. "I suppose I don't have to ask why."

"Not if you already know the answer."

"Listen to me. I know you don't want to hear this, but sooner or later, you have to play the game. It's how things work. When you become a captain, you'd better not try to refuse your own quarters. That's not good leadership. Know what I mean? When you get to that level, everyone is watching. Like with your captain. He'll have to address what he did, letting you take over his show out there."

"You heard about that?" Reznik said.

"Did I hear about what happened to the minister's son? What do you think? Everyone knows. Whether or not one feels inclined to discuss it openly is another matter."

Reznik sighed. "Anyway, Captain Havora made it seem that matters regarding him and the Assembly were resolved."

"I wouldn't be so sure about that." Renard paused. "Anyway, how are you holding up? You look rather ... indisposed."

"I've not been sleeping all that well," Reznik admitted. He had taken on a paleness that gave him a sickly appearance.

"Still in a lot of pain? The doctors can give you some goods to deal with it."

"No, it's not that. Not only have I been busy with my new duties, but I seem to be haunted by the encounter I had with that Amelaren soldier."

"I'm sure you realized he was no ordinary soldier. Not even an elbar. That was War Chief Tallen."

Reznik's eyebrows shot up. "How do you know?"

"Glen told me what happened. Based on the description, it had to be him. When I told Glen that, he almost lost it."

"No wonder," Reznik said. "An Amelaren war chief." There was a sense of awe in his voice that Renard almost never heard. "I've dreamed about it. That moment. Sometimes I can't block the attack. Sometimes I'm watching myself get cut down. Me, then others around me." He sighed. "I could have done more. I should have done more. He shouldn't have gotten that close to our lines. Or maybe we should have seen the ambush coming. At least we could have started retreating earlier."

Renard gazed into the distance at the snowy Alcone peaks.

"You can't keep bearing the weight of the world on your shoulders. It was your first campaign. You can't expect to be able to handle everything all at once. You're lucky to have gotten away with your life."

He paused.

"What happened to Remington was unfortunate. I didn't know him well, but he was a good man."

Reznik stared at his reflection in the lake. "He might have made a good captain one day." He shook his head. "And Dyson. You should have seen the look on his face. Do you know the story between those two?"

"Dyson and Remington? The two of them worked patrol in Kantor after graduating from Kendrall. They were on the same shift, though not paired together, I believe. One night, Dyson tried to help an Atherian who was getting beaten by some boozers. He was outnumbered, and they weren't too pleased with the interruption. His throat was slashed."

"And he lost his voice."

"Right. Would have been worse, but Remington happened by and took care of the drunk bastards. That's how the two of them became as close as brothers."

"How do you know all this?"

"If it's a Kantorian tale, it will get told to me at some point. And Remington was an estated, after all. A bit higher up the food chain than I am, in fact."

Reznik raised an eyebrow and shrugged. "I imagine Avet Lane is having a tough time as well."

When Renard gave no indication that he knew who that was, Reznik reminded him that he had been extremely pleased to make her acquaintance after the Argiset battle.

"Ah, of course. A fine lady."

"Apparently she and Liam were family friends. I hadn't really thought about it until now, but she didn't have much of a reaction at the time of his death, and she made no mention of it when she visited me the other day."

"I see," Renard said in a distant tone.

There was a moment of silence, after which Reznik said, "What do you think will happen now?"

"Hmm?" Renard continued to stare into the distance, seemingly not paying attention.

"I haven't had a chance to speak with Captain Havora about this. What is the army's next move?"

Renard stared blankly at Reznik for several ticks before his expression cleared. "Oh. Well, as far as I know, our main priority is to set up defenses at Argiset. Pressing on is going to be very difficult unless we establish a forward base there first. I also think the military needs some time for things to cool down."

"That makes sense, but I find it hard to believe that the Amelarens will simply stand by and watch us fortify Argiset."

"There is that, of course, and I agree, but there's a bigger issue at hand."

"What's that?"

"It is highly unlikely that the Amelarens are not fully aware of the threat Aldova presents. They remember what happened the last time they tried to attack. They know what will happen if they try again. Despite that, they still ambushed Elsin and set off this war." Renard's hazel eyes bore into Reznik's blue ones. "General Leynitz thinks something is amiss, and I agree."

Reznik pondered this for a moment. "I see what you mean."

"But not much use in indulging hypotheticals. We lost the initiative and the momentum. We need to rethink our position. In the meantime, the high command is petitioning the defense ministry to step up recruitment efforts."

"I don't know how I feel about that," Reznik admitted.

"Nor do I."

Another lengthy pause followed. Finally, Renard pushed himself off the wall and stretched.

"Come on, I didn't come here for this. Enough of this serious talk. It was good catching up with you. I still feel guilty for not finding you sooner."

"Don't worry about it," Reznik said, smiling faintly.

"I'm famished. What do you say we go grab some dinner?"

"Let's go."

Reznik motioned for Renard to lead the way and the two of them began to stroll along the bridge back into the fold of Aldova.

Interlude

By four arc, Orlen and the other war chiefs, with the exception of Tallen, had taken their places around the circular table in the war room of Solterra-Volek. Lebb, in his usual boisterous manner, was rapidly spewing an assortment of trivialities in the direction of his unfortunate neighbor, Yura, who maintained a stony face and mostly ignored him. Occasionally, Izven and Xanos exchanged quiet banter. The others in the room were generally inert, though one element stuck out—a tanned girl of about eighteen, standing behind Zefrid, who sat to Orlen's right. The girl wore a mat of wild blue-dyed hair atop her head that matched her eyes. Her expression was detached to the point of boredom or perhaps even obliviousness.

At the sound of footsteps that resounded through the sparse, cavernous crown of the fortress, all present turned their attention to the double-door entrance, where Tallen approached.

"Ah, here comes Tallen to grace us with his presence," Shira pronounced mockingly.

"What is she doing here?" Tallen said, pointing accusingly at the blue-haired girl. Lebb shifted in his seat, while Izven and Yura followed the trajectory of his finger with their eyes. The others remained unfazed. The girl stared at him owlishly.

"Sit down, Tallen," Orlen said crossly.

The war chief made his way to the single empty chair directly facing Orlen and sat.

"Let us recount the current state of our enemy," Orlen said, ignoring Tallen's outburst.

"We lured them into the gorge and sliced their formation to pieces. According to Tallen, they lost well over six hundred soldiers, while we had around three hundred and fifty in causalities. This number reflects our men lost at Argiset as well. Is this correct?"

He looked over at Tallen, who nodded.

"And how many have we captured?"

"Only twenty-eight originally, and two have died since arriving at Ertel Ridge," Tallen said.

"Very well." Orlen returned his attention to the other war chiefs. "This is the type of war we will wage on them from here forward. It is a matter of crushing their spirits as much as it is of numbers. Their movements have been purely defensive since that battle. We ambushed them at Elzamir; we broke their resolve at Ertel. Things are progressing smoothly."

"Ilarud has been waving his fists over the loss of Argiset," said Izven.

Lebb's gaze kept darting in the direction of Tallen, who sat with his arms folded and eyes narrowed.

Orlen laughed cryptically. Everyone waited for him to say something, but no words came. Gradually, it became clear that there was some sort of standoff between Orlen and Tallen, although neither looked at the other, and a creeping tension filled the room.

Typically disinclined to assert himself, Zefrid leaned forward, pressing his hands on the table, evidently waiting for something to happen. Finally, he tapped a pale, bony finger and said in a faintly prodding tone, "Warlord, I believe we had a matter to discuss?"

Orlen paused for effect before saying slowly, "Indeed, we do. As I was saying, our ambush at Ertel could not have been executed more precisely or effectively. The few losses we took were inevitable, but I can conclude that our young feigren has performed well. Come forward, Olifa."

The girl standing behind Zefrid cocked her head to the side and shuffled her feet as she approached Orlen, who rose and nudged his chair out of the way to make room for her. The two of them stood side by side as Orlen placed a hand on her shoulder. Olifa shied away from the touch, though she straightened after she met the gaze of Zefrid, who gave her a stern nod.

"Welcome to our proud collective, Olifa," Orlen pronounced, his voice filling the room. "You are now the newest war chief of the mighty Amelaren Army."

Olifa displayed little reaction beyond a lift of her head and a crooked smile in acknowledgment.

"This is premature!" Tallen broke out, his arms still crossed. "The girl may have skill, but she is no war chief. She had no regard for her superiors during the Ertel battle, and now you place her as an equal among us?"

"What are these allegations?" Zefrid, softly though indignantly, demanded.

Tallen was not prone to such outbursts. His flare-up had already subsided, and he addressed Zefrid in a firm and even tone. "Your little pet enjoyed slaughtering the Coranthians who were drawn into our trap, but she found it unnecessary to follow the commanding war chief's lead in driving them back through the Highlands."

"I'll not have you accuse her of cowardice, Tallen," said the elderly man.

"I'll not have you feign misunderstanding. You know very well what I'm saying. Apparently, bloodlust is her only fuel. She is less than capable when it comes to anything beyond killing."

Zefrid frowned. Many of the other war chiefs were now visibly uncomfortable. Olifa maintained a blank expression, as if the current conversation were not even taking place. For his part, Orlen seemed willing to allow Tallen and Zefrid to continue their volley.

Shira's eyes flashed. Brushing back strands of long blond hair that had fallen over her left ear, she cut in venomously, "Tallen, it's not like you to blame others for your own missteps. It's your own fault that some Coranthian whelp cut open your leg."

Tallen did not appreciate the interruption.

"What if it had not been my leg but your porcelain face?" he shot back. "What would you think of such a scratch?"

Shira bolted up from her chair and uttered slowly and clearly, "What the fuck did you just say?"

"Let's move on," Orlen said.

Ignoring him, Shira stared piercingly at Tallen until the latter glanced down at the table, unable to withstand her unrelenting baleful gaze. "Would you like to try it, Tallen?" she taunted, sensing her imminent victory. "Never mind a fledgling Coranthian avet. Do you think *you* can scratch me?"

"That's enough," Orlen boomed, his voice filling the room. "Let's settle this right now. Sol, you have not made any mention of Olifa's involvement in the drive through the gorge. Can you account for Tallen's claims?"

Eager to look away from the confrontation between Shira and Tallen, the other war chiefs turned their attention to Sol, who had not said a single word since entering the room. Sol never wasted his breath and always said only what was necessary when he was so obliged. Those with only a cursory impression of him were likely to deem him perpetually inattentive, but everyone in the Solterra-Volek war room knew he had absorbed each word. He never hesitated, and when addressed, his eyes gleamed from beneath tar-black wisps of dyed hair, and he promptly responded with a soft voice that contrasted with his ominous stature.

"While Olifa was key to the coordination of the ambush, Tallen is correct in that she was not diligent during the pursuit of the retreating Coranthians."

"Then you are only half right, Tallen," Zefrid said before letting out a small, almost inaudible sigh. "Her leadership skills do not seem lacking. Perhaps it is merely a matter of motivation."

"Why not let her speak for herself?"

Eight pairs of eyes turned first toward Yura, who uttered the words, and then to Olifa.

"And so," Shira said after a pause, "does the girl have anything to say?"

After a moment, Olifa appeared to realize she was expected to speak. Again she tilted her head oddly. "Sorry I didn't back you up," she said to Tallen, "but I understand my responsibilities if I am to be a war chief, and it won't happen again."

This seemed agreeable to most of the war chiefs, Zefrid and Yura in particular. Only Izven appeared ambivalent toward Olifa's answer.

"Well, Tallen? Does that satisfy you?" Orlen challenged.

"If it satisfies *you*," returned Tallen, who took note of how his peers reacted and felt it would be inopportune to press the issue.

Orlen, too, weighed the expressions of his subordinates. He had originally planned to discuss other matters at the meeting, though sensed it prudent to reconvene at another time.

"So there it is. That will be all for now. We will meet again in two turns to discuss our plans for the coming cycles. In the meantime, I want you all to rest and put your affairs in order. You can be sure that we'll be sufficiently occupied."

He glanced at Shira, who remained standing. She took his cue and made her way to Yura, bending down to whisper something in her ear. The latter rose and followed Shira to the door and out of the war room. This spurred the rest of the war chiefs to take their leave as well. Izven and Xanos exited together, while Zefrid left with Olifa shortly afterward. This left Orlen, Tallen, Sol, and Lebb alone.

While Orlen took Sol aside and began to speak in a low voice, Tallen stayed in his seat, not bothering to acknowledge Lebb, whose eyes were trained anxiously on him. Eventually, Sol left, but Lebb still lingered. It was only after Orlen finally tired of waiting and impatiently waved him away that he came to his senses and hastened from the room, leaving Orlen and Tallen alone.

• • •

Later that afternoon, a sunny haze presiding over an unseasonably warm day, Tallen and Lebb strolled along the northern edge of Lake Navrek. Lebb began babbling as soon as the two met. He was quick to disparage Olifa and dismiss her as unfit to be a war chief, even offering a few choice words regarding Shira, none of which he or anyone else would dare to say in her presence. Tallen was grateful for his friend's support, though gradually became annoyed when Lebb continued far longer than was necessary. Finally, Tallen was forced to look around to make sure they were not in earshot before pleading for Lebb's silence.

Soon, the two spotted Izven and Xanos, rowing a small, burnished boat on the lake. Izven was an avid rower and fisher and, recently, he had taken on Xanos—who was uncommonly agreeable to most favors asked of him—as a companion on these excursions. The two had pulled in close to shore soon after Tallen waved them in.

"I'd like to speak with Izven privately, if you don't mind," Tallen said.

Izven dipped an oar into the shallow water and drove the boat forward onto the dark brown sand.

Xanos got to his feet and stepped nonchalantly out of the boat. Izven motioned for Tallen to get on; Tallen obliged, taking care not to rock the boat, and took the oar handed to him by Izven. Xanos pushed off the boat with his foot, sending it on its way. As he rowed with Izven, Tallen stole a look back at the beach. Left alone with Xanos, Lebb gingerly paced back and forth at an uncharacteristic loss for words, not having any idea how to approach the other man with conversation.

When Tallen and Izven had rowed about fifty meters, the latter drew up his oar and fastened it onto a latch on the side of the boat. Tallen followed suit, leaving the boat in the care of the Navrek waters, which were tranquil almost to the point of stillness. From his perch in the boat, Tallen was able to take in a remarkable panorama. The north was blanketed by the rolling trees of Volqua Forest, the western, mountainous part of which wrapped around the mouth of the Gharad River, while Solterra-Volek loomed over Navrek to the east. The lake reached far to the south and west, beyond which stretched the great Central Grasslands. Lost in the moment, Tallen could understand why Izven indulged in such simple pleasures.

Izven's voice broke into Tallen's wandering thoughts. "What did you want to talk about?"

Tallen brought his focus back to Izven's plain but firm countenance. Aside from the small cross-shaped scar at the lower right corner of Izven's mouth, and the fact that he was uncommonly well-groomed and clean-shaven for an Amelaren, little stood out about the older war chief's features. Those who did not know him would not have found him impressive but for the fact that he was a renowned warrior and capable leader. Once fierce and exceedingly indignant, he was now completely free of brusqueness and incorrigibility, though he still preferred to keep to himself.

"I think you know." Tallen sighed. "You may be in the warlord's good graces, but I've always been able to trust you for an honest and independent opinion, Izven."

"You put on quite a display this morning," Izven mused.

"Why didn't you speak up then? Do you not agree that Olifa is not worthy of regard as an equal? We already have to deal with one incompetent war chief."

"You are too harsh on Yura, Tallen. She suffers enough rebuke from her sister."

"There is no reason for Shira to show her leniency." Tallen sniffed. "Let us return to the matter of Olifa."

"Olifa is not the problem. I do not disagree with the warlord's judgment of the girl. You saw her in action. You should know better than anyone that she is capable of fulfilling the role, and an additional war chief will be vital as this war progresses." Staring pointedly at Tallen, Izven shifted his weight to make himself more comfortable. "I do not think you should direct your bitterness toward her. Are you simply upset that you were unable to personally exterminate more Coranthians?"

"Why do you say that?"

Izven scratched at the scar under his lip. "I suspect you wanted to mount even more bodies to justify the sacrifices our brothers made at Argiset."

Tallen tried to hide his vexation at Izven's insight.

"Unknowing sacrifices. They did not deserve to be cut down, all the while expecting us to save them."

"I think it would have been worse had they known the truth," Izven replied. "It was a difficult situation."

"I wonder if the sacrifice was necessary."

Izven had a response ready, but decided not to delve further into the topic. "Was there anything else you wanted to discuss?"

Tallen shook his head, clearly disgruntled. Wanting to divert him, Izven inquired about the overall status of the troops after the Ertel battle, about which they spoke at length. After twenty or thirty reps, Izven craned his head skyward and picked up his oar.

"It will rain soon. Let us return."

With that, Izven began to row again. Tallen also picked up his oar to paddle the boat back to the northern shore. He had forgotten his original grievances against Olifa and was now preoccupied with Izven's diagnosis of his consternation.

When they reached land, Xanos, who patiently stood where they had left him, extended a rodhook to bring the boat to shore. Lebb was spread out on the sandy beach. He had grown tired from pacing. Having spent an excruciating half arc with Xanos without saying as much as five words to him, Lebb was relieved to rejoin Tallen's company. The two strolled in the direction of Solterra-Volek, separating themselves from the two older men, who lagged behind.

Although Xanos sported his typically tattered leather clothing, peppered hair, and an unkempt mustache, he maintained a steady and stoic presence. On the other hand, Izven became agitated and wished to air the thoughts he had withheld from Tallen. After several reps, he broke the silence.

"Olifa will be a capable war chief. Unfortunately, her appointment only strengthens the old man's hold on the warlord. Even you must have noticed how the warlord is buying into the words mumbled into his ear. You heard it yourself this morning."

"This again?" Xanos said dispassionately. "Zefrid's plans have worked so far, have they not?"

"He is no war chief. He'll never see battle. He sits outside the hierarchy and enjoys his ability to sway the warlord with his silver tongue. He's nothing more than a miscreant."

"He has had the warlord's trust for a long time, yet now you complain? I don't see why the warlord shouldn't at least entertain Zefrid's ideas. Whatever works, I say."

"I'm not comfortable with the sort of scheming that Zefrid employs."

"I still fail to see why it is such a terrible thing for Orlen to give his confidence to Zefrid."

Izven had always been annoyed that Xanos was allowed to refer to Orlen by name instead of with an honorific and, aside from Shira, was the only one to hold this privilege.

"Zefrid is committed only to himself. Surely you can at least sense that. For now, he is loyal and competent, but I don't doubt for a second that he will turn the warlord against us should we not behave to his liking … You think about that. I can only hope we will soon have no more need for him."

Xanos shrugged lethargically. "I wouldn't know. There's no reason to think about it. Orlen has taken all factors into consideration. I'm sure everything will work out."

Izven drew to a halt.

"You really don't give a damn about anything, do you? I might as well be talking to a chalva." Despite his words, he knew that, just as if he were actually addressing a bland white flower, there was no risk that Xanos would divulge any part of their conversation to anyone, so great was his complete detachment from anything other than his duties on the battlefield.

"Why are you so inflamed?" the stocky war chief asked. "You worry too much and look too far ahead. What's the point? All that matters is the task at hand. Immediacy, Izven."

"And yet there is nothing immediate about anything you do."

"You are free to think that."

Xanos resumed his pace, prompting Izven to follow. By now, he was used to these inconsequential exchanges with Xanos. It was, indeed, as if nothing had been said at all. Out of habit, he tried to read the expression in Xanos's face, even though he knew it would be a fruitless endeavor. But, as was often the case, the calm that the other's steady brown eyes directed back at him was reassuring and ultimately infectious. As inscrutable as Xanos was, Izven had never found him to be bad company.

Gradually, Izven found himself reverting to form, though his insides continued to churn. He knew that the big picture eluded him and wondered whether Orlen was subtly distancing himself from his war chiefs for unknown reasons. The thought filled Izven with unease about his own future.

Chapter 9

(987.3.30–34)

—1—

Northwestern Corande was well-known throughout the country for its juxtaposition of two adjacent sectors, Bronsdale and North Bronsdale, which stood in marked contrast to one another. During the final years of his reign, Creon Coranthis commissioned the development of an entertainment district in what was then still a sparse capital. Over time, it became a haven for the estated who wanted nothing to do with commoners and tradesmen, those not of peerage were generally shunned. As a result of Bronsdale's exclusionary nature, the city's unestated population seized the opportunity to build its own version of the district, and North Bronsdale sprang from a modest collection of vendor-lined streets to become as large as its neighbor.

Creon's successor, King Cyril, was greatly interested in integrating the two Bronsdales, hoping it would pave the way for the homogeneity between classes that he saw burgeoning in the city of Kantor. To his bitter disappointment, North Bronsdale, which initially drew the enthusiasm of both estated and unestated, was unable to sustain any sort of long-term cultivation. Within the Assembly, Lynderan fundamentalists—led by Rudolf Eurich, father of Sebastian—used their influence to alienate any estate that persisted in such "wasteful" allocation of resources into the "commoners' corner." Thus, despite Cyril's judicious planning, North Bronsdale fell victim to the Assembly's rhetoric and subsequent restrictive

policies. Without adequate funding for maintenance or further construction, the district was quickly abandoned by most of the initial investors
and came up for grabs by commoners who saw the opportunity to make
it their own. Restaurants, bars, and lounges, some of questionable repute, took root. Street vendors moved into many of the empty buildings,
for which some had not completed construction. In many ways, North
Bronsdale became an extension of Henn, the lower-class neighborhood
in northwest Corande that was in all measures a slum. Eventually, it grew
to become more than twice the size of Henn and was given a boost
by the infusion of middle-class support. A small collective of tradesmen
and merchants from Audliné, the most populous district in the capital,
intervened shortly after North Bronsdale had descended to the cusp of
ruin and restored some of its original polish. In particular, a concerted
effort was made to preserve the integrity and upkeep of the areas in and
around Bronsdale Plaza. This large, circular arena was designed by Cyril
to be the cornerstone of his original vision for the community. An air of
respectability reinvigorated the district, which currently functioned as a
social milieu that was both open and diverse, if slightly dilapidated and
disorderly.

The rebound of North Bronsdale did little to buoy any hope of co-
alescence with Bronsdale proper, which continued to serve as the capital's
locus of arts and entertainment for the estated. At the geographical and
cultural centers of Bronsdale was Layne Hall, the largest theater in all
of Coranthia, built concurrently with Castle Coranthis and decreed by
Creon to be one of the capital's landmarks. For that reason, only the
most elite establishments were permitted within its vicinity. In addition to
harboring a number of smaller auxiliary performance venues, the streets
surrounding Layne Hall offered an overwhelming assortment of refined
cuisine and drink, local and regional, domestic and imported. These out-
fits were typically financed by Lynderan estates and catered equally to
nobles, the occasional estated upper-middle-class Coranthian seeking a
special experience, and foreign visitors, who often traveled by luxury caravan from Lymria, entering through Corande's southwestern gate. Shortly
after Samsen ascended the throne, the Assembly approved a proposal to
erect a five-meter-high fence separating the two Bronsdales—traffic between them permitted only through several guard stations—to reinforce
the exclusivity of the prized theater district. The submitter of the proposal
chose to remain anonymous, preventing any possible repercussions against
his or her person, and was in turn was protected by the Assembly, which
was far from concerned with concealing its contempt for what it saw as

an encroachment from the north. Samsen and the Cabinet conceded on this issue. They did not wish to strain further relations with the nobility, which, by 974, had deteriorated to what was practically outright hostility between the two sides. Many of the largest estates had committed an exorbitant amount of resources into financing the construction of Aldova Fortress and were locked into a bitter dispute with the Cabinet over the issue of reparations. And so Bronsdale Crossing, as it came to be known, remained the symbol of the divide between estated and unestated, southern isolationism and northern integration.

Ferdin Velmann had never harbored much affection for commoners. He would be among the last to fall in with Eurich and his band of Lynderan elitists, but he found people of meager upbringings to be coarse and repugnant on the whole. Moreover, he felt that he was in a better position to make such claims, having spent a great deal of time around the unestated. He knew that many of the Assembly stooges had never set foot inside North Bronsdale or Henn, nor so much as ventured a meter north of Corande in their lives. He marked those who could claim exemption from ignorance as irrefutably hypocritical. By Velmann's logic, the only way for them to come to the same conclusion about commoners was to make contact with these lower denizens, just as he had. Despite his aversion to the plebian lifestyle, Velmann was a frequenter of the Plaza, as North Bronsdale was informally known, and bore no qualms about it. He harbored certain interests that could not be fulfilled merely by what Bronsdale had to offer. Having grown up inundated with conventionally upper-crust luxuries and pastimes, many of which had become wholly boring to him, he found the offerings of the Plaza dynamic and refreshing. He knew firsthand that he was most certainly not the only Corandi noble to feel this way. He typically ventured into North Bronsdale in disguise, wearing commoner garb and a wig. He thought it a most prudent measure to take, even more so whenever he ran into familiar faces during his visits, faces belonging to those for whom outside knowledge of their exploits would inevitably result in uproarious scandal. These people were not keen to take the precautions that Velmann did while navigating the Plaza. Velmann had even chanced, on occasion, to see a number of his hedonistic peers grandly leading around guests, some of whom were wide-eyed foreigners. It was plain to see their itch to satiate some adventurous and base appetite. What flabbergasted Velmann was how apparently confident they were that there was not the slightest possibility of being compromised in such an environment. Velmann made a point to remember these instances and immediately set them down against the account of whomever he happened across, though it ultimately served only to remind him that he was equally guilty of such indulgences.

He had originally planned an excursion that night precisely to oblige his salacious urges, though a series of unpleasant encounters at the castle left him in a foul mood. Normally, this would further fuel his desire to stalk into the depths of the northwestern underbelly of Corande, but he found himself craving conversation. As he departed the palace, he stopped to invite the other members of the Cabinet to join him in his customary room at the Desrabian Gardens, a lounge of opulence dwarfing any other in Coranthia, not least because of its location directly opposite the entrance to Layne Hall.

The Gardens stood four stories high and was regularly scheduled as the host of a number of social functions. Its traffic was notably in correspondence with any heavily anticipated premiere or event at Layne, during which patronage would suitably swell. Desrabian Gardens was owned by the Countess Aldina Hurtzwald, widow of the late, esteemed Count Oscar, and stood as a monument to her formidable rank within the Coranthian nobility. Since the countess inherited the building, she had been determined to redecorate it to live up to its namesake in a way that would satisfy her. Painstakingly nurtured flowers of all types, gathered from all over Coranthia, were on full display. It was impossible to turn in any direction without being overcome by their diverse patterns, shapes, and colors. Long vines of aresca, fully matured with bright yellow flowers, were strategically arranged along the walls; perfumed dark purple ralgian roses picked from the Alcone Mountains lined the ornamental waterway that enclosed the main floor of the atrium; pheni stalks, imported from the Doromalian Empire, emerged from intricately carved pot stands between the tables within the public section in the main area; and large arrays of bouquets wrapped around the carved columns that rose to the glass ceiling along the perimeter of the atrium. The private rooms occupied the outer ring formed by the upper three floors, located directly above the waterway. Each of the rooms had two balconies, facing the building's exterior on one side and the atrium on the other. The rooms were paired off, sharing a common entryway that also served as a landing for a flight of stairs running from the first to the fourth floors. The servers entered the rooms from these entryways, so as not to disturb any guests engaged in affairs on either balcony.

While Velmann did not enjoy interacting with the countess, he went to considerable lengths to charm her for access to a room with a frontal view of Layne Hall. This seemed not only natural but necessary for a man of his status and tendencies. He chose a room on the third floor with the measurement that the second floor was not exclusive enough, while the top floor was somewhat impractical for someone who demanded reasonably prompt service. Upon entering the Gardens, he pretended not to recognize the smiling hostess who greeted him, and her smile wavered immediately. He was not in the mood to deal with this and urged her to lead him to his accommodations.

The hostess hastened to lead him up the stairs to his room, where Velmann threw himself onto the couch with a weary sigh. He leaned back, letting his shoulder-length brown hair fan over the back of the couch.

"I think we met during your last visit, Your Excellency," said the girl meekly.

He resisted the urge to acknowledge her words. Instead, he pressed the back of his head into the couch, closed his eyes, and asked, "What is today's specialty, miss?"

The girl mumbled something in a low and hoarse voice.

"What was that?" Velmann murmured.

"My name," the girl whispered. "It's Lusanna."

He sighed impatiently. "What is today's specialty, Lusanna?"

Her lip quivered as she proceeded to tell him it was jelaire leconet, an extremely expensive Lynderan fine wine.

"Fine, let's have it."

Lusanna bowed hurriedly and left.

When the wine was brought a short time later, she was nowhere to be seen. Another hostess, whose name he knew to be Samantha, appeared in the doorway of Velmann's suite. The new girl remained in the room, watching as he fiddled with the bottle after refusing her offer to open it for him. She seemed unwilling to leave until finally he sent her away with a hint of annoyance, tasking her to bring another bottle but to hold it until at least one of his guests arrived. Samantha bowed and exited, leaving Velmann to work on his drink as he tried to sort through the jumble of thoughts in his head. Everyone who knew him found him to be exceedingly sociable, almost intolerably so at times, but he was often silent and almost sluggish when alone. Here was a man who drew his vigor from the presence of others.

He considered opening the sliding door to the balcony but thought it too muggy outside. He settled for drawing back the curtain, unleashing the radiance of the streetlamps and the brightly lit frame of Layne Hall.

Several giant scrolls draped over the front columns of the edifice in a cascade of maroon, advertising an upcoming performance of the recently premiered Spring Symphony of Gerald Farrell, who would be conducting the Lymrian Orchestra.

Unlike many of the city's other districts, Bronsdale tolerated only minimal advertising. Aside from a few displays and banners hung on major venues, forms of solicitation, such as flyers and caravan ads, were rare in areas frequented by nobles, who generally condescended toward the practice. At that moment, Velmann spotted a particular caravan making its way down the road. The caravan was large, its canvas painted in bright colors. A group of lanterns inside the vehicle illuminated the large painting on the canvas, which depicted a burly man smashing an enormous hammer against a glowing sword set on an anvil. Bright orange and red sparks flew from the sword; the tag read:

Sworded Affairs: We Get to the Point
Elling Street, just west of Capital Circle

It had become increasingly popular for various establishments within Coranthian cities to use the wagon canvases to display advertisements. Velmann had always loathed advertisements and found in recent years they had become almost offensively garish. Given his current mood, the sight of one of these in a district he considered a safe haven from such annoyances almost lit a powder keg under him. Velmann felt a strong impulse to throw open the door and yell down at the driver of the vehicle, though ultimately restrained himself.

Regaining his composure, he sighed and lumbered to the other side of the room and threw those curtains open as well. Peering down at the atrium, he noticed how empty the Gardens were that evening; the cluster of public tables was filled only to half capacity as the nightly music began to emanate from the piano at the center of the floor. Some player poked away at the keys while a reasonably attractive young woman crooned away. Velmann looked on disinterestedly for a rep before turning around and planting himself on the couch once again, loosening his belt two notches to provide relief for what had, over the past several years, become a rapidly enlarging belly. He did not know how much time passed before Samantha, smiling from ear to ear, returned with both the second bottle of leconet and Weston Grandville.

The Minister of the Treasury thanked the hostess and dismissed her. He sat on an adjacent couch, arranged perpendicularly to the one occupied by Velmann, and popped opened the second bottle. After procuring a glass from the stand beneath the large cocktail table in front of him, he began to pour from the bottle. Velmann, whose eyes had been languidly following Grandville's movements, stirred and sat up.

"No, finish this one first," he muttered, waving the container in his hand.

"Seems like you don't need any help with that," Grandville returned, raising the glass to his lips to take a sip. He hummed approvingly as he downed the wine.

"So what's wrong with you?" he said, noticing the shade cast over Velmann's face. "Eurich still twisting your arm?"

"I had a rather noxious exchange with him earlier." Velmann unconsciously gave the bottle a slight shake. "Eurich and his lapdogs think they can hold Leynitz's failure over my head ..."

"Perhaps both of you are letting it get out of hand," said Grandville. "It's hardly necessary, Ferdin. We are all at fault for underestimating the warlord. Ourselves, the Assembly, the generals, the king. Leynitz chose to absolve us to avoid another blowup between you and the First Chair. Surely you realize this."

"Marsell Leynitz, First Knight of Coranthia," Velmann snorted. Ever the paragon of chivalry, defender of incompetent children who play at being soldiers."

"Pray you do not say that in Elliott's presence," Grandville said sternly.

"Leynitz works for me. I tell him when he's allowed to take the blame."

Even though Grandville knew that alcohol fueled Velmann's words, his patience had worn thin when it came to the unending feud between Velmann and Eurich.

"So what you're saying," Grandville said, "is that you dislike the fact that the general preempted you and stepped forward himself? You want to be able to save face by making an example of him?"

Though Velmann did not respond, the look of frustration on his face was sufficient confirmation. A lengthy silence followed as Grandville turned to his drink, while Velmann tilted back his head and stared blankly at the ceiling, his mood entirely unimproved.

Sensing that he would do better to be more diplomatic, Grandville said evenly, "You're just fanning the flames at this rate. You know we can't afford infighting during a war."

Velmann scowled.

"Nor can we afford the intolerable games we apparently let the Assembly play with us. With the way Leynitz bungled the march on Ertel Ridge, he'll have no goodwill left the next time he screws up. I'll make sure of it."

Before Grandville could reply, there was a knock at the door. Samantha returned, still smiling, though less broadly and with a hint of fatigue, her face ached from bearing her frozen mask of hospitality. Accompanying her was Martin Verinda, who regarded the young woman with amusement.

"What will you have, my Lord?" Samantha chirped, her enthusiasm ringing somewhat artificially.

"Nothing," Verinda said, entering the room and stepping aside. "Thank you, young lady. I will not be staying long. I'll have only a glass of whatever these two are already drinking."

"Please let me know if you change your mind," Samantha said, giving the three ministers a hurried bow before leaving.

"Hello, Martin," Velmann said as Verinda took off his cap.

"What kept you?" Grandville asked. "Where is Elliott?"

"And what's this about running off now?" Velmann added.

Grandville shifted to his left and motioned for Verinda to take a seat next to him. As Verinda obliged, Grandville fetched a second glass and filled it with leconet.

"Thank you. Elliott had some business to tend to," Verinda said, holding up the glass Grandville handed to him and inspecting its contents. "My apologies for my tardiness."

"Think nothing of it. You didn't miss much. Just another of Ferdin's drunken rants," Grandville said, glancing at Velmann.

"Pah! I'm not drunk …"

"I bumped into Lord Gregor, and we had a rather lengthy, spontaneous conversation." Verinda paused momentarily before switching topics. "I also apologize in advance for not being able to stay. Lady Verinda is expecting me home early tonight. I have to accompany her in the morning to assist in the party preparations."

"You met with Lord Gregor?" Grandville asked.

"Ah, how is the old windbag?" Velmann said simultaneously.

Verinda took a gulp of leconet and smiled crookedly. "The lady is quite well. I will pass along your regards."

Grandville burst out laughing.

Velmann smiled begrudgingly. Despite his sullenness, he enjoyed the joke, even if it had been at his expense.

"If Lord Gregor accosted you, it was a foregone conclusion that you'd be kept late," Grandville said.

"Yes, he has maintained his penchant for prolixity, but as usual, his words are worth consideration. We discussed, yet again, the possibility of diverting manpower and resources to deal with the growing bandit situation in the Outlands. He still does not seem to be willing to give any ground on the issue."

"Why is he so adamant about this?" Grandville wondered aloud.

"He's in no position to do anything anymore. Sounds to me like you're just humoring his idle chatter."

"Actually, Ferdin, the matter is becoming increasingly pertinent. Outlander avets have already begun to opt-out of their service. I suspect some of them feel compelled to return to defend their homes against the chaos wrought by bandits."

"An undesirable scenario in the long run," Grandville said.

Verinda nodded. "It seems to me that we have two equally risky approaches to the problem. We could pass a mandate to lengthen the service quota—that would surely draw the ire of the people—or, as an alternative, we could police the Outlands more rigorously, which would take away from our manpower against the Amelarens. That said, I am hesitant to commit to either option. It is a dilemma for which I have no good answer."

Velmann laid down the now-empty bottle he had been holding and fiddled with the ring on his right index finger. "You realize that either of those options," he said, slowly and impatiently, "would provoke Eurich even more. He'll rally his goons to threaten withdrawal of war funds."

"And what of the bandits now?" Grandville asked Verinda.

The Minister of the Interior rubbed his smooth pate. "No progress, unfortunately. I know that a collective exists. It might have been patchwork or temporary in years past, but presently there is definitely an organized presence in the Outlands."

"Have you been unable to confirm or deny this?" Grandville said. "Don't you have your network of Outlands messengers?"

"Messengers? You mean spies?" Velmann remarked pointedly.

Grandville wrinkled his brow.

"Any leads that my sources came across have been derailed," Verinda said. "I am rather amazed that the trail is so cold."

"I would not afford these bandits much credit. It's only a matter of time before you make some headway."

"I fear we may not have the luxury of time," Verinda said.

"Come, enough of this serious talk," Velmann huffed. He pulled himself up and made his way to the door. "I'll be back with more wine. I need a new flavor."

Before Grandville could come up with a new thread of conversation, Velmann reappeared. True to his word, he had brought with him an unopened bottle, and it was plainly not leconet.

Verinda stood and placed his cap on his head. "My sincerest apologies, Ferdin. As I said, I must retire early tonight."

"I suppose we'll be seeing you tomorrow." Velmann grinned. "You really need to join us more often, Martin."

"I'll be sure to make up for it next time. Good night, gentlemen." Verinda said, and, with a nod, he left.

Grandville gazed at Velmann, who remained where he was, blinking torpidly, having not seemed to notice he had left the door open. "We can have that bottle at your mansion, Ferdin," he said, getting to his feet.

"What are you talking about? We'll have it right here. It's all too stuffy back with … I need fresh air, you understand?"

"We'll get fresh air on the walk over."

"I'm in no mood to go home early, Weston." Velmann waved the bottle in the air with annoyance.

"Don't be so imprudent. You cannot be in one of your spells tomorrow." He planted himself in front of Velmann, effectively blocking him from the couches.

"Being difficult, aren't you?" Velmann turned and ambled into the entryway. Grandville followed, closing the door behind him. He relieved Velmann of the bottle to secure it. Even though he did not want either of them to drink any more that night, he did not want to risk mishandling a container of fine wine. With his other hand, he took Velmann's arm and guided him down the stairs.

"Fine," Velmann declared, as if their course of action had not been determined until he issued a final proclamation. "We'll have it your way, only you're not allowed to take flight the moment we arrive."

As much as that was exactly what he wanted to do, Grandville knew he had to stay with his friend until he was sure there would be no further adventures for the night.

"I wouldn't think of it," he said reassuringly.

—2—

By royal decree, Sophelia Anamarie Coranthis commemorated the end of her twentieth year on the Thirty-Fourth Day of the Third Exile with a fête in the grand ballroom of Castle Coranthis. Dignitaries from every corner of Coranthia converged on the palace. Several envoys from the Doromalian Empire were also in attendance. Aside from the princess herself, they received the most attention from the other guests.

Princess Sophelia took no issue with this and wished everyone would leave her alone. She had long since ceased to harbor enthusiasm for her annual public birthday celebration. She harbored no desire to preside over any sort of function, much less be the center of attention at one.

By now, the procedure was familiar. She was required to arrive well before the official commencement of the affair, since what kind of proper lady, to say nothing of a princess, would do otherwise? Each and every guest was obligated to approach her as she sat on a dais set atop the stage and offer their rehearsed congratulations and other flattery before taking a position at one of the tables across the floor. Annoyed by such an artificial consuetude, Sophelia often reminded herself with resignation that it could be worse; she was only too glad that the guests were not also required to bear gifts.

Accompanying her on the dais, to either side, were her father and brother. The dais seated only the royal family. Esther Milderich, Sophelia's governess, did not attend these events, and Isabelle Martina Verinda, the princess's personal guard, spent most of her time at the nearby ministers' table with her parents, Martin and Harriet Verinda. Occasionally, Isabelle drifted along the edges of the room, blending in with the stationed members of the Royal Guard, allowing her more freedom to observe the proceedings while avoiding the spotlight that surrounded Sophelia.

Typically, Samsen and Adrian would leave to engage in pleasantries with the guests. At times, Sophelia followed suit, though more often than not, she remained rooted to the dais, staring out at innumerable faces, both known and unknown, as they streamed into the ballroom. This would last until her boredom became too oppressive, at which point she would wade into the crowd and pass the time with inconsequential conversation. Eventually, she would be expected to dance with her father and brother, and, while she liked to dance, she did not enjoy the thought of having to put on a show. She knew that remaining on the dais would expedite such nonsense and sought to leave her chair at the first opportunity that night. When Samsen and Adrian rose, she immediately followed suit. Perhaps she felt slightly empowered by the alcohol coursing through her body; she had discreetly finished two full glasses of wine brought to her by Adrian while seated. She watched as her father made his way to the Doromalian table and, not feeling entirely comfortable with the notion of conversing with the foreign guests, followed her brother instead.

A collection of individuals belonging to the uppermost circles of Coranthian society sat among the row of tables closest to the dais, which was not really a row at all but a ring that enclosed a wide, open area, which was what remained of the dance floor. At the table closest to the western wall sat Mathias San Gregor, the Second Chair of the Assembly. Gregor, in his advanced age, did not have many close friends left and no longer spent much of his personal time with members of the nobility. While one might have expected a man of his rank to be in the company of an impressive assemblage, his attendance of the party was a solitary one.

"Surely you are aware, Countess," he said with a wry smile, to the woman who sat across from him, "that your stock can only go down if you continue to indulge me much longer."

Countess Aldina Hurtzwald laughed haughtily. Her voice was strong and reverberant, complementing her strong jawline, piercing brown eyes, and high cheekbones. Her raven hair was twisted in an elaborately braided coil, fixed in place with an assortment of gold pins that matched her small, lambent earrings.

"Believe me, good sir, that is comfortably outside the realm of possibility. Besides, I quite enjoy talking to those who actually have original thoughts to share."

"And fittingly, here is the prince. Hello, Your Highness."

"Hello, Lord Gregor. My Lady."

Adrian bowed to Countess Hurtzwald, who shook her head fervently and all but begged him not to "demean himself before this old woman."

"You are making the rounds, I suppose?" said Gregor.

"Indeed, and—"

"And your sister seems to have taken an interest as well!" Hurtzwald exclaimed.

"Greetings, Countess," Sophelia said timidly. "And Lord Gregor."

"You look simply stunning, my dear Princess," Hurtzwald gushed.

Sophelia wore an off-white full-skirted gown that grazed the floor; her garments shone only slightly more than her creamy skin. The ruffled satin dress featured embroidery and blue lace tied around the midsection. She donned a sparkling aeron crown that matched her fiery blue eyes, as well as silk opera gloves and a gold-trimmed blue ribbon that secured her long blond hair, which draped behind her shoulders and flowed straight to her slender waist.

She had already received many compliments on her appearance that evening, but found herself intrigued by the countess, who seemed much less stiff and infinitely more genuine than the other ladies of the court. She knew of Hurtzwald's reputation as undaunted and self-assured and felt some measure of satisfaction that this assessment did not appear inaccurate. She flashed her best smile and thanked Hurtzwald for her kind words.

Adrian glanced at them and said to Gregor, "Would you mind taking a walk with me, sir?"

"Of course, Your Highness."

The Prince led Gregor away from the table, leaving Sophelia alone with the countess.

"I have a question for you, Lord Gregor," said Adrian when he felt they were out of earshot, not only from the two women but also from the other guests. They stood almost against the wall, with Gregor leaning slightly on his cane. "What is the situation in the Assembly regarding the upcoming inquiry? I know you will be frank with me."

"Are you asking on behalf of General Leynitz, perhaps?"

"Not on anyone's behalf. I simply want to know. Is it so strange for me to be independently motivated?"

"I apologize, Your Highness. It is good for you to take a more active role in our internal affairs."

Adrian sighed impatiently. "Not you too, Lord Gregor."

"You are right. I do not mean patronize you. The Assembly grows rowdy, as you might expect. Certain people believe the general was over-confident and ill-prepared for the Amelaren strategy. Of course, that is not my presumption. You should expect that I will maintain objectivity at the hearing."

The prince nodded in acknowledgment.

A collective roar of laughter arose from the Doromalian table across the room. Samsen and the envoys appeared greatly entertained by a conversation with Jacqueline Havora and Harriet Verinda, wives of the agriculture and interior ministers, respectively.

"I'd like to throw these armchair generals of ours out to Argiset or Ertel and see how much better they do," Adrian said. "But I suppose they are merely falling in line behind Lord Eurich, who is still only interested in preserving his own resources."

Gregor remained silent. Having not received the reaction he expected, Adrian raised an eyebrow and turned his attention to the ballroom. He pointed to a man seated alone at one of the rear tables.

"And there he is," the prince said, "all the way in the back. At least he's not bothering to put on a show of enjoying himself."

The haggard, dead-eyed expression on Sebastian Eurich's normally sharp face held no significance to Adrian, though Gregor found it jarring.

"He looks quite strange, if you ask me," the older man said, half to himself.

Adrian's attention had returned to the table where his father and the foreigners continued to chat buoyantly. He reflected on Samsen's clearly manufactured joviality, which was a far cry from the usually staid demeanor he and Sophelia were accustomed to seeing from their father.

"I have to ask," he said to Gregor without turning his head, "how you manage to keep yourself in the game, holding onto your position as Second Chair. I mean no offense, of course, but I cannot imagine having any sort of desire to remain engaged in matters of the court, or any other affairs at your age. I've only just begun involving myself and am already quite tired of it all."

Gregor adjusted his cane to alleviate a faint cramp in his left leg. "You give me too much credit, Your Highness."

"Do I, Lord Gregor? Then will you tell me why you haven't simply retired to a carefree life at your estate? You've served in the Cabinet and on the Assembly. What more is required of you at this point?"

Just then, the king called for attention, effectively ending the conversation between the two of them. Although Adrian diverted his gaze, he could sense that Gregor had been none too eager to respond to the question.

"The birthday dance!" Samsen hollered, his voice ringing throughout the ballroom. "Sophelia, where are you?"

The string orchestra brought to play, almost incessantly, throughout the party was split into two sections, seated in identically shaped pits surrounding the dais. Samsen left his place at the Doromalian table to say something to the concertmaster, a tall, skinny male violinist, who nodded and gestured to his fellow musicians. They raised their instruments in unison and drew the opening measures of a waltz.

The princess sat where Adrian had left her at Hurtzwald's table, having become increasingly engrossed in her conversation with the countess. Her countenance exhibited disappointment at the interruption.

All eyes fixed on her as she rose from the table and made her way carefully to the polished dark wood dance floor beneath a massive crystal chandelier, where her father awaited with an outstretched hand and a wide smile, one that seemed a touch too broad to her.

"Come, my dear," Samsen said in his deepest voice. He swept her hand in his, and the two twirled across the empty floor as an appreciative murmur rose from the crowd.

Countess Hurtzwald, sipping a glass of redeye—a cocktail of red wine and Doromalian grain liquor—trained her eyes on the king and princess. She took no notice of an approaching Minister Grandville until he was already seated beside her.

"My word! You startled me, Lord Grandville. What is the matter?"

"How are you, My Lady?"

"I am perfectly well and enjoying myself greatly. His Majesty and Her Highness are flawless on the dance floor." Her gaze remained on Samsen and Sophelia.

Grandville decided to dispense with idle chatter. "My Lady, I'd like to continue our conversation from last night. You'll understand that I chose not to alert Lord Velmann that anything was amiss at the time."

Hurtzwald shook her head slightly, but did not turn to meet his gaze. "I have nothing more to say."

"There must be at least some justification for your actions," Grandville said pointedly. "He has been most generous to your establishment. He is an impulsive man, but not a reckless one. I'm sure that whatever he has done—"

The countess barely suppressed her displeasure as her ruby-red lips curled into a snarl.

"This time. Whatever he has done *this time*, you mean." Her voice rattled like the ice in her glass. "And this time was inexcusable. He may not always be reckless, but Lord Velmann either has no control over his impulses or little regard for me. Either way, he is no longer welcome at the Gardens."

Samsen and Sophelia completed their pirouette across the floor just as the orchestra tied off the music. Cheers and applause echoed throughout the room. With a shy smile that made her look all the more radiant, Sophelia bowed slightly and made as if to return to her chair on the dais.

"Wait! Your turn, Adrian!" Samsen declared, pointing at his son, who gradually drifted toward the open floor, away from Gregor, who remained against the western wall, standing apart from the other guests.

Adrian shrugged and strode forward. "All right, sister," he said loudly enough for all to hear. "Shall we?"

Sophelia shook her head ever so slightly, but her smile lingered. She offered her hand to Adrian and off they went at the concertmaster's cue as the music resumed.

"Her Highness is a sight to behold," Hurtzwald marveled. "I was not nearly as beautiful as she when I was her age. As for the prince …"

The countess locked eyes with Grandville, curling her lips into a coy smile.

"It has been quite some time since he's been spotted in the presence of female company, no? I'm sure you've heard the rumors, my good sir. Do you have any thoughts on the matter?"

Grandville resisted the change of subject. "Please, Countess, at least tell me what Lord Velmann has done to anger you so."

Hurtzwald glanced at him with annoyance.

"One of my hostesses. I warned him specifically to stay away from her. I told him in no uncertain terms. It is as simple as that."

She gave the empty glass in her hand a disapproving shake.

Grandville decided not to press further. Instead, he said, "Very well, My Lady. I should remind you once again, however, that his patronage is a boon to your business, and he may take it upon himself to dissuade others from frequenting the Gardens if you decide to ostracize him permanently."

He was about to leave when she said, "Wait, Lord Grandville. I would like to ask you something."

Looking around for a waiter, she raised her glass in the air and tapped it with a perfectly maintained rose-polished nail. A waiter standing three tables away hastened to her side and promised an immediate refill. After the servant had gone, she gave Grandville her full attention as he remained, awaiting her address.

"Surely it has not escaped you how much you've sacrificed by remaining so loyal to him. Tell me, why do you still hold him in such favor, even now?"

He stared at her impassively for some time before standing. "I wish you a pleasant and enjoyable evening, My Lady."

Hurtzwald shrugged with equal placidity. "Likewise."

As Grandville slinked inconspicuously around the array of tables toward the ballroom doors, Adrian and Sophelia concluded their waltz to another round of applause. The countess rose from her seat and led the cheers, deliberately making eye contact with the princess and flashing her warmest smile.

While Samsen and Sophelia returned to the dais, Adrian headed to the ministers' table where Velmann sat two chairs from his wife, Cassandra. Although Jacqueline Havora and Harriet Verinda spent most of the evening occupying the Doromalians, if one were to ask the foreign envoys who between them made the stronger impression, they would have agreed it was neither, but rather Cassandra Velmann, who sat two tables away and never said a word to them. She had the sort of rarefied beauty that was the envy of queens; no one present was a match for her magnetic, voluptuous bloom. Between husband and wife sat their son, Marcus. Although he was only thirteen, it was obvious to all who regarded him that he was heir to the flawless physiognomy and fair complexion that blessed both of his parents.

"That was delightful, Your Highness," Cassandra said, smiling at Adrian as he pulled up a chair.

"Nonsense," he said. "I'm sure I looked quite silly out there." He turned his head and waved at a waiter, signaling his request for a drink.

Velmann's eyes drifted toward the currently idling orchestra. He approved of their playing and thought it a cut above the quality of performance given by even a good Lymrian ensemble; unsurprisingly, the king had spared no expense, ensuring the best entertainment for his daughter's gala. As these thoughts ran through Velmann's head, an impulse seized him like a vise. He pulled Marcus's sleeve.

From across the table, Adrian, who had just received a glass of white wine from the hustling waiter, watched as Velmann spoke quietly with his son. Though they had only a brief exchange, Adrian could see a glimmer of excitement in the boy's eyes. Marcus stood and walked to the concertmaster. The guests did not pay much attention until the orchestra, on instruction of the concertmaster, began to warm up once again.

Marcus boldly approached Sophelia, who sat frozen in her chair, and spoke in a clear, firm voice.

"Your Highness, I would be honored if you'd allow me a dance as well."

A hush fell over the room. All eyes fell upon Sophelia, who began to redden. Trying to sneak a glance at her father, she saw him back at the Doromalians' table, but could not make out the expression on his face from where she sat on stage.

"Very well," she said, her voice projecting outward for everyone to hear. She stepped from the stage onto the floor. Even in her seven-centimeter heels, she was slightly shorter than the sprouting Marcus.

A feverish buzz swept through the crowd, and, in particular, the ladies in attendance. The orchestra played a slow, dulcet number, immersing the ballroom in a layered romantic melody.

At the ministers' table, Adrian looked on as Sophelia and Marcus stiffly danced to the music. He had not heard the conversation that transpired between Velmann and Marcus, but it was obvious what had been said. Therefore, nothing about the scene, which played before his eyes, surprised him. But lack of surprise did not translate to indifference. On the contrary, he simmered inside, resenting how Grandville and Velmann treated him as the myopic juvenile he had been before Tellisburg, without regard for even the possibility that he was now fully aware of how they and most everyone in the room functioned as part of the all-encompassing pretenses of the nobility.

After spending so much time away from Corande, Adrian found it ironic that he was now loath to stay long. He pitied his sister, watching as she played her part in the artifice. He reminded himself that once he was finally established, there would no longer be any need for worry. Although the process would be gradual and deliberate, he would not rest until he became the kind of ruler he had always aspired to be, and one in whom his father and their predecessors would take pride.

He was, after all, the heir to the throne. He was Coranthia's future, and he would see to it that the people of his country, and especially those gathered in the room, accepted and rightfully acknowledged that fact.

Chapter 10

(987.4.09–11)

—1—

The Citadel of Creon, located at the southwestern corner of Corande in the estated sector of Lateur, was founded by Creon Coranthis himself. Despite having retained some of its defensive capabilities from its original establishment as a military structure, the Citadel currently served multiple purposes. It connected the banks of the Sarigan River with the western city walls to its north. The heavily guarded gate within the structure was one of the five entrances into Corande, allowing nobles to enter the Lateur district directly from outside the city and bypass any interaction with unestated citizens in the capital proper. The large central and southern wings were home to the Citadel Academy, the premier nonmilitary educational institution of Coranthia, exclusively estated in its student body.

Drake Wing, the much smaller northern branch, was the seat of convention for the Assembly of Coranthian Lords. Here, in the northwestern corner on the third floor, was a small room where military hearings held jointly by the defense ministry and the Assembly chairs were conducted. One hundred and thirty-four days after the defeat of the army at Ertel Gorge, one such set of hearings began.

• • •

A loud rapping rang harshly on the wooden double doors, which opened slowly to reveal Nash Havora. He trudged through the doorway, past the two members of the Royal Guard who stood to either side, and walked down the aisle, which resembled a ramp, to his prepared seat at a small table facing the inquiry panel; the table was only a temporary fixture, hauled into the room specifically for purposes of the inquiry. Minister of Defense Velmann headed the panel and presided from the central seat of a dais at the back of the room. To Velmann's right sat Sebastian Eurich and a portly noble; to his left sat Mathias San Gregor.

As Nash took his seat, he glanced at the wall above Velmann where a golden banner hung to display Caliri's Scepter, the emblem so prevalent throughout the Citadel and noble-dominated districts of Lateur and Bronsdale; it was the same as the one emblazoned on the Coranox, though showcased here as a distinction of class rather than part of a grander unified symbol. The structure of the room resembled a small auditorium, with the inquiry panel seated on the dais in front of him and the audience in rows of seats behind him. Minister Elliott Havora and his wife, Lady Jacqueline, sat in the first row behind Nash and watched their son with apprehension. Next to Jacqueline was Countess Hurtzwald, who occasionally turned to speak with another noblewoman seated in the second row.

Among the spectators were General Leynitz and Colonel Dyers, who sat side by side. They were set to attend inquiries of their own, which would take place the following day. To the surprise of almost everyone present, Prince Adrian was also in attendance, seated alone in the back row. Finally, an assortment of other nobles peppered the remaining seats. The audience numbered sixteen in total, though their spread made the room seem almost filled to capacity.

Ferdin Velmann's gaze bore into Nash as the captain took his seat. Eurich was busy inattentively shuffling through papers. The portly noble sat aloofly. Gregor, on the other hand, smiled reassuringly and locked eyes with Nash. Nash adjusted his spectacles and returned the smile.

"Please be quiet," Velmann boomed, raising his right hand. "Today's session will commence shortly."

Countess Hurtzwald leaned in to whisper to Jacqueline. "Don't worry, my dear. Nothing will come of this. Lord Velmann's voice is the only one that counts, and for all his bluster, I doubt he is keen to place any blame on your son."

Lady Havora gave the countess a weak smile.

"Now," Velmann began, "we are here today to conduct an inquiry into the conduct of Captain Nash Havora during the previous campaign, specifically the battle at Ertel Gorge. This will be the first in a series of inquiries to take place over the next two days. Joining me on the panel are the first, second, and fourth chairs of the Assembly: Sebastian Eurich, Mathias San Gregor, and Richard Drake."

At the mention of his name, Eurich cast a fleeting glare in the direction of Velmann and then quickly straightened himself.

As Velmann paused to take a sip of coffee, Nash squirmed in his chair. The Minister of Defense had a reputation for whimsy and flippancy, but when it came to military affairs, he was deadly serious and more intimidating than even the most severe of senior officers.

"Should we determine that the captain behaved in a dangerous or inappropriate manner, we shall reconvene at a later point to determine the proper course of action." He glanced to his right. "Count Eurich, you may begin."

Eurich ran a hand through his hair to check that it was properly combed and offered a small, smug smile as he fidgeted in his seat. "Captain Havora, we have several eyewitness accounts of your actions at Ertel Gorge. Some of them claim that your behavior and inability to command your company resulted in the death of your vice captain, Quincy Parsons. Furthermore, you allowed your company to fall into a state of disarray while an avet seized control."

Eurich paused for several ticks to scan the audience. "Let the record state that the avet in question is Reznik Sylvera from the 9th Squad of Captain Havora's upper platoon." His gaze drifted to Nash. "Have you anything to say regarding this testimony?"

"Excuse me, Count Eurich," Nash said firmly. If I am to be judged on others' interpretations of what transpired, then I think I have a right to know who my accusers are."

Richard Drake, whose family name adorned the section of the Citadel in which those present found themselves, rapped his fingers on the table as his wiry gray hair fell behind his shoulders. His double-chinned face pulsed a mild shade of red. "That is of little consequence, Captain. What matters is whether the events in question did occur, and testimony from multiple soldiers suggest that they did."

Nash shook his head. "I disagree, Your Excellency. I think the origin of these accusations is of great relevance. Are the reputation and trustworthiness of a source no longer important?"

"We have on record multiple statements from avets and sergeants corroborating the statement," Velmann said. "We are not accusing you of anything. We merely ask for your own account of what transpired."

Eurich frowned disapprovingly at Velmann.

"So, no officers corroborated these reports?" Nash countered, hesitantly emboldened by this reveal.

"They did not," Velmann confirmed.

"But," Eurich cut in, "it is rather difficult to acquire testimony of your second when he is no longer with us, is it not?"

A cup of water rested on the table before Nash. He raised it to his lips and drank.

"Sir," he said after setting the cup back down, "I maintain that Vice Captain Parsons charged ahead to engage the enemy of his own volition. He was not following my orders."

"So you say," Drake condescended.

Gregor spoke for the first time. "Assuming the vice captain died as a result of his own poor decisions, Captain, you still have yet to explain what happened during the battle or address the claim that you lost control of your company."

Nash sighed.

"The panel seems to have difficulty honoring my request to name my accusers. I cannot offer a proper defense without this information."

"Regardless of their identities, we do have the statement of your present vice captain, Reznik Sylvera." Drake raised his hands in the air. "Frankly, Captain, I'd like to give you a chance to defend yourself, but you seem to be grasping at straws. The statement received by the now Vice Captain Sylvera corroborates the other reports. He stated that you promoted him as a result of his accomplishments in battle. Is that not consistent with what other eyewitnesses said? That you ceded control to him and acknowledged this by making him your new second. You must understand how this is suggestive to us, do you not?"

"Which is it, Captain Havora?" Eurich demanded. "Did you lose control of your soldiers? Or did you reward the reckless actions of a newly graduated avet by promoting him to vice captain? Actions that subverted your authority, no less."

Nash furrowed his brow and stared at the table. He had no response.

"That's enough," a powerful voice rang from the audience. Everyone turned to see General Leynitz, who had risen from his seat and was making his way down the aisle toward the table.

"What's this about, General?" Velmann wagged his finger. "This is not your inquiry. Wait your turn and do not meddle in this."

Leynitz offered a disarmingly warm smile in return. He approached Nash and placed his right hand gently on the table.

"Gentlemen, what is there to gain from this? We are at war, and you are occupying my officers by putting them through these ridiculous sessions." He turned to face the audience. "Our overwhelming victory at Argiset aside, this was the captain's first true battle, as it was for many of the soldiers and officers, and not an ideal setting to begin one's career as captain. This fault is entirely mine. I am aware that an officer's lack of practical experience is not a permissible defense of inappropriate conduct, especially of a captain, but I bring it up as a reflection on the overall state of our army. There is no substitute for real battle experience, something lacking among most of the soldiers on our front lines, including officers. Stand up, Captain Havora."

"General, you are out of line," Velmann warned.

"Don't you listen to him, Captain Havora," Eurich added through clenched teeth.

Nash stared at Leynitz, who nodded, and stood. He stepped aside for the general, who took his place in the chair.

"Lord Velmann, place any blame you have for what happened at Ertel on me. I am at fault for insisting that we rush into Amelaren territory without having gradually escalated our encounters with the enemy after a ceasefire of almost two decades. I am the only one who should stand trial."

Velmann was nonplussed. "General, this is hardly a trial. This is merely an inquiry into the events of that battle. Your theatrics are not appreciated."

"And yet, you speak of determining the correct course of action in response to Captain Havora's testimony. That sounds like a trial to me."

Gregor leaned forward, hanging on Leynitz's words, while Drake stared blankly ahead, as if he did not understand what the general was saying. Eurich made a valiant attempt to contain his anger from leaking through his countenance, albeit with little success.

"Frankly, it does not surprise me, in hindsight, that chaos ensued. I urge you not to place the blame on Captain Havora. I personally believe that he did a fine job and that he will continue to do so going forward. He is also an excellent judge of character. I will be certain to review his choice to replace Parsons, but I expect his reasoning was sound."

Leynitz trailed off, taking a few ticks to collect his thoughts.

"But that is not my point," he continued with a wave of his hand. "I alone am responsible for our failings at Ertel. I pushed for an offensive with insufficient planning and poor strategy. I failed to account for the enemy ambush. I was unable to adjust to the difficulties imposed upon me by the terrain to efficiently relay orders to my brigade."

As Leynitz listed strike after strike against his record, the expressions of those on the dais began to change. Each grew increasingly uncomfortable at hearing the general admonish himself. Even Eurich's expression softened.

"General," Velmann said, interrupting Leynitz before the latter could say more, "you are far too harsh on yourself, especially in the presence of your soldiers and noble peers."

Leynitz leaned back in his seat. The normally faint wrinkles under his eyes and around his mouth seemed more pronounced.

"Gentlemen, let us not do this now. I will be happy to meet with you behind closed doors."

It was rare to see Ferdin Velmann so unsure of himself; the Minister of Defense shifted in his seat, noticeably uncomfortable. "Fine," he said at last, staring directly into Leynitz's eyes as his voice hardened. "General, we shall discuss this with you tomorrow. We will convene not here but in my office. I will send word when I have set a time."

Before Leynitz could respond, Velmann raised a finger.

"While your assumption of responsibility is noted, I must ask that Colonel Dyers be present as well. Certainly you do not claim that you alone were responsible for every facet of the operation. The panel has some questions for him that must be answered. I assume you have no objection to this?" His gaze drifted toward the audience, where Dyers sat by himself.

"Very well, Minister," Leynitz agreed. "I take no issue with that."

"Nor do I," Dyers called from the back, prompting several members of the audience to turn their heads.

"Does this satisfy you all?" Velmann asked the other members of the panel.

The three chairs of the assembly each nodded, albeit hesitantly.

"Then we are adjourned," Velmann said, waving his hand. Without waiting for anyone else, he rose hastily and nimbly exited through a side door.

After Eurich had gathered his belongings, he departed with Drake in tow. The two chatted in harsh, hushed tones as they exited. Gregor was last; he smiled and gave Leynitz and Nash a slight bow before leaving, walking slowly but steadily with the support of his cane.

Nash and Leynitz turned and walked back up the aisle. Halfway, Nash stopped and began, "General, I—"

Leynitz shook his head.

"I meant what I said, Captain. The blame is mine." He paused before adding, "And you have my full support."

"Thank you, sir."

Nash offered his superior a salute and was again surprised as Leynitz extended his hand instead. The two shook, Leynitz's grip firm and assured, Nash's meek but grateful.

Leynitz exited through the double doors. As Nash watched, he felt a hand on his shoulder. Startled, he turned to see the smiling faces of his parents. It was clear to anyone who saw the three in that moment that Nash was a younger version of his equally diminutive father, although he had inherited his mother's radiant blue eyes, long thin nose, and pallid skin.

Elliott Havora strengthened his grip on Nash's shoulder and pulled him closer. "Don't worry about it, son. I will talk to Lord Velmann. We'll make sure an understanding is reached."

Nash shrugged off his father's grip. He adjusted his spectacles and shook his head. "Father, that probably will not be necessary. For whatever reason, the general has absolved me of all responsibility. I don't really know why."

"You should let your father help," Lady Havora said with concern. "A little extra push won't hurt in this case."

Countess Hurtzwald hovered around the family, eavesdropping on the conversation. Havora shot her an unfriendly look, but she took it as an invitation to speak.

"That was an interesting turn of events, was it not?" she said, smiling broadly at all three of them.

"Countess," Nash said with a small bow.

Hurtzwald appreciated the gesture and offered the same in return.

"I had no idea, Young Lord, that you were such good friends with the general."

"Honestly, I barely know His Excellency," he said sheepishly. "I've had the opportunity to speak with him in person maybe twice. I'm not sure why he did that for me."

"Hmm, yes," the countess mused. "Well … I suppose he does feel rather guilty for the disaster that befell his campaign."

"I hope he will be able to avoid any severe punishment," Nash said worriedly.

The countess laughed merrily. "You need not fear. No real punishment will befall him. No, what I suspect is that poor Colonel Dyers will be forced to shoulder the blame. Save your sentiment for him." She chuckled, projecting an air of muted certainty, as if to indicate that she knew she was right and had every reason to flaunt her confidence, though chose not to do so. "Would your family be so gracious as to bless me and several other guests with your company this evening? There is this lovely Kantorian place in the southern part of Bronsdale."

Nash shook his head. "Perhaps my parents can join you, but I must decline, Countess. Maybe another time."

Hurtzwald frowned, though did not seem offended. "I am sorry to hear that. Best wishes to you, then. Jacqueline? Elliott?"

As the Havoras and the countess continued to talk, Nash excused himself. He was disinterested in their conversation and had noticed that Prince Adrian remained seated in the back. Nash made his way to the prince and sat beside him.

"That was quite a show," Adrian grinned.

Nash wiped his sweaty brow with the sleeve of his uniform. "Quite. Also rather embarrassing for me."

Adrian shook his head. "I thought you did a good job showing your mettle, but …"

"But?" Nash pressed.

"You probably wouldn't have slithered out of the questioning had the general not intervened, it's true. I also must say that you exhibited abominable judgment in your choice of vice captain."

"Thanks," Nash said sarcastically. He leaned forward, resting forearms on the back of the row in front of him, and slowly laid down his head.

"Hey, now," Adrian said, "I was only kidding. You did well today, and despite all of this"—he waved vaguely at the air—"I'm kind of jealous. I know the campaign was a disaster, but I wish I had been out there fighting alongside the other soldiers."

"It's not quite as glorious as you may think, Prince."

Adrian frowned. "Don't patronize me, Havora."

"That was not my intention."

The prince stood. "Anyway, I'm glad you came over. I was waiting for a chance to say hello. It's odd that we've seen each other twice within such a short period, isn't it? Rather rare these days. Hopefully the next time we meet will be under more pleasant circumstances."

Nash raised his head. "Yes, I agree."

"How long will you be in Corande?" Adrian said.

"I'm not sure," Nash responded glumly. "It could be a few days or even a whole cycle. I suppose it will depend on what becomes of the general's inquiry tomorrow."

"If you're around for a while, let me know. We can meet for drinks sometime."

The corner of Nash's lips curled up in a small smile. "Sure. I'd like that. At this rate, I may be stuck here until the yugo championship."

"I do hope you're joking. The Harvest Festival is almost a cycle away. But if you do happen to be here, you should join us for that. And now, I must go. I have a dinner to prepare for."

Nash nodded. "Tell Sophelia I said hello."

"I will. Tell Sylvera I said he better not mess things up for you."

Nash laughed a little. "I fear the truth may be the other way around."

Adrian raised his eyebrows but said nothing, and he took his leave. Nash stared after him for some time before stirring.

His parents were still chatting with Countess Hurtzwald; several other nobles had eased themselves into the conversation as well. He contemplated joining them but ultimately decided against the idea. After several reps, he rose from his seat and left the room in a hurry without saying a word to anyone.

—2—

Sebastian Eurich sat on a fenninwood park bench in the center of Bronsdale Plaza. While the plaza itself was mostly used by commoners, the occasional noble could be spotted walking through or enjoying a rest on one of the many benches surrounding a fountain in the center of the plaza that boasted statues of Creon and Caliri, which were of comparable size to those in the North Foyer of Castle Coranthis.

He found the plaza an ideal place to meet in the middle of the day without being noticed. It was always crowded but not overly so. People went about their business; no one gave a second thought to the sight of a conversation between a noble and a commoner. Even Eurich had to admit that there were some benefits to the utter lack of deference granted to nobles by many commoners, at least in Corande.

Eurich watched as a flock of reas birds swooped down and scattered some white doves that were pecking at scraps on the ground. The count snorted at the arrival of the interlopers before diverting his attention to his shirt. Carefully, he pulled a gold object attached to a chain from his left pocket and stared at it.

"Pretty fancy timepiece you have there, Count," came a soft male voice from nearby.

Eurich looked up to see a tall, rugged man with long brown hair and a stubble on his chin. The man smirked at Eurich.

"That is what it is, if I'm not mistaken?"

"You're late, Hunt," Eurich said with agitation. He started to put his timepiece back in his pocket.

"Wait, if you please, sir," said the man known to Eurich as Mason Hunt. "Is there a second clock on that thing? I've seen the occasional timepiece on nobles, though never one with a second clock. May I see?"

Eurich was reluctant to part with his antique; nevertheless, pride overcame mistrust and he gently handed over the piece.

Mason stared at the object. Etched along the outer edges of the pocket watch were the numbers one to ten, denoting the time of day, and slightly offset from the center was another clock with its own hands and etchings. This second clock had twelve points rather than the usual ten, marked by a strange set of symbols that Mason did not recognize. They appeared to resemble letters more than numbers. Each clock had a distinct tick hand; both hands moved at the same rate. The hand of the second clock took fewer ticks to complete one turn around, although Mason did not count exactly how many.

He slid his finger over the protective transparent screen. The material was completely foreign to him. When Mason lightly tapped it with his nail, it made a hollow noise.

"What is this?" he said.

"It's known as reil. It's stronger and lighter than glass and immune to glare."

"Where does it come from?"

"That's the question, isn't it? Reil has only been found through guild excavations. No one even knows its composition."

Mason raised an eyebrow skeptically.

"It's one of a kind," Eurich declared proudly, holding out his hand. "I paid more for it than you probably make in an entire year."

Mason returned the piece. "Any idea what the smaller clock is for?"

"No," Eurich shrugged, returning it to his pocket. "Curious, isn't it? Now take a seat. I don't have all day."

Mason sat on the bench, allowing ample space between Eurich and himself. He took a comfortable slouching position, his legs outstretched and crossed. Reaching into his jacket, he produced a flask and enjoyed a swig before offering it to Eurich, who was taken aback.

"No, thank you," he said crossly.

Mason shrugged and took another swig. "Well, what's this about?"

"I have a job for you," Eurich said in a low voice.

"Really? Music to my ears."

"I have no need for your flippant commentary. Just listen."

Mason cocked his head.

"I will have you transferred to the 9th Squad of the 26th Company," Eurich continued. "I need you to be my eyes and ears there. I want full reports on the company's activities and any suspicious behavior you observe from either officer."

Mason raised his eyebrows. "That's all?"

"That's all." Eurich nodded, glancing warily at the other man. "And try not to get your head lopped off by an Amelaren ax, of course. It'd be rather difficult to complete your task if that were to occur."

Eurich's comment seemed to have little effect on Mason. Instead, the commoner suspiciously narrowed his eyes. "Usually you call me to do jobs that require a bit more ... Why don't you get your lapdog Nelhart and his men to check in on them for you?"

Eurich laughed dismissively and scratched at his right hand.

"The surveyors are not suited for this task. I'm beginning to question how useful they will be moving forward. This requires discretion. The surveyors stand out like drunken nobles wandering through a Kantorian brothel."

"Point taken," Mason responded, swigging from his flask. "Is there anything I'm looking for in particular?"

"No." Eurich shook his head. "I just want a full report. If anything, focus on the captain's behavior. The more information there, the better."

"Fine," said Mason. "But I'm just one man. There's no way I can keep an eye on him at all times, especially if I'm going in as an avet."

Eurich chuckled again. "Don't be foolish. Surely you don't think you're the only one I'm sending?"

Mason shrugged to show he neither knew nor cared. "Why are you doing this, if you don't mind my asking? I heard some gossip about the captain's inquiry. Or the inquiry that didn't take place, rather. Something to do with that?"

Eurich replied haughtily, "I care not about the young captain but about shifting power away from the leeches surrounding the king." The count became stern and glowered at Mason. "It would do you some good to learn some manners in public, you ape. I understand that the code of conduct in the military is less ceremonial, but you should not be so carelessly casual toward everyone. You have no idea how fortunate you are that I will tolerate your utter lack of decorum."

"Sorry, milord." Mason bowed his head slightly and took another drink.

Eurich could not tell whether the gesture was genuine; this only frustrated him more.

"But what do you mean by *shifting power*?"

"That does not concern you." Eurich could feel his boundaries being tested. "You are my employee, not my partner. All you need to know is that what I do is for the benefit of the king."

"Fine," Mason said again. "But since we are on the topic of employer and employee, how about we discuss my payment?"

"Later. I assure you that compensation will be more than fair. Despite the fact that this job is less colorful than the ones I usually ask of you, a bonus may be involved this time, depending on the information you bring back to me."

Eurich handed Mason a folded slip of paper. As the latter read, his eyes lit up. "I see. Well, Count, I'm at your disposal. After all, we've had a long and fruitful history together, haven't we?"

"Yes, yes," Eurich responded, eager to dispense with small talk. "Also, you would do well to quit some of your … habits. I will not be kind to failure."

"My personal life is my own, sir. I know you are not overly fond of me, but my record speaks for itself, does it not?"

Eurich said nothing. He wondered whether Mason would be surprised to know that he actually thought well of the man. While he considered commoners to be unrefined and publicly espoused them to have vastly inferior capabilities, privately he had nothing against them. He realized that many were a lot like himself, only lacking money or power. On the other hand, he thought Mason was trustworthy for a simple reason—the man had nothing in the way of ambition. Eurich preferred to employ people like Mason. They were content to do their jobs, and there was little chance of betrayal. Eurich was uncharacteristically guilty of turning a blind eye to Mason's less admirable qualities; they had indeed managed a productive working relationship thus far.

"I'll be sure to bring back something good," Mason continued with the same unwavering nonchalance.

"See to it that you do. Let me be clear, Hunt. This is only one part of my current agenda, but it is an important task."

"If you say so. I don't care to be privy to any sort of political gamesmanship. We have a deal."

"Very well. You may leave now."

Mason put away his flask and hopped to his feet. He gave Eurich a little bow before walking toward the streets of North Bronsdale.

Eurich pulled the timepiece from his pocket again and stared at it thoughtfully. Although he hoped to have successfully projected a sense of urgency, he considered his investment in Mason Hunt, and others like him, to be relatively minor. Any useful information they brought back would serve only to supplement his existing designs.

The inquiry into the Ertel campaign would not be resolved in the manner he wished. There was little he could do about General Leynitz's eagerness to martyr himself. Fortunately, it was no longer of great importance. He and Drake had come to the conclusion that it was sufficient to acknowledge, even emphasize, the level of failure suffered by the army. Recalling the meeting with Samsen and the Cabinet almost three cycles ago, during which the king resolved to declare war on Amelares, Eurich smiled to himself sardonically. What was originally an alarming setback had turned out to be the seed of a new opportunity.

Chapter 11

(987.4.27–34)

—1—

From atop their horses, Reznik and the Curtland twins gazed across the wide expanse of Argiset Plateau, where a mock battle between the 26th and 28th companies was underway. As vice captain, Reznik was permitted to ride a horse during the exercise, although he and the twins abstained from participating and merely looked on as the soldiers below engaged. His current steed, a dark brown midsized half-breed named Gin, was likely temporary, as Nash had insisted that Reznik give him time to find a suitable ride.

Rain pouring from the dark sky muddied the field. Although wet weather was rare this time of year, the Coranthian Army could hardly afford to allow such matters to deter their regimen.

There had been no raids for over a turn. Although the 26th and 28th were both due for leave in a matter of days, Jasmine Curtland had suggested to Reznik, who had been left in charge of the 26th temporarily after Nash was summoned to Corande, that they lead their companies in war games as a means of keeping the troops sharp, while avoiding overexertion. Colonel Dyers had elected to store some of the debris left over from dismantling the slipshod Amelaren fortifications. These bricks, stones, and other bits of rubble were littered liberally across the western flats during war games, simulating obstacles or, in concordance with various natural features, marking changes in terrain.

The present skirmish designated the staging of an Amelaren attack to the 28th, leaving the 26th to mount a suitable defense. Though vice captains typically led such training skirmishes, using the opportunity to hone their leadership skills, this was currently not true of either company. Essentially co-captains, the Curtlands appointed two of their squad leaders to act as temporary vice captains. Meanwhile, Reznik had selected Bethany, now the leader of the 9th Squad, to serve as the commander of the 26th during the exercise. The 9th Squad had also risen in prestige within the company as a result of Reznik's promotion, mounting additional pressure on the rest of the squad to perform well.

As the two companies approached one another, the front row of the 26th raised their shields. The soldiers of the 28th had no shields and were only partially armored to reflect the increased mobility of the Amelarens.

Madeline marched near the head of the 26th's formation, falling behind Bethany. She served as the 9th Squad's sergeant in Bethany's stead. Madeline felt uncertain about her new leader. Initially, Bethany had strongly refused the promotion to sergeant when Nash gave it to her, but he overrode her protests and eventually she relented. Generally, she had been sullen and withdrawn since the Ertel campaign. Madeline's attempts to reach out to her were politely, though firmly, rebuffed, and a distance had formed between Bethany and her squad.

The one person Bethany did grow closer to was Philip. It seemed to Madeline that they developed a friendship stemming from shared grief. Philip was similarly morose for a long time after the Ertel-Ghend battles, though had recently regained his intensity, and as the 26th continued to dig in at Argiset, his spirits improved markedly. He marched alongside Bethany now; the two exchanged a look before Bethany turned to address the company.

"Formations ready! Let's—"

"Let's give them hell!" Cyrus Marcole shouted from behind Philip, startling Bethany and drawing a few enthusiastic cries from the other soldiers.

Lately, Cyrus had become more approachable. Madeline found his hostility to be a front for his inexperience and insecurity. Ironically, he became more willing to integrate himself with the other soldiers as he hardened through battle, although certain soldiers, particularly those in positions of authority, still rubbed him the wrong way. Occasionally, this friction caused a verbal or physical fight to ensue. Fortunately for Cyrus, he eventually showed sufficient restraint, but his outbursts did little to earn him friends outside the squad. Nevertheless, Cyrus had developed an odd synergy with Josef Reinbach. While not quite friends, the two of them were sparring partners who worked well together in battle.

Jacob Nilson, the 14th Squad's sandy-haired, brown-eyed sergeant, marching next to Bethany and the 9th Squad, turned to his command and shouted, "Pipe down. This is just a training exercise."

"We should take this seriously, Sergeant," Josef urged.

Reznik, Jasmine, and Rosalina continued to observe the proceedings. As Reznik scanned the ranks of the 26th, and the 9th Squad in particular, he noted the absence of both Patrice Konith and Amy Trenton. Patrice, like most medics, was allowed to opt-out of these exercises; most of the officers at Argiset agreed it was not worth the risk of accidental injury to mandate medic participation in mock battles. Patrice typically watched from the sidelines, standing by in case anything went awry, but today, she had been called to the makeshift medical bay for assistance.

Amy Trenton remained indoors as well, claiming illness. The prevalent opinion among the squad was that she had lost her will to fight after Alphonse's injury. With some hesitation, Nash had privately suggested some form of discipline, but Reznik did not consider her vital to the company's efficacy. He also believed that many of her squadmates were sympathetic to her situation and would react negatively to any sort of punishment for her perceived malaise.

Reznik was so focused on the battle and lost in thought that he did not notice a man on horseback had approached from behind.

"Vice Captain Sylvera?"

Startled, Reznik turned his horse to face the owner of the voice. A tan young man in his midtwenties, with short-cropped blond hair, sat atop a brown zephyr. He wore a military uniform, the standard for noncombatants, and hastily saluted Reznik, who returned the gesture.

"What can I do for you?" Reznik asked.

"Hello, Windsor," Jasmine said.

Reznik glanced questioningly at her.

"I am General Leynitz's adjutant," the man said in a soft voice.

"I see," Reznik said. "We have not met."

Windsor nodded in acknowledgment.

"The general has returned?" Jasmine said. "We did not expect him back so soon."

"He has been here for several days," Windsor replied. "It is necessary for him to oversee construction of the top floor."

Reznik and the Curtlands exchanged glances. Reznik wondered why the general had not publicly announced his return.

"Vice Captain." Windsor's voice brought him out of his thoughts.

"Yes?"

Windsor did not reply immediately. As the four stood in momentary pause, the only sounds came from the rain pattering down on the field and the faint cries of the soldiers from the two companies sparring. Rosalina was the only one who was paying any heed to the exercise. Reznik and Jasmine waited for the adjutant to continue.

"The general calls for your presence in his quarters for dinner tonight at eight arc."

Reznik was puzzled. "Me?"

Windsor directed his gaze to meet Reznik's. "This is not a request but an order, Vice Captain. Eight arc, general's quarters. Do not be late."

Without another word, Windsor galloped back toward the Highpost, leaving Reznik and the Curtlands staring at each other in confusion.

—2—

That evening, Reznik found himself obediently seated at General Marsell Leynitz's dining table. The general had recently returned from Corande after being absent for the better part of the past cycle.

Construction of the third and topmost floor of Argiset Highpost was far from complete, but the general's quarters were spacious though bare. A large bed made of Kantorian oak abutted the northern wall. Several solistone lamps provided marginal lighting. A large cherry wooden desk stood opposite the entrance, close to the eastern wall.

Reznik sat opposite Leynitz and Colonel Hector Osterfeld, who faced him from the other end of the dining table, which lay perpendicular to the general's desk. They had been served grilled flank of valdwen, a bulky deerlike herbivore with a round head and large hooves—common throughout the Amelaren badlands and forests of eastern Coranthia—along with several sides of assorted vegetables.

Upon noticing Reznik's disinterest in the food, Leynitz asked, "Is something the matter, Vice Captain?"

"Not at all, sir. I'm just not particularly hungry."

Osterfeld scoffed as he speared a thinly cut and delicately seasoned slice of meat and shoveled it into his mouth. He chewed slowly and with obvious enjoyment, loudly smacking his lips after swallowing each bite.

"Most soldiers have never tasted Lynderan spices such as these, Vice Captain."

Reznik said nothing, having no desire to engage the colonel. Since Osterfeld's promotion, a number of nebulous rumors had gradually made their way through the Coranthian ranks. While none were particularly detailed or substantive, Reznik had the clear impression that Osterfeld was not a man to be trifled with or to provoke. In his limited interaction with Osterfeld, he found the colonel imposing and somehow unnerving. Nevertheless, he had never been singled out or treated unfairly by Osterfeld, so he was unsure as to whether his apprehension was merely self-induced paranoia.

Hesitantly, he cut a piece off the valdwen on his plate and skewered it and a few vegetables with his fork. The food was exquisite, as Osterfeld had implied, and Reznik found himself savoring the rich texture of the meat, the fullness in the small slices of potato and crisps of cabbage, and the sharpness of the wine.

Meanwhile, Osterfeld rapidly cleared his food and was finished before Reznik had touched the second half of his dish. Leynitz ate sparingly, though gulped his wine hastily before seeking a refill. He repeated this process several times before turning his attention to Reznik.

Although Reznik enjoyed his meal, he remained uncomfortable and suspicious. After observing him for a while, Leynitz said, "I see that you are ill at ease. Don't hesitate to speak your mind, Vice Captain."

Reznik straightened his back.

"I must admit I do not know why I have been so privileged to join Your Excellency for dinner," he replied.

Osterfeld smiled condescendingly and gave a half shrug.

Leynitz raised his brass cup to his lips and took another large gulp of wine. "Since being stationed here the last half cycle, the 26th has made quite a name for itself. I suppose your experience at Ertel has paid off. I am most impressed by your company's results against the Amelaren raids …"

"Did you call me here to compliment my company, sir?"

"No, of course not." Leynitz paused to down more red wine. A small stream dribbled down his handlebar mustache. "You look like you have something to say."

Reznik nodded. "Sir, do you know when Captain Havora is expected to return?"

"Captain Havora will not return before the 26th Company takes its scheduled leave."

Reznik waited for Leynitz to continue.

"The captain's business at Corande will take longer than expected. Minister Velmann has mandated that the captain remain at Corande rather than return to the front to serve only two turns at most. You are to relay that to the company at your discretion."

Leynitz greedily consumed the last drops of wine in his cup and wiped his mouth with his lavender silk napkin, taking great care to clean his mustache.

Reznik was amazed at the speed with which the general put away his drink.

Leynitz cleared his throat, reaching for the bottle yet again.

"We failed the Coranthian people at Ertel Gorge. We underestimated the Amelarens." Leynitz paused, making an effort to continue. "I underestimated them. If anyone should be blamed for our incompetence, it is I. Unfortunately, despite my best efforts, Captain Havora and Colonel Dyers and several others are considered to be more preferable scapegoats by certain people."

Leynitz regarded his empty cup.

"Now the captain is stuck in Corande. And Dyers and his troops are to be sent to that miserable outpost at Tull Rock, despite his exemplary efforts during the battle at the gorge. These matters are out of my hands."

Osterfeld narrowed his eyes. "Sir—"

"Nevertheless, Ertel has not set us back. Our blitz was unorthodox and did not succeed in the way I had hoped, but if we are to win this war and truly defeat the barbarians, we need more forward and open thinking, and less interference and backlash from those who seek to use this situation to advance their own agendas."

"Sir, perhaps you should—"

"Do not interrupt, Hector."

Leynitz refilled his drink, glaring at Osterfeld. After topping off his cup, he slammed the bottle on the table. "I am concerned only with winning this war and bringing as many of our troops home as safely as possible. Usually, I do not engage in politics, and the statesmen refrain from telling me how to run my army." He raised a finger. "Usually."

Reznik watched and listened intently.

"Now that complications have brought our offensive campaign to a halt, I must indulge these so-called leaders of our citizens. Even though it would be best for the Assembly to know as little as possible about military operations, I'll have to throw the surveyors a line, won't I?"

Though clearly displeased with the general's loquaciousness, Osterfeld nodded in agreement.

"In any case," Leynitz said, "let us move on to business. I would like your frank opinion of the captain. How do you rate him as your commanding officer?"

Reznik shifted uncomfortably, caught wholly unprepared for the abrupt change in topic. "Has Your Excellency seen our combat reports?"

"I have been informed as much by the colonel here."

"So far, we have worked well together," Reznik said evenly.

"Answer the question, Vice Captain," Osterfeld snapped.

Reznik kept his eyes on Leynitz. "Captain Havora is much better versed in logistics, support formations, and obviously medicine. I merely direct the troops in battle."

"A good captain should excel in all of those areas." Osterfeld returned, barely suppressing a sneer.

Leynitz looked at the colonel and then back at Reznik, who had resumed eating as means to avoid eye contact with his superiors. Osterfeld reclined in his chair and clasped his hands behind his bald head, apparently waiting for Leynitz to speak.

After two reps without a word from anyone, Leynitz broke his silence.

"Vice Captain, I shall tell you why we invited you here today," Leynitz said. "We wanted your opinion of Captain Havora, not to help us evaluate him in his role but to gauge how you might perform in his stead."

Reznik put down his fork.

"Before you ask how such an idea came to us, you should know that it was your captain himself who made the suggestion. When I met with him in Corande, he spoke to me about the possibility of this role reversal. The two of you have provided identical reports on the shared leadership of your company."

"I have been vice captain for barely two cycles," Reznik said, dumbfounded. "I imagine Your Excellency does not speak of anything immediate?"

"No, of course not," Leynitz said, exchanging a glance with Osterfeld, who nodded back. "This would not happen anytime soon, if at all. Still, it is commendable for him to realize that he is incapable of adequately fulfilling the role assigned to him and to be willing to step back in favor of one better suited to the task. Even if my endorsement of him at his hearing seems myopic as a result."

Detecting the bitterness in the general's tone, Osterfeld raised his eyebrows and sniffed, bringing his folded hands over his head and placing them on the table, leaning forward as he did so. "We agree with Captain Havora on a preliminary basis. From what both of you have said of how the 26th is run, and from what I have seen myself, we may consider such a move over the next year or so. I've done my research, Vice Captain. Your performance since transferring to Aldova and your record at Tellisburg are impeccable. You've done quite well for an Outlander."

"Thank you, sir," Reznik said. "I cannot claim all the credit. Were it not for my comrades and instructors, I would not be where I am today."

Osterfeld grunted with approval. "Hard to hope for a better teacher than General Hagen. In any case, Vice Captain, remember what we have told you, but do not dwell on it."

"What the colonel means to say," Leynitz said, his voice becoming deeper and more forceful, "is you are not to mention this to anyone. Not a single person."

"I will say nothing of this to anyone, sir."

Again the two commanding officers looked at each other. Seeing the meal was finished, Osterfeld motioned toward Reznik. "In that case, we have other matters to discuss. Would you mind seeing yourself out, Vice Captain?"

Eager to leave, Reznik stood immediately, saluted, and headed for the door. He stole a glance back toward his superiors and saw they were staring at him, Osterfeld whispering something inaudible to Leynitz, who let out a grunt and nodded.

"Enjoy your upcoming leave, Vice Captain," Leynitz said.

Reznik nodded. "Thank you, sir."

He left the room and walked unevenly down the hall.

—3—

On the thirty-first, after three days of training, the 26th Company officially began its leave and was replaced on duty by the 16th. The preceding night was one of transitional quartering, and with the Highpost incomplete and the outdoors unseasonably cool at night, members of the 16th packed into the mess hall and medical bay, sleeping on benches and floors wherever there was room, moving into proper quarters sometime after three arc the next day once the 26th had vacated.

While it was customary for soldiers to be granted sixty days of leave per year, commonly referred to as their "cycle and two turns," the actual amount of time permitted was more generous and scaled according to distance from deployment. Given the distance between Jardis and Argiset, Reznik and Madeline were permitted a maximum leave of seventy-five days before they were to be expected back at Aldova.

Upon reaching Aldova, most of the 26th scattered. Some rushed immediately onto the first available caravans to Inner Coranthia, while others opted to spend part of their vacation making use of the guest facilities at the fortress complex. Reznik and Madeline decided to stay one night before continuing home. They wound up sharing a caravan with Bethany and Philip, who were headed to Kantor. Bethany informed them that she and Philip planned to pay their respects to the Remington family; it would be an especially long journey for her, as her hometown of Densley, deep within Lynderas, was the farthest Coranthian town from Aldova, and Kantor was in the opposite direction. The four traveled together to Irsa Bastion, located at the northeastern corner of Inner Coranthia, almost halfway between Aldova and Corande. Irsa served as the main base for soldiers deployed to guard the Outlands. The largest fortification in northern Coranthia, second only to Aldova, Irsa was capable of housing over a third of the Coranthian Army. It was where the group would split.

The three-day ride was uneventful and there was not much in the way of conversation. Bethany remained as reticent as she had been since Liam's death, and her melancholy spread to the other three. Upon arrival at Irsa, Bethany and Philip transferred to a caravan bound for Kantor. Reznik and Madeline bade them farewell and settled for the night, planning to board another caravan the following day to Hayes Junction, a large trading post located at the major intersection of the Outlands, where the roads from Calena, Corande, Kantor, and Irsa met. Once at Hayes, they would catch one final caravan to Calena and finally Jardis.

• • •

There was an unofficial station in the woods on the northern outskirts of Irsa, where an entire congregation of caravans formed a circle within the trees, numerous campfires scattered near freshly cut stumps. Reznik and Madeline claimed one of these sites and set up two small tents. Guest rooms inside Irsa were available for their use, but the two shared an unspoken aversion to spending time in military quarters during a period of leave.

Having bottled up his thoughts since meeting with Leynitz and Osterfeld, Reznik desired all the more to release them after spending time in the company of Bethany and Philip, who reminded him of where he had been not long ago. After they finished dinner that evening, Reznik broke his oath by telling Madeline of what he had talked about with the general and colonel regarding his possible switch with Nash.

Madeline's eyes widened as she listened. When he finished, he abruptly turned his gaze in another direction and held it, stubbornly silent.

"Do you really think it's going to happen?" she asked, knowing he was waiting for her to speak first.

"Certainly not during our leave." Reznik folded his arms. "General Leynitz didn't say it directly, but he needs to find a way to do it without giving the Assembly something to pounce on."

"Meaning you or the captain will need to give him a reason to do it."

Reznik frowned.

"What's wrong? Isn't this what you want?"

"I'm not sure I've earned it."

She chuckled, prompting Reznik to raise an eyebrow.

"Oh, you're amused?" he said.

"Somehow, I'm not surprised. Rez, you do realize that you're not a noble. Do you think they would consider promoting any unestated who did not deserve it?"

"I'm just thinking about what's best." He scratched his chin, suddenly looking uncommonly flustered. "I don't feel ready."

This did catch her by surprise. "You're thinking too hard about something that may not happen anyway," she said after several ticks of silence. "You and I both know that you will be ready when the time comes. So what's the use in worrying about it now?"

Reznik nodded. "You're right. Thanks, Maddy."

Madeline smiled. "Have you thought about what you'll say to your mother when you see her?"

"I suppose I should."

"I can't wait to be home again," she said.

Reznik returned her smile and rose to his feet. "Maddy, I'm turning in early. You should too."

"Good night, then."

Madeline watched as he stepped into his tent. She wished she could have said more to put his mind at ease, but she had been unprepared to see Reznik so uncertain of himself and was unable to articulate her reassurance in the way that she wanted. Frustrated, she turned her attention to the fire. After several reps, she relocated to a large stump nearby and sat down to lean back and rest her head atop it. She stared up at the sky at Rhynon and the barely visible Faerila and the stars that gleamed around them through a window in the blanket of treetops.

Chapter 12

(987.4.34–5.41)

—1—

Although Irsa Bastion stood roughly equidistant between Calena and Aldova, the friendlier terrain and straight roads between Irsa and Calena made the second leg of the trip back to Jardis much faster. Two days later, the caravan, originally scheduled to arrive at Calena late afternoon, pulled in early at around four arc. Having intended to spend the night, Reznik and Madeline found themselves wolfing down a quick lunch and rushing to catch a wagon out of Calena that would get them to Jardis that evening. Unfortunately, one of the wheels came off their wagon, and while the driver expertly avoided any injury to passengers, the replacement of the wheel stalled their progress. When they finally reached Jardis, it was well past eight arc.

The village square was empty. Only a small circle of lit rodtorches, kept ready for nightly use, greeted the two. Reznik took one of the torches and led the way down the dirt path toward Madeline's house. As they arrived, Madeline stared despondently at her dark, vacant abode.

Reznik began, "I'll come by tom—"

"There's a light on in your house!" she interrupted, pointing farther down the road.

The glow from within the kitchen of the Sylveras' radiated from the window into the darkness.

Reznik knitted his eyebrows. "What is she doing up so late?"

Together, the two walked down the road to Reznik's house. As they approached, shadows pranced and flickered from within the house. The light faded as if someone had carried a lamp out of the room. Several ticks later, the front door to the house swung open to reveal Edith holding an oil lamp, which she immediately set down on a stand beside her.

"Trying to sneak back home, are you now?" she said accusingly. She raised her hand, beckoning her son. Reznik walked briskly up the path, dropping the small bag he brought from Aldova at the doorstep. After hanging the rodtorch on the small ring stand next to the door, he hugged his mother tightly.

"My son, a vice captain," Edith said softly. "I'm so proud of you."

When Reznik pulled back, he saw the moisture in Edith's eyes in the dull glow of the lamp. He smiled warmly.

Madeline stood several steps away, not wishing to disturb them. Edith unfastened herself from Reznik and approached her. "Maddy, welcome home."

The women embraced and before she knew it, Madeline felt tears streaming down her face.

Edith refused to allow her to spend the night alone. Reznik was obliged to give up his bed to Madeline, sleeping in his mother's reclining chair in the living room; he offered no complaints.

—2—

The next day, Madeline unpacked her belongings at her house before returning to the Sylveras' for lunch. As they ate, Reznik asked his mother about the state of the village. More specifically, he wanted to know how the old army crossbows held up during the year.

"As a matter of fact," Edith said, "we had a chance to try them out during the last raid."

Madeline's jaw tightened.

"The crossbows were distributed as you had specified," Edith continued. "Almost every nonmilitia household was given one. Still …"

"When was this?" Reznik asked.

"Three turns ago."

"What happened?"

"They came for crops in the middle of the night. Thankfully, no one was hurt. We were able to protect some of the fields, but—"

"Were the *bandits* hurt?" Madeline interrupted.

"Almost certainly, but all managed to escape."

"That won't discourage them from returning," Reznik said.

Madeline shook her head. Her blood pulsed with anger; her thoughts failed to coalesce into words.

Edith reached out and touched her hand lightly. "William is an able watchman, but sometimes he lacks the conviction to act as you've suggested. That applies to most of the villagers. We are only concerned with protecting our homes and families. You know this."

Reznik frowned. "That's not enough. Bandits deserve no mercy. If only you could lead them …"

"But I no longer can. I am just stating the facts."

"And the damage?" Madeline asked, finally finding her tongue. "What was hit worst?"

"They mainly targeted the balis and rice fields. We lost several hogs as well. There was an attempt on the horses, but it was thwarted."

Madeline sighed. "We will need to convene with the watch again. The sooner the better."

"Not until after the festival," Edith said firmly. "The last thing we need is a dampener on the harvest and preparations."

Madeline opened her mouth in protest.

"I agree," Reznik said.

He put his hand on her arm and nodded reassuringly.

"All right," she conceded. "Let us wait until after the festival."

—3—

Traditionally a celebration of the annual crop to take place on the first day of the Fifth Exile, the original notion of the Harvest Festival was lost on people who lived in large cities; they merely saw the day as an opportunity to hold enormous feasts. For many farming villages, the occasion was more about family and community. In Jardis, the event was usually held on a different day every year to avoid being easily targeted by bandit raids; this year, the villagers took a small measure of solace in the fact that a raid was unlikely, as they had just suffered one only a short while ago.

On the seventh, the villagers of Jardis congregated in the square at five arc, where Elder Potts led an overview of the harvest. The year's crop had been above average in both quantity and quality, which softened the blow that was suffered after the recent raid. The elder professed a heightened anticipation for this year's celebration, as young Penny Jenkins had recently won a local culinary competition and was eager to try out her new recipe for genberry pie, which she prepared for the celebration. Finally, the elder led cheers—officially welcoming Reznik and Madeline home. In describing their trials on the battlefield and Reznik's ascendancy to officership, the elder called them the "pride of the village," and from the villagers' reactions, it was apparent that many agreed, much to Madeline's gratitude and Reznik's embarrassment. That evening, families returned home to enjoy modest suppers before turning in early. The main event of the festival was to take place the next day and everyone made sure to get sufficient sleep.

Many of the villagers were already awake by half-past-two arc the next morning. Men, women, and children alike scrambled out of bed and bundled up to weather the chilly morning. They worked as the sun rose, each family engaged in a different task. Two rows of long tables were lined up in the square. William Cadrene and several of the older men assembled a ceremonial booth, reserved for the elder, next to the bell. Meanwhile, other villagers erected their own stands around the square for food preparation.

The entirety of Jardis's populace spilled slowly into the square. At noon, the elder, who watched the proceedings from his booth, mostly undisturbed, rang the bell four times, signaling the cooks to present the fruits of their labors. Gradually, the villagers loaded a vast assortment of food onto the long tables. There were staple dishes of the Outlands: a variety of pastries made from wheat and vegetables such as yoa, balis root, and garvine. One cluster of plates housed a variety of meats, the most abundant being reas. Moving farther down the table, however, the dishes grew increasingly personalized, as many households put forth their special family recipes; the main attraction was, of course, Penny Jenkins' pie. The setup allowed people to take whatever they wanted, with the understanding that no one was to hoard any single offering, allowing everyone to sample everything. The villagers separated into small groups as they sat around the square and partook in a communal meal.

Afterward, the tables were cleaned and everyone returned home for an afternoon respite. Some took naps, while others began preparing for the evening straightaway. As dusk approached, Reznik and several others took charge of lighting the rodtorches in the square and stowing the tables in the basement of the Cadrene house, replacing them with a number of small firepits. According to tradition, the evening meal consisted of a wide assortment of stews; each flavor was brought out in a huge pot to be stationed on one of the firepits, which had all been lit. When the preparations were complete, the elder rang the bell four times, just as he had earlier in the day, and the villagers gathered to feast once more. Despite the noticeable precautions taken—a stockpile of weapons, readily available at the first sign of danger, lay scattered on the elder's lawn—the atmosphere was loose, the square brightly lit, and the villagers in good spirits.

Initially, Reznik and Madeline sat alone. They took in the scene as they ate. Edith's spicy reas stew was one of Reznik's favorites; he watched as she stood beside the enormous pot she used to serve the villagers who lined up one behind another, each with a bowl brought from his or her home. Edith and Madeline had spent nearly two full arcs brewing the stew, and it was so popular that Reznik had been worried there would not be any left for him later.

As he dug the last few spoonfuls from the bottom of his bowl, Reznik began to scan the crowd. Madeline stared at him curiously.

"What are you looking for?" she asked.

"Albert told me earlier that Thomas Polke came back for the holiday."

"I haven't heard that name in a while," Madeline said with a frown.

Reznik's mouth twisted unpleasantly. "Our erstwhile neighbor returns from his distinguished travels as a bully-for-hire in order to snag a free meal."

"Keep it down," Madeline muttered, elbowing him and glancing off to the side. He followed her gaze to see Karen Alton, the butcher's daughter, approaching with Lucille Barlow, the fourteen-year-old only daughter of the best yoa croppers in the village. Trailing behind them was Albert Dunning, who stopped within several paces.

"Good evening," Reznik said.

"Hello, Reznik," Albert replied, in a small voice.

Madeline waved him over. "Come closer, Albert. Don't be silly."

Albert stepped gingerly around Karen.

"How are you?" Reznik said.

"Fine, thanks," Albert said, brushing back stray strands of dark brown hair and keeping his eyes firmly trained on Reznik. "I wanted to tell you something. I was at the elder's house earlier today."

Reznik lapped up the last of his stew and signaled for Albert to continue.

"Mr. Polke met with him to discuss stationing here after the new year."

There was a loud clang as Reznik dropped his spoon into the bowl.

"Stationing," he repeated hollowly.

Madeline ran a hand through her hair agitatedly. "You don't mean his band of mercenaries?"

Albert pursed his lips. "I had nothing to do with it. The elder just told me—"

"And what did the elder say?" she demanded. "To Polke, that is."

"He agreed to the proposition," said Karen, prompting both Reznik and Madeline to swivel in her direction.

"You knew as well?" Reznik said.

Karen pursed her lips and gestured toward Albert. "He told me earlier, before the festival started. Actually, I was leaving the elder's just as he arrived. But I had no idea then."

Madeline shook her head. Reznik's gaze lingered on her in that familiar way; she knew he was mulling something over carefully.

"I knew we shouldn't have waited this long to talk to the elder," she muttered ruefully.

"We promised Mother," he reminded her. "But I should tell her about this, at least."

After a moment, he got up, uttering a quick "excuse me" as he wove his way through the square, heading toward where Edith was seated beside Sharon Dunning. Madeline and the others stared after him.

"So is Thomas here tonight?" she asked, glancing at the girls.

"Somewhere," Lucille shrugged. She stood slightly apart from them, arms folded across her chest. In spite of her youth, Lucille was a skilled tailoress, having taken up the hobby during her uneventful tenure as the elder's assistant. She had a passion for the newest fashion trends in Calena and channeled it into making clothes of her own design. Her attire frequently gave her a much more mature appearance than her age would suggest. Tonight, she wore a simple but elegant black blouse and skirt.

"He didn't bring any of his cohorts, did he?" Madeline asked Albert sarcastically. "To present the elder with a more convincing case?"

"Oh, come on," Karen said. "What does it matter? Let's just enjoy the food. And the music."

Their attention turned toward the elder's house, where several villagers had set up with instruments, mostly flutes, fiddles, and guitars. Having finished their meals, they began to play in crisp tunes, enhancing the ambiance provided by the setting sun and blustery winds.

"When was the last time Reznik picked up his fiddle?" Karen mused. "What are they playing, anyway? I don't recognize it."

"Is it something you wrote, Albert?" Lucille wondered.

Albert scratched his head, avoiding eye contact with Lucille. "I told them to play it while everyone was still eating. It's just background noise."

"Oh, give yourself some credit," she said. "I like it. It's soothing."

"Thanks." Albert's lips twitched into a small smile. "I really wish we had a piano. I know how expensive they are, but it would have been much better than using guitars to complement the other strings. I think ..."

Catching himself, he cleared his throat again and turned to face Karen. "Anyway, what of your meeting with the elder? What was that about?"

Face reddening, Karen looked down and smoothed the folds in her plain magenta dress.

"He asked me to take over his teaching duties after the winter."

"That's great news!" he exclaimed.

"He's passing the children off to me. It just means I'm getting old," Karen smiled wryly, her green eyes flashing.

"Don't listen to her," Lucille chimed in. "She can't wait to take over."

"Well, you're the obvious choice," Albert said. He glanced around as he lowered his voice conspiratorially. "And now you can say goodbye to the butchery, right?"

"Yes. Now I can talk to Father and ... Well, Stanley was probably going take over for him anyway. Maybe he won't even be needed for the watch anymore, since it sounds like we may be getting some outside help."

She glanced uneasily at Madeline, who flashed her a faint smile.

"Really, that's great," Albert said again, nodding.

"It is," Madeline echoed.

Karen stared at her thoughtfully.

Several ticks later, Reznik reemerged from the crowd, this time walking in a straight line toward Madeline through a group of dancing villagers. The musicians had begun to produce strongly rhythmic, upbeat fare. The vigorous chords of the guitars took over as the revelers tapped their feet and swayed to the music.

"We're going tomorrow, Maddy."

Having been distracted by the strangely uncomfortably dynamic she felt between the others, Madeline acknowledged him with a slow, languid nod, but when she lifted her gaze to meet his, the familiar intensity emanating from his blue eyes brought her back into focus.

"I'll expect you at the elder's house, then?" Lucille said to Reznik.

"Oh, yes. Sorry, I don't remember when you're over there."

"Very often nowadays," she replied with a shrug. "He needs the extra help. Would anyone like some more food?"

Lucille offered a short parting wave and drifted away from Reznik, Madeline, and Albert, whose gaze wandered to follow her.

"I'll come with you," Karen called out, hurrying off after her.

Reznik rubbed his forehead, suddenly looking weary. He trudged over to the bench where he and Madeline previously sat and planted himself back down.

"There's something else I'd like to talk to you about, Reznik," Albert said.

Madeline eyed the lanky young man curiously.

"I'll leave you two alone then," she said. "Be back later."

She spun around and walked away.

After she was out of earshot, Reznik relaxed on the bench and stared piercingly into Albert's eyes. "I'm not the person to be asking for that sort of advice, you know," he said.

"What? What do you—"

"You should talk to Madeline about Lucille. She'll be honest with you."

Albert's face turned bright red.

"I hope you haven't confided in Karen about this," Reznik continued. "I'm not sure I would trust her to take your side."

"That's not what I wanted to ask," Albert protested.

Reznik blinked. "Oh. My apologies."

Albert's shoulders slumped, his long gangly arms dangling at his sides.

"No, I haven't told Karen," he said with a sigh. "I finally told Stan a little while back. Not that it matters. It's a lost cause, I know that."

Reznik said nothing and waited for Albert to continue.

"Although, you know, actually, I might be able count on you to be direct with me, Reznik. I knew you'd have noticed. Hearing your honest opinion is better than having people give me false reassurance. So I might as well ask you if you think there's any hope for me."

"You're right," Reznik replied immediately. "It's best for you to give up on that and move on."

The way Albert's face twisted made plain that he was not at all prepared for such a blunt dismantling. He walked around to Reznik's other side and slumped heavily onto the bench, lowering his eyes.

"Sorry," Reznik offered.

Albert took a deep breath.

"Right. Well, anyway, I wanted to ask you about enlisting."

Reznik raised an eyebrow in surprise.

"Why would you want to be a soldier?"

"It's what I should do. There's a war going on. I should serve."

"You should stay here. Help with the farm and look after your sisters. Look after the village. There's nothing wrong with that."

"No, that's not good enough. Joining the army is the best way to make something of myself."

The two sat in silence for a rep before Reznik shook his head and said, "You don't even believe your own words."

"I believe it's a path out of Jardis."

Albert's eyes simmered as he glared briefly at Reznik before looking away.

"Yes, I understand," Reznik said, "but you know as well as I do that it isn't the right one for you."

A look of grim determination crossed Albert's thin face.

"Better that than a dead end."

"Not everyone is meant to be a soldier, Albert." After a rep, Reznik attempted to lighten the mood. "Perhaps you should consider taking up yugo and become a famous athlete instead."

Unable to decipher Reznik's sarcasm, Albert stared at him dumbfounded. "What in Creon's name are you talking about?"

Suddenly, another voice cut in. "Well, look at you, Vice Captain Sylvera."

Recognizing the voice, Reznik looked up. Albert scooted aside and slinked away, allowing Thomas Polke to saunter forward.

"Real nice seeing you, kid. You fighting the good fight? Killing Amelarens everything you thought it would be?"

"Hello, Thomas," Reznik returned.

Thomas glanced across the square to where Madeline stood with Karen and Lucille; the three faced one another in a small huddle near the musicians.

"It's been forever since I've seen you and Maddy. It seems she really doesn't like being called that anymore. When did that start?"

"She is selectively tolerant of that address," Reznik said.

Thomas snorted. "Sure, I get it."

"How long will you be staying?"

"Business as usual, huh?" Thomas grinned crookedly and ran a hand through his greasy dark blond hair. "I'm just here for the party. I'll be gone in a few days. Got a bit of work to do over in Warrenhill."

"Just here for the party?" Reznik echoed. "Is that right?"

Before Thomas could reply, William Cadrene, who had decided to eavesdrop on the conversation in passing, added, "Why are you always in such a hurry to go? At least stay a few days."

"He's off to make his profit from bandit raids," Reznik said.

Thomas frowned. "Be careful there, kid. Don't go thinking you can talk over us now that you got a fancy title. Means nothing here."

"You just said yourself that you're on your way out of here for a job," Reznik said.

"What are you doing out there anyway?" Thomas retorted. "At least I'm defending our homes instead of mindlessly killing some brutes out east for the fat cats in the capital."

"You're delusional," Reznik replied, "if you think anyone in this village actually thinks you're as righteous as you claim to be."

Thomas's pale lips twitched, but he restrained himself.

"William, you see how he carries himself? Thinks he can talk down to us, judge us. Well, I can't say I didn't see this coming." He shrugged contemptuously and sauntered off, losing himself in the crowd.

"Always the soft-spoken one, Reznik," William sighed.

"And what is your opinion?" Reznik returned.

"I don't think myself qualified to have one. All I can say is that nothing ever changes." William grabbed his prematurely graying mustache. "You know what happens when the bandits get driven from one place? They attack another one. Round and round it goes. So what if people fight back?"

"Depends on who's fighting back. Are we talking about people like Thomas and his mercenary friends?" Reznik shook his head. "If we want a real effector of change, we're going to have to do a lot better than the likes of them."

"Oh? Are you going to be the one to change things, Reznik?" William chortled. He drifted off without waiting for a reply.

Left alone, Reznik stared vacantly at the sky, lost in thought. Rhynon's pulsing crimson glow seemed appropriately reflective of his mood, which had fallen so suddenly and irreconcilably far away from the sounds of bubbly chatter and mirthful music that continued to fill the air around him.

—4—

Reznik awoke in the morning and went downstairs to find that Madeline had come over early. She was already wolfing down a large serving of eggs, toast, and porridge. Edith sat beside her, waiting for her son before she partook in breakfast.

Edith rose as Reznik joined them at the table. She brought servings for each, and they began to eat. After all three finished, Madeline insisted she take care of the dishes, leaving Edith and Reznik to talk.

"You are going to the elder about Polke's men?" Edith said to Reznik.

"We are. I see Madeline wasted little time telling you."

Edith nodded. "I'm coming with you. I may not be leading the watch anymore, but I can still give the elder a piece of my mind."

Reznik smiled. "I'm glad you feel that way, Mother."

Madeline was also pleased when she heard of Edith's decision. The three left the house, stepping into the morning mist. As they walked down the road toward the square, Edith, who had wrapped a faded red shawl around her shoulders, began to cough lightly.

As winter approached, it wasn't surprising to find Elder Potts not in the wooden rocker outside his house. Reznik knocked on the front door. After ten ticks, during which he did not hear any movement from within, Reznik tried again. This time, there came the shuffling of footsteps, strong and brisk—they did not belong to the elder.

The door opened to reveal Lucille Barlow, dressed in a plain white blouse and a dark green skirt. "Good morning, everyone. Come to see the elder?" she asked.

"Indeed," Reznik said without missing a beat. "Is he available?"

"Certainly. Come in. May I, Mrs. Sylvera?" She moved aside to hold the door open and extended her free hand, offering to take Edith's shawl.

"Never mind, Lucille. I'll keep it on."

Reznik went through the entryway and into the common room. Elder Potts sat on a large, old cushioned chair that seemed too wide and too deep for him; it was unlikely the elderly man would be able to rise without assistance.

"Good morning, Elder."

"Reznik," Norman Potts rasped in a soft but firm voice. "Madeline, Edith."

Gently, Reznik shook his knobby hand. Madeline came forward to do the same. While the three exchanged pleasantries, Lucille brought chairs for the guests, arranging them neatly in a semicircle facing him.

"Thank you, Lucille. Please." He uncurled his hand, gesturing for Reznik, Madeline, and Edith to sit. As they obliged, he continued. "Lucille has been indispensable to me. My knees are becoming creakier as the days go by. At my age, I'm afraid my days of doing daily laps around the square are winding down." He chuckled lightheartedly.

Reznik did not mince words. "Elder, what is this I hear about Thomas Polke bringing his business into the village? This seems incorrigible to me."

Potts rubbed his stubbly chin and cast a glance at Edith, who sat with her arms crossed and stared blankly at him.

"Who informed you of this? I suppose it must have been Albert."

Reznik ignored the question. "Elder, how can you entertain the thought of having a band of mercenaries living in Jardis? You strongly disapproved when Thomas left the village. We all did. And now you're—"

"Is he demanding payment for his services, Norman?" Edith interrupted. "To defend his own home?"

Potts slowly shook his head. "He did, however, request to act as an intermediary for all fees paid to his colleagues. He said it would be a convenience for everyone involved."

"He said that with a straight face?" Madeline said incredulously.

"It works out well for him," Edith said. "He can skim off however much he wants, and his cronies will be none the wiser."

Standing to the side, Lucille Barlow dared not join the conversation. Her cool blue eyes darted back and forth between everyone in the room.

"Excuse me, Mother, but you did not let me finish," Reznik said during a pause in the exchange. "While you and the elder discuss these arrangements as though they have already been decided—"

"They have, Reznik," Elder Potts firmly cut in. "It was my decision. In case you've forgotten, I am the authority in this village."

Reznik remained undeterred. "I still have the right to ask for an explanation, Elder. Why impose such an unnecessary and repugnant burden on Jardis when we have always defended ourselves, no matter how—" He stopped to glance at Madeline, who hung on his every word. "No matter how dire the circumstances?"

The elder made an effort to lean forward in his sunken chair. "Reznik, I know you may forget this simple fact, but we are not soldiers." His voice remained temperate. "Have you been told of the previous raid? It has been almost a cycle now."

"They did not want to hear about it before the festival," Edith said, glancing pointedly at her son.

"And I suppose you did not want to inform them of the details," the elder said to her.

Edith frowned.

"Gail Levitt was taken hostage during the raid. We had no choice but to lay down our arms and allow them to take what they wanted."

Madeline's eyes widened.

"What else could have been done? What if it were your mother in that position, Reznik? What if it were Madeline?"

"That's enough, Norman," Edith said quietly.

"I do not mean to be combative. Understand my justification for spending what little money we have on these hired swords. You can be assured that I have no qualms about putting their lives at risk to defend our homes and livelihoods while the rest of us adhere to protecting our families. Had Abby been able to keep watch on Gail ..."

He paused to drink water from the mug on the lampstand beside his chair. "After three years of quiet, two attacks within three cycles is unsettling. Raids are occurring with greater frequency throughout the Outlands. Surely you understand why I agreed to this."

"I do understand, Elder," said Reznik, "but it is still unacceptable to me, no matter how one looks at it, and I'll tell you why."

The elder stared at him curiously.

"I think you either misunderstand or overestimate the mercenaries you've invited into our village. I thought you, of all people, would be familiar with these types. How sturdy is their commitment to our safety in the face of mortal danger? What good is the money we give them if they do not live to waste it? I find it highly likely that they will simply abandon us when it suits them."

"I suspected you might feel this way, Reznik," Elder Potts said with a wry smile, leaning back in his chair, still unfazed by Reznik's forceful tone. "I will take your words into consideration."

This gave Reznik only the slightest pause. "Thank you for doing so, Elder." He rose. "I think I shall be going now. In light of our discussion, I don't think there is time to waste. Regardless of your decision, I will meet with William immediately to revise the defense protocols for the watch. Madeline?"

"I'll walk your mother home and then join you," she said.

"Very well." He bowed slightly to the elder. "Goodbye, Elder."

"Good day to you."

Lucille scampered behind Reznik to open the door. After they had gone, the elder's gaze lingered on Edith. "It would seem he still believes you should have taken over for me last year. He does not think you would have made this decision."

"I wouldn't have. But that's irrelevant. He respects your judgment, even if you'll never convince him on this issue."

"I still believe it," he added.

Edith sniffed. "That I should have accepted, you mean?"

He nodded.

"I know you made the offer as a way to keep my mind off Sebastian. My being elder would not have been best for the village. I can tell you that with certainty."

The elder smiled wryly. "Modesty does not suit you, Edith."

"Oh, I assure you that I have none."

Edith rose from her chair. Madeline followed suit.

"I hope you will consider what he said."

"Of course, Edith," he replied, after clearing his throat.

"My wishes for your improved health, Elder," said Madeline.

"Thank you, dear."

Lucille pulled open the front door as the two women prepared to leave. She reached out and tugged on Madeline's sleeve as the latter walked past to follow Edith out the door. "I've never heard anyone speak to the elder like Reznik did," Lucille whispered with bated breath. "That was unbelievable."

"He was being bullish, as usual," Madeline said.

"Yes, the nerve of him!" Lucille said, giggling.

Ignoring her, Madeline exited the house to find Edith already walking out to the square. The temperature had dropped since arriving at the elder's house. Madeline hurried over and took off her button-up sweater, offering it to Edith for extra warmth.

"Oh, please." Edith pushed Madeline's hands away. "Do you really think I'll take that? I kept my mouth shut in there so as not to embarrass you."

She began to cough again. Madeline walked beside her, still holding the sweater uncertainly in her hands.

"Go on." Edith waved as if swatting a fly, quickening her pace without looking back.

Madeline sighed, turned around, and began walking toward the eastern gate, where she knew she would find Reznik.

—5—

Thomas Polke swung his wooden sword over his head in an arc toward the red head of Stanley Alton, who raised his own stick to block the attack.

"Good!" Thomas exclaimed. "Stan, I'm impressed."

"Even though you're taking it easy on him?" Dane Landsman snickered, leaning against a nearby post as he observed the spar with arms folded across his chest.

"Thomas!" came a loud, stern voice. Since there was no one else manning the gate, the three turned their attention westward as a cloaked shadow emerged slowly from the fog.

Thomas lowered the wooden sword to his side, tightening his grip. "And good morning to you, Reznik."

"Where is William?"

"I told him I'd cover for him in the morning. Better to let him get some rest once in a while, you know?"

"Now I understand what you meant during our conversation last night." Reznik's pace remained steady as he spoke. "You think you'll be able to protect Jardis. For a price, of course."

"That's ridiculous. I simply offered the services of some people I know. The elder accepted. I stand to gain nothing but the security of my home."

Stanley backed away from Thomas. Dane uncrossed his arms and leaned forward on the post, his eyes lighting up with interest. Reznik stopped three meters in front of Thomas. The two men faced each other squarely. They both wore neutral expressions on their faces.

"It's the elder's decision," Thomas said.

"Is that right? And what if he had said no? Would you have remained here on your own?"

Thomas frowned.

"You and I made our choices," he said. "We both fight the good fight. We're not so different, you know."

"Stop trying to convince people that you're doing anything for anyone other than yourself. Maybe the elder agreed to your proposal, but you're on their side, not ours."

The thin veil of civility finally faded from Thomas's face. His eyes blazed, and his lips contorted into a snarl.

"You've always been a real prick, you know that? I've killed to protect this village too. I fought next to your father. What the hell have you done? Run off with Madeline to your fancy military academy and then on to fight the king's battles out east. And for what?"

Reznik said nothing; his gaze remained steady. This only further enraged Thomas.

"Oh, that's right. The two of you are going to become champions of the Outlands. You think I don't know about your silly dream? And you call me delusional? Tell me, what good was all that to Gail anyway? Where were you when she was snatched up and used as currency for our crops?"

After several ticks of silence, Reznik replied, "From where I'm standing, nothing you've said disproves the notion that you're merely a cynical opportunist. In fact, I'm more convinced of it than ever."

"You're in no position to judge me," Thomas said between gritted teeth.

Reznik replied, "You're not part of the village anymore."

"And you are?"

Seeing that Stanley no longer stood beside him, Thomas looked around. "Stan, give me your trainer."

Stanley Alton stared down hesitantly at his wooden sword. He slowly stepped forward, laid the stick gingerly in Thomas's outstretched hand, and retreated again.

Bringing his arm forward, Thomas flung the wooden sword at Reznik's feet.

"Come on. Prove to me that your training was worth something."

Reznik made no attempt to acknowledge the practice weapon on the ground in front of him. Instead, he angled his head upward, his blue eyes widening, the corner of his lips curling slightly. "Prove to *you*?"

Thomas's eyes iced over. After several ticks of silence, he raised his wooden sword and rushed at Reznik.

"Oh, shit!" came Dane's excited voice from behind him.

Reznik leaned to his right as he easily dodged Thomas's first swipe. "I don't owe you anything, Thomas. The way you're acting only confirms your lack of character."

Thomas feinted another swipe before pulling the sword back and thrusting it at Reznik's head. Reznik ducked and scrambled to the side, inadvertently kicking Stanley's sword from where it still lay on the ground.

"You need to wake up," Thomas said as he bent over to pick up the displaced trainer. "Do you actually think you speak for anyone in Jardis?"

Reznik continued to move to his left. Thomas did the same, now wielding both wooden swords as the two men circled each other.

Thomas lunged. Reznik stepped nimbly backwards, avoiding swipes from both swords.

"You left this village the day you headed to Tellisburg, long before I set out on my own. You don't have anyone here, Reznik. Only your mother. And Madeline. I've never understood what she sees in you."

Reznik narrowed his eyes.

"Sure, we looked up to your folks," Thomas continued, "but for some reason, you think that puts you above everyone else. Nobody holds you in nearly the same regard, Reznik. You can spew your bullshit all you want. Your self-righteous fantasy won't come to pass. You have nothing to offer the real world."

He tried another overhead swipe with his right hand and followed up with his left, sharply jabbing in anticipation of Reznik's movements. Instead, Reznik raised his hands, turned into Thomas's body, grabbed his left wrist, and whirled him around. At the same time, Reznik swept his leg under Thomas's, dropping the latter face-down on the ground, before releasing Thomas's wrist and stepping back, still unarmed.

Thomas propped himself up on his elbows and glared at Reznik, angrily coughing and grunting. Something sparked a glint in his eye. He tensed himself as inconspicuously as possible.

"At least I have my values," Reznik said. "Maybe if you had any sense of yours, you wouldn't feel so threatened by mine."

Reznik leaned over, ready to extend a hand, then staggered backwards, temporarily incapacitated by a shower of dirt thrown into his eyes.

Having released both wooden swords, Thomas launched himself at Reznik. The two tumbled over one another. Thomas rolled off quickly and sprang to his feet. In his hand was the knife he had seen strapped to Reznik's belt underneath the latter's cloak.

As Reznik got up, Thomas brought the weapon up close to his face to admire its craftsmanship. He gripped the hilt and pulled. There was a brisk shrill as the blade slid out of its sheath.

"Where the hell did you get this?" Thomas said in an awestruck voice, turning away slightly.

"Give it back," Reznik said as he got to his feet.

"Hah! I'll keep this for myself, thank you very much. I bet it'll sell for quite the tidy sum."

Reznik's jaw tightened. "That's mine. Return it right now." He stepped forward threateningly.

Thomas whirled around and pointed the blade directly at Reznik. "I don't think so. Think of this as payment for your arrogance, kid."

Reznik took another step forward.

Thomas's eyes widened. "Hey, hey! I mean it." The point of the blade wavered. "This is mine now."

"You're trash, Thomas. That knife is worth more than you are. Now hand it over."

"You little shit!" Thomas yelled. Suddenly, he charged.

Dane cried out, "Whoa, whoa! Hold on!"

Reznik tensed as he prepared to wrestle the blade from Thomas, but before either could react, another person darted in from the side and rammed into Thomas, toppling him over and rattling the knife free from his grasp. His attacker scooped up the weapon and planted a boot atop Thomas's other arm, causing him to shout in pain and release the scabbard he still held in his hand.

Madeline returned the knife to its sheath, her eyes blazing as she glared witheringly down at Thomas. He scrambled to his feet and returned her harsh gaze with a blankly defiant look, but after a few ticks, the fog lifted, and he came to his senses.

"Sorry, I wasn't thinking. Things got out of hand. I wasn't really going to do anything anyway."

The shell-shocked expression on Thomas's face was enough to convince all of them, even Reznik, that he was truly contrite.

"If we go to the elder with this, he'll run you out of the village," said Reznik. "Or I could go to my mother. She'd build a pole in the square high enough to hang you."

"I really am sorry," Thomas mumbled.

Reznik waved his hand awkwardly, eyebrows furrowed in annoyance.

Madeline took a deep breath and looked around at Stanley and Dane, who had joined the three in a small semicircle. "We won't tell the elder. In fact, we won't tell a single person. This has nothing to do with anyone other than Reznik and Thomas. It was a disagreement between them, nothing more. Is everyone clear?"

"Thank you," Thomas said. "I appreciate that."

Madeline braced for an argument from Reznik, but to her surprise, none came.

"Hold on," Dane interjected. "I won't agree to keep quiet about it unless Reznik apologizes for being an ass."

She sighed and glanced wearily at Reznik, who shrugged and stepped forward to extend his hand.

"I apologize, Thomas. Nevertheless, I meant most of what I said, and I'm sure you did as well. I hope we can settle our differences at some point."

Thomas squinted and gave a slight roll of his eyes, but shook Reznik's hand. "Very well."

"Good enough for me too," Dane said with a nod. "Stan?"

"I won't tell anyone," Stanley agreed meekly.

Thomas set off alone, back up the path toward the square. Dane and Stanley returned to their post at the gate, leaving Reznik and Madeline to stroll through the eastern fields.

"Let's walk the perimeter, since William isn't here yet."

Madeline nodded. "You certainly let him off easy."

"From what he said to me, I thought it better to let things be." Reznik snuck a peek at the holster on his belt to which he had returned Leland Hagen's knife. "Thanks for the assist, by the way."

"What would've happened had I not shown up?" she wondered aloud.

"It doesn't matter. What matters is that you did. And you said the right thing, Maddy. Whatever happens will stay between the two of us. And as long as Thomas retains that impression, the village won't suffer for it."

"What do you mean?"

"If I tell the elder, Thomas would lose his precious contract. If he can't make money through his mercenary friends, he'll surely hold a grudge against everyone, not just me. I don't know how that would manifest, but I don't want to find out. I don't trust him." He kicked at the dirt. "We already made our case to the elder. The village is everyone's responsibility, not just mine or yours. Let's see where things go from here."

"You're really content to leave things as they are?" Madeline asked incredulously.

Reznik shrugged.

She stared at him in wonderment. The two walked on in silence as they continued their trek around the outskirts of Jardis.

—6—

Thomas Polke left the next day, though most of the villagers remained unaware of his departure for several days; some later expressed surprise that he seemed in such a hurry. Word spread that Thomas's mercenaries would arrive after the winter. While many Jardisians expressed misgivings about sheltering strangers, most were accepting of hiring the sellswords after the elder pled his case at a gathering in the square, during which he conveyed Thomas's promise not to take profits for himself and to make all mercenary activity subordinate to the militia.

With the matter settled, preparations began in earnest for the coming change in season. With the arrival of the cold, the people of Jardis transitioned to a more insular lifestyle. Although the latest raid had resulted in significant losses of crops, most villagers expressed muted concern, given it had been an overall bountiful harvest.

Winter came early in the Outlands, and Jardis, one of the northernmost villages, was among the first to experience the hailing of snow and winds. While its people had long since grown accustomed to the annual harshness, they were habitually inclined to withdraw into their homes and spend their days harnessing warmth from their fireplaces, stovetops, and internal firepits, which doubled as water heaters. Most houses had a thin-walled storage annex, where vegetables could be kept fresh in the freezing cold.

The militia remained vigilant, but the active rotation was much smaller than it had been; like most Outlanders, bandits were rarely active during the winter, obviating the need for a large number of armed villagers. Instead, the militia's duties consisted mainly of chopping firewood or hunting small game in the Kinnan Woods, usually in sizable groups. Reznik and Madeline were asked to tag along more often than not and willingly obliged.

Aside from these occasional excursions into the forest, they remained mostly within the more intimate social circle of the Sylveras, Dunnings, and Altons. The three families were tightly knit. When Harrison and Maya Agilda were alive, they had been part of the group as well. Madeline, of course, fit right in and grew nostalgic when the families gathered for supper. The Sylveras' house was the most spacious and usually the accommodation of choice.

After supper, the parents would typically occupy the kitchen and the now-grown children—Reznik, Madeline, Albert, Karen, and Stanley—took over the living room. Over the course of two turns, Reznik and Madeline imparted their experiences as soldiers on the battlefront. Karen remained mostly silent but was always attentive, while Albert and Stanley made no attempt to hide their fascination. In turn, the three relayed stories of the village and their friends and neighbors. Alana and Anita, Albert's younger sisters, ricocheted between the living room and the kitchen; the evening usually ended for the Dunnings when they tired and had to be put to bed.

One night, after the Dunnings had gone, Reznik asked Stanley to accompany him on an evening patrol. With permission from his parents, Stanley agreed. The two set out, leaving Madeline and Karen in the living room. Edith continued to chat with the Altons in the kitchen; the girls could hear their voices faintly emanating through the door.

"You know, Maddy," Karen said, cupping her own mug of tea in her hands, "I've been thinking a lot about your stories, about all you've been through in such a short time. Does it feel strange to be back here after all that?"

Madeline smiled but gave her a quizzical look. "Why would it be strange? This is my home. This was all I knew for so many years of my life."

"But this isn't your life anymore, is it?"

"Military life isn't real life," Madeline replied, taken aback. "Military life is just time spent looking forward to going back to where you belong. I'm out there to do a job, that's all."

"So that's what makes you different from Thomas?"

Flabbergasted, Madeline slowly shook her head.

"I didn't mean it that way," Karen quickly disclaimed, staring at her hands. "I heard about the incident."

Madeline sighed. "Stanley couldn't keep it to himself, could he?"

"He had to tell someone."

Madeline shook her head again.

"It's fine," Karen said. "I'll make sure no one else knows. But how can Reznik possibly expect us to stand our ground on our own with what little we have? It's wholly unreasonable."

"He doesn't think so," Madeline returned. "Regardless, he accepts the elder's decision, and so do I."

"And what would you do? If you were in charge, would you bring in the mercenaries?"

"I'm not sure, to be honest."

"I heard about your meeting with the elder, Madeline. You and Reznik. And Edith. Lucille told me."

"Of course she did."

Before Karen could reply, the kitchen door swung open and in walked Edith, followed shortly by John and Mary Alton.

"Come, Karen," John said. "We should be heading back now."

Karen glanced at Madeline and shrugged and then stood up. Edith and Madeline bid the Altons farewell.

Madeline put the kettle on the small stove, washed and dried the dishes, and cleaned the table. She brought the boiling kettle into the living room and prepared to pour some tea for the two of them. Meanwhile, Edith settled into her favorite chair in the living room, a large, cherry wood recliner with thick wool cushions.

Edith adjusted the light blue shawl that was wrapped around her shoulders. Although she had aged considerably in the past year, she was still a beautiful woman and nothing brought it out as well as her modest but radiant smile. It spread across Edith's face, wry and knowing, warm and comforting all at once. "I don't know if you've been carrying that look around all day, my dear, but your face seems so heavy. It worries me."

It was rare for Edith to be this tender. Madeline's insides stirred violently. The clamped emotions she had suffocated for so long began to churn. Before she knew it, her hands were shaking.

"I thought I'd be able to make it through the whole cycle without feeling like this," she said quietly.

Edith's smile disappeared. "What's wrong?"

Madeline drew a deep breath. "I don't … I'm not sure." She drew another deep breath. "I've killed people before. I did it to defend my home. The justification doesn't change when you become a soldier, fighting foreign people in foreign lands. It's the same commitment I had when I'd drive away bandits here."

"But it's not the same," Edith said softly.

Madeline nodded stiffly. "I know that it's normal for people to become desensitized as soldiers, but I think the opposite has happened to me. I think I'm reacting even more to these things now that I am back home. The raid, the mercenaries. I don't know what to make of it."

Edith said nothing.

"Did Reznik tell you what happened the day before Thomas left? I'm sure he must have."

"Yes, he did."

"So you know what I'm talking about then. For once, he was the one who showed restraint, and he was right to do so. But I don't know how he feels about all this. Or if he'd understand how I feel." Madeline sighed and loosened her grip on the arms of her chair; her hands were bright red from the pressure.

"I am sure that when you need him to, he'll show you just how well he does understand you." Edith's eyes glowed in the flickering lamplight. "His father was much the same way."

Madeline was not fully at ease, but Edith's words had a calming effect on her, and she changed the subject to try to push away her anxiety. When Reznik had still not returned half an arc later, she decided to take her leave and return home. Bidding Edith a good night, she shut the door quickly behind her to prevent the cold evening wind from swirling inside.

—7—

Reznik and Madeline spent most of the last four days of their leave drilling the watchmen in all matters of defensive tactics. They discovered that the stockpile of old crossbows was unpopular with the villagers, who preferred the familiarity of their modified home and farming tools. Reznik forcefully persuaded William Cadrene, Dane Landsman, and many other members of the watch to retrain with the crossbows, while Madeline gathered maps of the village, marked important chokepoints, and made suggestions for potential lookout spots, particularly along the northern border of Jardis.

On the last day, while Reznik and William made one final pass around the western end of the village, Madeline led the rest of the watch in drilling near the eastern gate and tower. Shortly before noon, Karen came to visit, bringing with her a cart of pork sandwiches, for which the villagers were most appreciative. Madeline had not seen her since the night at the Sylveras'.

The two young women ate together, sitting among a row of eroded stones that had been planted as makeshift seating beside the gate long ago and, over the years, had come to be permanent fixtures. They chatted pleasantly and took in the white-coated hills in the distance, blanketed in the first heavy snow of the season, which had arrived only two days earlier.

As they finished their food, Karen grew quiet. That was when Madeline noticed how pensive her friend seemed.

"What's the matter, Karen?"

Karen took a deep breath. "I'm sorry for what I said the other night."

"Don't worry about it," Madeline returned immediately. "It isn't anything that I haven't thought myself over the past cycle."

"And now it won't be two turns before you have to leave. Leaving already. Again."

"You'll be too busy teaching to notice!"

"Maybe so."

"I bet you've already started to think about lesson plans."

"I do want to arrange for more frequent book deliveries from Kantor. I don't know if we'll be able to afford them after the raid though."

That caught Madeline off guard. Several ticks passed before she thought of a reply.

"Let's make a trip to Kantor during my next leave. You'll be settled in too. We'll take care of it then."

"Yeah, settled in," Karen said, her voice faintly pulsing with wistfulness. Her gaze seemed to drift away toward nothing in particular. "First the butchery, now the classroom. I'm just moving from one holding area to another."

Madeline waited for her to continue.

"I can only imagine what the eastern wilderness must be like. I've never even been to Corande. Who knows if I'll get the chance to? I'm jealous of you, Maddy. Of you and Reznik both."

"Jealous of having to fight a war?"

"You know what I mean."

"Are you unhappy here?"

"Unhappy? No, I wouldn't say that." Karen pulled her maroon shawl tightly around her. "I just wonder sometimes what's out there. Even though I know this is where I belong."

Madeline wanted to object, but before she could say anything, Karen stood. Madeline followed suit and was caught by surprise when Karen wrapped her in a long embrace.

"I won't see you off with a whole crowd this time," Karen said after they pulled apart. "I'll say goodbye here and now, the way I want to."

Madeline felt a pang in her heart when she saw her friend's green eyes glistening.

"Next time you return, I'm going to make you sit in on one of my classes. Maybe you can give me a few pointers on how to conduct myself more like your fancy-pants academy instructors."

"I wouldn't ever wish that on you," Madeline returned with a laugh.

The two of them stood in silence for several ticks. Slowly, Madeline's hand moved to the crimson Coranox on her necklace and began tracing its outline.

"You never take that off, do you?" Karen asked.

Surprised, Madeline realized what she was doing and let her hand drop back to her side.

"I suppose not," she said with a laugh.

"Do you still think back to that day?"

"Sometimes …" Madeline clasped the pin around her neck and stared off into space.

After a moment, Karen hung her head slightly. "Sorry, I didn't mean to—"

"Oh no, it's fine," Madeline said, shaking her head. "I was just thinking about what this pin means to me now."

Karen waited for her to continue.

"This symbol is supposed to remind me of how I fight for my country, but more often than not, it reminds me of home. I miss my parents every day, but I grew up without them. I grew up with you, with all of us together."

"So even when you're so far away, you'll still be thinking of Jardis," Karen remarked.

"Yes, and sometimes I wonder if the path I'm following is the right one. Maybe there's no way to know for sure right now."

"Either way, I'm sure you'll do what's best, Maddy. You always have. That's what I came to realize after I said those stupid things the other night. You won't let people down, least of all yourself."

Madeline smiled and released the pin from her grip. "Thanks, Karen."

Karen put her hands on both of Madeline's shoulders and squeezed. They locked eyes.

"Most importantly, please, please stay safe."

Now it was Madeline's turn to hug her friend just as tightly. "I will."

Chapter 13

(988.1.02–03)

—1—

Winters in Moriana typically began during the Fifth Exile and spanned the entire Reunion. All Coranthians were accustomed to below-freezing temperatures, ice storms, and heavy blizzards during this period. Due to the harsh weather and an intermittent stream of Amelaren raids throughout the fall, construction on the Argiset Highpost was delayed. Eventually, as the weather worsened, the attacks tapered off, allowing General Leynitz to spend the majority of the Fifth Exile overseeing construction of the new fort, now mostly finished. During the Reunion, he was summoned back to the capital by King Samsen. To the chagrin of many Corandi nobles, Leynitz politely declined to grace them with his presence at most New Year parties, opting instead to rest in the comfort and quiet of his spacious quarters in the Citadel before meeting with the king on the second day of 988.

• • •

Samsen and Leynitz sat facing each other at a game table in a small room attached to the Castle Coranthis library. Two unlit solistone lamps lay atop tall posts behind each of their chairs.

The marble game pieces on the table took the form of various shapes, crafted to represent wielders of different weapons. After much thought,

Samsen moved a white swordsman piece away from one of Leynitz's lancer pieces and then leaned back, signaling the end of his turn.

"I was disappointed that you decided not to attend Sophelia's birthday party last year, Marsell. Surely the Assembly was not to blame for keeping you away? You should have been there to celebrate her twentieth." He chuckled. "I remember when you and I were that young ourselves."

Leynitz picked up the lancer piece and nudged it one space forward, and then he grabbed a twelve-sided silver die lying in a specially designed pocket that protruded from the side of the table and rolled a five. He handed the die to Samsen, who rolled a two and removed the swordsman piece from the table, dropping it into a small bin on the windowsill.

"I was busy with preparations. I must hasten back to the Highpost soon, Your Majesty. It must be completed on schedule. Now that the winter is over, it is certain that enemy raids will resume shortly."

"That shall not stop us from fitting in our match of kenzan."

"Yes, here we are," Leynitz agreed.

"Have you spoken with Elliott?"

Leynitz captured another of Samsen's swordsmen. He wondered whether the king was even trying. "I did meet with Lord Havora," he said. "He shared his son's thoughts and promptly apologized profusely for them. I presume you know of what I speak?"

The king smiled and stroked his beard. "I understand Elliott's mortification. Young Havora proposes to undo all you've done for him regarding the Ertel inquiries."

"The young Lord is thinking critically about how to improve our army and his performance as a soldier, and that is what is important."

"Marsell, you are impervious to the Assembly's pressure, as usual," Samsen said in an appreciative tone. "Why must someone like you always be the exception?"

"I am not the only one. Your move, Your Majesty."

Samsen nodded and turned his attention to the game. For a while, both refrained from saying much as the match eased into a groove. Gradually, Samsen retreated his pieces, prompting Leynitz to push his forward. The die often fell in Leynitz's favor.

"Lord Eurich's trips to Aldova have become more frequent," Samsen said after Leynitz captured yet another piece. "He is only interested in making noise. Don't let him get to you, Marsell. You answer only to Ferdin and me."

"The way I see it, Your Majesty, the generals must act as representatives of all Coranthians now more than ever. Unfortunately, I fear the only way to satisfy all parties is to satisfy none. I stress again that I have absolutely no desire to be involved in any politics. I will only focus on doing what is best for our troops and ensuring our victory in this war."

"Well said, Marsell. Exactly what I wanted to hear from you."

Leynitz dipped his head gratefully. "Thank you."

"I haven't seen your manservant around," Samsen remarked.

"He would not appreciate being called that."

Samsen let out a hearty laugh. "Come, now. All in good humor."

"I granted Windsor a personal leave. He requested to be in the company of his father, who is once again bedridden."

Samsen raised his eyebrows. "You've gone soft, Marsell."

Leynitz frowned. "If ensuring the well-being of those under one's command, even off the battlefield, fits the description of soft, then so be it."

"You've still changed quite a bit," Samsen said.

"Your Highness, the military serves all people of Coranthia. There is value also in the naked gratitude that Windsor's estate expressed after I granted him leave. Surely, all of our soldiers' families deserve whatever relief we can afford them, relief from wondering if their loved ones will be victims in the next battle, for example."

Samsen nodded. "I admit that your empathy serves you well. How are things on the front?"

Leynitz smiled, his mind wandering back to times long gone. In peacetime, Samsen had regularly called on him to speak casually about military affairs, and their meetings often devolved into dry status reports. This had previously annoyed Leynitz, but now, he felt a strong and unexpected appreciation for the trite and mundane. As the king had to contend with more and more challenges, both domestic and foreign, such meetings were indeed few and far between these days. Suddenly, Leynitz did not mind that Samsen did not appear to invest much effort in their kenzan match.

"Construction at both Tull Rock and Argiset will be completely finished within half a cycle," Leynitz said. "In fact, we overestimated both the time and money required to fortify Argiset. It turns out that the Amelaren materials, while inadequate for the foundation, were useful in buttressing the walls and columns. Of course, our engineers deserve most of the credit for this."

"Are they running at full manpower?" Samsen inquired.

"They are, Your Majesty."

"And the supply lines?"

"Elliott has personally ensured that they remain on schedule and meet our quotas."

"Good," Samsen said. He leaned back in his chair, a look of relief on his face. "Then I'll expect you to spend more time at Argiset."

Leynitz knitted his eyebrows. "Of course, Your Majesty. That is where I'll be directing our offensive—"

"Two other reasons," Samsen cut in, holding up his hand. "First, the more you remain on the front, the less chance for Lord Eurich and his merry band to meddle in your affairs. A few surveyors might tag along, but you can handle them. The second and more important reason I want you there is that I may send Adrian to the Highpost. I'll want you to look after him."

Leynitz stroked his mustache nervously. "Your Majesty, would it not be better for His Highness to remain at Aldova? I cannot say when he will feel ready to head to Argiset—"

"When Argiset will be as safe as Aldova, you mean?" Samsen cut in haughtily, sporting a stern gaze. "That is clearly impossible. This is not up for discussion."

"As you wish, Your Majesty."

Samsen motioned to the board. "Shall we finish the game? It's time for my counterattack."

As his gaze darted across the board, Leynitz realized he had let his guard down. He felt the sting of his carelessness as Samsen brought his line of archer pieces forward and, after several rolls of the die, obliterated Leynitz's advancing lancers. It was now clear that Samsen had sacrificed his front line in drawing Leynitz into the trap he had set with his archers.

"Beware of short-sighted aggression, Marsell."

The parallels between the game and the Ertel Ridge campaign hit Leynitz hard; he could not help but feel that this was far from an unintentional jab from the king, who clearly retained his abilities as a strategist.

Leynitz held up his arms. "It's your match, Your Majesty."

"And rightfully so," Samsen laughed, standing up. "Now, let us meet with Sophelia. I trust you have some time before you need to leave. I'm glad we had this talk."

Leynitz rose from his seat as Samsen turned to leave. After the king had taken several steps, Leynitz decided to clarify his earlier point of contention.

"Your Majesty."

Samsen stopped and turned slowly to face Leynitz.

"I hope you did not misunderstand me," Leynitz said. "My main concern is the matter of whether His Highness himself is willing to take the reins. My misgivings have nothing to do with his safety. The Highpost should be fully reinforced by the spring, and His Highness will undoubtedly be a fine soldier and leader. I will accompany him for as long as he is stationed there."

"I am glad to hear that, Marsell. The boy wishes to show that he can stand at the front like his old man did. It was bound to happen."

Samsen stepped forward and offered his hand. Leynitz shook it gently and then released it. The king nodded somberly and turned to exit the room.

Leynitz took a moment to review the game board—still frustrated by his loss—before taking his leave.

—2—

After several days of persistent snowfall, the king tracked down his son on the third day of the new year and told him he was to set out for the fortress with General Leynitz the following day, hoping the newly favorable weather conditions would hold until he reached Lake Sanmoria.

Sophelia was present during the conversation. She convinced the two to dine together that night and convene for breakfast the next day as well. Fully satisfied with the arrangement, she made her way to the royal mews, where she awaited her father's arrival; they had already made plans to ride that afternoon. To her dismay, not only did Samsen postpone their riding session until after six arc, but he also informed her that he would be unable to dine with her and Adrian that evening.

"I'm truly sorry, my dear," the king said as they led their horses out of the royal mews, "but I have a meeting that cannot wait. I had to choose between one and the other. I thought you would prefer to ride, so here I am."

Sophelia smiled and tried her best to look pleased, though could not hide the disappointment in her eyes.

"And what of breakfast tomorrow?"

"That will not be rescheduled, of course," Samsen said, giving her a comforting smile. "We will prepare everyone's favorite before Adrian is to set out."

Sophelia hoisted herself onto an eager Abelina, whose white coat and dark gray mane—draped across a slender frame—glistened in the setting sun. As usual, father and daughter had not seen much of each other over the past two cycles, and Sophelia could sense the restlessness in her mount, who snorted eagerly.

When the durioness was barely over a year old, Samsen bought her from a breeder in Mardena. He had never seen such a beautiful horse, but Abelina was a strong-willed creature who refused to let most people near her. Initially, Samsen regretted buying the animal, as she was unmanageable. Then one day, shortly after Queen Evangeline's passing, he spied Sophelia near the stables talking to Abelina. Everyone was amazed at how Sophelia had been able to calm the horse and touched at how the princess had found comfort in a new friend after the loss of her mother. On Sophelia's fifteenth birthday, he gave her Abelina as a gift. Since then, Sophelia and Abelina had formed a deep bond.

Samsen brought out a black, sinewy spardnell that Sophelia did not recognize; his rotation of horses was always in flux, and a new one was favored almost every cycle; the one it would replace was typically shipped to Aldova. In one graceful motion, he climbed onto the horse and motioned for Sophelia to lead the way.

The two embarked on their traditional route through the northeastern recesses of the palace grounds, collectively known as the Cardetz, which would take them through the paddock surrounding the mews and Farin Wood.

Sophelia remained reticent as they weaved in and out of the trees at the outskirts of the grove, making their way east. Samsen, wanting to console her but, unsure of how to proceed, decided to explain why he would have to cut their time short that day.

"Your father has finally managed to sway the Empire to provide assistance in our war against the barbarians," he said, "and the emperor awaits my accommodation of his envoys in Mardena, where we will finalize the agreement. Such is why I must make arrangements with the utmost expediency."

Sophelia acknowledged him only with noncommittal hums. Riding behind her, he sensed she was hardly paying attention.

"If you were to acquaint yourself with these matters, Sophie," Samsen said, trying not to sound reproving, "you would make a fine hostess for the Doromalian envoys when they arrive."

The princess tugged lightly on her reins, prompting Abelina to slow down. Samsen veered around and pulled up next to them as Sophelia turned to him.

"Is that what you want from me as your daughter? Or as the princess?"

A look of surprise crossed Samsen's face. He did not respond for several ticks. "Both, I would say, but it is only an indulgence. I will not ask you to hold company with people from the Empire if you do not feel comfortable doing so."

Sophelia dug her heel lightly into Abelina's side. They sped to a canter as she rode ahead of her father. "I wonder which role holds the greater burden?" she wondered aloud, without turning to look at Samsen.

The king spurred his spardnell to catch up with his daughter. "What is this really about, Sophie?" he asked, pulling up alongside her. A hint of frustration colored his tone. "You must have something specific on your mind."

Sophelia's blue eyes flashed. Wisps of her blond hair, jarred loose from the tight bun gathered at the back of her head, fluttered in the breeze. Her riding posture was regal: straight but not rigid, assured, and relaxed. Samsen marveled at his daughter's image, one that acutely reminded him of Evangeline.

"What is my role supposed to be, Father?" Sophelia asked firmly. "Things are changing all too quickly. This war has magnified, accelerated everything. A year ago, I would have never imagined that Adrian would be on the front lines, fighting against the Amelarens." She tilted her head back, gazing skyward. "It just makes me think: What should I be doing?"

"My dear, you shouldn't look at it that way. Your brother is not acting purely out of obligation. I'm sure he has told you as much."

As he said this, a pit began to form in Samsen's stomach. He was unaccustomed to speaking so frankly with his daughter about her personal affairs and could not presently call on Adrian or Isabelle, Sophelia's personal guard, to mediate.

They rode on in silence, leaving the air filled with sounds of rustling flora and rhythmic hoof beats.

Finally, Sophelia said, "Regardless of my brother's imperative, no one would dare to openly question his actions. He is the Crown Prince. I am but a woman, the first blood princess of Coranthia. So how am I to present myself?" She gazed challengingly at her father.

"It is your precedent to set," he replied. "And I know it will be a fine one."

The blueness in her eyes flickered. "Very well. Thank you, Father."

They had traversed almost the entire length of Farin Wood. To their south was a small pond into which a stream emptied, both of which were artificial, having been diverted from the canal down through the rolling pastures between Farin and Dagnus Woods.

Samsen pulled beside her and glanced upward. The angle of sunlight was already sharp and continued to close by the rep.

"We should head back," he said. "We rarely have chances to talk like this, and I am glad we are making the most of them."

Sophelia smiled distractedly.

As they retraced their route southwest, riding straight through the field without bearing into the trees, she engaged Samsen in idle chatter. At first, he indulged her happily, but eventually, he became disappointed that their moment of openness had passed and began to wonder why she had again distanced herself. He went over their conversation in his mind and tried to recall her reactions to his words. Finally, as he thought back to the end of their exchange, he came to the realization that he might not have said what she wanted to hear.

—3—

The notion lingered in his mind throughout his hasty supper. He carried it with him to his later meeting with Velmann and Grandville.

Samsen chose to hold the conference in a parlor in the southwestern wing of Castle Coranthis, several doors from the grand ballroom and on the opposite side of the corridor. This chamber was among Samsen's favorite places to host a small group of guests. The southern face of the room was taken up by a floor-to-ceiling window that offered a majestic view of the Sarigan and the Nelia Woods, a small forest across the river directly opposite Corande. The inner space of the room was adorned only with several chairs and a modest chandelier hung low from the high ceiling. The walls were lined with the richest quality of lehrwood, a Lynderan analog of mahogany. A small fireplace, built into the eastern wall beside to the window, had been lit by servants in advance.

The king settled in early and sat reading a report from Aldova sent by General Leopold San Mortigan as he waited. Velmann was the first to arrive and flopped onto an open chair. After a rep, Samsen looked up and set the report aside on a small stand to his left between the two. Velmann, who had been nonchalantly examining his nails, reached for the report and began to flip through it with similar disinterest.

Moments later, Grandville entered. He checked the clock on the western wall to make sure he was not late. Unlike Samsen and Velmann, he had come from outside the palace grounds. He hung his long, dark gray coat on a rack, and then moved to take a seat on Samsen's other side.

They sat silently for some time, as Samsen appeared lost in thought. Finally, the king looked at Grandville, who waited expectantly, and then at Velmann, who was still half-heartedly leafing through the report.

"Given that the emperor has refused our invitation to Lymria, I think it only appropriate that I also refrain from attending the signing ceremony."

"No question," Velmann said, setting the papers down on the stand. "It seems they are still incapable of treating us as equals, not as second-class former colonists."

"We must be careful though," Grandville said. "You're right in taking such a stance, but we have to butter them up if we are to remain in their good graces."

"While we still need them, you mean?" Velmann said.

Samsen raised an eyebrow toward Grandville. "I suppose you already have a more specific notion in mind, as usual."

"They might see your absence as an insult, and the reality is, as Ferdin said, we need them more than they need us right now. I suggest we put together a select group of avets to escort the Imperial envoys around Lymria when they arrive."

"Be at their call, so to speak," Velmann said.

"Yes," Grandville said.

"I see the merit," Velmann admitted reluctantly after a moment's pause.

"How difficult would that be to arrange?" Grandville asked.

"General Mortigan could draw it up easily enough."

"I have not yet agreed to this," Samsen cut in crossly. "You are suggesting we parade our soldiers as lackeys and servants before so-called Doromalian dignitaries?"

"Not just any soldiers," Grandville replied. "They should be mainly of Doromalian descent. And a few Lymrians, perhaps."

Samsen shook his head. "I fear that this will be demeaning to our men, and we will appear as though we're obviously pandering to the Imperials."

"The Doromalians are too full of themselves to consider such things," said Grandville. "We will have Lady Havora put her touch on the procession. It will go smoothly."

Velmann took a pipe from his pocket and put it in his mouth, running his bite over it as he spoke. "I suppose we need to keep the Doromalians happy, at least until Norev agrees to deal with us directly. Then we can bypass the Empire completely."

Samsen raised an eyebrow.

"The Empire does not have a monopoly on premier guild services, that's true. But why would Norev elevate our status?"

Velmann shrugged and then shifted his gaze to the window, examining the night sky.

"Wishful thinking, Ferdin?" the king pressed wryly.

"In any case, I agree with Weston on the issue of the stewardship," Velmann said. "And let us worry about entertaining our guests. You should stay here in Corande."

Samsen stroked his chin. "I'll leave it to you, then, although I would like to see General Hagen when he arrives with the first shipment of hand cannons." His eyes rose to the ceiling as he took a moment to admire the chandelier. "I have been toying with the idea of establishing a foreign ministry. There would be no better candidate to take charge of it."

Grandville furrowed his brow. "I agree, but ..."

"But?" Samsen prodded.

Neither of the ministers spoke. The king sighed. He knew what they were thinking, but wanted one of them to be direct. Seeing that he would not be able to elicit the answer from them, he provided it himself. "Elevating him to a Cabinet position would paint a target on his back, despite his record."

"Eurich will never go against him directly," Velmann said, "but you know he'll start something."

"Besides," added Grandville, "Hagen is comfortable where he is. He stands outside the institutions and answers to you directly."

"You're both right," Samsen admitted. "I only wish there were some way to reward him. The man deserves my personal congratulations."

"He deserves that and more," Velmann added. "I will see to it that he receives your accolades."

"What you should see to," Samsen rejoined, "is that we have a cache of hand cannons distributed among our soldiers before year's end."

"Right, right." Velmann twirled the pipe in his hand.

Another lull followed.

"It's settled then," Samsen said after a rep. He leaned back in his chair and briefly closed his eyes. When he reopened them, his expression abruptly became weary. He waved his ministers away. "You may go now. I think I'll be off to bed early tonight."

"Very well," Grandville said. "Good night then." Without missing a beat, he rose and strode to the door. Within ticks, he was gone.

Velmann remained in his chair, gazing evenly at Samsen, who cupped his mouth to stifle a yawn.

"What is it?" the king asked, bleary-eyed.

"You seem to be often tired these days."

"I'm fine, though thank you for your concern." Samsen stared at the chandelier. "The truth is, I've been preoccupied lately with thoughts of the pups." He laughed dryly. "Running a country is but a trifle compared to raising two children on your own …"

His voice grew somber as he shifted in his chair to face Velmann squarely.

"Do not take Cassandra for granted, Ferdin. You are most fortunate to have her."

"I remind myself of that every day." After a pause, Velmann asked, "How is Sophelia?"

For Samsen, the lingering impression left by the riding session surged to the fore once again. He drew in a deep breath and sighed. "Good question. Has she seemed different to you lately?"

Velmann did not reply immediately. A trace of uncertainty crept across his face.

Samsen pounced on it. "What is it, Ferdin?"

"Well, why do you ask?" Velmann deflected.

"We had an interesting conversation today," the king mused. "Apparently, she wants to know what her duties should be as a princess, and I think she meant how she could contribute on a level comparable to Adrian's."

Velmann caught himself shaking his head and abruptly stiffened his neck, though not before Samsen noticed.

"Come, out with it," the king urged.

"Fine," said Velmann. "All I'm thinking is that she isn't the one you should be focused on at the moment. Adrian is setting off once again in the morning, is he not?"

"I'm not worried about him," Samsen said. "He is ready to come into his own. And with that, it is best I not crowd him. Sophelia, on the other hand …"

Seeing Samsen so unsure of himself, Velmann nodded sympathetically. He sensed it would be of no use to linger and stood to leave. The king got to his feet as well. The two walked to the door. As Velmann reached for the doorknob, Samsen clapped him appreciatively on the shoulder. "Thanks for hearing me out."

"Just like old times, right?" Velmann grinned and bade the king good night.

Samsen lingered inside the parlor. He wandered the room aimlessly, lost in thought, until he reached the fireplace on the eastern wall. Above the mantel was a portrait of Queen Evangeline, drawn three years before her death. She sat with her hands resting in her lap, gazing out the window, her straight blond hair down, her dark blue dress simple but sleek, her expression serene and dignified.

It was one of his favorite portraits of his late wife, one in which he had always found comfort, and he stopped in front of it, taking her in forlornly with his eyes. He remained that way for a long time.

Chapter 14

(988.1.31–36)

—1—

Prince Adrian's arrival at Argiset Highpost at the beginning of the First Exile mandated a significant increase in security. By midcycle, a total of seven companies had gathered at the Highpost. About half a cycle's work remained before the fort would be completed.

Two turns into the First Exile, Amelaren raids resumed with increasing intensity. Numerous skirmishes drove General Leynitz to deploy scouts toward the Ghend. Their subsequent report informed him that an enemy encampment of well over a thousand warriors was posted just outside the western end of the gorge. It seemed clear that the Amelarens amassed a larger force to reclaim Argiset and that the raids were merely portentous of a much graver threat.

When this assessment reached General Leopold San Mortigan at Aldova, he ordered a meeting be scheduled for the thirty-first, which all officers currently stationed there were required to attend, to discuss the situation.

• • •

"I feel that the obvious recourse in light of this new information should be nothing short of immediate deployment of reinforcements to Argiset."

This statement by Mortigan, delivered matter-of-factly to a room of colonels, captains, and vice captains, followed his conveyance of the report sent to him by Leynitz. Mortigan sat in a high-backed chair behind a long table that spanned the length of the dais. Seated around him were colonels Osterfeld, Albrecht, and Lurande. There was one other person at the table: Sebastian Eurich. Having come to Aldova for a visit on the Assembly's behalf, he was invited to take part in the meeting as well. The captains and vice captains took up the first three rows of seats in the audience; even though the room was much smaller than other auditoriums, most of it was empty.

"Over the past half-cycle," Mortigan continued, "the frequency and intensity of these raids have increased. The colonels and I all feel the Amelarens are planning to wear down the defenses at Argiset before launching an all-out attack."

The general's deep voice echoed across the small sixth-floor auditorium. As he spoke, his shoulder-length graying brown hair rustled across the collar of his officer's coat, which was adorned with an aeron Coranox on the left breast.

"We have not yet established a firm enough foothold in the Highlands. It is paramount that we address this threat to the Highpost seriously." Mortigan scratched his short, also graying, beard. "While I am sure that General Leynitz is fully capable of defending our fortifications, I wish to take no chances this time."

At the end of the table, Eurich smiled wryly. There was an almost imperceptibly faint murmur among the lower officers.

"I have already sent messengers ahead to Tull Rock with orders to Colonel Dyers. Four companies in total will be sent immediately to Argiset: two from Tull Rock, and—from here—the 10th and 22nd. In addition, the 26th and 28th will leave from here tomorrow to replace those rotating out from Tull. In total, our manpower at Argiset will be twelve companies strong. Colonels, I trust you take no issue with these arrangements."

Osterfeld, Albrecht, and Lurande were already nodding in unison.

Then came a voice that reverberated throughout the mostly empty room, clear and firm, almost indignant. It came from the third row. "Forgive me, General. If I may offer a word?"

Colonel Lurande, a stocky, square-jawed man who had an obvious habit of readjusting his combover, turned his nose upward as he tried to pinpoint the source of the voice in the crowd.

"I do not recognize that voice," he said. "Who is that? Stand up."

"Arthur Sorel, sir. Vice Captain of the 17th."

A tall, fair-skinned man stood up. His posture was stiff, his spine almost rigid. His dull-green eyes stared straight ahead.

Lurande gave Osterfeld a sidelong glance. "One of yours, Osterfeld?" he said in a voice low enough that only those on the dais could hear. Osterfeld ignored him.

"Go ahead, Vice Captain," Mortigan acknowledged with a nod.

"Thank you, sir," said Sorel. "I do not mean any disrespect, but I believe the rotation of troops may be a mistake."

The room fell into abrupt silence. Mortigan glared at Sorel.

"And your justification?"

"It would leave Tull Rock short two companies. Even for only for a few days, wouldn't it be better to err on the side of caution? Why were the officers not consulted before the messengers were dispatched?"

Eurich leaned forward to look across the dais at Mortigan. "What is this, General? You are being all too tolerant of such insubordination."

Sitting to Mortigan's right, Colonel Albrecht drummed his fingers on the table. The tapping of his fingernails rattled loudly throughout the room. He was a middle-aged man with several small scars blended into the wrinkles of his face, and he spoke clearly and calmly, though with a hint of impatience. "Vice Captain Sorel. While the general is generous enough to allow you to speak freely, need I remind you that you will ultimately be held responsible for your conduct?"

Nervous chuckles rippled throughout the room and subsided, just as quickly, when Osterfeld bellowed for silence.

The man sitting to Sorel's right quietly, though firmly, motioned for him to take his seat.

Eying Eurich wearily, Mortigan gave Albrecht an appreciative nod.

Sitting in the front row, the captain of the 10th Company raised his hand. "I have a question, General."

"Yes, Captain Wolbay?"

"Why the rotation for Tull Rock and not Delmond Cleft? We would be able to reinforce Delmond much more quickly. We would not have to move anyone from Tull Rock, and the companies leaving Delmond would still reach Argiset sooner than any deployed from Aldova."

"We do not have full security on the road between Delmond and Argiset, Captain," Mortigan said. "Amelaren encroachment in that region has been reported over the last year. Colonel Kendrall's companies are to remain as they are at Delmond. Tull Rock is our best option for the most expedient reinforcement of the Highpost."

"I apologize, sir," Sorel said, still standing, "but I cannot stress enough that this matter should have been discussed more thoroughly."

"On the contrary," Eurich snapped. "I think you have stressed it quite sufficiently, Vice Captain."

"Lord Eurich," Mortigan said, an edge in his voice, "while I appreciate your input, your capacity in this meeting is merely one of observance."

Eurich scowled impishly.

"Enough, Vice Captain!" snapped someone from the first row.

Sorel, who made a habit of facing people directly when addressed, angled his frame to see who had spoken. Osterfeld's successor as Captain of the 27th, Ferris Schaeffer, a tall man with a youthful face, short red hair, and a long slender nose, glared disapprovingly at Sorel.

"What makes you think, Vice Captain, that the general did not confer with the colonels before taking action? And what obligation does he have to consult the lower officers?"

Sorel smiled thinly. "I could see how one might feel that way if he knew himself incapable of making meaningful contributions to the discussion—"

"Vice Captain Sorel!" Albrecht interrupted, sternly waving a finger. "You are certainly making an impression today, but not an advisable one."

Lurande had an unmistakable sneer on his face, while Osterfeld remained aloof. Eurich appeared to be holding back an outburst with great effort.

"My apologies, sir." Sorel bowed and finally took his seat. The man to his right shook his head and threw him a disapproving glance.

"Vice Captain Sorel, we understand your concerns," Mortigan said. "We have considered a multitude of scenarios that may unfold based on our decision to rotate out troops."

The general leaned back in his chair and probed the audience until his eyes rested on Sorel, who looked down immediately upon making eye contact. "The plan will move forward tomorrow as detailed earlier. I am adjourning this meeting." Having regained most of his composure, Mortigan took a deep breath as his voice reverted to his base tone. "Good day, officers. Dismissed!"

He rose from his chair, walked to a door on stage, and exited. The colonels filed out after him, followed by Eurich, who avoided eye contact with everyone and kept a distance from the colonels.

When Eurich was gone, the lower officers dispersed, breaking into smaller groups.

"I have to say I agree with Vice Captain Sorel," Reznik said to Nash in a low voice, not noticing that Arthur Sorel and the man who sat next to him were walking past and stopped when they heard Reznik speaking.

Noticing them, Nash sighed and nodded at the other two men. "Captain Eldrid, Vice Captain."

Sigmund Eldrid, captain of the newly recommissioned 17th Company, was a stern man in his early thirties with short brown hair and sunken eyes. His most notable feature was the long scar running vertically down the left side of his face.

"Hello, Captain Havora," he said. "Arthur might have served a better impression had he resisted the impulse to trade quips with Captain Schaeffer."

"What can I say?" Sorel replied. "The man pushes my buttons. In any case, I thank you, Vice Captain Sylvera. Since we no longer have an official chief strategist, I feel our superiors can sometimes be a bit shortsighted. Someone like Eric Bellard would certainly have spoken up."

Nash's expression soured at the mention of the name. Noticing this, Sorel shrugged and raised his hands defensively. "I'm nowhere near the man he was," he qualified, "but something had to be said."

Nash relaxed and shook his head. "I did not mean to convey any disapproval."

Sorel stepped forward and extended his hand to Reznik, who eyed him uncertainly in return. "I don't believe we've made our acquaintance officially. Pleased to meet you."

After a few ticks of hesitation, Reznik shook Sorel's hand. "Likewise."

The four left through the rear doors and headed for the main stairs, where they went their separate ways.

—2—

The next day, the 26th and 28th companies set out for Tull Rock. On the third day of travel, the two companies set up camp one kilometer east of Elsin Point, the remains of which were recently reinstated as an outpost. It was still more than half a day's travel to the fort at Tull Rock, and the captains decided against overexerting their companies.

The lights of the many campfires flickered at the edge of the forest. Around one of these fires sat the 9th Squad of the 26th Company, currently led by Bethany Lane. The squad had suffered no further losses since the Ertel campaign. Liam Remington, killed in action, and Alphonse Trenton, discharged after the amputation of his left arm, had been replaced by Mason Hunt, a scout, and Nicole Desanolis, a swordsman.

Amy Trenton never returned from her year-end leave. Nobody knew what had become of her, but Madeline assumed she simply did not want to leave her family. She suspected many of her squadmates thought the same. There were no enforced laws against desertion by commoners; there were enough enlistees to refill any vacancies and few of the high officers paid attention to the occasional missing avet unless the party in question was an estated of some repute. Nevertheless, Amy's absence left the 9th Squad with only eight members after Reznik's promotion to vice captain.

There was a noticeable segregation among the members of the 9th Squad as they sat around their fire. Bethany sat by herself, apart from everyone else. The two new members sat on one side and were slightly farther away from the others. Madeline, who sat closest to Mason and Nicole, decided to be more accommodating.

"So, how long have you served, Avet Hunt?" she asked.

Mason scratched his stubble and sucked on a limp, hand-rolled cigarette, a rare sight for Madeline; Outlanders rarely partook in smoking of any kind.

"I suppose, if you count it up, going on eight years, though not much action until now," he said with a chuckle.

"Funny you say that," Madeline said. "It was strange to see Elsin as we passed by. You'd have thought nothing ever happened there. But that was the reason this war started."

"Indeed, indeed," Mason said. Significantly older than most of the squad, he was still a handsome man at twenty-nine and had not suffered any unkind effects of aging. He gave Madeline a wink, which she did not feel was necessary in the slightest.

"Couple more and you'll be set, is that right?" said Cyrus Marcole, who was jabbing at the fire with a poker.

"Looking forward to registering an estate," Mason grinned.

Josef Reinbach, who wrote in his ledger as he often did, raised his head, his pen frozen midstroke. "How's that now?"

Mason blinked. "What?"

"You will be given an estate for your service, even as an avet?"

Cyrus chuckled. "*Lord* Reinbach here doesn't know the terms of service for us unrefined folk."

"Did you really not know, all this time?" Patrice Konith said.

Josef shrugged.

"Unestated can become estated after ten years of service," Cyrus said. "Or upon retirement as an officer. That's the draw for most of us, isn't it?"

"Ten years, really?" Josef said with wonderment. "That long for compensation? It seems altogether scarce, doesn't it?"

"Scarce?" Patrice said in confusion. She rummaged through her medical bag, only half-listening, though she could hardly be blamed. Josef's idiosyncratic Coranthian had improved surprisingly little over the past year.

"I know what he means," Cyrus said. "We are given our dues upon retirement even if we don't make it to ten years or get a promotion. Just not an estate."

All of this was apparently new to Josef, who rubbed his forehead. "What is the service quota for unestated?"

"Two years."

Nicole spoke up for the first time since they sat down. With short brown hair that barely reached her neck and a crooked nose, she was the youngest and newest member of the group, having just graduated from Barrington at the end of the Reunion.

Josef angled his head contemplatively. "So unestated enlisted in the military can leave after two years, but if they stay for ten they will get an estate. Do you receive anything for only two years of service?"

"A lousy pension," Mason said.

Patrice cast her eyes downward to her bag, consternation creeping into her round face.

"What are you looking for?" Madeline asked.

"Oh, nothing." Patrice tied her bag closed and stood up. Hauling it over her shoulder, she sauntered off in the direction of the officers' tents.

Madeline watched as Patrice left. The two of them had become closer over time, though Madeline wasn't exactly sure if she'd consider them good friends. Patrice was generally kind and agreeable, though somewhat socially awkward and occasionally prone to mood swings and anxiety.

"I thought the minimum service requirement was only a year," Josef spoke, redirecting all eyes to him.

"That's just for you estated folks," Nicole responded.

"Unestated are required to serve twice as long as estated? As I understand it, their conditions for real advancement are quite steep. It seems imbalanced to me," Josef mused.

There came a short bark of laughter from Cyrus. "We commoners are expendable and easily enticed. The system works."

"Some of us do not do this only for material gain," Nicole said quietly, staring at her feet. Philip's approving nod went unnoticed by her.

"I concur," Mason said, gnawing on what remained of his cigarette. "Don't get me wrong, I want my mansion and all that, but ten years is a hell of a long time to put in if you really don't have any other motivation. Might as well not waste your youth as a soldier and risk your life, just to get a nice house and lowly title. What do you think?"

His question was directed at Josef, but the latter had apparently lost interest in the conversation after his previous statement and was again busily writing.

Cyrus frowned and mumbled something, though no one could make out what he said. He abruptly withdrew his sword and began judiciously sharpening it.

Mason appeared unwilling to let the thread of the conversation go. He addressed his previous question to Nicole: "Well, what about you? You can't be a day over, what … eighteen, nineteen? You sure you want to …"

He cast a sidelong glance at Bethany, who sat by herself on a log, slightly apart from everyone else, though within earshot.

Madeline had been occupied with a phalsen she roasted over the fire. She listened only vaguely as she ate, but her ears pricked at Mason's words. She followed his gaze and stared at Bethany, reflecting on what an enigma the new squad leader had become. The period of leave after Liam's death did not seem to have rejuvenated her. She often came across as cold or bored. Even Philip did not have much luck rousing her from her diffidence.

Nicole frowned. "There's no need to presume what I want or do not want."

"Well, I wouldn't want any of my younger siblings enlisting, that's for sure. They're better off at home minding the farm. One of us in the army is enough," replied Mason.

"How old are they?" Nicole asked.

"Let's see. I'm the oldest. My oldest sister is twenty-six. We're practically the third and fourth parents. Then there's sixteen, thirteen, ten, eight, and seven."

This information invoked looks of surprise from everyone.

"That's quite the litter," Cyrus said. "Don't see that much these days."

"Indeed," Josef said with a nod. "I was under the impression that unes-tated birth rates had declined significantly over the past decade."

"In the Outlands, sure," Mason said. "But there are still a few big fam-ilies in Lynderas. I guess we might be a bit better off there. Still not well off though."

The squad soon dispersed. Madeline wanted to crawl into her tent and sleep, but there was something she could not let lie. She made her way through the camp until she reached the officers' area. The officers had in-dividual tents, each with their horses tied nearby. Madeline recognized the scarring along the side of Reznik's new zephyr, Gambit. She approached the tent just beside him.

"Reznik?"

"Come in," came his muffled voice.

Madeline brushed the covers aside and entered. He sat cross-legged on his groundspread, which was essentially a minimattress. The first volume of *A History of Coranthia* lay open on his lap in the dim candlelight.

"How many times have you gone through that? Do you never tire of it?"

He snapped the tome closed and laid it aside. "Was there something you needed?"

Madeline frowned at the curt nonreply. She sat down on the ground opposite him.

"I want to talk to you about the squad."

His blue eyes drifted briefly before refocusing on her. "Sure, what is it?"

"Sergeant Lane seems in a perpetual malaise. I have no reason to doubt her capacity to lead the squad, but she's disengaged and distant. It's like she's a completely different person now."

Reznik ran a hand through his wavy hair. "Does anyone share your thoughts?"

"Patrice admits to feeling awkward around her at times."

"What of … Avet Desanolis? That's her name, if I'm not mistaken."

"Keeps to herself. The opposite of Avet Hunt, I'd say."

"Oh, yes. Mason Hunt," he huffed, as if trying to purge the name from his mouth. For reasons unknown, he did not harbor a favorable impression of the man.

"What do you think?" she asked after he had lapsed into silence.

"I trust your account, of course," Reznik said. "I don't speak much with Sergeant Lane. If the squad has to worry about what's bothering her, it could lower morale." He pressed his lips together. "I guess we may need a new sergeant."

"Who?"

"You, obviously, would be the best choice."

As she turned this over in her head, not without apprehension, he grinned the familiar grin that she was used to seeing when they were not in uniform. It was like the flip of a switch; suddenly, she felt at ease.

"Are you sure?" she murmured.

"What kind of question is that? We can't make the switch in the middle of an operation, though, unless the situation is really dire." He uncrossed his legs and stretched them in front of him. "It won't be a problem. Nobody will question your appointment."

She nodded, not having fully processed the notion of becoming sergeant. She knew she would spend quite a bit of time turning it over in her head in the foreseeable future.

"I'll bring it up with the captain." Reznik smirked. "You know, you could have just gone to him directly. Besides, he's in charge of the upper platoon, and you already meet with him often enough, what with your insistence on learning all about his secret concoctions. You think I don't know about that?"

Madeline wrinkled her nose. "I've probably seen more of him than I have of you lately," she said accusingly.

"And that," he said, "gives me another reason to promote you. Having you at the sergeant meetings will make them much more bearable."

"Wow, good save there."

Reznik laughed softly. "We'd best retire for the night and prepare ourselves for tomorrow."

"Yeah, you're right." She rose, though only partly, as the tent was not made to accommodate a fully upright stance. "Good night, then."

"Good night, Madeline."

She brushed the tent covers back and stepped out.

When she returned to her squad's campsite, only Mason and Bethany were still to be seen. The others had presumably settled into their tents. Mason seemed as forward as ever and attempted to coax Bethany into conversation with forays into an assortment of topics. The latter showed little interest in matching his verbosity but did appear to pay attention.

As she circumvented them, keen not to draw attention to her presence, Madeline was struck by pangs of discomfort and regret. She had gone behind Bethany's back. There was once a time when it was unthinkable for

Madeline to consider Bethany ill fit to take a leadership role. Madeline remembered when Reznik thought Bethany more deserving to be captain than Nash, but now he was considering demoting her from sergeant without reservations. Things were different, of course; Reznik's opinion of Nash had changed, and Madeline's experience made for a good candidate in her own right. Still, she could not help feeling sadness for Bethany.

She crawled into the tent the two shared, shook off her boots and coat, and lay down on her own uneven and flimsy groundspread. The moment her head hit the pad, she felt extremely tired. The light and crackling of the fires outside faded as she drifted off to sleep.

The rough and occasionally hazardous terrain comprising even the most negotiable route from Argiset to Tull Rock required all mounts to be left at Elsin so as not to slow either company; officers traveled alongside their subordinates on foot. The soldiers toughed staggering cliffs, ridges, rocky slopes, and rapid elevation changes almost the entire rest of the way. Despite covering a relatively short distance, the second leg of the journey to Tull was significantly slower than the first.

Spurred by the tireless command of the Curtlands, the 26th and 28th companies navigated the tail end of the narrow, uneven, and forested terrain at the feet of the Alcone Mountains to the north and northwest at a relatively quick pace. While Mortigan and Havora had estimated their arrival on the morning of the thirty-fifth, the contingent pushed forward late into the night of the thirty-fourth with the expectation of reaching Tull near new arc.

Reznik and Nash had begun to descend a steep foothill when they heard the voice of Jasmine Curtland as she broke through the rear line of her company.

"Captain! Captain Havora!"

Accompanying the co-captain of the 28th was Reznik's friend Glen Emerett, who had recently been promoted to sergeant of the 2nd Squad, as well as the leader of the 5th Squad, Torin San Aldorett, a young man with deep-set eyes and shoulder-length black hair.

"What is it, Captain?" Nash asked with concern.

Jasmine wiped away beads of sweat from her forehead. "Sergeant Emerett scouted ahead and saw smoke and fire in the direction of our fort."

As she spoke, she motioned toward Glen, who offered Nash a quick salute.

"In all likelihood," she continued, "Tull Rock is under attack."

Reznik could not see far through the trees and cliffs from where they stood. Earlier, he thought he had seen light in the distance but paid it little heed. Now, he detected a faint scent of smoke.

"Have you given the order to rush the fort?" Nash asked.

"No, not yet," Jasmine said. "We need to discuss how to proceed."

"We must not rush in carelessly with our current formation," Reznik said. "Filing out of the forest into a battlefield of which we have no surveillance would be disastrous."

After the three officers offered ideas on their course of action, they quickly drew up a plan. Jasmine set off immediately, with Glen and Aldorett close behind, and reunited with her sister. The soldiers in front of them snapped to attention as the Curtlands passed. When the two reached the head of the procession, Jasmine turned to Glen and Aldorett, who stood first in their respective lines.

"We will advance on the fort and split once we are within two hundred meters of the clearing. You will each lead your file along the tree line. We will encircle the fort and join the battle when Rosalina signals, so pay attention. I know you will see and hear things that will make you want to break ranks, but *do not* do so under any circumstances. We have outlined the most efficient procedure. Noise will be kept to a minimum. Avets will acknowledge by signal only. Is this understood?"

"Yes, Captain!" Glen and Aldorett answered in unison. The other soldiers within earshot nodded once but said nothing, as per their orders.

With that, the two Coranthian companies began their approach on the fort at Tull Rock. The 2nd and 5th squads of the 28th separated at the point designated by Jasmine, who anchored there to direct traffic with the 6th Squad at her side. Rosalina forged straight ahead from the mark to scout the battle as Aldorett circled to the north of the eastern clearing and Glen to the south. When Nash and Reznik, leading the 26th Company, reached Jasmine's position, she left to join the southern flank. Shortly after, Rosalina, who crept back and forth along the inner edge of the tree line, trying with little success to gauge the battle, independently turned north to join the Aldorett-led half of the 28th. These movements were methodical and exact, despite poor visibility and mobility, and took around ten reps to complete.

The soldiers hurtled through the uneven undergrowth, hearts pounding, breathing accelerated. They heard flames crackling, swords clanging, and people screaming, but they lacked a proper view of the battlefield, as there was still significant separation from the clearing. They fanned out and waited tensely. Most looked into the night sky through the branches of the trees that had not yet fully leaved.

"Look, there's Rosa," Jasmine said. She pointed to the sky, where half a dozen crossbow bolts coated with lit selim sap sailed over the clearing. "Time to move. Now."

Without waiting for acknowledgment, she raised her ax and charged.

Standing beside Glen, Douglas Drake glanced apprehensively at his friend, who caught his eye and nodded before springing forward to follow Jasmine as she burst from the cover of the trees.

Across the square kilometer of the military installation and geographical landmark that was collectively known as Tull Rock, Coranthians and Amelarens tangled in a blur of weapons, bodies, debris, and flames. The Coranthian storehouse, which lay between the two main buildings of the fort, had been set ablaze by a burning fallen watchtower. To the west, Amelarens swarmed the small two-story barracks, while increasingly desperate Coranthian defenders struggled to hold them off. A group of soldiers attempting to join the fray from the entrance of the command post to the east were hemmed in by more Amelarens who had driven directly into the heart of the encampment and split the defending forces into two groups. The twisted, irregular rock formations winding through the clearing hosted a number of strategic chokepoints that had been all but overrun by the Amelarens, who used the advantages offered by the positions at higher elevations to pick off isolated soldiers.

The sudden arrival of Coranthian reinforcements did not immediately draw the attention of the Amelarens besieging the barracks, who were preoccupied with a number of crossbowmen shooting from the second-story windows. This allowed Jasmine, leading the charge of the southern flank of the 28th Company, to run unimpeded to the nearest warrior and bury her ax into his neck. At the same time, Rosalina Curtland and Sergeant Aldorett led the other half onto the battlefield from the north.

Jasmine and Rosalina each began to carve a path through to the barracks. As Jasmine barreled directly into the enemy ranks, Glen and Gertrude Chandlin, an avet in his squad, supported her on either side. Douglas followed closely behind, doing his best to poke his spear at whatever blind spots opened between the three leaders. He was joined by two other lancers. The makeshift vanguard met with little resistance, blitzing through the Amelarens, many of whom were caught by surprise and began to fall back.

Standing at the tree line southwest of the barracks, Reznik and Nash had a clear line of sight to where Jasmine's group engaged the Amelarens.

"Looks like we may have given the enemy too much credit, Reznik," Nash said. "The 28th has practically walked up to the barracks. This is actually rather odd."

Reznik frowned. "Something is wrong. Why was there a breach if that were the case? I find it strange that we were able to cut through despite the fact that the defenders were pushed back into the buildings."

"No point in dwelling on it now," Nash replied. "Let us join them."

Reznik nodded and turned around to where most of the 26th huddled within earshot. There was no reason to remain quiet.

"Forward!" Reznik cried, briefly catching Madeline's eye before looking away.

A roar went up from the avets as Nash and Reznik led them into the open.

Jasmine and Rosalina converged on the front door of the barracks. Jasmine grinned upon seeing her sister completely unscathed, without even one flowing hair out of place.

She approached the door and began to pound on it. "This is the 28th Company! Open up immediately!"

"Captain Curtland? Is that you?" a male voice called from within.

"Open the door, damn it!" Jasmine returned.

Within ticks, the door flew open. The man standing before Jasmine wore a captain's uniform.

"Captain Frasier," Jasmine said. "It's good to see you."

Lowell Frasier, captain of the 11th Company, bowed slightly. "Likewise. Please come to the second floor with me. Leave your soldiers to hold the perimeter."

"Take a few with you and leave the rest to me," Rosalina said, before Jasmine could even turn to address her.

Jasmine scanned the personnel around her before counting off Douglas Drake and the two lancers. "You three come with me. Emerett, Chandlin, you stay with Rosalina."

Douglas followed the two sergeants up the stairs and then around to the hallway. Looking out the small window, Douglas could see Rosalina setting up positions around the barracks. Further down the corridor, crossbowmen continued shooting at the Amelarens, who retreated east toward the burning storehouse.

"The 11th and 39th were ordered to rotate to Argiset," Jasmine said to Frasier. "What happened?"

"Overruled by the colonel," Frasier replied. "He thought the fort would come under attack, so everyone stayed. And he was right."

"Four companies strong. And yet you're in this predicament. Why were you driven back so easily?"

"We have not been able to make much sense of their movements. They besieged the buildings but have not tried to break down the doors. On the other hand, the initial attack was brutal and relentless and drove our forces apart. Most of the 19th and 39th have been annihilated. Captain Shelton barely managed to withdraw into the command post. Incidentally, the colonel seems to be doing well there."

"What of Captain Parisse?" Jasmine inquired.

Frasier averted his gaze, but the answer was written across his face.

Jasmine sighed. "Who is leading the enemy?"

"I do not know," Frasier said. "We have spotted one or two warriors in elbar attire, but nobody of higher rank. The enemy armor is painted a dark color, so, at night, it is difficult to tell exactly who the leader is."

"I find it unlikely that this attack is being led solely by elbars," Jasmine said in a low voice.

Frasier nodded.

"I'm still trying to process the fact that they were able to move such a large force up the cliffs to the east," Jasmine continued, kneading her brow. "Was no one on watch?"

"We lost contact with the scouts," Frasier said grimly, "which means either they were extremely stealthy or they sent out a group in advance to neutralize our lookouts."

"Give credit where it's due," Jasmine growled through her thin lips. "First Ertel and now this. We can't afford to keep underestimating them."

She moved away from the window, allowing Douglas to regain his place. Torin San Aldorett, who had also made his way into the barracks, squeezed in next to him.

"Well, now we've evened the playing field, at least," Jasmine said, placing her ax and shield on a small table nearby. She wiped her hands with a handkerchief and then reached back to retighten the hair clip that held her long locks in a coil. "I don't suppose you were able to save anything in the storehouse?"

Frasier managed only an awkward shrug.

"And why have they not tried to burn this building?" Jasmine wondered. "They wanted to keep the barracks intact but not the storehouse?"

"I do not know that, either," Frasier admitted.

Jasmine shook her head exasperatedly.

Outside, most of the 26th had swarmed the barracks. Reznik ran to Rosalina's side. The senior Curtland had her back to a large boulder at the foot of the paths leading to the middle of the compound and was occasionally peeking at the gaggle of Amelarens that shuffled around the storehouse.

"Are they regrouping?" Reznik asked.

"Hard to say," Rosalina replied. "We have limited vision. They currently control the high ground."

It was this fact that prevented the Coranthians from simply rushing uphill to engage the enemy.

Reznik said, "We have to go. Now. We cannot allow the Amelarens the luxury of fortifying their position around the command post. I'll take the northern path, and you take this one. Advance with full shields."

Rosalina nodded, and as Reznik headed off to prepare the 26th, she gathered most of the 28th around her, issued orders, and placed herself in the middle of her soldiers. The swordsmen rushed to the front and began to make their way up the hill through the rocks toward the Amelaren position. Glen stayed close to Rosalina, while Chandlin anchored the rear. On the northern path, Reznik arranged his troops similarly and marched directly behind the shield bearers of the 26th, while Nash brought up the tail end of the formation.

The Amelarens did not idle and immediately began to pelt both groups of soldiers by throwing axes, arrows, and stones. Some of the missiles penetrated the Coranthian walls of shields and downed several frontliners. Both companies advanced steadily. Some Amelarens tried to launch their projectiles over the shields, but these shots were weaker and generally ineffectual. Several warriors rashly attempted to climb the surrounding rocks to obtain clear downward shots, and this made them victims of target practice for Rosalina and other crossbowmen who anticipated their every move. Lit braziers provided sufficient light for the Coranthians to navigate the winding paths, though also allowed the Amelarens to focus fire on them. In effect, each trail was a no-mans-land in which it was extremely disadvantageous to remain long.

Jasmine and Captain Frasier watched the situation unfold from the second floor of the barracks, maintaining hold over a small group of defenders left to secure the building.

"Move too quickly and the ranks are exposed," Frasier remarked. "Move too slowly and they'll be whittled down."

"Time to join the party," Jasmine said, picking up her equipment from the table.

No sooner had she started down the stairs than a group of warriors burst forth from the southern tree line, the same place from which the Jasmine-led flank of the 28th emerged earlier. Before any remaining soldiers patrolling the perimeter of the barracks could react, the Amelarens fell quickly upon Rosalina's group, hacking through what was mostly a congregation of scouts and medics designated to the rear of the formation.

As if on cue, half of the Amelaren warriors around the charred storehouse charged down the hill, rushing the now-pincered troops on the rocky paths. Rosalina, who had only just begun to face the rear attackers, was forced to redirect her attention to the frontal assault. The other half headed down the northern path to clash with Reznik, Nash, and the 26th, who maintained their form, having remained relatively undisturbed.

Sensing that the jaws were about to clamp down on the 28th, Rosalina scrambled for a diversion. She hoisted herself up on one of the lower-hanging crags to the north and climbed atop the rocky partition, separating the two paths. She caught a glimpse of a female elbar with a bow on her back running toward the barracks. Rosalina immediately gave chase, following the alpha warrior along the tops of the rocks as inconspicuously as she could.

Jasmine cracked open the barracks front door in time to see the elbar simultaneously kill two soldiers and hurry around the bend, ostensibly circling to where the 26th battled the Amelarens anchoring the central hill. From her position, Jasmine could not see the 26th but did catch a glimpse of Rosalina darting across the partition in the same direction. For a moment, Jasmine wondered whether Rosalina had made the right decision and whether leaving the company to fend for itself was worth the pursuit of this lone Amelaren. She did, though, implicitly trust her sister. She felt a twinge of regret; bloodlust pulsed through her in anticipation of facing the elbar, but as a captain, she could not abandon the 28th. She joined the fray outside the barracks.

Nash and Reznik had led the 26th in establishing a foothold near the storehouse remains. The plan was to reunite the 26th and 28th there, and when Reznik saw that the other company had not yet broken through its contingent of assailants, he directed his troops to cut a path along the southern rock wall of the trail through to the hilltop. He kept an eye out for any elbars or war chiefs and spotted none.

With Rosalina's divergence, the 28th was in temporary disarray. Glen tried to shepherd the soldiers up the hill. He had made his way to the lower end of the formation just as the elbar ran off, and he did his best to hold off the Amelarens with whatever support he had in order to buy time for his fellow soldiers to maintain their shielded advance. Eventually, they were indeed able to push through to the hilltop.

Reznik spotted the 28th and drove the 26th straight toward them. Meanwhile, Rosalina continued to chase the elbar, but had trouble keeping pace with the Amelaren warrior, even as she abandoned caution in favor of an all-out run. It wasn't long before the elbar came up on the rear of the 26th. The elbar removed her bow and climbed the rock formation that followed the path. As she moved, following the rear of the 26th, she began firing arrow after arrow into the formation.

Three men dropped before Nash realized what was happening. The soldiers next to him began shouting.

"Behind us!" Nash shouted. He turned around to see only the dimly lit path they had been following, and no enemy. Within a tick, two more soldiers dropped, shouting as they clutched their wounds. Nash swiveled his head and looked around, though saw nothing. More arrows rained in, several ticks apart.

Panic overcame the captain and his soldiers. Nash was uncertain of the best course of action. He did not know where the shots originated and how many archers were upon them.

"Shields, guard yourselves and those without heavy armor! I'm going to make my way to the front to inform the vice captain. Right now, we need to keep moving."

Nash left the rear in disarray, pushing his way to the front toward Reznik. He did not have any ideas of what to do and hoped for the sake of their soldiers that Reznik did.

Shortly after Nash left the rear, Rosalina stopped running, finally catching up to the elbar. As the latter slowed, Rosalina prepared to take a shot. She removed her crossbow and took aim at the elbar, who continued to dart back and forth along the edges of the rock, maintaining erratic movements to maximize the confusion of the soldiers below.

As the elbar stopped to fire another set of arrows, Rosalina pressed the trigger. Her bolt flew straight into the side of the elbar's head. The female warrior collapsed and fell off the rock formation onto a group of soldiers who shouted in surprise.

Rosalina watched for a few ticks as the soldiers scrambled to make sense of what happened. She returned the crossbow to its holster and continued along the rock formation to the front of the 26th.

What remained of the 26th and 28th companies reunited as one force. With the extra maneuvering room at the hilltop, they were in a much better position to take the Amelarens from all sides, and they now faced the ambushers to the southwest. To the north, and on the other side of the storehouse, stood the rest of another elbar's contingent. The Amelarens continued to besiege the command post. The charred remains of the storehouse had finally extinguished, and, as a result, the battlefield had grown darker; the scouts who carried rodtorches hurried to light them.

Nash pushed his way through the mass of reorganizing soldiers to Reznik, who eyed the young captain curiously as he gasped for breath.

"What happened to you?" Reznik asked.

"There is someone following us up the path, picking us off left and right," Nash said between heaves. "Maybe more than one."

Reznik opened his mouth to reply, but at that moment, Rosalina shouted a warning and leaped from atop the western partition, landing neatly in front of several astonished avets who quickly recovered and absorbed her into the Coranthian aggregate.

"I apologize for taking so long to catch up, Captain," Rosalina said to Nash. "It was just one. A female elbar. She will not be giving us any more problems."

Nash gave her a grim look and was about to respond when a deafening crash distracted him. Nearby, the reinforced walls of the command post gave way. Soldiers began to pour out both sides, surprising the Amelarens who were oriented to attack the building head-on from the west. Droves of soldiers launched directly into the enemy ranks; the relatively plodding siege quickly turned into a frenzied melee.

Reznik and Nash only partially saw what happened and inferred the rest.

"I understand now," Nash said. "The colonel waited until we established a footing here. Now he has made his move."

Colonel Theodore Dyers emerged from the opening in the northern wall, riding his steed, Iria. He raised his sword, as if it was an instrument of divine wrath. His bullish face, his mounted status, and the fact that both he and his horse were completely covered with the armor of Coranthian blue and gold made him an imposing sight.

The colonel rode to the central hill, carelessly trampling a warrior along the way, and pulled up beside the storehouse, drawing the attention of all who saw him, including a single massive warrior and a male elbar.

"I must say, I am quite surprised," Dyers bellowed as he swung to face the warrior and elbar, drawing a menacing snort from Iria.

The warrior beside the elbar was large, even by Amelaren standards, though held only a plain sword and wore standard armor. Ostensibly, he was a common foot soldier. To onlookers, it appeared Dyers was addressing the elbar.

The colonel continued, "I have fought your kind many times and usually you are all too keen to be the center of attention, be it through carnage or attire. It took quite some time to identify you. The visibility conditions are quite poor, but I knew one of you was out there. This could not have been the work of elbars." He chuckled. "You're a sly one, aren't you? Honestly, I was not sure who I would find. It is an honor to fight against the great Sol."

War Chief Sol stepped forward as he pushed the elbar aside and spoke in a soft, thickly accented Laestran. "The honor is mine."

He bowed deeply, almost to his ankles, and then walked slowly and purposefully toward Dyers.

"Humph," Dyers growled, and yanked the reins again to reorient Iria.

Nash heard someone near him yelp in a strained voice. "Sol? Did he say *Sol*?"

"Stay focused," Rosalina cut in sternly. "Captain Havora, we need to take this opportunity to reunite with the 7th. That may be what the colonel intends by drawing all this attention to himself."

"I agree," Nash said, regaining his composure. "On the other hand, we still have the barracks defenders to consider."

"We must follow His Excellency's cue," Rosalina said.

Nodding, Nash raised his voice to address the soldiers: "Move east! Link up with the 7th and 39th!"

The tentative standoff between the elbar's forces to the north and the combined 26th and 28th ended as the Coranthians began to shuffle eastward toward the mass of soldiers and warriors battling near the command post, which was now all but abandoned. Unfortunately for the two companies, the elbar had no intent of letting them out of his sight. He roared to signal the charge of the warriors around him.

Reznik realized the elbar's contingent would be upon his forces before they could reach their allies to the east. He informed Nash, who planted his feet and yelled, "26th, halt!"

Half the Coranthians atop the central hill immediately stopped. Rosalina turned and stared inquisitively at Nash.

"Captain Curtland, please proceed. The 26th will buy you time to reach the colonel's forces."

Rosalina hesitated only briefly and then nodded, staring directly into Nash's eyes, then into Reznik's. Then, to the 28th: "You heard Captain Havora. Move!"

The elbar did not understand Laestran but caught on immediately and whooped again, intensifying his run to almost an all-out sprint, prompting his warriors to do the same. The soldiers of the 26th stood prepared to meet them.

Rosalina visually estimated the weakest concentration of Amelarens in the mass of warriors, separating the 28th from the Coranthians on the other side. She emptied her supply of bolts as quickly as she could while making sure each shot counted; she was able to down half a dozen enemies before holstering her crossbow to pull out her knife.

Dyers trotted slowly toward Sol, who eyed the colonel and brandished a fork-tongued sword with his right hand, which he removed from a sheath attached to the back of his jade leather armor. Sol held the weapon loosely and only half-raised. His face was the portrait of inert, almost deathly calm, even as he broke into a run. Dyers took a deep breath and spurred his horse to speed up.

Twin flashes of steel pierced the darkness once, twice, thrice. Dyers grunted from a glancing blow that was so strong he nearly fell off his horse, but he remained uninjured and undeterred. He smacked the rump of his horse with the handle of his sword. Iria whinnied and readied herself to charge again.

With Sol fighting Dyers and the elbar focused on the 26th, there was no discernible command holding together the Amelarens fighting on the eastern side of Tull Rock, while each of the two Coranthian companies on either side coordinated with the discipline of the other. Within reps, the 7th had managed to maneuver around the Amelaren force such that the former was able to link with the 28th, and the latter was pushed back toward the empty command post.

The elbar was enveloped in a killing frenzy. Nash and Reznik attempted to steady their soldiers, but the elbar's disruptive and relentless brutality imposed the intended effect on many of the avets, especially those less experienced, who became all but paralyzed with terror. Unlike Sol, the elbar lacked discipline in his attacks and reveled in the carnage. One of his mighty ax swings cut completely through the armor of one soldier, tearing the soft flesh underneath and spilling the inner contents. As the unfortunate victim wailed and collapsed, the elbar kicked him aside and split the forehead of the soldier behind him without even blinking. Those following him fed off his furor and many tried their utmost to match him blow for blow.

Captain Jane Shelton of the 39th Company, who had formerly commandeered the troops at the command post under Dyers, approached Rosalina. Shelton was a young, portly woman whose unimpressive stature contrasted her hardened black eyes and scarred upper lip, which shaped her mouth into a permanent half-sneer. She had served many years under Dyers and earned the respect of her subordinates.

"Vice Captain Curtland," Shelton said quickly and urgently, "my orders from the colonel were to retreat once you met up with us."

Rosalina Curtland nodded; she was not one to dissect the decisions of her superiors.

"Then we shall."

"What about the 26th?" Shelton asked.

Rosalina looked briefly behind her and turned back to face Shelton. "They will join us later. We should consolidate ourselves first."

"All troops fall back to the barracks!" Shelton hollered.

From the other side of the storehouse, Dyers permitted himself a small smile of satisfaction. He continued to swipe ineffectively at Sol, though despite being a larger target, the colonel had little trouble holding his own against the feared war chief.

Unfortunately, the 26th was in complete disarray and suffering heavy casualties, even as Reznik stepped in to stifle the elbar's rampage. Nash separated himself from the fight, stealing off to the side. He was not idling or cowering but racking his brain for a way to turn the tide in the Coranthians' favor as he watched Reznik and the elbar battle. Fumbling in his waist pouch, he withdrew a book of matches, as well as a small flask of selim, normally used to light his rodtorch; Rosalina had used hers earlier on her crossbow bolts, converting them into signal flares. Taking a deep breath, he began to edge closer to the fracas, lining up behind the captain.

His eyes darting around him, Nash unwrapped the starter cloth from the end of his rodtorch and lit it with a match. As he crept behind Reznik, he uncorked the stopper from the vial of selim and replaced it with the starter, just as the elbar's head popped into view. Seized by a rush of adrenaline, Nash darted from behind Reznik and hurled the vial at the elbar with all his might. The makeshift cocktail worked exactly as Nash had intended, striking the elbar square in the chest and erupting in a billow of fire.

Everyone except Nash froze at the unexpected development. The elbar did not react immediately either and then roared, more in surprise than pain, and thrashed about as the selim bomb flared and lashed at his skin and armor.

Reznik opened his stance, ready to take the offensive, his eyes locked in fierce concentration on the elbar. A stumbling beacon of flame, the elbar blindly swung his ax, desperately shaking himself as if to extinguish his predicament. His wildness made him dangerous. Reznik had to pick the right time to strike. When the elbar could stand it no longer and dropped his ax, Reznik wasted no time. He leaped forward and drove his sword through the elbar's armor, puncturing his stomach. The elbar let out another cry. This one was sharper, singularly piercing. He fell. The entire sequence took no more than half a rep.

Just as quickly, a trio of warriors, unnoticed by Reznik as he had honed in on the elbar, flanked the vice captain, recognizing the danger their commander was in. They were too late to stop Reznik but carried through and struck him. Reznik reacted in time to evade the first two, though never saw the third.

Then he heard a woman behind him shout. "Philip!"

Reznik whirled to his left. Philip Dyson was doubled over before him, writhing in pain. The hilt of a dagger protruded from his chest.

Bethany Lane charged, crossbow in hand, followed by the 9th and 14th squads. Arrows from her crossbow, and those of other soldiers, flew one after another, piercing three warriors' chests. The soldiers attempted to reach Philip, who had slumped over.

Reznik stood stock still as warriors gathered around the fallen elbar, who had ceased to emit any sound. Bethany could not reach Philip before the enemy caught them.

Just as the Amelarens were about to surround the exposed squads, a Coranthian ax flew through the air and split open a warrior's skull. The Amelaren next to the victim glanced upward to the top of the partition and was met with a boot to her face. Jasmine Curtland used her body to soften her landing and launched herself at the nearest Amelaren. Several more soldiers followed from atop the partition. Another wave of Coranthians rushed up the southern trail. Jasmine had finally purged the barracks sector of Amelarens, opening a path for retreat.

Reznik, Madeline, Bethany, and Patrice pursued Philip, who crawled toward the northern trail, making his way through Coranthians and Amelarens who paid him no heed as they continued to grapple with one another.

Reznik grabbed Bethany's shoulder and pulled her roughly.

"It's too late."

Bethany stared at him blankly, then: "You have to help him! We can't leave him behind!"

"We don't have time for this," he said. "We have to go or we're all dead."

Reznik briefly caught Madeline's eye. Her sadness was undeniable. She and Patrice instinctively sprang forward at Bethany's plea, but Reznik remained firm.

"Pull back," he said. The three women complied, though only after a moment's hesitation.

The eastern group soon caught up with them. Jasmine called to Rosalina, relief in her voice. "There are reinforcements coming in from the north," Jasmine said. "Frasier put up a front at the barracks. We have to retreat through the southwest. Get everyone out, now. Where's the colonel?"

"The colonel suspected as much," Captain Shelton called, running alongside Rosalina. "He's … facilitating our retreat."

The Amelarens had resumed their occupation of the central hilltop and now controlled the command post as well. Two-thirds of the Tull Rock compound was completely under Amelaren control. North of the storehouse, Dyers and Sol dueled at length, neither giving way, Dyers rounding and charging repeatedly on his steed, while Sol remained defensive, throwing only a few ineffective pokes when Dyers was not immediately bearing down on him. Just as the Coranthians began their retreat down the southern trail, however, Sol managed to stab Iria in the hind leg. The durioness wailed in pain. Dyers was thrown, rolling several meters as he landed, then sprang to his feet, sword at the ready. Many warriors had crowded the two in eager anticipation of the outcome. They understood they were not to interfere; this battle was their war chief's and his alone.

Although still uninjured, Dyers knew he stood less chance against Sol as the battle wore on. Dyers had expended more energy, being constantly on the attack; Sol was younger and faster, and the colonel's armor served to weigh him down. He was aware of the warriors stalking amid the shadows around him. It was time to make his move.

Dyers held his sword in an overhead stance and charged Sol. The war chief tensed and dug his feet into the ground, preparing for a direct clash. Dyers bellowed mightily and brought down his sword. Sol raised his fork-tongued sword to block the blow, but dropped on his back at the last possible moment. This allowed him to kick upward, under the arc of Dyers' sword, and strike the colonel with precision in the solar plexus. Dyers grunted. His arms retracted to his midsection, the sword pulled back. Moving along the rough dirt as easily as if on ice, Sol slid downward, jumped behind Dyers, and kicked him again in the lower back. Dyers flailed helplessly as he fell, sprawling on the ground. Sol reached back with his right arm and then thrust with all his strength at a small slit between the other man's armor and the back of his helmet. The pronged sword plunged into the side of Dyers' neck. The colonel spasmed, kicked his legs feebly, and then was still.

Hearty cheers rose from around the central hilltop, signaling that the Amelaren victory was secure. Sol withdrew his weapon and walked toward the command post.

The Amelaren celebration at the bottom of the hill could be heard by most Coranthians. They immediately knew what had happened and exchanged grim looks; a tortured expression worked into Shelton's visage.

Patrice appeared beside Reznik.

"We've found Avet Dyson," she said, the sadness in her voice subdued by her exhaustion.

Reznik followed her. Philip was not far. He had managed to sneak back to the southern trail and extract the dagger from his chest, but the blood loss and severity of the injury had been too great. His body lay limp against a tree, head turned to the side.

From the north came rumblings of more warriors. The Amelaren reinforcements had finally arrived. The now deserted barracks was all that separated the Coranthians from the surging enemy torrent as they withdrew along its southern wall and southwest into the forest.

Chapter 15

(988.1.41–43)

—1—

The 26th and 28th companies returned to Aldova six days later, accompanied by a host of other soldiers. A small group of scouts rushed back to Aldova to contact Mortigan, who was stunned at the news he received and sent half of them back toward the incoming companies with the message that their officers should meet him and the colonels immediately upon their return.

On the afternoon of the forty-first, following an anxious lunch, colonels Albrecht, Osterfeld, and Lurande filed into Mortigan's eighth-floor office, by far the largest in Aldova, at the end of the Hall of Champions. Two portraits—one of Mortigan and one of his father with the king—hung behind the general's place at the large cherry wood desk where he was seated. Matching half-empty bookshelves lined the wall to Mortigan's right. A large table facing the bookshelves bore the only semblance of clutter within the room. Stacked atop it were numerous maps of Coranthia, the Dynan Midlands, and the Sanmorian Highlands. A clock hung over the table. The only other objects in the room were a richly textured blue banner with the Coranox hanging over the doorway, a steel solistone light fixture hanging from the ceiling, and four identical velvet chairs in front of the desk, three of which were now occupied by the colonels. In all, the room was sparsely decorated despite its size, in contrast to Leynitz's much smaller but overwhelmingly ornate office. Mortigan was long past decorating his military quarters; he saw no reason to grant it the same adornment he did his mansion in Mardena and favored more professional décor in his office.

The high officers waited uneasily and were served coffee to pass the time. The only bachelor in the group, Albrecht, had little to contribute to the idle chatter about family matters. Eventually, he was the one to broach the impending meeting.

"Back to the matter at hand, gentlemen? At the very least, I am grateful that Lord Eurich has already departed. Who knows how he'd interfere if he knew?"

"It is only matter of time," Osterfeld replied, scrunching his eyebrows together. "Once the surveyors catch wind, they'll be off to the races."

"We could forestall that for as long as possible, if necessary," Lurande said.

"Let's not get ahead of ourselves," said Albrecht. "We will wait to hear the full story."

The entourage from Tull was expected around six arc. As Mortigan ordered, the officers from the returning companies went straight to his office. When Landsett, Mortigan's secretary, announced their entry, the colonels moved their chairs around the desk so all four faced the door. One by one, the low officers stepped through the door into the inner room where their superiors awaited.

The general silently counted them. First to enter were the Curtlands. Then came Captain Frasier and Vice Captain Hayes of the 11th, followed by Captain Shelton of the 39th. Finally, Reznik and Nash entered. Mortigan waited several ticks before realizing there would be no one else joining them.

He studied each of their faces and knew his fears had been realized. No one appeared willing to offer the first word.

"Someone had better tell us what happened," he said softly.

Several of the lower officers exchanged glances. Just before Mortigan opened his mouth to repeat his request in a sterner tone, Jasmine Curtland stepped forward. "Very well, General."

It took Jasmine fifteen reps to recount the events at Tull Rock. Heavy silence hung like a thick fog inside Mortigan's office.

The general had propped his elbows on his desk, hands clasped, obscuring his mouth. Mortigan was lost in thought. He shifted slightly in his enormous leather chair.

As usual, Osterfeld seemed detached. He sat back with his hands folded on his lap, staring straight ahead; his mouth did not even twitch. The other colonels failed to match his impassivity, as worry spread plainly across Albrecht and Lurande's faces.

"The colonel's sacrifice affects me deeply," Mortigan said finally. He unwrapped his hands and lowered them slowly to the table. "So does the bravery of all who lost their lives at Tull Rock. The extent of our losses leave me no choice but to decommission the 7th and 19th for now. We need a new colonel for the 7th, but there's no time. Those remaining from the two companies will make up for losses in the 39th, Captain Shelton. It seems you will need to choose a new second as well."

Shelton nodded grimly.

"All other companies returning from Tull are to remain at Aldova on reserve," Mortigan continued. He glanced at the colonels sitting around him. "There will be time to honor the dead, but we must immediately respond to the Amelaren threat. Fortunately, the 3rd Battalion has already prepared to march."

He affixed his gaze on Osterfeld.

"I would like you to reinforce Argiset with the remainder of your soldiers. Go through the Pyrean Valley and secure the northern approach to the plateau."

"Of course, sir," Osterfeld immediately returned.

"While not the fastest route to Argiset, approaching the plateau from the north will allow us to head off any Amelaren advancement from Tull Rock. We are taking precautions against a repeat of the unfortunate scenario that has unfolded. The difficult terrain between Tull and Argiset is the best deterrent against their movement, so even if they leave Tull Rock immediately, which is unlikely, we stand a good chance of catching them at the Valley."

"General," said Osterfeld, "perhaps it may be best for the battalion to deploy this evening? My troops are already set to depart. It should not take much longer to finalize preparations."

Lurande nodded. "Good."

"The cold has not yet dispersed," Mortigan said to Osterfeld. "Camping in this weather can still be quite unpleasant."

"Thank you for your concern. I do not think it will be a problem."

"So be it, then."

"Sir, we volunteer to go," Reznik Sylvera said, to the surprise of the high officers.

Nash Havora nodded and added, "Vice Captain Sylvera and I have discussed this. It would be unbecoming for us to be one of the only companies in the battalion not deployed to Argiset."

"Then we would like to go as well, sir." Jasmine Curtland stepped forward in line with Reznik.

Rosalina followed her sister's cue. "We were able to minimize our own losses," she said, "and if the 26th sees fit to go, it would be inappropriate for us to stay."

Mortigan studied the faces before him, each painted with grim determination.

Lurande shrugged. "Let them go."

"Easy for you to say," Albrecht retorted.

"Do you have an objection, Colonel?" Mortigan asked.

Albrecht frowned.

The general glanced again at Osterfeld. "I will leave it to you."

Osterfeld sat silently for a rep, deep in thought. The others awaited his decision with interest.

"Then we will leave in the morning," he said finally to the companies' officers. "You are to obtain a full night's rest tonight. I believe the extra preparation time will be beneficial now that the battalion is set to march at full strength. The addition of the 26th and 28th will be a welcome one. The crown prince will be grateful for your support."

Reznik and Nash exchanged glances.

"That is all," Mortigan waved them off.

As Reznik turned to leave, he noticed, on either side of the doorway, the two glass display cabinets that housed several ornamental weapons. Among them was a knife with an aeron blade and a gold Coranox painted on the hilt. As he exited the room, he unconsciously touched his belt where his own knife was strapped.

—2—

Reznik wandered Aldova's dimly lit corridors. It was well past one arc. The occasional guard saluted him as he strolled past. He made his way to the dormitory levels and soon found himself standing outside Madeline's room. He stared at the door for several ticks, knowing he was not allowed to enter. There had not been a chance for them to talk privately since the events at Tull, and he greatly wished to speak to her and the rest of the squad about the death of Philip Dyson.

After half a rep, he decided to move on. Ahead of him, the northern end of the hallway opened to a small lounge where several chairs and sofas faced the breathtaking view of Lake Sanmoria and the southern spur of the Alcones Mountains through the large, reinforced floor-to-ceiling windows. Still wide awake, Reznik headed forward and took some time to relax by himself, reasoning that nobody else would be up. He was surprised as he approached the end of the hallway when he heard female voices emanating softly from the lounge. He leaned against the wall to remain out of sight; as a result, he could not see the women who were talking.

"I'm sorry, Beth," came one of the voices.

"Thank you, Jasmine. If I had only kept him closer …"

"He acted on his own," Jasmine Curtland said. "He sacrificed himself to save your vice captain."

"Yes, I know. It's just …" Bethany Lane emitted a sigh choked with emotion. "First Liam, now Philip. I still haven't gotten over Liam."

"I know," Jasmine said with great sympathy. Reznik had never heard her take such a soft tone.

"I'd known him since he was a baby. We rarely saw each other after he left for the academy … I was so happy when I learned we were assigned to the same company last year." Her voice was thick and heavy; she coughed to clear her throat. "I'm rambling. You already know all this."

"It's all right," Jasmine replied soothingly.

"I've had a lot of time to think about this. I have to honor both by not dwelling on their deaths. At the very least, I have to try."

"Yes, I agree. That's a good way to approach things."

"I get the feeling that Vice Captain Sylvera will not tolerate much more of my malaise."

"And what do you think of him?"

Only faintly cognizant of what he was doing, Reznik peeked around the corner. The two women sat facing one another, perpendicular to his line of sight.

"Rarely do I see another commoner with the kind of poise and discipline he has. And he's an Outlander. He reminds me a little of you, Jasmine."

Jasmine chuckled. "Let's not give him too much credit."

"He does try to overcompensate, I think. I get the impression that he bears a great burden for someone else. It strikes me as odd."

"Well, I certainly don't have that problem," Jasmine said with a sniff. "Interesting to know, though. I'm always curious about other unestated officers."

Bethany finally laughed. Her mood seemed greatly improved.

"Always sizing up the competition, aren't you?"

"You know it."

Bethany cleared her throat. "Thank you for talking to me like this. I know you need your sleep for tomorrow. I do as well."

"Anything for you, Beth. You know that. Rosa was really starting to worry, you know?"

"Oh, I'm sure she was," Bethany said slyly. "She does all the worrying for the two of you, right?"

"Of course, of course."

The two women broke into laughter. Quickly, though casually, Bethany tilted her head slightly and made eye contact with Reznik. They stared at each other for several ticks before she nodded faintly at him, her eyes and smile softly reassuring.

Collecting himself, Reznik nodded in return and then pushed himself off the wall and began to tread lightly back down the hallway. The tension he previously felt had lifted. As he made his way through the faded solistone light, his mouth slowly curled into a small smile.

—3—

The Osterfeld battalion departed for Argiset along the same route taken by the initial offensive at the start of the war nearly one year ago. To the west of the campsite that the Coranthians had previously used was a site, southeast of Pyrean Valley, which came to be known as the Pyrean-Argiset Junction, a waypoint between Aldova and Argiset. The junction was situated a short distance before the road to Argiset and split into northern and southern paths. The former led to Pyrean and would be taken by Osterfeld's troops. Before continuing, the colonel decreed that the battalion would camp briefly at Pyrean-Argiset until two arc, with the object of arriving at the valley by next sunrise. After the soldiers set up camp, Osterfeld called a cadre of volunteer scouts to set out for Pyrean at nine arc so they could report back to him just as the rest of the battalion arose.

• • •

It was the dead of night. Blades of grass and small brush rustled as wind blew gently across the highlands. The scurrying of phalsen, the hooting of owls, the whistling of insects—these sounds were accompanied by the low rhythmic march of the Coranthian Army as it emerged from the forests.

At the head of the 5th Company, Colonel Hector Osterfeld rode a large gray durion named Deni, a majestic beast with a thick, flowing mane and a long tail. Beside him, Captain Ferris Schaeffer, now leading Osterfeld's former company, the 27th, kept pace on his own horse, Lunsdal.

"Schaeffer, get me Keller and two other scouts. I want them to go ahead," Osterfeld said in a low voice. Francis Keller, a sergeant in the 27th, had served with Osterfeld during the Coronation War and remained Osterfeld's most personally trusted scout.

"Sir, why'd—" Schaeffer started.

Although stoic at large meetings in the presence of the generals and other colonels, Osterfeld was an entirely different person in the field, unapologetically brusque and domineering. He interrupted Schaeffer almost immediately.

"Yes, the scouts reported back an arc before we left camp, but that is plenty of time for the situation to have changed. I won't have any of your insolence now, Schaeffer."

Schaeffer gaped at the colonel, his mouth snapping shut.

"Now, Captain," Osterfeld almost hissed.

"Yes, sir," Schaeffer said. He jerked his reins and trotted off. Osterfeld watched Schaeffer and his horse fade into the shadows. He could barely see twenty meters in front of him. Rhynon and Faerila were ensconced behind a thick layer of clouds; visibility was poor compared to that of the previous night.

Two reps later, Schaeffer returned with a middle-aged man and two younger soldiers, one male and one female, in tow.

The soldiers saluted Osterfeld, who gestured in vague acknowledgment.

"Your Excellency," the older soldier said with a small smile, "the captain said you wished to see me?"

"Sergeant Keller, I want you and the other avets to go on ahead to Pyrean Valley. Go as far north as you can. You are not to return until either you have verified an Amelaren presence or our forces reach the valley."

The two avets exchanged glances and then looked at Keller.

"Certainly, sir," the sergeant said. "We are happy to oblige."

He saluted. The other two followed suit, and then all three took their leave.

Schaeffer stared after them, amused at the sight of the two younger scouts matching Keller gesture for gesture.

"Captain, I want three more groups. A scout sergeant and two avets in each group, same as with Keller."

Osterfeld's voice brought him back into focus.

"We need a dispatch to cover the southern end of the valley and another two between that group and Keller's," the colonel continued. "What are you waiting for?"

"Yes, sir," Schaeffer grumbled, setting off to carry out his order.

—4—

The four groups of scouts, each from different companies, took less than one and a half arcs to complete their mission, and all had returned by three-arc fifteen, meeting the battalion, which was less than thirty reps away from the valley. Daylight had come, though with a foreboding and drab gray mist. It was oppressively overcast; the clouds stifled the golden shine of Helistos.

The scouts checked in with their commanding officers and then reported directly to Osterfeld. Soon, the colonel gave orders to halt all advance and take a short rest. He called a meeting of officers. Eleven captains and vice captains from five companies formed a cloak of soldiers and horses around him. They stood to the side of the trail, out of earshot of the other soldiers, most of whom eagerly relieved themselves of the weight they carried by leaning against rocks or trees, or simply planting their rears on the ground.

"Let us review the scouts' reports," Osterfeld said to his officers. "I have spoken to Sergeant Keller. His group reached the entrance of the valley just north of the Utrep Scars, at roughly two-arc thirty. Call that Keller Point. By then, the Amelarens already streamed through to the southeast. What were their numbers?"

"Sergeant Keller reported about five hundred warriors emerging from the bend," Schaeffer said. He shot a glance at his vice captain, Gaston, a young, handsome man with sharp features and hair that flowed down to his waist. Assigned the task of recording the discussion, Gaston wrote hastily on a pad.

"How does the timeline match up with the other groups?" Osterfeld said.

"Sergeant Nilson's group reported the sound of war drums, but no visuals on the enemy," Reznik Sylvera said. "Time was two-arc seventy."

"Two and a half kilometers to the south of Keller Point," said Schaeffer, who glanced again at Gaston to make sure that the latter was taking down the figures.

Jasmine Curtland spoke next and gestured on the map. "Sergeant Emerett observed the head of a large group of Amelarens here, moving through at two-arc sixty-five. Estimated numbers of three to four hundred from what he could see."

"Three kilometers farther to the southeast," Reznik continued.

Osterfeld nodded, his eyes falling on Sigmund Eldrid.

"Sergeant Abberdine saw nothing at two seventy-two," the captain of the 17th said, indicating a mark on the map close to the southeastern end of the valley, "but war drums could also be heard. She was here, two kilometers south of Emerett."

"Two kilometers south of Emerett," Gaston droned as he scribbled.

"What is a reasonable estimate of their total size?" Osterfeld demanded.

"Eight hundred, perhaps?" Nash Havora ventured.

"Four hundred from the back and four hundred from the front?" Vice Captain Arthur Sorel said with a frown. "I'll be the pessimist and say at least a thousand."

"That would be problematic indeed," Eldrid remarked.

"Then there is no chance to cut them off before they reach Argiset," said Gregory Valteau, veins bulging in his bald head. Valteau had recently returned to active duty. For most of the previous year, he had served as an instructor at Barrington Academy while his 35th Company was decommissioned, before a surge of new recruits allowed Osterfeld to replenish its ranks.

Eldrid and Sorel exchanged grim looks.

Osterfeld posed another question: "How long before they reach the plateau? Anyone?"

Reznik responded immediately, "Colonel, given our information, I would say nine arcs, but more realistically, eight, and more conservatively, seven."

His assertiveness drew curious glances from Sorel and Schaeffer.

The burly colonel absentmindedly stroked Deni's back, lost in thought.

"Then we must depart immediately!" Schaeffer concluded. "If only we had not made camp—"

"It's unlikely that would have made a difference," Reznik interjected. "We still would have had little chance to catch the Amelarens, even if we had left Aldova immediately upon receiving the initial report. Our original plan was to reach the entrance well before they did, then intercept them."

"I don't understand how they could have moved so quickly," Sorel said, "unless they went straight through Tull Rock after driving out our troops."

"That is most likely the case," Osterfeld surmised. "They had to do just that to ensure unimpeded movement through Pyrean."

"There is no doubt that Argiset was the primary objective all along," Reznik said. "It would be reasonable to assume that the Amelaren forces to the east of Argiset are waiting for a cue from the Tull Rock contingent so that both groups may beset our forces at the plateau simultaneously."

"Go on, Vice Captain," Sorel urged.

"Assume they expected us to come to this conclusion, which would explain why they rushed through Tull Rock. They will anticipate our similar haste to Argiset, though are counting on getting there first and taking the initiative before we have a chance to consolidate with those already at the plateau."

"This scenario, then," Eldrid said, "would allow us to use their maneuvers against them if we properly time our strike. These Amelarens who have just traversed Pyrean Valley are likely exposed to their rear."

"Exactly."

"We should send messengers straight to Argiset to warn General Leynitz of the impending attack," Eldrid urged, "and ensure him we will reinforce him from the west, on the other side of the attacking force."

"Yes, that's the idea," Reznik said. "Pincer their pincer. But we need the fort to trap the Amelarens, so catching them before they reach it will be less than ideal. That would also prevent us from reinforcing the fort if the eastern Amelaren force attacks. We would need to send out additional scouts as we approach the plateau to track the enemy's movements and position the battalion accordingly."

Eldrid and Sorel nodded approvingly. Nash looked between Reznik and Osterfeld, trying to gauge the colonel's assessment of the discussion.

"I cannot agree to this," Schaeffer said, speaking calmly but firmly. "You are proposing we intentionally wait for the enemy to engage our troops at Argiset and begin killing our countrymen."

"This may save many more lives in the end, Captain," Eldrid said.

Reznik added, "We stand a good chance to gain the upper hand if this works."

"And General Leynitz is more than capable of following the plan," Sorel said.

Schaeffer waved a finger at Sorel. "Acting on this specious plan of yours will essentially handcuff the general to await our arrival. Do you think he'll find that agreeable?"

"I am inclined to side with Captain Schaeffer," said Valteau. "The chance of success with such a risky move strikes me as relatively low."

"Perilously low," Schaeffer scoffed.

Nash came to Reznik's defense. "What other choice do we have? Either we engage the western Amelaren force under circumstances we cannot control while being further separated from Argiset, or we attempt to fortify our allies from the southwest, which would be a difficult detour from our present location and would put us in the same pincer the Amelarens have planned for Argiset."

As Schaeffer grasped for a retort, Osterfeld spoke for the first time since Reznik put forth his idea. All eyes turned to him. "I want the sergeants who led the scouting teams called immediately."

He motioned to Fleissmann, the current vice captain of the 35th, a former sergeant appointed to officership from the company's survivors after Ertel. "Let us not waste more time than we already have."

"Yes, sir," said Fleissmann, turning his horse abruptly and trotting away in search of the scouts.

"Eldrid, Havora, Curtlands." Osterfeld rang off the captains of the scouts sent to survey the valley. "I trust you chose these soldiers as I chose Keller, for their skill, familiarity with the region, and their ability to approach the enemy without being compromised."

"Yes, Your Excellency," Nash said.

Jasmine echoed Nash's acknowledgment. Eldrid simply bowed.

"Good. Now, regardless of how we proceed, it is imperative that General Leynitz is informed of the incoming pincer attack. I intend to send the sergeants ahead to carry out this task." Osterfeld's gaze drifted to each of them in turn. "The fewer the better, both in speed and stealth. I want a three-man team, with Keller in charge. That means one of you will lead a separate group back to Aldova to apprise General Mortigan of the situation. Decide among yourselves who that will be by the time Fleissmann returns."

Reznik leaned as far to his right as he could while maintaining his balance atop Gambit and whispered into Nash's ear. The young captain listened intently to his deputy's words. When Reznik finished speaking, Nash nudged his horse forward.

"That won't be necessary, Your Excellency. I volunteer Sergeant Nilson to return to Aldova."

"Any particular reason, Captain Havora?"

A brief shade of uncertainty flickered across Nash's face, though left as quickly as it appeared.

"I believe Sergeant Emerett is better qualified for the mission to Argiset, and Sergeant Abberdine's more experienced."

"Are there any objections?" Osterfeld asked Eldrid and the Curtlands.

"No, sir," Eldrid said.

"No, Your Excellency," Jasmine added.

"So be it."

Reznik took out a pen and sheet of paper from his pocket and began to write, using his stirrup to support his strokes. Nash glanced curiously in his direction, but no one else seemed to notice. When he was done, Reznik folded the paper twice and approached Nash.

"What is it?"

"I know you carry that strange adhesive on you," Reznik said, making sure he was not overheard. "I need it to seal this note."

"What's all this about?"

"Please, not now. Just give it to me."

Nash frowned but complied. Reaching into his bag, he retrieved a small brush, as well as a vial of clear liquid indistinguishable from water to the naked eye. He handed the items to Reznik, who unscrewed the top and poured a small amount of the viscous substance onto the brush. He smeared it over the edges of the paper and folded it together.

Several ticks later, Fleissmann returned with the four scout leaders. Keller, Nilson, Emerett, and Abberdine lined up in front of Osterfeld, who issued the order in his rumbling voice to depart immediately.

Reznik examined each sergeant in turn. He knew Francis Keller by reputation, and beyond the grizzled older man's no-nonsense expression, there was not much to read in him. Of course, he was familiar with Glen Emerett and Jacob Nilson. Glen's recent promotion to sergeant had been all but inevitable. Nilson had been sergeant for some time and thought very highly of himself. He carried on in a manner that made this apparent to everyone who interacted with him. The sergeant was also superficially vain, taking time to ensure that his long sandy brown hair was in pristine condition, even on a campaign. Still, Nilson's skills on the field were impressive, and both Nash and Reznik had come to see him as one of the more reliable squad leaders in the 26th, even if he was difficult to get along with on a personal level. Furthermore, he always followed orders unquestioningly.

The most curious case was Mary Abberdine. Reznik had never met her. She was a young woman with long brown hair tied in a bun. Nothing seemed out of the ordinary about her. What was strange was the effect Mary had on the other officers. A number of them seemed reluctant to look directly at her. Aside from her commanding officers Eldrid and Sorel, only Osterfeld, the Curtlands, and Vice Captain Gaston remained unabashed.

The briefing lasted only several reps. After Osterfeld dismissed all the officers, Nilson proceeded to where Nash and Reznik sat atop their horses upon receiving a beckoning wave of the hand from the latter. As Nilson approached, Reznik climbed off Gambit to speak to the sergeant face to face.

"Vice Captain, I am disappointed I was not selected to go to Argiset," Nilson said, slightly lowering his head.

"Don't be," Reznik said, smiling faintly. "I have another task for you that is just as important." He held out the now-sealed note. "You are to deliver this straight to General Mortigan and no one else. No questions asked. Understand?"

Nilson stared suspiciously at the leaf in Reznik's extended hand and reached to take it carefully. "Of course, sir. In that case, I would be honored."

"Good."

"Sergeants, it is time for you to head out," Osterfeld announced. "We must resume the march."

Nash gestured toward Nilson. "Take two others back to Aldova."

"But don't take anyone from the 9th Squad," Reznik interjected. "I want them all here."

It seemed reasonable for Reznik to want his former squad to stay with him. Nilson nodded and headed off to conduct his mission. Meanwhile, Glen, Mary Abberdine, and Francis Keller had formed their own small group off to one side. Osterfeld gave them a dismissive hand signal. They saluted and took their leave as well.

Nash dismounted his own horse and pulled Reznik aside. "Now you're—"

"What's so special about Sergeant Abberdine?" Reznik asked.

Nash blinked in surprise but quickly recovered. "You don't know who she is?"

Reznik pondered the question for a moment.

"Is she related to the Abberdine family of the Conservatory?"

"The same."

"But that means she's an estated woman … serving in the army? I guess that explains the awkwardness."

"She's a unique case. Let's leave it at that. Now, you're going to tell me what that was all about."

"What?"

"Don't play dumb. What is in the note?"

Reznik looked around to make sure that no one was paying attention. "I wrote a letter to General Mortigan suggesting he send any extra troops on hand to retake Tull Rock."

"You *what?*"

Reznik repeated his statement.

"That's not the issue," Nash said agitatedly. "You bypassed the chain of command. Why did you not bring this up with Colonel Osterfeld?"

"What does it have to do with him?" Reznik countered bluntly.

Nash's jaw went slack. "Are you serious?"

"If the Amelarens rushed through Tull Rock, there is a chance it is now undermanned or simply abandoned. We should be able to take it right back if General Mortigan has the available manpower."

"Which he may not!" Nash said anxiously. "You totally disregarded protocol. If this blows up …"

Reznik sighed. "I'll take full responsibility."

"I just don't know what you're trying to accomplish by gaming the colonel. It's quite obviously unwise."

"Remember the meeting before we left for Tull? We don't have time for discussion— reasonable or otherwise—about what to do. We can't risk inaction."

Unsettled, Nash shook his head disapprovingly.

"Don't worry," Reznik said. He cracked a small smile, not in the least bit fazed. He strolled to where he had left Gambit. "Come on, we need to get back in formation. Our prince is waiting for his rescue! We mustn't keep him or the general waiting."

Nash sighed and followed suit. Once atop Alma, he took a moment to gaze at the horizon to the east. Gray clouds still blanketed the sky, and all he could see in the distance were kilometers of rolling hills.

"Nash!" Reznik called from behind.

This broke Nash's concentration. His face darkened and a small knot formed in his stomach as he trotted after Reznik.

Chapter 16

(988.1.45)

—1—

After waiting an entire year, Prince Adrian was pleased to be on the front lines at last. Unfortunately, the enthusiasm faded within days of his arrival. Enemy raids ceased during the winter; Adrian spent most of his time mulling around the fortress, occasionally overseeing pieces of its construction. The routine grew tiring quickly. It seemed he was once again consigned to do nothing of consequence, except now he was far away from home in the Highlands.

This ennui finally subsided with the recession of winter. The Amelarens began to amass a large force just outside the entrance of the Ertel Gorge, and it seemed only a matter of time before they attacked. The action for which Adrian yearned was imminent. He grew anxious as it approached.

• • •

The prince stood on a stone platform in the center of an enormous open-roof courtyard. To either side of him were General Leynitz and Colonel Lariban. Both officers were dressed for battle. Leynitz donned his heavy steel-trimmed armor, while Lariban sported a lighter set of steel armor. Adrian wore only the armor of a common swordsman.

A small bead of sweat trickled down the prince's pale face. The weather was quite cool, but the stuffiness of his armor, in conjunction with his nerves, caused him to perspire. He glanced up at the sky. Roughly half an arc had passed since Leynitz's scouts informed the general that the enemy was finally advancing from the east. He assumed Helistos was slowly beginning to set in the west, but could not be sure given the thick clouds hovering overhead. In several arcs, it would be dark.

Adrian sighed. He had never fought at night, or in a large-scale battle of any kind. He fingered the hilt of his sword, Antilus, which was resting in its sheath against his waist. Though his light plating was reasonably comfortable, he felt naked wearing it. He missed his royal armor. He did not complain aloud, for it was not prudent to wear anything that would distinguish him from a common soldier in the upcoming battle. Leynitz did not wish to take any chances when it came to the prince's safety; the general keenly remembered his promise to the king.

"Pike!" Leynitz yelled across the room at a man standing near a wooden door along the wall. The man was supervising several other soldiers who took turns hauling large wooden crates from the room on the other side of the door.

Upon hearing his name, Captain Cecil Pike of the 29th Company saluted the general and shouted back. A thin man in his mid-thirties, he had long brown hair that protruded from his helmet and rested on his shoulders. "Sir!"

Leynitz shook his head disappointedly. "You should have been done with those weapon crates an arc ago."

Pike frowned and turned to his troops. "You heard the general! Move it! We don't have much time!"

The soldiers from the 29th Company redoubled their efforts.

General Leynitz's shouts interrupted Adrian's thoughts of the upcoming battle. The prince chuckled softly to himself. He never much liked Pike and could not figure why the man was made a captain. He had never witnessed Pike in battle, but had the displeasure of interacting with the captain on a few occasions. Pike's carefree demeanor rubbed Adrian the wrong way and reminded him of another person at the Highpost he did not particularly like. Adrian scanned the ranks for Renard Renault. Over a hundred soldiers were present in the courtyard, making it difficult to single out one man.

The courtyard was an open area spanning seventy-five meters in both length and width, which served as the nexus of the newly built Argiset Highpost. Single doors on both floors led to hallways within the main fort. Balconies protruded from the second and third floors, enabling communication and transport of supplies with pulleys and levers. Two large wooden gates on either side of the room served as main entrances to the fort. The doorways were wide enough to fit ten people in formation side by side. They were controlled by gears and switches located on walkways along the walls. In the center of the courtyard was a series of stone steps leading up to the large platform on which the prince, general, and colonel stood. The courtyard doubled as both an auditorium for addressing troops and an area to prepare deployment for battle. It was massive enough to hold all who were currently stationed at Argiset.

Several soldiers already lined up near the central platform in their respective platoons and companies. Others, such as those in the 29th, shuffled across the room to haul supplies and equipment. Many of the smaller doors in the room led to armories, supply rooms, and other storage areas. Tied to stakes behind the platform in the center of the room were the mounts of Leynitz, Lariban, and Adrian: the durions Silvermane, Vermillion, and Maximilian, respectively.

The Highpost itself spanned one hundred and twenty-five meters east to west and two hundred fifty meters north to south. It was well under half the size of Aldova in terms of area-per-floor and only rose three stories to Aldova's ten. Furthermore, the fort's architecture was unremarkable. The structure was a square-shaped fortification made primarily of alacore and a concretelike mixture. Aside from a few windows, large iron-reinforced wooden doors for both entrances, and four incomplete watchtowers in each corner of the structure, there was not much of note about the structure's appearance. The watchtowers barely rose above the fort's roof and were not yet functional. Coranthian crossbowmen could fire from the rooftop but were offered little in the way of protection from enemy projectiles. The northern wall had also yet to be properly reinforced.

"Something troubling you, Your Highness?" Leynitz said.

Adrian turned to meet the general's gaze. "I'm wondering how this place will hold up."

Leynitz smiled softly. "Prince, are you prepared to fight?"

Adrian narrowed his eyes and stared at Leynitz. "I am."

"Just like your father. I remember him as a younger man, charged with determination. I know you'll do just fine."

"My father was a hero who saved our country …"

Adrian turned away.

Leynitz arched his left eyebrow. "Times are different now, Prince. I did not mean to infer you should measure yourself against your father in the same way." He paused thoughtfully. "You should consider yourself lucky you were not forced into combat at a younger age. No boy should have to experience that."

"But—"

"There are many ways to serve your country and be a hero to your people," Leynitz continued. "More importantly, I am certain your father is proud to have you as a son."

Leynitz's words made Adrian feel better. The general had always cut an impressive figure in Adrian's eyes. More importantly, he was a good man and a capable leader; he always seemed to know the right things to say and do. There was no doubt in Adrian's mind that he could trust the general with his life.

In the corner of his eye, Adrian saw the western gate open abruptly and three sergeants entered the courtyard. They moved quickly, cutting through the crowd toward the central platform. Adrian stared at them with mild curiosity as they made their way across the room. He immediately recognized Glen Emerett when the three approached the bottom of the stairs to the central platform. They saluted Adrian, Leynitz, and Lariban, though only the prince noticed their presence.

"Emerett," Adrian said softly. A hint of disgust laced his tone. He decided to ignore the three sergeants and redirected his gaze elsewhere.

"General!"

Francis Keller's shout was drowned out by the bustling noise. Fortunately, Lariban heard the man and turned. He placed his hand lightly on Leynitz's shoulder and motioned to the three scouts at the foot of the stairs, which caused the general to take notice.

"General! I am Sergeant Keller of the 27th. These are sergeants Abberdine and Emerett of the 17th and 28th. We bring urgent news directly from Colonel Osterfeld. Permission to approach?"

General Leynitz furrowed his brow. "Yes, please. Tell me what news you bring. As you can see, we are preparing for battle, and I have little time to waste on anything that is not an absolute emergency."

Keller and the other two walked up the stairs to the central platform.

"Then we shall not waste your time, General," Keller said, "Our fortification at Tull Rock has fallen. We lost the 7th and 19th companies, including Colonel Dyers. The enemy that attacked Tull was led by War Chief Sol, and currently they have around eight or nine hundred warriors."

Activity in the courtyard grinded to a halt. Stunned soldiers stopped in their tracks to digest Keller's words.

Keller continued, "Upon learning of our defeat at Tull, General Mortigan deployed Colonel Osterfeld's battalion to cut the enemy off before they made it through Pyrean Valley. Unfortunately, we did not make it in time. At roughly two arc this morning, we confirmed the enemy had made it as far as the Pyrean Valley entrance and were headed this way. At the Colonel's behest, sergeants Abberdine, Emerett, and myself snuck past the enemy and came to warn you. The Amelaren Army will arrive in approximately two arcs."

"Two arcs?" Adrian said, straining to maintain his composure. "And we have the enemy marching to attack us from the east as well."

"I see," Leynitz said gravely. "Continue."

Keller hesitated and glanced at Mary Abberdine, who nodded for him to resume.

"Colonel Osterfeld's battalion has little chance of catching up to the enemy forces before they arrive. Rather than try to overexert themselves to do so, the officers felt it more prudent to pursue them at a distance and wait for the ideal moment to attack. Specifically, they request that you divide your troops to defend both sides of the fortress. Once the enemy is entrenched in battle on the western side, the battalion will take the enemy by surprise, attacking from behind. This should allow us to deal quickly with the Amelaren forces on the western side of the Highpost. Then we can move in to support the forces protecting the east."

Leynitz emitted an incredulous chuckle.

"But we scarcely have enough troops to defend the eastern side of the fort as is," Adrian protested.

Lariban replied flatly, "Prince, while it is true we do not have enough troops here to combat this new threat, we are offered little choice. If the enemy is indeed attacking from both sides, we are forced to respond appropriately. Many will die today, but with reinforcements on their way, there is a chance, however small, that some may survive."

Adrian's face grew pale. He gripped the hilt of his sword tightly.

Leynitz glared at Lariban, who seemed to come to a realization and bowed slightly toward Adrian.

"My apologies for my lack of tact, Your Highness."

After several ticks of silence, Leynitz spoke. "Thank you, sergeants. The three of you may remain in the fort for the upcoming battle. You deserve a rest. I imagine you are all quite tired, and I would not have you fighting in your condition. Go see Sergeant Boyer of the Lower 3rd, over there." Leynitz pointed to a man standing near some supply crates in the southwestern corner. "He will see that you are properly accommodated. You are dismissed."

After salutes were exchanged, the three sergeants descended the stairs and made their way to Boyer.

"General, let me lead the troops to the east," Lariban said. We will depart early and make contact with enemy forces before they arrive. That should buy some time."

Leynitz nodded. "Very well. Take the 14th, 22nd, 25th, and 32nd companies with the Lower 3rd to meet the enemy. Go inform the captains and their troops. Leave as soon as you're ready."

"Yes, sir."

Leynitz glanced at Adrian. "I shall inform captains Rousseau, Pike, and Wolbay that their companies shall defend the western side of the fortress. Please wait here, Prince."

"I will fight."

The prince still shook slightly from nerves, but his voice was firm, causing Leynitz to stop midstride in his descent.

"I'm sorry, Your Highness." The general turned to face Adrian. "The situation has changed and the risk is far too great now. You are to remain inside the fortress with the Upper 3rd and myself. The 21st will remain behind as well."

Adrian glared at Leynitz. "General, I command you to let me and my soldiers fight!"

Leynitz shook his head. "Your safety is paramount, Prince. There will be plenty of other chances to prove yourself, I assure you. Please don't be so eager to throw your life away." He turned and resumed his trek down the stairs.

"General!" Adrian called.

When Leynitz did not respond, Adrian shouted again in a louder voice, drawing anxious looks from some of the other soldiers, but still Leynitz did not acknowledge him. Adrian remained on the platform for a while, frozen as if in a trance.

He finally came to when he heard Lariban's voice behind him, followed shortly by countless other soldiers' cries. Adrian spun around and watched as Lariban, riding Vermillion, led his three and a half companies through the eastern gate.

—2—

Twisting hard with his right hand, Lariban yanked his javelin from a fallen Amelaren warrior's torso. Blood poured from the wound and flowed over the body, pooling on the ground. As Lariban removed the weapon, another warrior charged him from behind. With blinding speed, Lariban pivoted and expertly thrust the javelin through the warrior's chest as if wielding a spear. The Amelaren ax-wielder stood in disbelief, his weapon held high over his head and ready to strike. The colonel retracted the javelin and watched as the warrior dropped the ax, stumbling backwards, gurgling and grabbing at the hole in his leather armor, blood spewing. Within ticks, he fell on his side and convulsed on the ground.

Lariban took a moment to look coldly upon his enemy before jamming his javelin directly through the warrior's skull. He was exceptionally gifted with the javelin; many in the military considered Lariban one of the best skirmishers in Coranthia. Unlike most javelin-wielders, he preferred to not use a shield and only carried limited ammunition on his back. While the lightweight spears were generally used as a long-range weapon and coupled with a shield for protection, the colonel opted for longer, heavier javelins, which could double as polearms.

Many within the army considered him a more dangerous man on foot than horseback, but in most battles he rode Vermillion to issue commands. Unfortunately, Vermillion was killed earlier in the battle. Given that his only order from the general was to hold off the enemy until reinforcements arrived, Lariban decided to leave the issuing of orders to the captains. He had not been granted permission to call for a retreat; therefore, the loss of his horse would not greatly affect the tide of the battle.

Lariban continued to plow through the enemy with the Lower 3rd, but wave after wave of Amelaren soldiers flowed from the east. There was no apparent end to them. He stole a glance behind him and estimated that the eastern gate was less than a kilometer away. Over the one and a half arcs since Lariban and his troops first met the advancing Amelarens, the Coranthians had slowly but surely lost ground.

The colonel raised his javelin to rally his troops.

"Do not let up!" he cried.

On the western side of the fort, the situation was much direr. Captains Lamonde Rousseau, Cecil Pike, and John Wolbay did their best to keep the enemy away from the western entrance but faced an enemy force nearly twice their size. Many archers stationed along the western wall of the Highpost, no longer safe from enemy fire, withdrew from their perches. With the majority of the Amelarens engaged in a melee with the Coranthian forces, it had become increasingly difficult for the archers to ensure they did not inadvertently shoot allies.

From atop his horse, Captain Rousseau of the 33rd, a tall, lanky man of thirty-three years with a thick black mustache and sunken brown eyes, drove his ax into the head of an Amelaren warrior who was by his side. Several other enemy soldiers surrounded him but were quickly taken down by Captain Wolbay, who had galloped over to Rousseau. Wolbay swung his sword wildly, dispatching the last warrior harassing the captain.

Rousseau whipped his horse around. "Thanks, John."

Wolbay nodded in acknowledgment. His blue eyes surveyed the battle before them.

Rousseau adjusted his helmet and turned his attention east where, several meters away, Captain Pike and Vice Captain William Anders fended off the enemy with the lances atop their mounts.

"You have things covered here?" Rousseau asked. "I'm heading to Pike."

Wolbay laughed dryly. "Covered, you say? I've lost a lot of my soldiers. But I'll be fine for a few reps."

Rousseau dug his heels into his ride and made his way to the captain of the 29th.

"Pike, this isn't good," he declared. "We're down almost half our soldiers. John lost his second as well. How are your forces faring?"

"We're having a splendid time of it, obviously." Pike paused to take on an attacking warrior. Rousseau maneuvered around him. Together, the two lodged their weapons into the foe. "But I do say, at this rate, I find it very unlikely we shall make it through the arc alive. I was not planning on dying today, so that would be a shame. I am sorry to hear about Vice Captain Calvin."

Pike afforded his vice captain a glance. "Anders, how are you holding up?"

Nearby, Anders freed his lance from the bowels of an Amelaren warrior and turned his horse to face Pike. "Yes, Captain?"

"You should thank Creon you're still alive!" Pike shouted. "Wolbay's second wasn't so fortunate."

Anders managed only a puzzled look in return.

Rousseau frowned. Pike was rarely serious or tactful, even in the face of seemingly insurmountable danger. This always rubbed Rousseau the wrong way, but Pike's skills in battle could not be denied. Therefore, he was surprised when Pike's expression sobered.

Pike said, "Tell your troops to hold out as long as they can. Remember that Colonel Osterfeld is on his way."

"Just a little bit longer," Rousseau agreed, as if to reassure himself. He took a moment to look toward the hills to the west before heading back to his own company.

—3—

Reznik sat atop Gambit, gazing steadily ahead at the condensation forming with each breath he took. While the worst of the winter snow was over, it was still rather chilly outside, and the overcast skies made it even worse. Before him stood a thicketed hill stretching north to south as far as the eye could see. The sounds of clashing metal and shouting soldiers came from the battle that raged at the Argiset Highpost on the other side of the hill. About a dozen meters behind Reznik stood the 26th Company, ready for battle. To his north stood the 17th and 35th companies; to his south were the 5th, 27th, and 28th.

Gambit jerked his head sideways and whinnied when he noticed someone approach them from behind. Reznik patted the horse's neck softly. Nash had procured the animal after returning from winter's leave. Gambit was a medium-sized, light brown zephyr with a black mane and tail. It was apparent from the scarring along the horse's left side that he had seen plenty of action. Gambit was skittish and, unless properly restrained, had the tendency to be disobedient when nervous. Despite these undesirables, Reznik treated his horse as a top-tier durion, and in turn, Gambit showed equal respect for his new master.

Riding Alma, Nash trotted up beside Reznik before coming to a stop. Neither spoke for a rep.

"It is hard to believe it has been almost a year since we were last here," Nash finally said.

Reznik turned his gaze south to the row of hills there and was struck by a specific point in the landscape that he recognized. He remembered when he stood on that same hill with his squadmates as a recent academy graduate, recalling the apprehension they all felt preparing for their first battle and how inexperienced they were. Now they were hardened and any apprehension was owed to impatience wrought by an inability to help their fellow soldiers. He was vice captain, no longer marching alongside his companions but out in front of them. If things had turned out differently, would Liam Remington be where he was now? Reznik forcibly evacuated these thoughts from his mind.

He shook his head. "I disagree. Things have changed so much since then. Honestly, it feels longer ago."

Nash tilted his head sideways, contemplating Reznik's words and shrugged. He then briefly glanced back at his company before turning his attention south to Colonel Osterfeld.

"We've been here almost an arc. We know what's happening past those hills, but we're just waiting around …" Nash sighed.

A sarcastic grin formed at the corners of Reznik's mouth. "It sounds almost like you are looking forward to this battle, Captain."

Nash grew wide-eyed and stared at Reznik. "N-No. No, that isn't what I meant at all. I just …"

When Nash realized Reznik was joking, he let out a nervous laugh, scratching the back of his blond head. He was still unaccustomed to Reznik's deadpan humor.

"I understand how you feel," Reznik said. "We are helpless to do anything at the moment, but if we don't execute the plan properly, many more of us will die today. The colonel's scouts will let us know when the time is right."

After ten more reps, Reznik watched five scouts scramble down from various spots on the hills outlying Argiset Plateau. They rushed toward Osterfeld's company. Shortly after the scouts met with the colonel, several more were dispatched to inform each company to be prepared to attack.

While Reznik drew his sword and shield, Nash took off his glasses and carefully placed them in the bag slung around his shoulder.

"I suppose it is time to go rescue the crown prince," Nash said.

He turned Alma to face the troops of the 26th and rode to his company, shouting to make himself heard over the noise beyond the hills. "Everyone! Remember to stay close together and stick to the plan. We need to cut all the way through enemy forces and meet the 17th near the Highpost entrance."

As Reznik rode up beside Nash, he could hear his captain's struggle for words.

Wavering slightly, Nash continued, "Be sure to stay in formation and make sure the flanks are a solid wall. Any weaknesses could put our entire company in jeopardy!"

Nash looked up and saw some of the other companies moving up the hills. Reznik caught a glimmer in the captain's eyes as Nash quickly turned his attention back to his troops.

"I have faith in you all! We didn't get this far because we were lucky. Let us show the Amelarens the might of the 26th Company!"

His soldiers refrained from speaking so as to not alert the enemy, but most of the company stamped their feet in acknowledgment. A number of the more veteran soldiers seemed impressed at Nash's short, confident speech, delivered with such efficacy.

Reznik nodded approvingly at Nash, who smiled and turned Alma toward the hills.

"Move out!" the captain commanded.

Reznik caught Madeline's attention before following. She was near the front of the 26th and the two exchanged smiles. Reznik mouthed a simple "be careful" before he lowered his helmet and caught up with Nash.

The 26th stopped just below the crest of the hill. Before long, the entire battalion was in line, awaiting Osterfeld's signal. When Aranow's trumpet sounded from the 5th Company, the Coranthians began to pour over the top of the hills, charging full speed to meet the enemy. Their stampeding thundered across the plains. Upon their allies' arrival, the remaining soldiers of the 29th and 33rd cheered enthusiastically. Several Amelarens at the rear of their formation turned when they heard the sound behind them to face a massive wave of soldiers headed directly toward them. Osterfeld's soldiers collided with the enemy in less than a rep. The Amelarens had little time to process what was happening, let alone prepare themselves to defend against the Coranthians. Instead, they acted purely on instinct and rushed to meet the Coranthian reinforcements head-on.

The 17th Company was the first to make contact with enemy. Led by both Captain Eldrid and Vice Captain Sorel on their mounts, the soldiers plunged into the enemy formation with weapons drawn, while maintaining a sturdy defense on both flanks. To the south, Reznik galloped ahead to lead the charge for the 26th, while Nash stayed near the middle of the formation to provide support with the crossbowmen and other medics. One by one, the companies in Osterfeld's battalion met the rear of the Amelaren formation. In particular, the 17th, 26th, and 28th made a concerted effort to drive deep into enemy lines in an attempt to break up the Amelaren forces.

With the arrival of reinforcements from Aldova, the Coranthians soon gained the upper hand on the western side of Argiset Highpost, now outnumbering the Amelarens there more than two to one. After several reps passed, most of the Amelarens had turned their attention to Osterfeld and his company, significantly lightening the burden placed on the 29th and 33rd.

From atop Gambit, Reznik used his shield to deflect a blow from an Amelaren swordsman and instantly countered with a swipe of his sword, lopping off the warrior's head. Gambit whinnied as blood sprayed onto his side from the fallen warrior. Another enemy approached from his flank, but Reznik did not give him a chance to get an attack in before jamming his sword into the Amelaren's chest. Reznik breathed heavily as he took a moment to survey the battlefield. Enemy forces were scattered and disorganized. The Coranthians were on the verge of breaking through.

He caught a glimpse of Nash issuing orders to fellow soldiers behind him. Officers on horseback had a huge advantage in terms of battlefield visibility, especially across flats such as these, but they were also easier targets for Amelarens. When Reznik saw Nash hop off Alma to treat an injured soldier, he noted that the captain's primary disposition as a medic in the heat of battle made it inefficient and impractical for him to keep a horse at all. On the other hand, Nash's responsibilities as the captain made it necessary to retain access to one. Fleetingly, Reznik remembered his conversation with Leynitz and Osterfeld the previous year.

Annoyed at having distracted himself, Reznik turned his attention to the enemy soldiers around him, wondering if Sol was among them. He had been unable to get a clear look at who was at Tull Rock but was given a description of the war chief after that battle. There was no sign of the war chief anywhere. Reznik wondered which company would have the unfortunate pleasure of meeting such a fearsome fighter in battle. He returned his focus to the task at hand and felt it a good time to leave the front to his soldiers and rendezvous with Nash as was planned.

"We're almost through!" he shouted at the soldiers. "I'm going to meet with Captain Havora! When we return, I expect you to have pushed through the enemy formation!"

The 26th cried out in acknowledgment. Reznik spun Gambit westward and galloped through the 26th's ranks toward Nash's position. When he approached Alma, he saw the captain wrapping up a bloody stump of a soldier's hand nearby. Reznik could not remember the injured soldier's name but knew he was a new recruit who had just joined Aldova since the 26th returned from leave. Reznik felt sorry for the young man and was reminded briefly of Alphonse Trenton. For some reason, the soldier did not appear to be in significant pain. Once Nash finished, the injured man thanked the captain and raised his sword in his good hand. He did an about-face and returned to defend the flank.

Nash used a cloth in his medical satchel to wipe the sweat from his forehead. Turning to mount Alma, he finally noticed Reznik. "Oh, I didn't see you there," he said as he climbed onto his horse.

Reznik frowned. "You sent that man back to fight with only one hand?"

"For someone so green, he was quite strong-willed. Reminded me of you." Nash laughed. "He was very insistent on returning to the front. I gave him something I've been working on to help dull the pain from his injury. He should be good to fight for another arc."

Reznik eyed his captain skeptically.

"I assume you did not come to interrogate me about my treatment methods?" Nash said.

"No. As you can see, we've mostly broken through the enemy ranks. The 17th is close as well, and the 28th appears to have already made it through. I think it is the right time for us to push through. You can meet up with Captain Eldrid, and we can all make our way to the Highpost."

Nash nodded. "Very well, let us go."

Just as they were about to leave for the front, Josef Reinbach barreled toward them through the ranks. Though he could not say a word, his appearance spoke for itself. Disheveled and distressed, he urged the two to follow, his Doromalian accent almost unintelligible as he struggled to complete the simple request.

A sense of dread filled Reznik. His thoughts turned immediately to Madeline. Reznik and Nash looked at each other. Josef turned and charged back through the ranks. The two immediately took off after him.

—4—

Madeline turned briefly at the sound of a galloping horse behind her and saw Reznik riding Gambit toward the rear of the formation. She whirled back around in time to deflect the ax of an Amelaren with her gladius, while Josef lodged his lance into the warrior's side to her right.

"Thanks," Madeline said. She nodded gratefully at Josef, who simply smiled through his helmet. On her other side, Cyrus hacked away at Amelaren soldiers, occasionally goading them on to attack him. Patrice was directly behind them, pulling back a fellow soldier who had received a wound to his side. Madeline had lost sight of Bethany, Nicole, and Mason. Despite the Coranthians' ability to hold off the enemy and protect their flanks, the squads were dispersing and mixing with others.

The four continued to work effectively in this manner. Several reps later, Patrice finished attending her current patient and signaled a nearby medic to take the soldier further from the front. Suddenly, her gaze focused on something to the north; she strained her eyes to get a better look. "Hey!" she shouted. "Madeline! Come here!"

Madeline turned to see who was calling her name. When she spotted Patrice, she called for Cyrus to maintain the effort and moved away from the front of the flank, letting him and Josef fill her spot while other soldiers moved forward to solidify the line of defense.

"What is it?" Madeline said, as she approached Patrice. Her squadmate did not turn to greet her but rather continued to stare northward and pointed.

Patrice stood on her toes to get a better look. "Isn't that your friend from the 28th?"

Madeline spun and looked where Patrice indicated, expecting to see Glen, but it wasn't him. She strained her eyes, trying to get a good look at what Patrice was pointing at. With so many soldiers around them, it was very hard to make out whom she was talking about.

"Is that Douglas?" she wondered aloud.

"Right," said Patrice. "Avet Stover, wasn't it?"

Madeline was shocked. "What is he doing all the way over here?" Then she corrected herself. "How did he get here?"

"Maybe the 28th has already cut through the enemy?" As soon as the words left her mouth, Patrice realized the implausibility of her answer and shook her head. "No, I don't know. Something's wrong with him though."

Douglas Drake was moving slowly through the ranks of the 26th, soaked in blood. His helmet was nowhere to be seen, and he dragged his lance and shield heavily at his sides. Ignoring the fighting around him, he continued to shuffle aimlessly while being pushed by nearby soldiers.

"I'm going to see if he needs help," Patrice said, breaking off into a run.

"Wait!" Madeline cried. She ran after Patrice and quickly caught her.

As they approached, the first thing Madeline noticed was the blank stare on Douglas's face. His mind seemed far away. Patrice reached out and lightly shook his shoulder. "Avet Stover," she said.

He ignored her and continued walking.

"Douglas?" Patrice tried again.

There was no response.

Finally, Madeline chimed in. "Douglas!" she shouted.

Slowly, Douglas stopped and turned his head to look at Madeline, but his gaze seemed to stare right through her as opposed to directly at her.

"I …" He dropped his lance and shield, falling to his knees.

Patrice and Madeline moved to catch him. They looked at each other.

"I don't know what's wrong with him, but we can't leave him here," Patrice said. "Let's take him away so I can examine him properly."

Madeline nodded, and the two propped Douglas on their shoulders to move him behind the front lines. Douglas walked, as they helped support him on their shoulders, but after a few ticks, he began to flail hysterically. He let out a scream before his feet gave way fully. The brunt of his weight knocked Madeline and Patrice over, on either side of him, as he slumped to the ground.

Patrice cried out in pain as she hit the ground. Madeline rose quickly to her feet to try to lift Douglas and managed to prop him upright on the ground.

"Are you all right, Patrice?" Madeline cried.

"My back …" Patrice gasped.

She attempted to stand but crumpled to her knees. Suddenly, Josef appeared and rushed to support Patrice. Madeline had no idea where he had come from, but she was grateful. Josef laid Patrice on her side. Madeline's eyes grew wide as she saw the large, broken spear tip jutting from near Patrice's abdomen.

"She must have fallen on it," Josef said, his eyes wide with concern.

Madeline looked for a nearby medic and saw none.

"Josef, fetch Captain Havora," she said.

He hesitated a moment, turning to glance at Patrice, then nodded and ran off.

Patrice rasped in a weak voice, "Don't be foolish. He's not going to drop everything and come."

Madeline shook her head before turning to look at Douglas.

"Don't move!" she barked.

Douglas did not seem to have realized what happened and simply sat with them, staring at the ground in a daze.

Madeline knelt beside her. The injured medic breathed more heavily now, sweating profusely. Blood pulsed from the wound in her back. Patrice tried to speak but could not. She cried quietly.

"The captain will be here soon. You're going to be fine."

Madeline pulled some glass vials from the pouch around her waist and reached into Patrice's medical bag for bandages, scissors, and forceps. Madeline stared at the wound and felt queasy. Patrice would be extremely fortunate if the spear tip had managed to miss any vital organs.

Large beads of sweat dripped down Madeline's face as she bit her lower lip and tried to think of how to proceed. This was very different from her lessons with Nash. She had never practiced on a wound this severe, and the fact that it was Patrice rather than than someone unknown made it that much more difficult.

"Madeline!" Reznik shouted from behind her.

She spun to see him and Nash as they rushed toward her. They had already dismounted their horses, leaving them in the care of two soldiers.

Reznik's face uncoiled with relief when he realized it was not Madeline who was injured. Without a moment's hesitation, Nash knelt beside Patrice, dumping the contents of his medical satchel. He assessed the wound, talking to himself.

"What happened here?" Reznik barked.

She quickly explained what had transpired. As Reznik listened, his eyes drifted to Douglas. A cloud fell over his face. It was rare for him to feel such fury. He walked briskly to Douglas and grabbed him by the arm. Douglas squirmed in pain as Reznik pulled him to his feet. Reznik glared at him and received only a blank stare in return.

"Avet Agilda," Nash said. "I'm going to need your help removing this. We don't know if any permanent damage has been—"

Nash stopped in amazement when Reznik, who still wore his gauntlets, slapped Douglas hard across the face, causing the avet to stumble back. Blood trickled down Douglas's lip. He gaped at Reznik in shock; the haze had finally seemed to lift from his eyes.

"Reznik!" Madeline cried. "What are you—"

She started to get up, but Nash grabbed her arm. She stared wildly at him.

"Please, focus on Avet Konith. I need your help."

"Do you realize what you've done?" Reznik bellowed.

Douglas stood and touched his bloody lip. Reznik hit him again and then grabbed him by the chest plate, just under the neck, and pulled him closer, menacingly raising his other arm.

"Stop! Stop!" Douglas cried out, having recovered his wits. "I'm sorry! I'm sorry!"

Reznik leaned in and whispered so only Douglas could hear.

"And if it had been Madeline? What then?"

He shoved Douglas away. Stumbling backwards, Douglas lowered his head, blood pouring from his nose and mouth.

"I'm sorry …"

Reznik expelled a deep breath and returned his attention to Nash. His hands shook. For once, he was uncertain of what to do next. "Captain? What now?"

Nash did not take his eyes from Patrice; he was busy applying an ointment around the wound and preparing to remove the spear tip while Madeline held her still.

"Vice Captain Sylvera," he said, "I cannot leave Avet Konith here, and it may take some time before I finish. I want you to meet with Captain Eldrid in my place and enter Argiset. Time is short and we need to know what the situation is on the other side. I'm counting on you."

Reznik took a deep breath. "Yes, sir."

He glared at Douglas, busy wiping the blood from his face.

"You're coming with me," Reznik said, grabbing Douglas's arm. "You are a danger to yourself and others right now. I'm not letting you out of my sight until we return you to the 28th."

The two mounted Gambit. Reznik spurred the horse and trotted to where Madeline knelt over Patrice.

When she looked up, he had a soft, sad smile on his face.

"Be careful," he said, echoing his silent address to her only a short time earlier, before they waded into the mayhem surrounding them.

She nodded. "You too."

Reznik's attention shifted to the fort ahead of him. He grabbed Gambit's reins and dug his heels into the horse's side, taking off at a gallop. Upon arrival at the western gate, Reznik saw that Eldrid was already there and appeared to have been waiting some time.

Eldrid arched his eyebrows as Reznik trotted up next to him. "Where's Captain Havora?"

"Preoccupied. He sent me in his place," Reznik responded.

Seeing Douglas perched behind Reznik, Eldrid frowned. "The Drake boy?"

A look of surprise washed over Reznik's face. "You know him?"

"Everyone knows the Drake family," Eldrid responded. "But no, I don't know him personally."

"I see … Well, it's nothing. I'm just looking after him."

Reznik's glowering countenance discouraged Eldrid from pressing the matter further. The captain turned his durion toward the gate. As they approached, a few soldiers along the wall noticed the two officers and shouted for the gate to be opened. The door began to rise. As soon as they could, Reznik and Eldrid galloped through the opening, and on cue, the gate closed immediately behind them

As they rode through the tunnel, Reznik recognized General Leynitz from a distance, pacing back and forth on the platform in the center of the courtyard.

"What is the general doing there?" Eldrid muttered. "I thought he'd be leading the charge."

A small detachment of soldiers—among whom was a captain, riding on a large horse—made their way toward them. Reznik could not immediately make out who the rider was, as it was already getting dark.

"Reznik!" the captain shouted.

As he entered the courtyard, Reznik recognized the horse's red coat.

"Reznik!"

The voice was now unmistakable.

"Renard. I didn't expect to find you in here. I thought you'd be out fighting."

"I thought I would be too!" Renard laughed. "I'm surprised to see you here as well, but I'm glad. And Douglas!"

Douglas nodded but said nothing.

Renard paused to examine them more closely. "What happened?"

"We can talk about it later," Reznik answered.

Renard nodded. "Well, for what it's worth, Glen is here too."

Reznik permitted himself a small smile. "That's good to hear."

"Captain Renault," Eldrid said, "we need to see the general immediately. Exchanging of pleasantries must wait."

Renard's expression sobered as he nodded in acknowledgment. "This way."

—5—

Lariban was beginning to feel fatigue. While his performance had not declined significantly, the long battle was beginning to take its toll on him and his men. The situation had not improved over the last fifty reps; on the contrary, it had grown worse. The enemy onslaught from the east continued without pause. Every time one wave of warriors was thwarted, another surged forward to take its place. The arrival of a cadre of cross-bowmen from the western side of the fort provided some much-needed relief, but even with the reinforcements, Lariban and the other companies were still losing ground. They were less than a kilometer away from the fort now, and since the fighting had started, the eastern detachment had lost roughly a quarter of their men. Captain Lowmann and Vice Captain Frost of the 22nd Company had sacrificed their own lives—as well as those of their soldiers—to buy Lariban more time.

The colonel dodged an ax that would have taken off his head had he been a tick slower. He skewered the warrior standing in front of him and casually slid the warrior off his weapon. Hearing a battle cry to his right, he pivoted with two javelins, one in each hand, and took aim. Before long, two more Amelarens joined their recently departed comrades.

Lariban paused to wipe the sweat from his face. "Troops, hold your ground! I will be back shortly!" he shouted, trying to make himself heard over the fighting. After the soldiers of the Lower 3rd shouted their acknowledgment, Lariban headed north in search of the 25th Company.

He bolted past the motionless bodies of Captain Petrof and Vice Captain Daniels, sprawled on the ground beside their horses, without slowing. His focus was trained squarely on the back of a huge Amelaren warrior tearing through what little remained of the 25th. Acting purely on instinct, Lariban leapt into the air, javelins in both hands, ready to strike down the Amelaren, but the warrior turned with lightning-quick speed to face Lariban. The intense countenance, silver streaked hair, and looming broadsword were unmistakable to Lariban. Taken by surprise, the colonel hesitated only a tick, but that was plenty of time for his opponent to shift his stance and knock Lariban aside.

Lariban gasped for air as he hit the ground and struggled to crawl backwards to gain some distance. His helmet fell off and one of his javelins broke with the fall, but he scurried to his feet with the other in hand.

Meanwhile, the Amelaren had returned his attention to finishing off the soldiers who had attacked him before Lariban's interruption. The few that still stood backed away in fear. Within a rep, he had taken down five men with ease, and the remaining survivors wanted no part of him. He looked at the man who had attacked him from behind. A wry smile of recognition spread across his face. "Colonel Lariban …"

Lariban nodded and spat blood from his mouth. There was no fear in his eyes; his expression remained as icy as ever. "War Chief Tallen."

He gripped his javelin tightly and charged.

Crouched near a second-story window, Adrian peered out to the east, gauging the battle between Colonel Lariban's forces and the eastern horde. The sun had finally escaped the veil of clouds rolling across the sky; the long shadow of Argiset Highpost cast over the battlefield happened to be a precise demarcation between the two sides. On one were the Coranthians, who tried to blend into the shade to mask their movements. On the other was the encroaching Amelaren force, a menacing mass of wending warriors.

Adrian heard a loud crash near the western gate, followed by a surge of voices. He sprang from his perch with several avets on his heels. Leynitz met him in the corridor, and the two hurried onto the balcony overlooking the courtyard. A small group of soldiers stood tensed, facing the entryway to the gate.

"Who gave orders to open the gate?" Leynitz barked in their direction.

In response, there came the sound of clopping hooves. Renard Renault, bent forward atop his durioness Phoenix, straightened upon entering the courtyard and pronounced, "I did, Your Excellency. To bring in some reinforcements that broke through the western horde."

"Humph," Leynitz grunted, but it was clear that he had no reason to object. "Well, maybe we can finally get an account of what's going on out there."

"If Your Excellency permits, I would like to ask the same of you regarding the battle outside those eastern walls. And what of our status within?"

The voice belonged to Captain Sigmund Eldrid, who approached behind Renard, voice tinged with urgency. When Adrian saw Reznik alongside Eldrid, his eyes narrowed, and he harshly sucked in his breath.

"I told you, Captain Eldrid," Renard said, almost chidingly, "that we are sufficiently established inside the fort. We have nearly two companies at our disposal and the Amelarens have not attempted entry."

"For now," Eldrid replied evenly. "Only a few of us have made it in-side. Colonel Osterfeld's main force has still not managed to clear the enemy's western detachment."

The general made his way quickly down a flight of stairs at the north-ern end of the courtyard.

Eldrid dismounted hastily. On either side of him, Reznik and Renard did the same.

"At ease, gentlemen," Leynitz said. "We'll not stand on ceremony now. Continue, Captain Eldrid. What of Colonel Osterfeld?"

"The colonel's soldiers are fighting their way through War Chief Sol's warriors," Eldrid said. "I was sent ahead with Vice Captain Sylvera here"—he glanced at Reznik—"to establish contact with the fort, but the Amelarens bore down on us. Most of our party was driven back."

"Our archers are set up along the upper floors," Leynitz said. "They have been instructed to make random movements to harass enemy troops." He stroked his mustache. "If Colonel Osterfeld makes good progress, it seems only a matter of time before he will link up with us here."

"I hope that is indeed the case," Eldrid said. "How is Colonel Lariban faring against the main force?"

"I am certain he will hold out as long as necessary."

"Had Colonel Osterfeld arrived a day earlier, we would not be in this situation," Adrian cut in, as he strode forward. He had been lurking near the bottom of the stairs, unnoticed in his avet armor, before emerging from the shadows.

Eldrid bowed. "Your Highness."

Reznik did not follow suit. "The colonel mobilized as quickly and as thoroughly as he could, Your Highness," he returned.

"I make no insinuation to the contrary," Adrian returned with a frown. "I am just stating the facts."

Leynitz and Eldrid seemed unsure of how to interpret the exchange. Renard gave a slight roll of his eyes.

"Perhaps it would be of greater prudence to discuss how to proceed," Reznik said evenly, making unabashed eye contact with the prince.

Though Adrian's nostrils flared, he did not hesitate. He turned to Leynitz. "General, this may not surprise you, but I believe we should throw all of our weight against the western detachment and bring the fight to them. The sooner we are able to join with Osterfeld's forces, the better."

"That is a gamble, Prince," Leynitz said. "We must accomplish our objective quickly. We lose our positional advantage by directly engaging War Chief Sol, and leaving the interior of the fort undefended is another huge risk."

"And what are we doing now?" There was a noticeable tremble in Adrian's rising voice. "Nothing. What good is holding the fort when all of our troops are outside?"

For a moment, no one spoke. The other soldiers in the courtyard watched with intense interest but kept their distance. All eyes were fixed on Adrian and the group of officers. Outside, the sounds of battle raged on.

To everyone's surprise, it was Reznik who responded. "While I am as concerned for our soldiers as you are, Prince, I respectfully disagree."

Adrian's eyes widened in disbelief. "You mean to say that you do not wish to hasten to their aid?"

"No, that's not it at all."

Now it was Leynitz's turn to be incredulous.

"Please do not waste our time, Vice Captain."

"Let him speak," Adrian said crossly with a wave of his hand. "I want to hear a better idea from you, Sylvera. And quickly, if you please, lest we stand around all day without taking action."

Reznik cast a glance at Leynitz, who frowned at him quizzically.

"Very well, Your Highness. I advise staying here, at least for a while longer, but not out of indecision. Having surveyed the battle before I entered, I can tell you with confidence that it will not be long before Colonel Osterfeld breaks through."

Adrian made no attempt to hide the skepticism in his countenance.

When he saw that the prince remained unswayed, Reznik continued, "I have another reason, one of simple numbers. The enemy's main force lies to the east. Am I correct?"

"Go on," Adrian said slowly, as if trying to decipher some sort of deceit in Reznik's words.

"War Chief Sol's detachment is effectively surrounded, no matter how conservatively we evaluate the situation. He is unable to enter the fort under current conditions, and Colonel Osterfeld is pressuring him from the other side. On the other hand, not only is the main force larger, but we must not dismiss the possibility that it can be reinforced further from behind their lines to overwhelm Colonel Lariban's troops. This is something we cannot control. Therefore, I believe any drastic movements at this point may cue whoever is heading the main force to enact contingencies we have no knowledge of and will have difficulty accommodating, given our delicate position."

His explanation complete, Reznik took several steps backwards, face frozen once again in blankness. He stared almost lifelessly at Adrian, as if he had not spoken at all.

Leynitz clapped his hands once, drawing all eyes to himself. "It would seem that we have two options, each with considerable merit. We will need to decide soon, but we should take some time to more thoroughly assess the factors at play. Nevertheless, let us be swift."

He pointed across the courtyard.

"From my understanding of the current distribution of enemy forces, the main detachment is shaded toward the south on the eastern side of the plateau, and so Colonel Lariban has moved to intercept them there. If we can track the Amelaren movements for about ten reps, we will have a better idea of how the battle is progressing.

"Vice Captain Sylvera, while I have also foreseen the possibility of enemy reinforcements from the east, it seems unlikely they would have any immediate effect on the battle given their present location. There is a natural bottleneck for any large force to ascend onto the plateau from the east. That is what makes this such a critical point of defense."

"Yes, sir," Reznik acknowledged.

"That is why," Leynitz went on, "if we are able to see that Colonel Lariban is sufficiently suppressing the eastern advance, we will do as His Highness suggests and commit as many of our forces within to attack War Chief Sol's detachment and rendezvous with Colonel Osterfeld."

"Good," said Adrian. He glared triumphantly at Reznik, who did not meet his eyes.

"Your Highness, you and I will take the southern wing. Captain Eldrid, Vice Captain Sylvera, I would like you two to direct the archers along the western windows and report status on War Chief Sol's forces. Let us reconvene here in twenty reps. Captain Renault, you will remain here and contact any of us, as is necessary."

"As you wish, sir," Renard said.

Leynitz nodded and walked toward the southern staircase on the other side of the courtyard. Adrian hurried after him.

Soon, they were out of earshot. Eldrid turned to Reznik and said, with wonderment in his voice, "I am surprised the prince did not demand your immediate dismissal and demotion."

"We have history together," Reznik said plainly.

"That much is clear," Eldrid remarked. "Shall we be going?"

"You may go on ahead, Captain. I need a word with Captain Renault." Reznik pointed to Renard, who was speaking to a group of avets from the 21st several meters away.

"As you wish. I will start on the top floor and work my way back along the walls."

Eldrid made for the northern staircase. He climbed the first set and turned on the landing, disappearing from view.

Reznik walked over to Renard and lightly tugged his arm. Renard dismissed the avets he had been addressing.

"Tell me you weren't thinking of more ways to rebut our fair prince before the general interjected," Renard said.

"I need a favor."

Renard noticed the tinge of bitterness in Reznik's tone. "Go on."

Reznik nodded toward the western wall, near the corridor leading to the gate. Oblivious to his surroundings, Douglas Drake sat slumped against it. The blood smeared across his lower face had dried.

"Is he all right?" Renard asked, knitting his eyebrows.

"I dragged him along with me. He's not hurt, just completely out of it."

"Whose blood is that?"

Reznik shook his head. "Don't worry about it."

"I'll keep an eye on him, then."

"Thanks."

Reznik looked carefully at Renard for a few ticks. He hadn't noticed until now, but something in Renard's eyes had changed. On the outside, he was his usual, jovial self, but Reznik noticed a weariness to Renard's gaze. "What is it?" Reznik asked.

As if his question had lit a spark, Renard broke into a grin. "Nothing, nothing. Stop stalling and get going. I'll look after Douglas."

Reznik wasn't convinced but had to go. He clapped Renard on the shoulder, surprising his friend with a rare gesture of plain gratitude. He briskly set off for the northern staircase.

Head hung between his propped knees, Douglas sat several meters from the threshold of the tunnel. The other avets who accompanied Reznik and Eldrid kept their distance and even avoided looking in his direction.

Renard walked straight to where his friend sat, leaned against the wall, and slid casually into a sitting position. "How are you holding up, Douglas? Glad to see you uninjured."

The portly young man did not stir. There was nothing to indicate he had even heard Renard's words.

Putting on his most comforting smile, Renard reached out and gently tapped Douglas on the arm. "What's wrong?"

Douglas slowly raised his head. His eyes were dry, though cloudy and red. He looked utterly lost. When he spoke, Renard sensed naked despair in his friend's voice.

"I don't belong here, Renard …"

Renard stared at him for a while without responding. His insides stirred sharply and unpleasantly as his smile faded. "Neither do I, Douglas. Neither do I."

—7—

"If Lord Velmann were present, I have little doubt he would have banished the vice captain to patrol duty in Otharon," said Leynitz.

Adrian chuckled. "I suppose he learned well from you and Mortigan. Formality is the last thing I am concerned with on the battlefield."

"He not only spoke on equal footing with you but had no reservations in doing so," the general remarked. "I would not have believed it myself had I not come to expect it from your accounts. My own experiences with Vice Captain Sylvera led me to believe him a rather reserved man."

"I cannot entirely blame him for his behavior toward me. It was my own doing, in a way."

The two paced quickly down the southern third-floor corridor on their way to a small armory located at the southeastern corner of the fort that offered a clear view of much of the plateau and served as the lookout room, also housing various ballistics and doubling as a sniper's perch.

"Why do you say that?"

Adrian shook his head. "You know how adamant I was against attending Tellisburg. My resentment manifested in a decidedly poor attitude toward the officers, the other cadets. I felt everyone owed me something. Sylvera was the only cadet who had the nerve to stand up to me. In hindsight, I acted no better than the most typically spoiled estated."

"I had not heard that," Leynitz said.

"Of course you wouldn't have. Everything that came out of Tellisburg about me was airtight. Marsell, do you honestly believe nothing in my report was an embellishment?"

"I wouldn't presume anything of the sort, Prince."

"A neutral answer," Adrian scoffed. "I expected as much."

"I am not insincere. I see no reason to doubt your report was anything other than accurate. And I know for a fact that you were, without a doubt, top of your class, and would have been even if you were from the Outlands. You should have more faith in yourself."

"Nevertheless, Sylvera and I locked horns for the entirety of my second year."

"And so you respect him? Enough to allow him to speak in such a manner."

"I don't know about that," Adrian said with a frown. "But as far as I am concerned, I have not yet done anything to prove myself worthy of the crown. His impudence serves as an adequate reminder that I must still earn my future duties and privileges. Though usually he's too frustrating to bother with."

The corners of Leynitz's mouth turned upward in amusement.

Glen Emerett, Mary Abberdine, and Francis Keller were already pressed against the windows when Adrian and Leynitz entered. Upon hearing the door swing open, Keller whirled around, almost running into the prince and general.

"Your Highness. General. The enemy is snaking along the eastern recesses and making its way around Colonel Lariban's forces to the north."

"What! Where is the colonel now?"

"Giving chase."

"Has the enemy broken through to the eastern gate?"

"No, the barbarians appear to be going around our defenses and are pushing farther north."

Leynitz's eyebrows shot up. "They plan to circle around and link with War Chief Sol," he said.

Keller nodded. "I think so too, sir."

Leynitz strode up to the windows and looked outside to confirm Keller's report. He saw immediately that all was as he had surmised. The amorphous swarm of Amelarens was no longer confined to the area leading from the southeastern entrance to the plateau. As Keller had said, it now made its way around Lariban's smaller and more spread out contingent of soldiers, seemingly avoiding confrontation in order to push through to the north.

"We must reconvene at the courtyard immediately," Leynitz said, turning away from the window and pointing at the scouts. "You three. I apologize, but it looks like I can no longer offer you well-deserved rest. You'll have to move out immediately. I want you to gather half the archers still stationed along the southeastern windows and meet us there."

"Yes, sir," Keller said. Glen and Mary acknowledged the order with brief salutes as they exited quickly.

—8—

Renard lost track of how much time had elapsed since Adrian and Leynitz left the courtyard. He tried to monitor the sounds from outside as best as he could from where he sat against the western wall. At first, the clashing of blades, and impact of shields and projectiles were distant, but they amplified as the reps passed, and, after a while, it seemed highly plausible that Osterfeld was making significant progress toward the western gate. Renard had just begun to consider rallying a small group to venture outside and investigate when Reznik and Eldrid returned from the northern wing, hastening down the stairs from the second floor. Reznik spotted Renard and practically ran straight at him.

"We have a problem. The main force somehow got past Colonel Lariban and bypassed the eastern gate entirely. There are warriors rounding the northern wall of the fort."

"They're trying to link both forces," Renard said.

"Indeed. What is the colonel doing?" Reznik wondered aloud.

"I don't doubt that Colonel Lariban did the best he could," Eldrid said, joining their conversation. "Given the disparity in numbers, it's a wonder he managed to hold the eastern gate for this long."

Reznik raised an eyebrow ambiguously. "I was talking about Colonel Osterfeld."

"Do you hear that?" Renard said, pointing at the wall behind him. "It's getting louder."

Reznik and Eldrid strained their ears. Eldrid nodded.

"That answers your question," he said to Reznik.

"Want to go take a look?" Renard suggested.

"Let's go," Reznik replied without hesitation.

"If you are both going, I will stay and wait for the prince and general," Eldrid said.

"The two of us will be enough," Reznik said. "Come on, let's not waste time."

With that, he ran into the tunnel. Douglas looked up languidly as he passed; Reznik did not even offer him a glance.

Two-thirds of the way through the tunnel toward the gate, a narrow door was etched in the northern wall, barely visible and almost impossible to distinguish without prior knowledge of its existence. Behind it was a narrow staircase leading up to a small nook between floors. It had a small window that offered a glimpse of the area just outside the western gate. Equally as camouflaged next to the door was a transceiver mount with the wiring running through the walls up to the nook. A single soldier with a disengaged but uneasy expression stood beside the setup.

Renard hurried after Reznik and caught him before the latter ran past the door.

"Hold on. Stop."

Reznik whirled around. "Why?"

Renard pulled the door open. "This is the emergency relay system for gate control. You stay here. I'm going to see what the situation is." He pointed at the soldier. "Wait by the gate."

The soldier roused from his idleness and did as he was told. After several ticks, Renard disappeared behind the door and ascended the stairs.

Reznik squinted in the darkness as he tried to make out the transceiver. After spotting it, he propped himself against the wall beside it, impatiently tapping his foot as he waited. Reznik had seen this technology before in Aldova and Tellisburg, but was surprised it had already been installed at the Highpost.

After two or three reps, which seemed to last an eternity to Reznik, Renard's voice rang out from the mount. "Reznik, can you hear me? If you're there, pick up the transceiver and hold down the button on top to talk."

Reznik lifted the device off its mount and did as Renard instructed.

"What do you see?" he asked.

"Never mind that," Renard snapped. "Get the gate open. *Now!*"

Rarely did Renard speak with such urgency. Reznik knew better than to hesitate. He slammed the transceiver down on the mount and ran toward the gate. The din outside was piercingly loud.

Two avets stood to either side of the gate. They looked anxious but ready to act. The one to Reznik's right was the soldier who had just been standing by the midhall door. Next to him was a large crank.

"Open the gate!" Reznik commanded.

The gatekeepers lined up next to the crank and began to roll it clockwise.

—9—

Osterfeld's initial push to the western gate was rebuffed after Sol regrouped his warriors. Although Reznik, Eldrid, and their small group of avets had reached the fort, the Amelarens clamped down on any remaining soldiers within the vicinity of the gate.

Madeline helped Nash carry Patrice beyond the combat zone. Nash recruited an avet to lay two blankets on the ground, onto which he and Madeline gently lowered the injured woman. Patrice fought to stay conscious and refused Nash's attempts to anesthetize her with a cloth dipped in one of his mysterious substances.

"Get that away from me," Patrice rasped.

"It will help with the pain," Madeline said as gently as she could.

Patrice jerked her head to the side. "No. The pain will keep me awake."

Madeline was at a loss. It seemed inappropriate of her to instruct a medic on treating an injury. Nevertheless, she wanted to do what she could for her squadmate.

"Have you stopped the bleeding yet?" Patrice asked Nash in a tense but remarkably steady voice. "I can't tell."

"Yes," Nash replied, "but I don't want you to move just yet."

He pulled a small vial filled with another liquid from his bag.

"This is to prevent infection. A special formula," he said cheerfully. "It doesn't even taste bad, I promise you."

He uncorked the vial and held it close to Patrice's lips. She glanced up at him, uncertainly. He smiled reassuringly at her. Slowly, Patrice craned her neck forward. Nash tilted the vial and poured the liquid into her mouth. Patrice swallowed and laid her head back on the blanket. Gradually, her eye movements became less rapid, before her lids closed and her breathing slowed.

Nash stood and took a deep breath.

"You knocked her out," Madeline said slowly.

"I wasn't lying," Nash said. "Palodine does prevent infection, but I had to add a sedative so I could cut her open."

"What? Why would you do that?"

Nash bent down and rolled Patrice until she was almost flat on her stomach. He pointed to the wound through her torn uniform. Madeline saw it looked much less severe than she had thought it to be from the amount of blood Patrice had lost.

"Part of the spearhead got lodged inside somehow," Nash said grimly. "I'm not much of a surgeon, but I'll have to do what I can …"

A chill ran down Madeline's spine, but before she could process her thoughts, someone grabbed her arm.

"We're going in again," Cyrus Marcole said, releasing his grip after she saw him. "The brutes are on the move."

Arthur Sorel and Jasmine Curtland appeared behind him on their respective mounts.

"Captain Havora, we're moving," Sorel called.

Nash shook his head and gestured toward the unconscious Patrice, then to where other injured soldiers lay around him. "I have to tend to the wounded."

"Vice Captain Sylvera is inside the fort," Sorel said. "Who will lead your soldiers if not you?"

Jasmine gave him a look. "What about you, Vice Captain?"

"I have been instructed to hold the rear lines with the colonel."

Frustration washed over Nash's face.

"Captain Curtland, can you—"

"Fine."

"Thank you."

Cyrus tugged gingerly on Madeline's elbow. "Come on."

Madeline tore her eyes from Nash and Patrice and forced herself to follow the two officers. She and Cyrus returned to where the 9th Squad was lined up alongside the rest of the 26th. Word spread quickly that the Curtlands would assume temporary command of the company.

"What's going on?" Cyrus asked Josef.

"The Amelarens pressed up to the northwest," Josef said. "The colonel sees an opening to make another push for the gate. Or such is what I hear."

"More or less," Mason Hunt agreed.

"Get ready!" Jasmine barked from atop her horse, galloping from the south to where the squad was lined up. The 26th and 28th stood side by side. Two hundred meters away, two-thirds of Osterfeld's soldiers were locked in combat with the Amelarens, entrenched another two hundred meters in front of the western gate. The volume of enemy warriors separating the Coranthians from their soldiers in the fort was thinning; Sol's detachment was indeed shifting northward.

Rosalina Curtland rode next to her sister, facing east, her eyes trained like a hawk's on the battle. She leaned forward, lowering her coiled body and holding her reins close to her horse's mane.

"On your go, Rosa," Jasmine said.

Rosalina produced her crossbow, fitted a flare bolt and shot into the air.

"Now!" Jasmine hollered.

For Madeline, there were no longer thoughts of Patrice lying on her side or Reznik hitting Douglas. There was only the adrenaline and survival instinct kicking in, the trigger that had by now been conditioned in her before every battle. Gladius in hand, she rushed alongside her squadmates into the fray.

Though few in number, the Coranthian reinforcements charged at full force. After ten reps of fierce fighting, the Amelarens retreated toward the fort's western gate where Coranthian crossbowmen appeared in the windows and rained arrows down on the warriors. The Amelarens shot their own arrows in return but were at a clear disadvantage with most of their troops concentrated north of the gate, preventing them from solidifying and blocking Osterfeld's forces from advancing. At first, it appeared only a matter of time before the Coranthians would break through, but the battle took a different turn as they began to steadily push the Amelarens back.

Southwest of the fort was a small thicket of dellews, short trees that commonly grew in small, isolated clusters. It was not large enough to conceal many people, but Sol had managed to pack in thirty of his best warriors. Lodged between the trees, they were part of the contingency plan for this exact situation. The arrival of the Coranthian reinforcements prompted them to burst forth from their hiding spot and strike, perpetuating the cycle of flanking; those on the offensive were once again forced to contend with a blindside attack.

"Turn around! Behind you!" Jasmine waved her ax in the direction of the oncoming Amelaren elites, most of whom were lightly armored, tall and hulking light-footed behemoths.

"Behind us!" Bethany cried from beside Madeline, relaying the message to her squadmates. Gone was Bethany's listlessness; in the heat of battle, she was as alert and focused as she had ever been.

Rosalina dodged the swipe of an Amelaren ax and instinctively threw the bolt in her hand like a dart; the missile lodged itself in the throat of a warrior, who fell to the ground, choking on his own blood. Still atop her steed, she weaved her way into the middle of the Coranthian formation and grabbed a handful of bolts. Hands moving at lightning speed, she fitted them to her crossbow and shot repeatedly and accurately at two of the charging Amelaren ambushers from the southwest. Both warriors were struck with a pair of bolts, though not critically. They did not even slow down from the impact and tore into the avets closest to them. Seeing this, Rosalina loaded another bolt and took a few ticks to aim carefully. Her next shot went between its target's eyes, but by the time the warrior went down, three more had replaced him, hacking away at the avets at the rear of the 28th.

Meanwhile, Jasmine continued to fight the Amelarens up front, briefly making contact with Vice Captain Kenneth Anders of the 33rd, informing him of the situation.

"Another of the war chief's traps, is it?" Anders growled, riding behind a wall of soldiers, rushing to meet the enemy. "I don't remember these brutes being quite so clever."

"Why isn't the colonel committing everyone to entering the fort?" Jasmine wondered.

"And abandon our path of retreat?" Anders returned, as he adjusted his helmet.

Just steps away from Jasmine, Madeline heard the exchange. She looked over her shoulder and then back ahead. There seemed to be only a few Amelarens between her and the fort. It would be a short sprint away.

"We should rush through," she said to no one in particular but loud enough for Jasmine to hear. The captain glanced at her and nodded.

"If Colonel Osterfeld is unwilling to supply more reinforcements, there's no reason for us to be out here fighting War Chief Sol's warriors by ourselves. We should try to regroup inside the fort and bolster the defenses as well."

"Very well," Anders said. "I will consult Captain Rousseau."

"You think we have time for that?" Jasmine spat. "I'll take responsibility. Just move with us and bring as many soldiers as you can with you. We need all the momentum we can muster."

Anders nodded timidly, while Jasmine had already moved on. She raised her ax and let out a shrill whistle. Friend and foe alike turned toward her.

"Everyone, head straight for the western gate! *Now!*"

With that, she spurred her horse and almost rammed directly into the nearest warrior, who stumbled aside to avoid being trampled though could not avoid Jasmine's ax slashing his face open.

"Rosa!" Jasmine called without looking behind her. "Back me up!"

It was an unnecessary request. Rosalina was already almost single-handedly holding off Sol's elites with rapid-fire shots and the superior mobility offered by her horse, but the soldiers around her were now forced to fight while moving backwards to cover the charge led by Jasmine at the front of the formation.

As the 26th and 28th pushed through avets and warriors alike, more Amelarens from Sol's main force broke off to intercept them. What was only moments before a sluggishly retreating group of warriors now closed in rapidly on the Curtlands' position. The two groups soon collided. Sol's warriors halted the Coranthian advance with the western gate fewer than one hundred meters away.

Jasmine looked around and realized that Anders had not rallied the 33rd to follow her lead. She saw the vice captain safely enclosed within a circle of his avets, sitting atop his horse with his shield half-raised though not taking any action. Captain Rousseau was not far from him, adopting a similar stance. The two officers had held back their companies to remain with the main body of soldiers. The Curtlands' command was separated from all nearby friendlies by a gaggle of Amelarens, many of whom now turned their attention to the 26th and 28th.

"You cowards! Are you abandoning the prince to save your own hides?" Jasmine shouted in frustration. Despite her words, she knew that to continue toward the fort would further isolate her troops and put them in grave danger. Doubling back to reunite with the others was the best option to prevent annihilation.

"Back to the main force!" she cried, turning and jerking her head to the side, barely evading an Amelaren hand-ax that whizzed past her left ear.

Madeline was incredulous. They had come so far, only to be repelled a few strides away from the gate. Something primal stirred within her. She had no intention of obeying this order.

"I'm going to make a run for it," she said, again to no one in particular.

Next to her, Josef looked stunned. "What?"

"Come *on*! We're here already!" Madeline's voice laid bare her desperation. "We can break through, even if it's just our company."

To her dismay, the collective group of the 26th and 28th had already reoriented and was pushing back toward the other Coranthians. She turned again to consider the path before her.

"I'm going," she repeated, raising her gladius and breaking into a run.

"Wait! Come back!" Bethany shouted, to no avail.

The suddenness of her movements caught some of the Amelarens by surprise. She was able to run right past several warriors before any knew what was happening but was stopped in her tracks by one who was more alert and ready for her. The man pointed a sword in her face. His posing allowed Madeline to lower her head and run directly at him. Caught off-guard, the warrior pulled his sword back in a panic to put some force behind a swing, but Madeline barreled right into him. Her gladius went straight through the man's torso. Instinctively, she shoved him to the ground to free her weapon.

"Go! Go!" came a Coranthian voice from behind her, and this time she whirled around. As she did so, her hair clip rattled loose and snapped away. Her hair flung wildly as she jerked her head to toss aside the crimson locks blocking her sight. Tailing her were Cyrus Marcole and Nicole Desanolis, as well as several avets from other squads, numbering about twenty in all.

"Why are you stopping?" Cyrus shouted. "Go! We're almost there!"

"Look!" said Nicole. "The gate!"

There came a rumbling of chains and bolts. The steel gate and thick wooden door behind it rose in unison. The sight and sound of the gate's opening came as a surprise to all. Some of the Amelarens froze, uncertain how to react. Meanwhile, the heads of numerous crossbows protruded from the second and third stories of the fort, through the windows directly above the gate, followed by a shower of bolts aimed at the warriors surrounding Madeline's group.

"We can't go back now!" one of the other avets yelled. "Move, Agilda! Get inside!"

There was no time to waste. Seeing the Amelarens distracted by the cover fire, Madeline raised her gladius and slashed at anything in her way. Several warriors fell to her blade. Madeline sensed the other avets behind her, who followed her lead, forcing themselves through with as much desperation.

Then there was nothing in front of Madeline except grass and dirt. The jaws of the gate roared open to reveal an entryway shrouded in darkness, except for a tiny beam of light emanating from the courtyard at the other end of the tunnel. A single soldier wearing an officer's uniform emerged from its shadows.

"Hurry up!" Reznik cried, standing several meters in front of the door. He raised his arm in the air. The door, having risen fully, creaked and groaned. Inside, the gatekeepers were prepared to release the cranks.

Madeline's run turned into an all-out sprint. The others were right on her heels. As they ran toward Reznik, the crossbowmen from the upper floors laid down a precise barrage of bolts, cutting off the warriors, giving chase to the small group of Coranthians dashing for the gate.

When Madeline reached Reznik, their eyes met briefly. Madeline's were wild and fiery, Reznik's cool and calm. He turned and headed back inside.

"Close it," he said to the gatekeepers after Madeline's group of soldiers had run past him.

The cranks turned much more easily in the opposite direction, and the gate came crashing down. A harsh clang reverberated throughout the tunnel as the gate snapped into its plants. With the outer grid of steel firmly in place, the wooden door began to descend slowly.

—10—

"You shouldn't have done that," Reznik said through clenched teeth.

Madeline had not yet caught her breath, panting heavily against the wall. They had entered the courtyard and stood near the far northwestern corner. Many of the soldiers present gathered in small groups. They were on edge and were made further uneasy by Leynitz, who watched stonily from the floor.

"What if Renard hadn't ordered the gate open? You should have regrouped with the main force."

This made Madeline angry.

"We were within a stone's throw of the gate. All of a sudden we're supposed to turn back?"

She bent over and gripped her knees tightly to steady her shaking arms.

Reznik began again, "If Renard hadn't been on the lookout—"

"It's not her fault, from what I saw," Renard interrupted, appearing from nowhere. "Maddy, I'm glad to see you."

Madeline glared at Reznik. "At least someone is."

"Charging the gate wasn't the wrong move." Renard gave Reznik a quick glance but continued speaking without missing a beat. "From my vantage point, the 26th and 28th had a clear shot, but then War Chief Sol sprung his trap. He's outmaneuvering everyone. I realize now that all along he has been baiting Colonel Osterfeld into trying to make a run for it so they can whittle away at our forces. The first time was when you made it through, Rez. Something about this entire situation feels very wrong."

"It won't work again," Reznik said.

"It won't have to," Renard replied. "Not if the war chief links with the main force to the east."

"But you said it was right to rush the gate."

Renard's eyes narrowed. "What, you don't agree?"

"It was too risky, too reckless," Reznik said.

"That's a surprise coming from you," Renard said. "I'd have expected you to do the same thing if you were out there. Would you just back off and let War Chief Sol regroup?"

Reznik frowned.

"I should report to the general," Renard said with a shrug. He headed for the southern stairway, leaving Reznik and Madeline alone.

Reznik's attention was diverted elsewhere. Madeline followed his gaze to the other side of the tunnel where Douglas sat despondently, apart from all the other avets. The blood was wiped clean from his face, although dried spots streaked the front of his armor. Glen Emerett stood awkwardly nearby to provide some measure of comfort. He offered occasional words in an attempt to engage Douglas in conversation.

"How is Konith?" Reznik asked, facing Madeline once again.

Her breath had returned to normal, but her muscles began to cramp slightly. "Nash was still working on her when I last saw them."

Reznik nodded and looked away. There was a long pause before he spoke. "Renard is right. I would have done the same thing. But it wasn't me out there. It was you. That's why I feel differently about it."

Madeline turned his words over in her head for a moment.

"I see," she said simply.

—11—

There was no discernible change in Leynitz's demeanor after Renard informed him of what he had seen outside the western gate.

"Very well, Captain," Leynitz said flatly. "Go find the prince. Conduct a scan of the upper floors and assure the bowmen are maintaining their rotations."

Renard ran off to carry out the order, once again leaving Leynitz alone on the balcony. The general looked down at the courtyard, surveying his soldiers below. He began to pace back and forth, lost in thought. Occasionally, he peered at the darkening sky. The arc continued past six. It had been two arcs since Tallen's forces first appeared on the eastern outskirts of the plateau.

Several more reps passed. Although Renard had not returned with Adrian, Leynitz decided to head back down. He had barely taken his first steps when he heard a crash from the eastern gate.

Leynitz quickened his descent. When he reached the ground level, he was intercepted by Eldrid, accompanied by several avets.

"Sir, Colonel Lariban has returned with the remainder of his command."

"Is that so?" Leynitz said.

Eldrid backed away to let Leynitz pass. The general marched toward the eastern tunnel. Lariban emerged from its dark recesses. He was disheveled—dirty and bloodied—though appeared uninjured. The survivors of the Lower 3rd followed. Captain Newitt and Vice Captain Lusk led the remainder of the 14th, 22nd, and 25th companies, and Captain Einhardt commanded the 32nd.

The blankness in Leynitz's face finally gave way to frustration. "You have quite the nerve to show your face after allowing those brutes to just walk right by you."

"The colonel fought War Chief Tallen to a draw," Captain Newitt protested. "We had to stay close to support him."

"Were your orders to engage him?" Leynitz roared, apparently unimpressed that his second-in-command had managed to stand toe-to-toe with an Amelaren war chief.

Robert Newitt, a wiry young man who scarcely appeared his twenty-five years, shrank under the general's withering glare.

"Forgive my failure, sir," Lariban said, unfazed by his superior's rage. "I was trying to fulfill my objective of holding them back for as long as possible. I did not expect the enemy to prioritize anything over a direct confrontation."

His words gradually calmed Leynitz. The general regained his composure during the long silence that followed.

"I don't disagree with that, I suppose," he said finally, reverting to his calm, measured voice.

"What now, sir?" asked Charles Einhardt, a strongly built man with a bald head and thin mustache. At forty-seven years of age, he had served longer in the military than either Lariban or Leynitz.

"Give me a head count," the general snapped.

At that moment, Renard emerged from the northeastern corridor and strode into the courtyard. Adrian walked alongside him. Leynitz waved them over, along with Eldrid, who was alone, leaning against one of the pillars near the opposite stairway. Soon, all captains present had gathered around Adrian and Leynitz.

"Your Highness!" Newitt cried with relief. "Thank Creon for your safety."

Lariban and Einhardt bowed.

"Enough." Adrian frowned.

"Well, gentlemen?" Leynitz said impatiently.

Newitt and Einhardt seemed reluctant to answer. Noting their disposition, Lariban said bluntly, "The Lower 3rd numbers only forty-seven. The 14th and 32nd were both severely thinned as well. We lost Vice Captain Darville. Newitt and Einhardt command about seventy-five soldiers."

"I see." Leynitz gave Einhardt a stern nod. "Darville was a good man."

Einhardt lowered his head. "My apologies for having failed you, sir. Your Highness."

"And I presume the 22nd and 25th … "

"I took on the stragglers," Lariban said. "I regret to report that no officers survived."

Leynitz gave a sigh weighed with grief and exhaustion.

"Factoring in a rough estimate of casualties among our defenders inside, that puts us at about three hundred soldiers," Renard said.

Lariban swiveled to face him. "What of Pike, Rousseau, and Wolbay?"

"They reached Colonel Osterfeld, but were cut off by War Chief Sol on the way back. Only a few of Osterfeld's soldiers managed to break through." Renard gestured toward the soldiers lined up against the western wall. Lariban, Newitt, and Einhardt took a moment to look them over.

"What should we do now, sir?" Einhardt repeated to Leynitz.

"We must abandon the Highpost. We have no other choice."

"I agree," Lariban said immediately.

Newitt seemed dejected. "Is there no way to salvage our position? Perhaps Colonel Osterfeld can br—"

Leynitz cut him off. "They outnumbered us from the beginning. That itself was not a problem, but when War Chief Sol's forces arrived, we were forced to fight on both sides. The brutes whittled us down. Now, what good is the fort when we lack the manpower to defend it?"

Adrian smiled as he heard the echo of his own earlier words.

Eldrid shook his head ruefully. "And just when we'd finished construction."

"It's only a building," Einhardt countered with a shrug.

"We need to rendezvous with Colonel Osterfeld," Leynitz said. "We can't wait for him to come to us."

"The safety of His Highness comes first," Lariban said with a nod toward Adrian.

The prince stared at him challengingly. "No, Colonel, the survival of our troops as a whole comes first. I'll not subject myself to pandering. Those who lost their lives did so not for me but for all of us."

Lariban's typically blank face morphed into a look of surprise. "Very well, Your Highness."

"Well said, Prince," Leynitz said. "Now listen closely, gentlemen. The brutes are rounding the northern end of the fort as we speak. They will also attempt to keep a lid on both gates."

"How can we leave, then?" said Eldrid.

"There is a reinforced ladder that can be lowered from the second-floor southeastern lookout," Leynitz said. "There is another at the northwestern lookout, but we'd best not go that way."

"What of the horses?" Eldrid asked.

Leynitz had not considered this point and had no answer. The other officers exchanged apprehensive glances. They valued their steeds highly, but knew there was no efficient way to escort the animals out of the fort except through one of the gates.

"General, I have a suggestion. The horses can be used as a distraction." Seven pairs of eyes fell on Renard Renault.

"Continue," said Adrian, the only one present who did not have his personal mount with him. While he was at Argiset, he made use of reserve horses such as Maximilian; his prized durioness remained at Aldova.

"A group of riders will wait for as long as possible by the western gate after everyone else leaves to the south. When the time comes, the riders will rush out the western gate and head straight for Colonel Osterfeld. This will, hopefully, draw the enemy's attention and also reveal the colonel's location to the southern group. The riders will keep the Amelarens occupied for as long as necessary and then return to the main force."

Those gathered around him paused as they considered the plan.

"That is an excellent idea," Leynitz concluded.

Lariban raised a finger. "But who will lead the riders, Captain? Obviously, the prince and general will not partake in your proposed diversion."

"It is only fitting that I do," Renard replied. "And I will gather volunteers from the avets."

"I will go as well," Eldrid volunteered.

Lariban wiped some dirt from his forehead and said to Leynitz, "That seems acceptable to me, sir."

"Likewise," Leynitz said. "This is quite a daring maneuver, Captain. You have my commendation."

He looked around at the officers.

"Does anyone object to having your steeds temporarily commandeered?"

None of the other captains offered any protests.

"Then we will proceed with Captain Renault's plan."

Renard bowed slightly. Adrian glanced skeptically at him, but noting Leynitz and Lariban's satisfaction, he nodded his approval.

The general looked skyward. Rhynon and Faerila were visible amid the twilight. "It will be completely dark soon. We will wait for the cover of night to make our move. Gather all the soldiers and horses into the courtyard. There remains no reason to scatter them. Let us reconvene in ten reps."

The circle broke up. Leynitz and Lariban left together, while most of the others returned to their own companies. Eldrid offered to sweep the northern wing once again, rounding up any soldiers still stationed on the upper floors. Soon, only Adrian and Renard remained near the entrance to the corridor.

"Are you trying to play hero, Renault?"

Renard smirked. "You know me so well, Prince."

That prompted a short guffaw from Adrian.

"I suppose I need to find more riders," Renard said. "Thankfully, I already have a few in mind."

He started across the courtyard; Adrian fell into step behind him. As they neared the western tunnel, the prince recognized more than one face among the soldiers lined up against the wall.

When Madeline saw Adrian, she immediately straightened and bent over in a deep bow. Beside her, Reznik stared dispassionately at the prince.

"Your Highness. It has been a long time," Madeline said.

"Hello, Avet Agilda." Adrian rubbed his chin and scanned the other soldiers, spotting Glen and Douglas on the other side of the tunnel. "A class reunion of sorts, it seems."

She nodded. "Not under the most preferable circumstances, unfortunately."

Renard waved a finger at Reznik.

"Listen, I have something to ask of you," he said. He recounted the discussion with Leynitz and the officers, disclosing the particulars of his plan to use the horses as bait.

"You want me to ride with you and Captain Eldrid," Reznik deduced.

"You and Glen, for starters."

"Excuse me," Adrian said with a frown, sauntering off in the direction of the southern stairway to where Leynitz and Lariban were engaged in a private, earnest conversation.

Renard saw the corner of Reznik's mouth curl and warned, "Don't you start."

"What?" said Madeline, glancing at each of them in turn.

"If I were the prince," Renard said, "I'd be annoyed, too. I'd hate to be treated like some sort of fragile relic."

"Oh, how his pride must have been stung," Reznik said acidly, "when you asked me, of all people, to sacrifice myself for his sake."

"Who said anything about sacrifice? You think I'd sign myself up for a suicide mission?"

"I'm saying that's how he sees it," Reznik said.

Renard felt a tap on his shoulder. Captain Newitt stood behind him.

"Ah, Robert. Still in one piece, are you?"

"I had a few close calls out there," Newitt said, eyeing Reznik and Madeline suspiciously. "I need a word with you … er, alone."

Renard shrugged and followed Newitt.

"Adrian is no coward," Madeline remarked. "I'm sure he wishes there was something more substantial for him to do, that's all. I doubt he's solely concerned with how often you plan to show him up."

Reznik shook his head derisively. "Whatever. Let's go get Glen."

Madeline grabbed his arm. "Wait. What about Douglas?"

"What about him?" Reznik raised an eyebrow. "He'll stay with you on foot. You'll be with the general and Colonel Lariban and the prince. You'll both be fine."

"Oh, no," Madeline said, stepping forward and staring defiantly into his eyes. "No you don't. I'm riding with you."

Reznik hesitated. "I told you before that—"

"Don't you dare make excuses, Reznik Sylvera. If Glen goes, then I sure as hell will as well. So will Douglas. You know he's good with horses. You'll square with him, and that's that. The five of us are sticking together."

Reznik sighed. "Then we'll do that."

"You're not leaving me behind again," Madeline said, unblinking.

"I won't."

He remained still, until Madeline finally released him from her gaze. Then the two joined Glen and Douglas to inform them of their upcoming task.

—12—

Leynitz ordered almost everyone inside the fort to gather at the courtyard in anticipation of a breach of either or both gates; the courtyard itself was designed to be easily defended from the overlooking balconies. The southern wing was almost completely vacated, save for several scouts, as there was little Amelaren presence on the south side since Tallen's main force and Sol's contingent convened to the north.

The bowmen previously stationed within the southern wing relocated to the northern wing, where a tripwire defense was employed. While the majority of the Coranthians remained in the vicinity of the courtyard to prepare for Renard's evacuation plan, the bowmen continued to harass the aggregate Amelaren force that lurked near the exterior walls of the fort in attempt to convey a strong Coranthian presence still inside and discourage Tallen and Sol from ordering an all-out assault. No one knew how long the ruse would hold.

Leynitz requested reports from Lariban and Einhardt regarding whether the Amelarens had ladders. Lariban denied having seen any, but Einhardt was less certain. If they did, there would be little the Coranthians could do to prevent them from climbing to the upper-floor windows and forcing their way in. All these factors and circumstances weighed on Leynitz, who admitted to Adrian and his subordinates that they faced a significant risk by staying put and asserted it would be advantageous to make their move in the dark.

After Renard returned from his private audience with Newitt, he spoke with Reznik, who by then had recruited Glen and Douglas, per Madeline's insistence. The two of them decided that, with the exception of Eldrid, the riders should consist of soldiers from the 21st and 26th. Mary Abberdine and Francis Keller were to help Leynitz coordinate Osterfeld's soldiers upon reunion.

"Command structure will be easier this way," Renard said. "We have thirty horses, maybe a few more, including reserves. Bring all your soldiers, and I'll fill in the remaining spots."

Reznik could not order all of his subordinates to take the assignment without reservation. When he gathered all the avets from the 26th, several professed a lack of confidence in their riding abilities.

"Cowards," Reznik muttered to Madeline, hand covering his mouth.

"We don't have time to browbeat them," Madeline said. "We have enough. Just leave the rest to Renard."

In total, fourteen riders were recruited from the 26th, with the remaining avets temporarily assigned to the command of Einhardt of the 32nd. Madeline was glad Cyrus Marcole and Nicole Desanolis had not shied from taking up reins. She found comfort in knowing her friends and squadmates would be together in the coming arcs.

There was little more to be done before nightfall. While Reznik and Renard went to the stable to prepare the horses, Madeline took a seat as far from anyone as she could manage and passed the time inspecting her gear and stretching sore limbs. Tension rose during the reps leading to eight arc. Anxiety swept over her in concert with the full realization of how dangerous the task looming before her was, but more significantly, she feared an Amelaren attack before eight arc, when Leynitz planned to commence evacuation. The prospect seemed more likely than not; in fact, several officers expressed confusion as to why the Amelarens had not attacked already. Still, what worried her was not the threat but the effect an actual attack would have on the escape.

At seven-arc sixty, her fears were realized when a loud explosion sounded to the north. Moments later, a scout ran into the courtyard and announced that the Amelarens were planting bombs at the northern end of the fort, trying to blast their way in.

"Why there?" Adrian wondered aloud.

"Possibly a structural weakness of some sort," Lariban said. "The northern wing was built outward and completed not long ago. There are sections that lack reinforcement."

"No ladders, then," Leynitz said. "I need the status outside each gate."

Eldrid and Einhardt called several scouts and bowmen to report.

"The troops cannot provide an accurate estimate of enemy traffic," Eldrid told Leynitz. "It is proving difficult to see clearly. The Amelarens have gone dark."

"So we do not know that either gate is safe even though they are trying to break in from the north," Lariban said. "That would explain why they waited until now to attack. They share our preference for moving in the shadows."

"They think like we do, it seems," Leynitz said. "We have no choice. Renault, Eldrid, gather everyone from the northern wing and send them to the second-floor lookout. It's time."

"Go on, sir," Renard said. "We may need to depart ahead of schedule if the Amelarens break through."

He flashed Reznik a hand signal from across the courtyard to inform him they were to fit the horses and fall into position. Reznik stood beside Gambit, hitched to a pole and snorting lazily, and Lightstar, the zephyr whose master, Vice Captain Lusk of the 14th, would remain on foot under Leynitz. Reznik beckoned to Madeline, who was tying her hair back into a bun.

"Are you ready?" Reznik asked.

Madeline took a deep breath. "I think so."

"Okay then, you take Gambit."

"What? Why?"

"It'll be easier this way, trust me. Here, let me give you a hand."

Madeline wrinkled her nose. "Uh, I don't need your help getting on a horse, Rez. You know that."

"That's not it. Gambit is friendly, but he has to be shown that you're a friend. Just watch."

She allowed Reznik to help her onto his horse, albeit somewhat awkwardly. Just as he had said, Gambit gave an amiable snort and, having seen that his new rider had climbed aboard with the apparent blessing of his master, did not seem to mind her at all.

"There." Reznik turned to Lightstar. "Now let me worry about this one."

Dressed in his avet uniform, Adrian watched the two from the southern second-floor balcony. He felt a light tap on his right shoulder.

"Your Highness, we'd best be going," Leynitz said.

The prince turned and followed the general to the southeastern corridor. Accompanied by Leynitz and Lariban, Adrian fell in behind soldiers of the 3rd, 14th, and 32nd as they hustled down the long hallway to the second-floor lookout. The room was filled with soldiers. The wide double ladder had been lowered from the largest window; a group of scouts had already descended to the ground outside the fort and scattered to check for any sign of nearby Amelaren activity.

"Get ready, Your Highness," Leynitz said.

Adrian checked the straps of his plain leather scabbard, which held his royal blade, Antilus. No matter how dressed down he was, it would be unthinkable for him to carry less than the most resplendent weapon. Adrian drew it as quietly as possible. What little light Rhynon and Faerila emitted on this cloudy night reflected off the aeron; his clear blue eyes, taut and hardened, stared back at him from the glowing blade.

Peering out the window, Sergeant Keller received a signal from the scouts on the ground and weaved his way through the mass of soldiers to Leynitz.

"We seem to be in the clear, sir," Keller said. He kept his voice low, as all the soldiers did; they had to make as little noise as possible throughout the evacuation.

"Good," Leynitz said. "Move up and make sure everyone is pairing down with no interruptions."

Lariban squeezed through the crowd, leaving Leynitz and Adrian behind all the other soldiers, backs practically against the closed door. Along with Lariban, they would be the last to descend the ladder.

Adrian was still lost in thought, staring at the royal blade.

"Your Highness, focus," Leynitz said softly.

"This better work, Marsell," Adrian said heavily, sheathing Antilus.

"There is nothing of which I am more certain." The general pointedly stroked his mustache. "You have my word."

Two by two, the Coranthians climbed down the double ladder to freedom. Out in the open, they could more clearly hear additional explosions to the north, increasing in both frequency and magnitude. Those on the ground urged the remaining soldiers in the lookout to hurry, but the exodus remained methodical due to Lariban's supervision and the soldiers' discipline. At last, the time came for Leynitz and the prince to descend.

They did so quickly and fluidly and were followed by Lariban. Two scouts remained in the lookout to pull up the ladder before opening a smaller side window and rappelling by rope.

With what Leynitz deemed the most dangerous phase of the operation complete, the Coranthians assembled into formation and edged west around the southern end of the fort, hoping to reunite with Osterfeld as inconspicuously as possible.

—13—

In the courtyard, the riders awaited Renard's orders. They could plainly see the agitation in each other's faces. No one was immune to the mounting dread and anxiety as the explosions intensified in the northern wing.

"Why are we waiting? This is crazy," Cyrus Marcole kept repeating to himself. His voice grew louder until almost all of riders could hear him.

"Quiet!" Nicole Desanolis hissed, but her face was deathly pale and her hands shook from gripping the reins to Phoenix, Renard's horse.

There was another explosion, this time accompanied by Silvermane's whinnying. Leynitz had entrusted his durion to Renard, who struggled for several ticks to regain control.

"Stay calm, everyone," Renard said in an even voice belied by heavy breathing. "Let's move into the tunnel."

Reznik sent Glen ahead to dismount by the transceiver and proceed to the small nook above the gate. Glen was to give the signal to open the gate, rejoin the others, and ride out. The last two soldiers to exit the fort, Eldrid and, Renard's vice captain, George Stradt, would man the gate.

Two rodtorches, one across from the transceiver and the other closer to the gate, provided all the tunnel's lighting. The riders lined up in two files, silently seated atop their horses.

Renard picked up the transceiver. "What do you see, Glen?"

"Not much," came the reply. "Nothing from either friend or foe."

"Nobody wants to give away position," Renard said. "Let me know if anything changes. I'll give you the signal to get out of there."

"Okay."

The next explosion was a low, ominous rumble, accompanied by an assortment of fainter unidentifiable noises.

"What was that?" said Stradt, a lanky man with a scar on the right of his forehead and a long ratlike nose.

"I do not think we can wait much longer," Eldrid said to Renard.

"If we leave too soon, it will just be more time we'll have to spend running around out there," said Reznik, standing on point. "We are at risk either way, but it's better to stay inside for now."

"The hell with this, Captain," Stradt snapped. "Let's get out there and do what we need to do."

Renard held up his hand to signal for silence. "Do you hear that?" he said after two reps had passed.

"I don't hear anything," Madeline answered.

"The explosions have stopped. Which means …"

"Which means they're probably inside," Reznik finished.

"Most likely." Renard nodded at Stradt. "Now we go." He picked up the transceiver.

"Glen, you're done. Get down here." Slamming the device on its mount, he ran to where Silvermane waited and hastily mounted.

Eldrid and Stradt dismounted and scrambled forward to manage the gate crank. Glen reappeared and climbed aboard his horse.

Madeline glanced at Douglas beside her, riding Einhardt's steed, Flamefoot. He was alert and seemed much more comfortable on horseback. Madeline looked into his eyes, now lucid, and remembered how he came out of virtual catatonia when she and Reznik approached him to take on this mission. His reaction was as much as she could have hoped for; it comforted her to see him rejuvenated. When he caught her gaze, she smiled. He managed back a small grin, the most fleeting of reassurances. Soon, they heard voices emanating from behind, voices distinctly from inside the fort.

"They're overrunning the building." Renard's voice was a forcefully hoarse whisper. "Open the gate now! We're leaving!"

—14—

The Coranthian riders thundered out Argiset Highpost's western gate, thirty-three strong with Renard leading the charge. One avet directly behind him fired a bolt flare from her crossbow. The flare erupted into a shower of sparks, lighting up the darkness of the inert evening sky. The aural seal enveloping the western half of the plateau broke, unleashing a clamorous torrent of purposeful shouts from around them.

"There!" Madeline yelled. "Enemies to the right!"

All at once, more than a dozen large rodtorches burst alight, casting their flickering flames upon the faces of innumerable Amelaren warriors on the move, several of them unleashing ear-splitting war cries. Hundreds of warriors zeroing in on the riders could be seen in the distance.

"Renard, look for friendlies!" Reznik called. "I'm going at them!"

He turned Lightstar almost completely around. Drawing his sword, he fought to balance as horse and rider rushed headlong toward the oncoming Amelaren swarm.

Madeline fell in behind him, resolving not to let him out of her sight. She knew she would be hard pressed to do any significant damage armed on horseback with only with a gladius and knife but remained undeterred. Douglas, on the other hand, had not bothered to draw either of his weapons, as he kept up with the two. Madeline reminded herself they were to distract the enemy and not obliged to cut down every warrior in sight.

Meanwhile, Renard held his spear steady at his side and charged dead west. "Split up! Half and half!" he called out.

Cyrus Marcole, Nicole Desanolis, and Sigmund Eldrid followed Reznik. Among those who followed Renard were Glen Emerett and George Stradt.

Reznik brought his sword behind him and arced it forward with all his might, driving the razor edge through the armor of the first Amelaren warrior who rushed to meet him. Seeing a second raise his ax, Reznik yanked the reins hard instead of trying to swing his sword across his body. Lightstar whinnied and responded in exactly the manner Reznik anticipated, thrashing and kicking to his left. His left forward hoof brutally connected with the Amelaren's face, cracking the warrior's cheekbone and sending him flying. With that, Reznik spun to separate from the rest of the horde waiting to pounce on him.

Having discovered his horse, Flamefoot, was aptly named for his speed and maneuverability, Douglas lured a group of ten Amelarens away from the rest of the riders, circling back toward the fort. He occasionally allowed the warriors to close the distance before bursting forward to regain separation. Following his lead, Eldrid allowed Douglas to attract most of the attention but expertly weaved in and out of the pack, cutting a swath through the pursuers, who became disoriented from chasing Douglas while being subject to Eldrid's hit-and-run attacks. Cyrus attempted to keep pace with Eldrid but found himself veering too close. His horse collided with a warrior and almost threw him.

"Oh, shit!" Cyrus cried as he clung desperately to his steed, surrounded by several warriors. Eldrid galloped to his aid, slashing to force those converging on Cyrus to back away for a moment, allowing the avet to regain balance.

Meanwhile, Renard rode on, searching for any Coranthian presence. He finally spotted rodtorches in the distance and headed straight for the flames, hoping their bearers were friendly. Several ticks later, he exclaimed in relief when he recognized the face of another rider approaching him.

"Captain Pike, you have no idea how glad I am to see you. And them." Renard gestured to the eighty-some soldiers gathered behind the other rider.

Captain Cecil Pike shook his head. "I am ashamed we were driven away from the fort."

"Save your groveling for the prince," someone cut in gruffly. Hector Osterfeld emerged from the shadows atop his mount, Deni. "We need to get to him and the general."

"They're coming from the southeast," Renard said. "I'll lead you to them."

Pike, Osterfeld, the 5th, and the remnants of Pike's Upper 29th followed Renard and his riders. Osterfeld had commanded the rest of the main Coranthian force to sweep eastward in a wide blanket to maximize the likelihood of contact. As they moved, so too did the rodtorches borne by several of Pike's avets, giving up their position to the Amelarens, who had been preoccupied with Reznik's group up to that point. Another flare went up from the southeast.

"That's them!" Renard shouted.

A voice rang out in Amelaren, halting those who pursued the riders led by Reznik in their tracks. The voice issued a brief statement, and then warriors turned to consider Reznik, tauntingly waving his sword in front of them.

To the surprise of all, another war cry went up in the darkness to the south. More Amelarens poured from the western gate, which was left open. Those who had broken into the Highpost came right back out and were now closer than either group of riders to where the last Coranthian flare launched.

"Damn it!" Reznik cried. They were now boxed into the north and south. While they could head west to meet the main force, this would render them useless to help the group escorting Adrian from the south.

As Reznik turned to face the warriors spilling forth from the gate, a subset formed a wall blocking his group from the most direct path down the western side of the southern wing, while the rest headed south to intercept Renard and Osterfeld. Behind him, those from the north advanced steadily on his position. In either case, they were overwhelmingly outnumbered.

Reznik shot a glance at Madeline, who pulled up next to him. She had managed to stay clear of close combat and was no worse for wear.

"No choice, Maddy. We have to go straight through them."

"I thought as much. I'll be right with you."

With that, Reznik charged.

As Madeline drew closer to the human wall, she noticed in the flickering dimness that these warriors wore different clothes from those donned by the ones she had just been fighting; they were not uniforms in the conventional sense. They bore the jade armor she had seen on warriors during her mad dash past the enemy and into the Highpost earlier that day, which already seemed a lifetime ago.

"These are War Chief Sol's warriors," she told Reznik.

"Yes," he replied, "so be careful. We don't know what tricks they have up their sleeves."

The riders, in contrast, could not afford any trickery. Time was not on their side.

"Go!" Reznik yelled.

The riders came together. They moved in a compact diamond formation, staying as close as possible to one another, riding as one. Those on the outside drew their weapons to keep the Amelarens at bay.

Two horses broke from the others as warriors heedlessly threw themselves at the animals in an attempt to break the formation. One was Flamefoot. Madeline whipped her head in time to see Douglas veer away from the pack.

"Douglas!" she screamed at the top of her lungs.

An Amelaren tried to simply grab the sword from Reznik's hand. Reznik engaged him in a tug of war, eventually winning by smashing his boot into the warrior's face. He ended up digging his foot into Lightstar's sinews in the process, causing the horse to buckle wildly in anger.

"What happened?" he called out, continuing to struggle with Lightstar.

"Douglas!" Madeline cried out again. When she heard Reznik's voice, she turned to him with pained eyes.

Reznik clutched his reins tightly. "Captain Eldrid, take point!"

Riding along the left wing, Eldrid surged forward. "We lost two!" he called as he hacked off an outstretched Amelaren arm.

"Looks like this stupid horse wants nothing to do with me," Reznik said, somehow managing to sheath his sword before using both hands to take the reins. He gave Madeline a knowing look. "Aren't you glad I gave you Gambit?"

Madeline could hardly believe her ears. "What about Douglas?"

"Did you see him fall?" Reznik jerked around on his saddle.

She stared at him.

"Did you see him fall?" he repeated, leaning forward to straighten himself.

"No, but he got separated from us."

"He has a chance if he's still on horseback."

A shrieking whinny came from behind them. One of the horses collapsed on its side, and its rider was immediately surrounded by a group of bloodthirsty warriors. Human screams mixed in with the horse's cries. Madeline was relieved to see that Cyrus and Nicole remained behind her, though felt guilty knowing another avet had fallen.

"Listen," Reznik shouted, "if he only broke formation, he'd know to head west and meet Colonel Osterfeld. I'm sure he's there by now."

Madeline nodded. She wanted to believe him and desperately hoped he was right.

Another Coranthian voice erupted in panic. Cyrus Marcole was under attack from two Amelarens, one of whom had grabbed his horse's left hind leg. The horse tried to jerk free, but the heavyset warrior clung stubbornly. Cyrus frantically bashed the man's head with the butt of his sword repeatedly, to no avail. The horse stumbled away from the others. The second warrior plunged an ax into the beast's neck.

"Let me go!" Cyrus yelled. Two more Amelarens grabbed his left leg and dragged him off the horse. He disappeared in a sea of green Amelaren leather.

"Cyrus!" Nicole called to him, but there was nothing she could do. She had to keep pace with the remaining riders.

Madeline felt her mouth go dry. A sickening knot twisted in her stomach. Had she been on foot, she might have been paralyzed by the wave of helplessness that overcame her. She lowered her head and wrapped her arms around Gambit, willing him to go faster.

—15—

As Reznik feared, Sol's forces reached Adrian's escort before Renard and Osterfeld could.

"To hell with them!" Leynitz shouted. "Break through and protect each other!"

The officers formed a protective shell around Adrian, who grew increasingly disoriented. He had no clear view of his surroundings. All he heard were the cries of men and women, Coranthian and Amelaren, and the calamitous clash of wood and steel tearing and bruising flesh and bone.

The Coranthian elites made short work of Sol's first two waves of warriors, but there seemed to be an endless stream, and the avets and officers made slow progress as they fought their way westward. Their path took them up an incline, which made it impossible to see very far ahead, greatly hindering their ability to gauge enemy movement and numbers.

So overwhelming and cacophonous were the sounds of battle that it was difficult for Adrian to decipher any words at all. He heard a throaty bellow, followed by unintelligible grunting, undoubtedly from the mouth of an enemy.

The Amelarens slowly pushed the Coranthians back down the incline. Warrior after warrior emerged from the darkness to engage the battered and shorthanded Coranthian guard. Adrian gripped Antilus's hilt as he felt them coming for him. There had yet to be an occasion for him to raise his sword personally, but it was only a matter of time.

"We have to push through!" Leynitz yelled. "Where's Sergeant Keller? Keller! Go around to the south and find Osterfeld! He can't be far off!"

"Keller's dead, sir," Einhardt responded.

"We're running out of options, General," Lariban said. "Should we attempt a feint or retreat?"

"Neither. Push harder. I'll be damned if we're stopped here."

Captain Newitt remained closed to Einhardt, guarding Adrian's rear. His green eyes danced in the faint moonlight. He timidly held a hand toward Adrian, who was unsure how to interpret the gesture.

"What is it, Captain?"

"Your Highness, it has been an honor."

Suddenly, Newitt threw off his cloak, revealing a golden suit adorned with gleaming crimson jewels. Adrian was caught by surprise, but soon realized that Newitt wore nothing but regular armor with a coat of paint and fake trim that bore a passing resemblance to his own suit of royal armor. Then it dawned on him.

"Newitt!" he shouted anxiously.

The lanky young man brandished his sword and waved it high in the air. "Follow me!" Newitt cried with all the enthusiastic showmanship he could muster, diving into a crowd of warriors.

"Follow his lead!" shouted Vice Captain Lusk, striding forward at the heels of his captain. Einhardt echoed Lusk's order and followed suit.

Lariban gave Leynitz a grim look, half-shrugged, and then moved to engage the enemy as well.

"Sir, Your Highness, please follow me," came a female voice. Mary Abberdine lurked in the shadows with another scout, having taken cover in the surrounding bushes. "We'll go around as you suggested."

"We must go, Prince," Leynitz said. "They'll buy us some time. It appears Captain Newitt had this planned from the start."

Speechless, Adrian followed Leynitz as they skirted the same cluster of dellews from which Sol set his ambush of the 26th and 28th arcs earlier. They did not get far before another Amelaren war cry was unleashed nearby.

"Hurry!" Leynitz commanded. The small group quickened its pace, breaking into an all-out sprint. In the distance, they saw the flickering flames of rodtorches borne by Osterfeld's forces.

As they ran, Leynitz heard the sound of fainter, more rapid footsteps behind them. They were being chased by no more than two or three people.

Leynitz slowed and fell behind the others.

"General, what are you doing?" Adrian said anxiously.

At once, the pursuing footsteps quickened. Adrian and the scouts skidded to a halt.

Leynitz pulled up and whirled around, his sword ready. "Show yourself," he demanded.

Two men emerged from the shadows of a nearby dellew and grabbed Leynitz before he could react. The general dropped his sword but showed little surprise.

"I see. I should have known, though I wasn't expecting two of you."

Sol was massive, even for an Amelaren. He stood two heads taller than Leynitz and weighed nearly twice as much. The moonlight peeking through the clouds revealed his slightly squashed nose and the grimace on his wide, chiseled face. His short, wispy black hair fell in all directions. The other man was slightly shorter. He appeared several years older than Leynitz, though was in peak physical condition; he was not even out of breath after giving chase to the Coranthians. A well-groomed man with shoulder-length gray hair, he sported a small cross-shaped scar in the corner of his mouth. His umber eyes, which matched the color of his armor, gazed dully at the prince.

"Greetings, Prince Adrian," he said, speaking in Laestran. The words were laced with an unusually light accent. "My name is Izven." He gestured to the other man. "This is Sol."

Adrian's stomach churned. His veins turned to ice. The prince's eyes were immediately drawn away from the sword Izven held against Leynitz's neck, down to the glimmering shield-shaped pin Sol had affixed to his armor. It was a golden Coranox.

The prince curled his hands into fists as the significance of the pin dawned on him.

"Colonel Dyers ..."

Sol's lips curled up into an expression that was something between a bloodthirsty grin and a triumphant sneer.

"Have you no shame?" Adrian roared.

"Where are the rest of your dogs?" Leynitz said, struggled futilely to free himself from Izven's grip.

Izven chuckled. He spoke smoothly and with a hint of smugness. "Please, General. Just as you tried to sell us your decoy, so did we play along in our response. Sol informed me that the two of us would be sufficient to accost you."

"Is that so?" Leynitz shifted his weight. "I see two overconfident pig chieftains. I think you should have at least brought a few goons with you. Then again, I doubt they would have had the endurance to chase us this far."

Izven shook his head. "You disappoint me, General. Where is the Coranthian grace and etiquette you are supposed to champion?"

Leynitz smiled contemptuously, his mustache twitching. "You are wasting my time. Whatever your purpose may be, I suggest—"

"A trade, Prince," Sol said icily in broken Laestran. His gaze never left Adrian.

"We only want the prince," said Izven. "The rest of you can be on your way."

"Let him go, brute!" Adrian cried. There was a sharp *shink* as he drew his glowing sword and pointed it at Izven.

Sol's eyes glistened at the sight of the royal blade. "I want that too," he growled.

"Don't, Prince," Leynitz warned.

Izven said, "Don't worry, General. We won't harm the Prince. Now just—"

Hooves pounded as four riders emerged from the north. Reznik, Madeline, Sigmund Eldrid, and Nicole Desanolis had managed to break free from the Amelarens streaming out of the Highpost in the darkness.

Reznik and Eldrid charged straight at Izven, who hesitated before he released Leynitz and dashed to Sol's side. Still riding Gambit, Madeline galloped toward Mary with an outstretched hand.

"Come on!" Madeline cried. Mary did not hesitate to jump onto Gambit.

Eldrid reversed his direction and galloped to Adrian. He extended an arm, and Adrian hoisted himself onto the horse. Meanwhile, Nicole helped the other scout onto her steed.

Sol drew a sword from his right hip and another from a sheath strapped to his back. He moved to circle Leynitz, but the general had recovered his weapon and was ready for him. Sol attacked with one of his swords. Leynitz parried Sol ferociously, knocking the latter several meters backward. The war chief frowned and resumed his former position beside Izven.

"Easy, soldiers," Leynitz cautioned. "Don't try anything."

The horses stood some ten meters from Leynitz, who held his ground and fixed his gaze on the war chiefs before him. Sol and Izven stood motionless, sizing up their opponent.

Leynitz tightened his grip on his sword and tautly raised his hands level with his mouth.

"Your Highness, leave now."

"What are you talking about?" Adrian shouted. "Sylvera, grab the general! Do it now!"

"Stay away, all of you!" Leynitz roared. "I'll not have my position compromised. Now, Your Highness, you must go."

Reznik trotted to Adrian. "Listen to him. Let's go."

Adrian glared at Reznik with unbridled hatred.

"Leave, Adrian!" Leynitz commanded. "*Now!*"

The prince bit his lip hard, and blood gushed between his teeth. His eyes clouded with anger and despair.

Eldrid turned west and yanked his reins. He and Adrian rode off; the others followed.

Leynitz breathed a sigh of relief.

"I kept my word," he proclaimed as Sol and Izven readied their weapons. "Well, gentlemen, I'm not the Prince, but I hope I will suffice. Shall we?"

• • •

Three reps later, Adrian reunited with Lariban and Einhardt, who had led what remained of the escort north in their escape from the Amelaren horde. Newitt was nowhere to be found. Renard and Osterfeld reached the party within reps. Adrian was still disheveled, leaving Reznik to explain the preceding events to the colonels in the briefest of terms. After Reznik finished, Lariban and Osterfeld ordered a full retreat from Argiset Plateau with the entirety of the Amelaren Army bearing down on the Coranthians. It was nine-arc thirty. The entire battle had lasted under five arcs.

Interlude

Marsell Leynitz gasped for breath under the weight of Izven's boot, which was on his throat. Sol stood a few meters away, doubled over and panting; nevertheless, Leynitz was in far worse condition. Blood soaked through the general's uniform and spilled from his mouth.

"If only your soldiers could see you now," Izven mused.

The general grimaced, though said nothing.

"Well?" Izven roared.

Leynitz continued to glare at Izven with defiance and condescension, gagging on Izven's boot.

Izven relieved some of the pressure from Leynitz's neck, awaiting a response. The general remained silent.

Consumed with frustration, Izven removed his boot and swung his sword, severing the arteries in Leynitz's neck. The general convulsed, drowning in his own blood. A smile brightened the Amelaren war chief's wrinkled face, flashing a mouth of neat yellow teeth. Leynitz gurgled as his eyes glazed over. Soon he was still.

Izven turned to look at Sol. "You shouldn't have gone easy on him. See what happened to you."

Sol's eyes flashed with anger. "Leave me be."

He slowly moved to stand alongside Izven. The two watched as their elbars and warriors chased away the remaining Coranthian soldiers. The enemy was now in full retreat.

• • •

"What is to be done with this fort?" Zefrid said to begin the meeting as evening drew near.

Orlen and Shira had relocated to Ertel Ridge after year's turn, the other war chiefs at Solterra following shortly thereafter. Within four days of Argiset's fall, most of the war chiefs and Orlen, himself, had made their way to their newly captured fort. Only Olifa remained at Ertel. The warlord then commanded that Tallen return east to retain the command post. Tallen was reluctant to be left alone with Olifa, but Orlen told him in no uncertain terms that the two had to learn to work together, and Tallen had no choice but to comply.

Orlen summoned most of his war chiefs to Leynitz's private quarters one late afternoon. They sat around the general's dining table.

Zefrid's eyes drifted to each of the other war chiefs present in turn: Shira, Izven, Lebb, and Yura. "Any thoughts?" he asked of them.

Orlen did not appear overly concerned with the question. All sat comfortably in the ornate chairs surrounding the table. While the Amelarens ransacked the fort in search for supplies and intelligence, this room had remained spotless and unperturbed.

"What can we do?" Shira smiled, a fading ray of light tracing a line from her cold blue-gray eyes down her smooth cheek. "The Coranthians were kind enough to erect this stronghold for us to take, and we have taken it."

Zefrid rubbed his gnarled bony hands together. "Shira, by now it should be clear that this place is of no strategic value to us."

Lebb's nostrils flared, lips twisted in a frown. His cheeks bulged, distorting the two long, thin scars on either side of his face. He wagged a finger at Zefrid. His dirty tangled blond hair fell over the right side of his face.

"You need to lighten up, old man. We gave the Coros such a drubbing and you marginalize our victory?"

"What victory, boy?" Zefrid said. "Our objective was to capture the prince! From where I sit, it looks like we failed."

He leered at Izven, who did not meet his gaze. Izven could not argue against the senior chief's assessment. The most important part of the assault on Argiset—the capture of Adrian Coranthis—had not come to pass.

"I am surprised you thought it to be so easy," Yura interjected. "General Leynitz was a formidable foe. He was in command of Coranthian elites. No matter how prepared we were, there was no guarantee of success."

Well-built and eclipsing seventeen pegs in height, Yura would have been an imposing figure anywhere else, but in present company, she appeared almost diminutive. Her wavy auburn-dyed hair was neatly trimmed. Her face was well-formed and free of scars but lacked Shira's impenetrable coldness. To an outsider, she seemed wholly out of her element among the other war chiefs.

Lebb laughed nervously, breaking a brief stunned silence. "Look who decided to speak up."

Zefrid's mouth twisted into a reproachful frown.

"Where is Sol?" Shira said, eyeing Yura bemusedly. "The prince was as much his responsibility as Izven's."

"Sol is resting," Izven curtly replied, still refusing to look in Zefrid's direction. "He is nursing a few unfortunate cuts."

Lebb whistled softly. "The general must have lived up to his name."

Yura offered a knowing nod.

"Had Sol been allowed to engage the enemy head-on," Zefrid said, "and not be slowed by the torpid movements of the eastern force, the Coranthians would have had less time to devise a maneuver and distract us from our primary target."

He ignored Lebb's wrathful glare as he made this assessment.

Orlen cleared his throat. "Zefrid is right. We all know that Argiset Plateau is a no man's land. We gain nothing from attempting to hold it again. The western recesses of the Ghend remain perfectly defensible. They will serve as an appropriate front for our troops." He massaged his baldpate with his fingers before continuing. "The Coranthians have already discovered there is little chance for them to advance this deep into our territory. I suspect we will fall into a stalemate presently. Once they regroup, I have little doubt they will make another attempt on this fort. It is of much importance to their position but poses little threat to us, even if it returns to their hands. We will not risk severe losses if and when they return for their retribution."

"It sounds like you are suggesting we merely keep house here and wait for the Coranthians' cue to retreat," Zefrid remarked, tightened his jaw.

Orlen chuckled. "We will put this place to good use. I have heard that the Coranthians retook Tull Rock, as we expected they would. We will make a play for it again in the coming cycles."

Zefrid shrugged. "Pardon me if I don't sense the urgency in your proposal."

"As we have discussed many times before," Orlen replied, his voice assuming a stronger timbre as he rubbed at his cropped beard with the knuckle of his thumb, "we could control every square meter from here to Aldova and it still wouldn't make a difference. As long as the water fortress stands, their heartlands are impenetrable. That is our military limit. That is why we went for the prince. Had we managed to grab Samsen's heir, many additional options would have opened up."

"If our main force had moved more quickly, Sol and Izven may have been able to more efficiently coordinate capturing the prince," Zefrid conjectured.

"Could we please move on?" Izven said, grinding his teeth.

Zefrid offered an unpleasant grin. "We all know you didn't perform your duty, Izven. Again, I'm only suggesting things might have been easier had our army been more efficient."

Yura spoke, again surprising all those present. "Yes, we understand. You are trying to shovel more of the blame onto Tallen. How do you have the patience to be so lacking in directness in your old age?"

Lebb coughed to suppress a guffaw. Izven appeared more amazed than grateful in reaction to Yura's outburst.

Zefrid's eyes tightened into shifty beads. He leaned forward, the crook of his back arched indignantly. "What has gotten into her?" he grumbled to Shira. He was obviously insulted and of the opinion that his best recourse against Yura's remarks was a refusal to acknowledge her presence.

Orlen tilted his head to look at Izven. "I'm sorry, but your punishment for failure is to remain here and keep the Coranthians busy while we plan our next move."

"I understand, Warlord." Izven had a hint of resignation in his voice. "And Sol?"

Orlen raised an eyebrow. "You were in charge, Izven. Don't blame others for your mistakes."

Izven nodded quietly.

Orlen cleared his throat again, looking almost bored. "That is all. Dismissed, all of you," he declared.

Izven left quickly, Lebb following. Zefrid gave Orlen a stern look, but the warlord shook his head and waved his hand in annoyance. Zefrid hesitated briefly before making his exit. Finally, Shira and Yura left.

After another rep passed, Orlen emitted a deep, exasperated sigh and reclined in his chair.

• • •

An arc later, Shira and Yura found Orlen in a small, mostly barren room on the fort's second floor. General Leynitz's body lay on a stone slab. The body had been drained of its blood, which ran over the slab's sides and pooled on the floor. The women arrived in time to see Orlen detach the left leg with a mighty swing of the large ax in his hand.

Shira's mouth curled into a sneer. "Quite the display of brutality."

Without looking up, Orlen laughed, both amused and annoyed by Shira's observation. "You disapprove?"

He brought down the ax again and again, methodically working his way up Leynitz's corpse.

"It doesn't matter to me," Shira said, though she did not sound wholly dispassionate. "You seem to be taking some things out on the poor general."

"As usual, you see right through me," Orlen said. "Our meeting earlier has left me somewhat vexed."

He looked at Shira before focusing on Yura, whose eyes averted the carnage. "Ah, you're here too. You certainly took Zefrid to task earlier."

"The old man's manner is intolerable," Yura said.

Orlen shifted the ax to his other hand with a crooked smile. "I'm impressed you stood up to him."

"I won't have to worry about him for a while," Yura replied with a sniff. "Frankly, I hope I never see him again, Warlord."

"I told you not to call me that in private," Orlen said chidingly, almost good-naturedly. He was drenched from head to toe in Leynitz's blood. He seemed much more relaxed now. His gaze lingered on Shira, who stared piercingly back at him. The two locked eyes for a moment.

Yura shifted uncomfortably.

"The old codger has his uses, Yura," Shira said, breaking the momentary silence.

Orlen turned, raised the ax with both hands and brought it down emphatically, severing Leynitz's head along the same cut Izven had made earlier. He picked up the general's head, set it aside, put down the ax, and picked up a small scalpel from the corner of the slab. Clamping his palm atop the head, he gouged out both eyes and tossed them in the corner of the room with the other body parts.

"I will send this back to Coranthia," he said.

"Why?" Yura asked.

"A message to the Coranthians. We have yet to topple their water fortress, but we can get under their skin."

After expertly slicing off the ears, Orlen set down the scalpel on the slab and picked up the metal bottle beside it, removing the cap with his free hand. "I think King Samsen will appreciate the gift."

Orlen opened Leynitz's mouth and filled it with the bottle's contents. Within ticks, the insides turned black and emanated a foul smell. Orlen clamped the mouth shut and straightened his back as he dusted his hands. He turned again toward the women.

"So what did you want?"

"Have you decided when she will go?" Shira asked, motioning toward Yura.

"Within two turns."

"Very well." Shira nodded. "I will accompany her northward."

Yura scowled. "I do not need an escort," she mumbled, pressing her lips together.

"That is not your decision to make," Shira returned, her voice hard and crisp. "We will go together, unless Orlen says otherwise."

She shot a challenging look in his direction. Orlen shrugged.

"Then it is settled," Shira said emphatically.

Yura glared at her, but there was nothing left to say.

"Believe me, that will be the extent of my involvement, Sister. Beyond that, I will leave you to your ridiculous brashness." Shira glanced accusingly at Orlen. "And you, you enable her."

"She has a good idea. It is sure to benefit us in the long run."

Shira felt an unfamiliar flicker of uncertainty and anxiety pass over her face, and she swiveled away to make sure Yura could not see.

• • •

Later that evening, Zefrid received a visit from a warrior who told him that Orlen summoned him once again to Leynitz's old quarters. Zefrid wrapped himself in a musty green cloak and made his way through the corridors of the Highpost. As he ascended the stairs, the flaring pain in his joints told him a dampness would soon settle across the plateau, bringing rain with it.

As Zefrid approached the room, he noticed the faint smell of idafan, a lighter fluid. The general's quarters were lit only by a small oil lamp that lay on the table the war chiefs sat around earlier. Orlen and Shira watched Zefrid amble over to the table and sit. Zefrid tried to refrain from speaking first but felt his blood begin to boil as he recalled the egregious offense that besotted him. "Where is Yura?"

"Why?" Shira said, turning her head slowly.

"I wish to have a word with her."

"Come, don't be so thin-skinned, Zefrid," Orlen chortled, stretching his bulky, muscular arms out in front of him. "Besides, the girl did have a point. If you have a problem with Tallen, there is no reason to be reserved about it."

Zefrid scowled. "Why did you wish to see me?"

Orlen cracked his knuckles loudly. "We did not capture the prince, but no matter. We will proceed anyway. Let's not wait any longer. The time to put our plan into action draws near."

Zefrid's dull blue eyes lit up. "I was not aware we would be moving so soon," he protested. "I didn't know about this."

"That doesn't matter," Orlen said firmly. "I've decided it is time. We will move forward to take advantage of this opportunity."

The elderly advisor was taken aback but recovered. "Very well, Warlord."

"I would like to go over the basic elements," Orlen said.

"Xanos has been training my hand-picked warriors in Laestran and Coranthian fluency," Zefrid said. "You will have to ask him about progress on that front."

"So I shall," Orlen said, glancing to his left. "Well, Xanos?"

Xanos appeared from behind Orlen. He was hidden in the shadows of the poorly lit room. Zefrid started at the sudden and unexpected movement.

"They are ready," Xanos said.

"How many warriors do we need?" Orlen asked.

Zefrid cocked his head and vacantly stared off into the air for several ticks before replying. "Minimum of seven or eight. More if we need any interference beyond a basic distraction during execution. Or if you want reserves."

"Reserves for an operation like this—can we afford that?" Shira wondered. "More warriors equals higher risk of exposure."

"My warriors are not all setting out at once," Zefrid said. "And once a spearhead is entrenched, additional flow of infiltrators should prove less difficult."

Xanos nodded slowly. "We'd need more time to train additional tongues, in any case."

"And yet we will be making our first attempt soon?" Zefrid said.

"Yes," Orlen said. "Xanos will arrange the return of Leynitz's head with the first group of your warriors. They will set out from here during the next cycle."

Zefrid squinted. "Returning his head? What purpose will that serve?"

"As I have said previously, Zefrid, we must employ methods other than brute force on our way to victory. This will send the Coranthians a statement they cannot ignore." Orlen's smile was twisted and unpleasant. "While General Leynitz's head is being delivered, your warriors will enter Aldova along the agreed route. So you see, Zefrid, there is another purpose for this delivery. With the Coranthians' attention focused on our envoy, we will have an opportunity to infiltrate."

"Then let me make the arrangements."

Orlen raised his hand. "That will not be necessary, Zefrid. Xanos has made all arrangements. You need only assemble a group of warriors for the next wave."

Zefrid's eyes widened with a hint of resignation, seeing there was little room for his input on the proceedings. "I see."

"Will there be anything else?" Xanos asked, not having stirred since he was last addressed directly.

"No, that will be all."

"Well then, good night to you all." Without missing a beat, Xanos strode past them, opening and closing the door as he left in one fluid motion. Zefrid glanced mistrustfully after him.

"Zefrid."

The old man turned to face Orlen again. A stiff breeze through an open window made him pull his cloak closer to his body.

"I know you have been reluctant to bring others into the discussion on this matter, but it only makes sense to consult Xanos. His knowledge is of great use to us."

"If you say so," Zefrid murmured after a lengthy pause. "As long as we succeed, I have no complaints, although I ask to remain informed of your thoughts. Now, I'm afraid this night air is a bane to my joints. I must excuse myself."

He stood and offered a slight bow before exiting, leaving only Orlen and Shira, still seated, the lamp now smoldering faintly.

Shira extinguished the lamp, rose, and walked to the window. She pulled back the gently billowing curtain, allowing the moonlight to stream into the room and the chilly air to whistle in through the window.

"A rough day for our elderly friend." Her mouth was drawn as tightly as it ever was, but her blue-gray eyes danced in the moonlight and there was an upward inflection in her voice. "First, he is humbled by the least imposing of us. Now he discovers he is no longer in charge of his own plan to destroy Aldova."

Such a moment of levity for her would have seemed exceedingly rare to most people, but Orlen was intimately familiar with her present demeanor.

He locked the door, then approached her from behind and wrapped his arms around her stomach. She breathed in deeply.

"*His* plan?" he said in a low voice, amused. "Yes, well, it seems he needs the occasional reminder that the final decisions are not his to make."

"You owe him nothing. He's more trouble than he's worth these days. Most of the time, all he does is rankle Tallen and Lebb. Even Izven regards him unfavorably."

Orlen gazed out into the night. "Whether or not that's true, he still helped engineer our war machine. And I have yet to find anyone with comparable logistical skills."

She turned her head and gazed into his eyes. Like hers, they shone frostily and brilliantly.

"What I am hearing is that you need a bookkeeper, not an advisor. You don't need Zefrid. You have the war chiefs. You have me."

Orlen flashed a smile that only she had the privilege to take in. He wrapped his hand around her breast as he bent down and kissed her. Her mouth and tongue joined fiercely with his. Shira's eyes brimmed with carnal fire when their lips parted.

"When I saw you covered in Leynitz's blood …"

"Yes?"

Shira's voice was a feline whisper. "I was so excited, I could barely breathe."

Orlen eased his hands up Shira's tunic. She exhaled a contented sigh and shook with anticipation.

"Soon, all of Moriana will bow to us," she said. "The fools of the Conclave think their archaic titles give them power. But you are the true leader of Amelares."

"You are quite right, my dear," he said. "Except …"

"Except?"

For a while, the two gazed into the night sky at the crimson beacon of Rhynon and the faint azurite pulse of Faerila.

"I do not deserve such a title, not before the king of Coranthia has yielded to me."

Chapter 17

(988.2.11)

—1—

Madeline sat by Douglas's bedside, watching him ravenously shovel spoonfuls of soup into his mouth. His condition had improved over the past four days, marking an extended stay in the medical bay, afforded only by the privilege of his estate. Some color had returned to his pallid face; fortunately, his appetite was as healthy as ever. He even cracked an occasional smile as they talked.

"You really like the food here, don't you?" Madeline teased.

His head twitched. "Not really. I'm just hungry."

Madeline had visited Douglas in the medical bay almost daily since their return to Aldova. At first, it was difficult for her. The death of Patrice affected her more deeply than she had expected. Though she wanted to blame Douglas for her squadmate's death, she could not bring herself to do so any more than she could blame herself or Nash for failing to save Patrice. She was immeasurably relieved to learn that, after separating from the rest of the riders at Argiset, Douglas had managed to find his way back to Osterfeld's main force.

He dropped his spoon in the bowl and stared solemnly at Madeline.

"Reznik hates me, doesn't he?"

Reznik had not visited Douglas once since their return. Madeline tried several times to convince him to do so, but he remained noncommittal.

She understood how Reznik felt, but it pained her to see him act this cold toward their longtime friend.

"No, he doesn't," she tried to reassure Douglas. "He's just been busy, that's all."

He shook his head skeptically. "No, he blames me for what happened. And rightfully so."

"Douglas … What happened to Avet Konith was an accident. Things like that happen."

"Things like how I completely lost it?" Douglas sunk onto his bed, head twitching awkwardly.

"My apologies, Avet Agilda. Visiting time is over."

Madeline jumped in her seat. She turned to face her interlocutor. "Dr. Halstead! You startled me."

Halstead cocked his head. "Sorry about that."

Madeline returned her attention to Douglas. He was clearly disappointed to see her go but said nothing. He looked directly into her eyes.

"Goodbye, Douglas." She gave him her best smile. "Get some rest. I'll see you tomorrow! I'm sure Reznik will come soon. He just has a lot on his plate. You know, being a high and mighty vice captain and all."

He managed a smile. "Thanks for coming, Madeline. Tell him hello."

"I will, and I'm sure Glen will come by to check on you later."

Douglas nodded and set his soup bowl aside before lying down.

Halstead escorted Madeline to the exit of the medical bay. Along the way, she glanced around, observing the sick and injured, as well as the medics and nurses rushing to attend to them. The medical bay and morgue were overtaxed since the soldiers' return from the Highpost. Hundreds were injured, and the army brought back as many dead as they could carry. Many more had since succumbed to exhaustion and illness, and still more of the injured or sick soldiers did not survive.

"Doctor, if you ever need any help here, I would be glad to come by as much as I am allowed," Madeline said as they walked. "I have some informal medic training."

Halstead kneaded his brow with his right hand. "We have been operating above maximum capacity for the last few days now." He paused. "I would hate to ask for help from main military personnel, but I will take your offer into consideration. Your captain tells me you've been working closely with him."

Madeline could smell the liquor on his breath as he spoke.

"How much longer do you think Douglas will be here?" she asked.

"I'd like to keep him for observation a few more days. He seems much better, but the twitching has me concerned." The doctor paused, lost in thought. "We've seen this kind of thing before after significant trauma, and it will likely go away with time."

"You don't sound very sure."

Halstead shrugged. "I can't say for certain. This is an issue of mind, not body. I have already recommended to his superiors that he be discharged or at least granted an extended leave of absence."

"Discharged?" Madeline pressed her lips together anxiously.

"Avet Agilda, some people do not have the mental constitution to handle war. Your friend is a perfect example of this. He has served his term in the military. He should retire. It is what most nobles do anyway. Come in, serve their year, and get out."

The doctor turned to face Madeline at the double door exit of the medical bay.

"If your friend continues to fight, I worry about the permanent effects his psyche might suffer. I simply can't recommend it."

Madeline stared at the floor. "Thank you, Doctor. I will be by again tomorrow."

A slight smile formed at the corners of Halstead's lips as he pushed open one of the doors to let her out. "Have a pleasant evening, Avet Agilda."

Madeline walked into the hallway and stepped into a sea of people as the door swung closed behind her. She weaved through the hall, taking care to not run into anyone. The fifth floor was particularly crowded. Several of the injured walked the hallways as part of their rehabilitation, and now that the life-threatening injuries had been treated, a steady stream of soldiers with lesser injuries visited the medical bay.

Six days had passed since the battle for Argiset Highpost came to its grim conclusion. The tired, broken, and beaten Coranthian Army had lost the fort and returned to Aldova. Although they suffered an immense defeat, the army found solace in a minor victory with the retaking of Tull Rock. General Mortigan sent Colonel Albrecht and his troops to Tull, where Albrecht met only minor resistance and easily recaptured the area where their outpost once stood. Due to the lack of Amelaren presence, it was clear the enemy was only interested in Argiset and had used Tull as a springboard to reach their primary target.

The loss of General Leynitz weighed heavily on the soldiers' hearts. One of the Coranthian Army's fiercest and greatest warriors was gone. Many members of the Engineering Company were also upset that the fort they had worked so hard to construct at Argiset was in enemy hands. In less than half a cycle, the Coranthians had lost a general, a colonel, four captains, and seven vice captains. Normally, a funeral would be held at Aldova or Corande in their honor, but serious logistical problems and low morale resulting from the severe losses indefinitely postponed funeral arrangements.

With three companies out of commission and five severely thinned, General Mortigan had his work cut out for him. He appointed Colonel Lariban as interim general until a new general could be officially appointed from Corande.

The 26th Company was not wholly decimated, but several of Madeline's comrades had died or gone missing, including Patrice and Cyrus.

Lost in thought, Madeline made her way down to the cafeteria. Watching Douglas eat had made her hungry. She regained focus when she spotted Renard talking to his vice captain, George Stradt, down the main hall on the second floor. She called Renard's name.

He stopped talking and peered over his shoulder, then waved in acknowledgment.

As Madeline walked toward them, Renard said something to Stradt. The vice captain nodded and walked away. Renard awaited Madeline's approach.

"Maddy! Good to see you!" Renard grinned as she approached and then frowned as Madeline playfully saluted him. "You don't need to do that."

"We're in public here," Madeline teased. "Need to keep it professional."

"It's good to see you. Sorry I haven't really been reachable. Things have been hectic since we returned. I've been scurrying about without much time for rest or relaxation. I swear I have a mound of paperwork back in my office that never gets any smaller no matter how much I slog through."

Renard had deep dark circles under his eyes. Despite his smile, he did not seem happy. Madeline had not previously noticed how pale and haggard he had grown. She had always assumed he was drained from all the paperwork and officers' meetings, but now she began to think it was something more.

"I can imagine," Madeline said. "You look pretty terrible."

"Oh, Maddy, how your words hurt me so."

She smiled. "Do you have a few reps now?"

Renard glanced at the large clock above the center stairwell. "A few."

They walked together down the hall slowly.

"So, how are you?" Renard asked.

Madeline shrugged. "Taking things day by day. Reznik is swamped like you are, so I haven't seen him much. I've been visiting Douglas in the medical bay every day."

"I suppose I should drop by as well," he said.

"I'm sure he'd like that. Glen goes too. Reznik, though … I don't think he wants to find the time, if you know what I mean."

Renard's expression sobered. "You're talking about what happened to your squadmate, yeah? That was an accident, though I know what Reznik is probably thinking. How is Douglas doing?"

"The doctor said the problem is all in his head and that he may recommend discharge."

Renard chuckled bitterly. "Discharge? That'll never happen."

"Why do you say that?"

"Come on, Madeline. Think about his parents. Would they ever let Douglas be discharged?"

"No, I suppose not, but staying in the army probably isn't what's best for him."

Something flickered across Renard's face, but Madeline couldn't pinpoint what it was. She thought it might have been sympathy, though was unsure.

"Well …" Renard glanced at the hall clock. "I really would love to continue the conversation, Maddy, but I do have things to attend to. I apologize."

"Of course! Sorry to keep you," she said.

"Oh, don't be!" His mouth curled into a warm smile. "And I'll be sure to visit Douglas as soon as I get a chance. Maybe I'll go talk some sense into Rez as well."

To Renard's surprise, Madeline leaned in and hugged him quickly, almost furtively, before continuing on down the hallway toward the cafeteria.

"That's not keeping it very professional," he murmured, smiling to himself.

—2—

Renard made his way out onto Aldova Crossway, the section of the bridge that served as an underpass through the second floor of the fortress. Descending a flight of stairs on the other side, he proceeded to the first floor where the prison was located. Two guards stepped aside when they saw Renard approach.

"Vice Captain Stradt has already arrived," one said.

Renard nodded. After entering the prison, he passed through a series of heavily guarded rooms that served as security checkpoints. Although Renard had talked to the same guards many times before, they were insistent upon reviewing his credentials and ensuring he carried no weapons.

Once past security, Renard joined Stradt and entered the prison cell holding area. As they walked past row after row of dank prison cells, several captive Amelarens rushed to the bars of their cells and yelled at the officers, though most prisoners were too tired or beaten to acknowledge them.

"These trips down here never get old, do they?" Renard said to Stradt with a stony countenance; there was no trace of his usual smile.

Stradt shrugged. "I learned the language to help out in this manner. I knew I'd be assigned here. Extraction and translation of information are vitally important, sir."

"That makes one of us," Renard said. "I detest this. I had no idea I'd be stuck with this duty. I guess that's what I get for making you my vice captain, isn't it?"

"On the contrary, sir. You were assigned to this with me because you are quite good at it."

Renard grimaced. The pair continued in silence through the hallways of the dungeon. The intermittent sounds of hacking coughs, angry cries, and groans of pain filled the air as they walked. Eventually, they came to a closed door flanked by two guards at the end of a long hallway. When the guards saw the officers approaching, they did not hesitate to let them in.

Inside the cramped, cold, and dark room, an Amelaren elbar lay strapped to a wooden table with a series of leather belts. His breathing was steady but labored. He made no move to acknowledge the officers' entrance. Renard noticed fresh spots of blood on top of the existing stains on the table. It was clear that he was not the first to interrogate this warrior.

This was not new to Renard; he and Stradt had been commanded to extract information from other prisoners on multiple occasions after initial attempts had failed. Renard credited their success to Stradt; he refused to believe it had anything to do with him. He could not communicate directly with the Amelarens, which reduced the effectiveness of the more diplomatic approaches he preferred in his questioning.

Renard shut the door and approached the head of the table. He stared down at the elbar. The warrior's face was bloodied, but his eyes burned brightly. The elbar glared back at Renard.

"Who told you our prince was stationed at the fort?" Renard asked calmly. Stradt translated the question.

The elbar's eyes grew wider, and he inhaled more rapidly for a few ticks before spitting upward into Renard's face.

Renard pulled out a silk handkerchief and leisurely wiped away the spit before repeating the question.

The elbar yelled something, but Stradt did not translate. Renard glanced at him expectantly.

"He didn't say anything worth translating," Stradt remarked.

"I'll be the judge of that. What did he say?"

"Death to you and your king."

Renard looked down at the wide-eyed elbar and forced a grin. He repeated his question twice more and received no response either time. After he decided to move the interrogation along, he walked around the table to a workbench at the back of the room. The bench spanned almost the length of the back wall.

Catching on to Renard's intentions, Stradt knocked on the door. After half a rep, there came a returning knock. Stradt opened the door. One of the guards carried a wrapped sack; its contents clanged ominously as he hoisted it onto the bench with a grunt. Untying the string that held the sack together, he unfurled the cloth to reveal an assortment of tools. Bowing slightly to Renard, who nodded in acknowledgment, the guard took his leave, closing the door behind him as he exited.

Renard calmly put on a pair of tanned leather gloves before picking up a wooden stake and hammer from the array of instruments laid out on the bench. Before the elbar could react, Renard whirled around, pried the elbar's left hand open with the hammer, positioned the stake over the center of the palm, and brought the hammer down hard on the stake, ramming it through the elbar's hand and into the table. The elbar screamed in pain; his eyes bulged as the stake pierced skin and bone. Renard and Stradt remained expressionless.

A stream of curses flowed from the mouth of the elbar. Renard looked at Stradt, who shook his head. Renard pounded the stake in farther.

"Who told you our prince was stationed at the fort?" Renard asked in the same even tone.

Again the elbar offered nothing to discourage Renard from continuing; he was no closer to relenting almost twenty reps later, continuing to hurl insults at Renard after another stake was pounded through his right hand. Renard moved to the right foot but, thinking twice, returned both tools to the bench.

Renard picked up a rank bandana and blindfolded the elbar. He removed his gloves and set them on the bench. Reaching into a pouch tied around his waist, he pulled out a pair of earplugs, which he inserted into his own ears. He grabbed another pair for Stradt, as well as a high-pitched whistle known as a shrieker. After he confirmed that Stradt had his earplugs in, Renard knelt by the elbar's left ear, put the whistle in his mouth, and began to blow as hard as he could. The elbar recoiled at the sound but said nothing.

After blowing the whistle into the same ear at random intervals for five reps, Renard repeated the question into the other ear. The elbar still refused to answer his question, but began to moan softly and convulsively.

Renard asked the same question once more. This time, the elbar spat a response. Renard noted the obvious relish with which the words were delivered. "What did he say?" he asked Stradt.

"Nothing useful."

"Translate."

Stradt cleared his throat uncomfortably. "This is nothing compared to what I would do to your mother."

Hearing his words repeated in Laestran, the Amelaren laughed mockingly.

Renard's previously deadened eyes flashed. "Fine," he said. "We're through playing."

Stradt did not move from where he stood.

Renard stared at him crossly. "Don't make me repeat myself. I recommend you put on some gloves."

He did as Renard suggested, reaching into his own pouch and producing a pair of gloves and a strip of tape.

Renard put his own gloves back on and removed the blindfold. He surveyed the items on the bench. His back turned, Renard asked Stradt if the elbar was watching him.

"Yes, sir."

Renard shook his head slightly as he grabbed a fistful of nails. He turned to the elbar, whose eyes were trained on him, and placed his hand over the Amelaren's nose. When the elbar gasped for air, Renard dropped the nails into his open mouth. Before the elbar could spit them out, Stradt swooped in and taped the elbar's mouth shut. The Amelaren unleashed muffled screams through the tape.

Curling his hand into a fist, Renard punched the elbar on the right side of his face. The elbar screamed louder as Stradt backed away. Renard picked up the hammer. Without as much as a jolted hair on his head, he punched the elbar again and brought the hammer down on the man's kneecap.

The elbar's wails caused his voice to break; he shook and sobbed through the bloodied tape. Tears streamed down his face. His eyes rolled aimlessly in their sockets.

Renard removed the tape. The elbar tilted his head and spat out a bloody mess of nails and bits of broken teeth that clattered on the floor.

"Someone … leaking … information," he heaved before emitting a helpless sob and slipping into unconsciousness.

A rep of silence passed as Renard stood over the prisoner.

"What do you think, Stradt?" he asked finally.

"As you suspected. Of course, he could just be putting on a show." Stradt came forward and jabbed a finger at the elbar's neck. The elbar remained still. Satisfied that the Amelaren was truly non-responsive, he stepped back again.

"That'll have to do for now, I suppose," Renard said. Like Stradt, he was skeptical, but the elbar's words also fueled his suspicions that the Amelarens knew too much of Coranthian military movements and that something out of the ordinary had happened at Argiset.

Renard pulled out all the stakes while Stradt opened the door and instructed the guards to summon the standby medic. Within the rep, the medic arrived and began to disinfect and bandage the elbar's hands and foot.

"Sir, would you like us to bring another prisoner for you?" one of the guards asked Renard.

"No," Renard said, removing his bloodied gloves and dropping them unceremoniously onto the cloth sack next to the stakes. "We are done for now. I am needed elsewhere. We'll take care of the other elbar tomorrow."

"Yes, sir!"

The guards saluted as the two officers made their way out of the dungeon.

Renard stopped and bade farewell to Stradt when they were near an exit leading out to Aldova Crossway.

"Sir, is everything all right?" Stradt called after he had already begun to walk away.

Renard stopped and turned in surprise. "It's not like you to express concern."

"What you did to the prisoner was not necessary."

"He coughed up information, did he not?"

"You took things a bit too far," his vice captain said, somewhat timidly.

Renard's countenance contorted in irritation. "It's rather stressful, you know? And what right do you have to judge me? This is our job. I—" He glanced at the floor. "Have a good evening, Stradt."

"Good night, sir," Stradt said hesitantly.

Renard made his way out of the dungeon up onto the Crossway. From there, he hurried to his quarters to clean up.

Half an arc later, he headed to the eighth floor and passed through the Hall of Champions to the massive double doors at the end. Mounted to the left was a large, golden face plate, engraved with General Mortigan's name. Elegant gold trim adorned the lacquered dark wooden doors. Renard hesitated before knocking softly.

"Come in," Mortigan called from behind the doors.

Slowly, Renard opened the double doors and entered Mortigan's office. Although Renard wanted to look around the expansive room, his eyes remained focused straight ahead. At the end of the room, General Mortigan sat behind a large, intricately carved wooden desk in his spacious, high-backed leather chair.

The velvet chairs normally in front of the general's desk were lined against the western wall. Newly appointed interim general Radley Lariban stood to Mortigan's right. Both men watched Renard as he walked toward them.

Renard stopped two meters before the desk and saluted. Lariban saluted in return. To Renard's surprise, Prince Adrian emerged from behind Mortigan's chair and stepped around the edge of the desk to Mortigan's left.

The prince took a few ticks to look over Renard. "Captain Renault."

Renard bowed slightly. "Prince."

CORANOX 363

CORANOX   363

"I wanted to thank you in person for your service at the Highpost, Captain. Had it not been for your plan, I might have suffered the same fate as General Leynitz …"

Adrian's obvious gratitude came as a shock to Renard, who was not used to witnessing such emotion from the prince, much less directed toward him. It was also clear that Adrian found it difficult to talk about Leynitz.

"Prince, you give me too much credit. A plan is nothing if not for its executors. All of our troops should be praised for their courage and resiliency under the circumstances. Captain Newitt also deserves to be commended for his extraordinary display of bravery. He had an idea while we were holed up inside the Highpost, and I helped him put the decoy together."

Adrian nodded and looked away briefly. "I am forever indebted to Captain Newitt for his sacrifice. His family and estate will be taken care of." His eyes refocused on Renard. "But let's not be modest, Captain. You saved my life and the lives of many other soldiers, and for that …"

Mortigan opened a drawer behind the desk and produced a small blue box. Inside was a golden Coranox pressed into the soft blue velvet lining. The pin signified the rank of colonel in the Coranthian Army.

"And for that," Mortigan continued from where Adrian left off, "you are the right man to take Colonel Dyers' mantle."

"The prince and I witnessed firsthand how impressive your leadership was, Captain Renault," Lariban added. "Or, I should say, Colonel. This is well deserved."

Renard stared at the pin for what seemed like an eternity. "I am deeply humbled by this honor, but I must decline."

"Excuse me?" Mortigan said after several ticks of silence that seemed much longer. While Adrian and Lariban had both started at Renard's revelation, the general had remained perfectly still, maintaining the same pose he had held since Renard entered the room.

"I mean no disrespect," Renard said. "I do not wish to be colonel. In fact, I plan to retire from the military once the 21st is granted its next leave."

Lariban stepped forward and said in a slow but biting tone, "Whether or not you mean disrespect, you certainly are showing it. We have suffered great losses and need young and capable men and women to step up and set an example for others. General Mortigan and I thought you'd be one such leader."

"I'm afraid you are mistaken, sir," Renard returned, unfazed.

Mortigan's face was unreadable as he spoke. "Is this truly what you want, Captain?"

"It is, Your Excellency."

"Then I will have Landsett draw up your papers. You have served your time and served it well. If your wish is retirement, so be it."

Lariban shook his head disapprovingly, his face a mask of incredulity. "It baffles me that you would give up such a promotion, Captain. I know that you are not a coward, so you must truly not value the glory that accompanies exemplary service."

"I await your final report, Captain," Mortigan said after a moment's silence. "To be submitted after tomorrow's interrogation, of course."

"Certainly, sir."

"Then you are dismissed," Mortigan said, waving his hand.

Renard saluted his senior officers and turned to leave. Outside the double doors, he was surprised yet again when Adrian caught up to him.

"I have a question for you, Renault."

He considered maintaining his pace away from Mortigan's office but decided to stand in the hallway and face Adrian, as the prince closed the double doors behind them. "Go ahead."

"Are you quitting because of your interrogation duties? I could easily have that taken care of for—"

"No, it's the food," Renard replied. "I can't take the gruel they serve in this place anymore. I miss my Kantorian restaurants."

Seeing the expression on Adrian's face, Renard felt he might have induced the same reaction had he dropped his drawers and defecated on the spot. "That was a joke, Prince."

Adrian shook his head. "Your timing needs work."

"I'll keep that in mind. It's true I no longer wish to be an interrogator, but that is certainly not the only reason."

Neither spoke for a moment as Adrian studied him closely.

"Very well, then," the prince finally said. "Good evening to you." He spun around and pushed open the double doors to Mortigan's office.

Renard walked down the hall without looking back, heading straight for his own quarters. Upon arrival, he walked to the back, where he kept a small minibar stocked with an assortment of wines, liquors, ice, and glasses. He poured a small glass of Kantor's Best, an ironically named cheap rye whisky from his home city that was popular among those seeking the most direct path to intoxication. He dropped into his leather chair, a sprawling, capacious seat he suspected once accommodated an officer far more massive. Renard faced the foot of his bed and kneaded his eyebrow with his free hand. He held his glass up, gazing at the distorted solistone light pouring through it and the liquid it contained. He downed the drink in one large gulp and leaned back, closing his eyes.

—3—

Reznik had stopped halfway down the Hall of Champions to watch as Renard and Adrian spoke outside Mortigan's office, obscuring himself from their view behind a pillar protruding from the wall. He could not make out their conversation, and it was not his aim to eavesdrop. Eventually, Renard left through an exit to a stairwell.

Adrian entered Mortigan's office, but came back out only a rep later when the double doors swung open. The prince sauntered down the Hall of Champions. He appeared distracted and did not notice Reznik coming toward him until they almost walked into one another.

"Sylvera," Adrian acknowledged blankly.

"Prince, a pleasure as always."

Adrian frowned. "What are you doing here?"

"I was summoned by Colonel Osterfeld."

"Of course you were," the prince said flippantly. "There seems to be quite a crowd up here tonight. I don't suppose you're here to resign too?"

Reznik raised his eyebrows.

"I don't know what you're talking about. You'd have no such luck, I'm afraid."

"No, I guess not. It doesn't surprise me that Renault is a quitter though."

Reznik's expression darkened.

Adrian stared for a moment and then guffawed. "What? He didn't tell you?"

"No."

"He tendered his resignation instead of accepting a promotion to replace Dyers." The prince rubbed his cheek absentmindedly. "Now we'll have to find someone else. Einhardt, maybe."

Reznik's eyes widened. "And nobody tried to convince him otherwise?"

"What do I care? Who turns down an honor like that? It's not my problem. Perhaps I should have expected as much from him."

"Don't be petty, Prince. Renard must have his reasons."

Reznik was keenly aware that his words lacked conviction. His mind was still trying to process what Adrian had just told him.

The prince shrugged. "I say once a slacker, always a slacker."

Reznik tightened his fists and clenched his teeth. In contrast, Adrian was clearly pleased at having riled him.

"And what happened at Argiset, Prince? If Renard is a slacker, what does that make you?" Reznik spat out. "Perhaps you'd best consider judging yourself first. After all, General Leynitz—"

Adrian's smug look vanished as he cut Reznik off. "Think very carefully before you decide to finish that sentence."

The prince leaned in, bringing his face close to Reznik's. They glared at each other silently for several ticks.

"I'd like to keep my appointment with the colonel," Reznik said evenly. "Good evening to you, Your Highness."

Adrian grunted and pushed past Reznik, continuing on his way.

Reznik walked slowly to Osterfeld's office. He stood motionless in front of the door for a rep; after composing himself, he took a deep breath and knocked loudly.

"Enter, Vice Captain Sylvera," Osterfeld's voice boomed from inside.

Reznik opened the door and stepped in. Like any colonel's office, Osterfeld's was much like that of a captain's, its slightly larger dimensions and higher-quality furniture the only significant differences. Every time Reznik entered this room, he felt uncomfortable. The office was not immaculate, though its arrangements always felt too deliberate, never overly clean or messy. Things were strewn about in a seemingly calculated fashion. The decorations were neither ornate nor bland. It all seemed artificial to Reznik; incidentally, he had come to feel the same way about the colonel himself.

To Reznik's surprise, Nash was already seated in one of the two chairs in front of Osterfeld's desk. Osterfeld motioned for Reznik to sit in the other chair.

"Please, Vice Captain, take a seat."

Reznik took his seat, nodding at Nash as he sat.

"Do you know why you're here?" Osterfeld grumbled.

"No, sir," Reznik shook his head.

The colonel twirled his mustache before producing a folded piece of paper from his left breast pocket and throwing it on the desk. Reznik and

Nash immediately recognized the note Reznik wrote following the officer meeting en route to Argiset, calling for a retaking of Tull Rock.

"Do you know now?" Osterfeld looked flatly at the two of them.

Reznik stared wordlessly at the colonel, while Nash shrank in his seat.

"Captain," Osterfeld said to Nash. "Were you aware of this?"

Nash nodded. His pale face grew damp with sweat. "Yes, sir."

Osterfeld turned his attention to Reznik. "Vice Captain, how dare you bypass the chain of command? This behavior is inexcusable. If you had something to say, you should have come to your captain, and he would have come to me."

"Sir, there wasn't—" Reznik started, but Nash cut him off.

"I told him to do it."

Both Reznik and Osterfeld stared at Nash in disbelief, although Reznik tried to hide his astonishment as best as he could.

"Excuse me?" the colonel exclaimed.

"I ordered him to send the note," Nash said. He appeared anxious, but his tone was firm. "There was no time to deal with the chain of command. I felt it imperative that this suggestion reach the general as soon as possible. I'm not particularly good at writing these kind of things, so I asked Vice Captain Sylvera to draft it for me."

Osterfeld stared at Nash for a few ticks in silence, leaned back in his chair, and started to laugh. Reznik and Nash exchanged puzzled glances.

"You realize, Captain Havora, what taking the blame for this will mean? You're in hot water as it is already. And I don't know what your father will be able to do for you."

Nash smiled weakly. "I understand, sir, but I am only taking responsibility for my actions."

Osterfeld sighed and shook his head. "Very well, Captain. As neither of you signed the note, and I only have Sergeant Nilson's testimony that he was handed the note by the vice captain to give to the general, I have no choice but to take your word." He stroked his mustache. "You may leave, Captain Havora. Vice Captain, you'll remain."

Obediently, Nash rose, saluted, and took his leave. Reznik sat still in his chair as Osterfeld stared pensively at him for half a rep without speaking.

"I know it was you, Vice Captain," Osterfeld said. "I know you wrote the note and ordered it sent."

Reznik said nothing.

"It is not in Captain Havora's capacity to do something so brash and stupid." Osterfeld wrinkled his nose. "I know he wouldn't dare bypass the chain of command. But you, Vice Captain, don't seem to have much respect for such things."

"Colonel, I—" Reznik began but was cut off.

"This is your one free pass, Vice Captain," Osterfeld said sternly. "Captain Havora is willing to take the blame for you, so I will do nothing." The colonel's frown gradually dissipated as he reclined in the chair. "He is throwing himself to the wolves, but it may be better this way."

He smiled at Reznik, who found the gesture awkward and slightly disturbing and tried his best to remain stoic.

"Your captain may not always be around to take the fall for your inappropriate actions. General Leynitz saw great potential in you as a soldier and a leader. I must say I'm beginning to see it as well, but you cannot pull a stunt like this again. You must respect the chain of command and follow protocol."

Several ticks passed before Reznik determined it appropriate to speak. "I will keep your words in mind, Colonel. Thank you for the advice."

"I'd like to see you succeed. We have suffered great losses in this last campaign, so as a result, there will be more opportunities for you to step up and show us your mettle. I am not trying to bring you down, but you can't simply do as you please. If you have something important to report, your captain, if he has any sense, will listen, and I can promise you I will act swiftly on anything of merit."

If Osterfeld's looser manner had intended to put Reznik at ease, it failed. He nodded stiffly. "Thank you, sir."

"You are dismissed, Vice Captain."

Reznik stood and saluted. Osterfeld returned the formality. Reznik turned swiftly and left the office. He was surprised to see Nash leaning against the wall just outside the door.

"Nash, why did you do that?"

"Now we are even," Nash said.

"Even? What do you mean?"

"You saved my hide back at Ertel," Nash grinned. "Now I've saved yours. Besides, how would it reflect on me as a captain if I had let my second go around me like that? That's no better than if I had let you take the heat."

Reznik cast his eyes downward with genuine embarrassment as the two retraced their steps down the corridor. "I'm sorry. It was a foolish decision. I still feel that you should have left it for me to deal with."

Nash laughed.

"One more thing to pile on my record won't make a huge difference. I see value in keeping your record clean."

"Thank you, Nash. I appreciate it." Reznik's tone harbored an earnestness usually reserved for his close friends. He hesitated before continuing but could not help himself. "I was right though, wasn't I?"

"About what?"

"About retaking Tull."

Nash's dumbfounded expression caused Reznik to break at last and start to laugh. Before long, Nash was laughing himself.

"Yes, I suppose you were," he said. "You really don't know when to quit, do you?"

"I guess not," Reznik agreed.

The two exited the Hall of Champions and made their way to the seventh floor. Along the way, Reznik found himself eager to tell Nash about his earlier exchange with Prince Adrian regarding Renard.

"That is most surprising," Nash said as they came to a halt outside his office. "I do not know Captain Renault very well, and I can't imagine what motivated this decision."

"I need to hear from him myself. We have been increasingly out of touch since graduation."

Nash nodded. "Both of you are officers. You have many matters to attend to even off the battlefield. I think he'd have made a good colonel. He's a smart and capable man. I hope Captain Renault finds what he wants, if not in the military."

"Yes," Reznik returned faintly. "I'm off to see him now. Good night, Nash."

"Good night, Reznik." Nash unlocked his office and went in, shutting the door behind him.

Reznik walked down the hall until he reached Renard's office. The door was ajar; light eked out through the crack. Reznik stopped and knocked firmly, pushing the door open.

"Come in," Renard said through the doorway. When he saw his friend, his face lit up. "Reznik! What a surprise! I did not expect to see you up at this time of night. Come, sit down."

Reznik stifled a yawn. "You're up pretty late yourself."

He had never been in Renard's office; it looked remarkably similar to Nash's, but sparer in its furnishings, not unlike Reznik's own office. It seemed to Reznik that Renard had not tried to make himself at home here.

Reznik took a seat at the desk across from Renard, who was surrounded by paperwork scattered across his desk.

"Late?" Renard chuckled. "This is quite early for me these days."

Renard put his fountain pen back onto its stand and leaned back in his chair. "They have me drowning in this stuff. It's good to see you, though. I don't think we've really had a chance to talk since we got back."

Reznik looked at his friend. Renard tried to maintain a positive appearance though looked weary and slurred his words; he appeared inebriated.

"You turned down a promotion to colonel?"

Renard laughed. "That was barely an arc ago. How did you find out so quickly?"

"Have you been drinking?" Reznik said.

Renard held up his thumb and forefinger pinched together.

"Only this much."

"I was on my way to meet the colonel and saw you as you left General Mortigan's office," Reznik said. "I ran into the prince shortly after you left."

"And he told you?"

Reznik nodded.

"He was quite understanding, I must say," Renard said. "He didn't give me a hard time about it."

Recalling his earlier encounter with Adrian, Reznik found it bizarre to hear Renard complimenting the prince. He briefly wondered how Adrian's demeanor toward his best friend could be so different from how it was toward him. This worsened his mood.

"I guess it's your own fault for getting us out of Argiset," he remarked.

"Saving the prince's life does have its downsides." Renard smiled thinly, more sober now. "But I've decided this military stuff isn't for me."

"Military stuff, huh?" There was a trace of irritation in Reznik's voice.

Silence filled the room for almost a rep before Renard spoke again. "I don't need to be in any deeper than I already am. I'm sick of these rules and responsibilities."

His words reminded Reznik of what Osterfeld said previously.

"Besides," Renard continued, "I've neglected my lounge back home long enough. I'm really looking forward to getting back to it and—"

"So you're turning your back on us, on your country, to go run a bar?" Reznik blurted out angrily.

Renard was taken aback by the outburst. "That's not really fair," he said, leaning back in his chair. "It's difficult to continue to fight a war you don't believe in. I know you may not understand or feel the same way, but that's how things are for me. I've had enough of this place, and there are different ways to further our cause than being on the front lines."

Neither spoke for a while.

"How long have you felt this way?"

"I'm not sure." Renard sounded hollow and unconvincing.

Reznik stood abruptly. "Well, then. Sorry to have bothered you. We can talk another time."

"Do take some time to visit Douglas, would you?" Renard said. "He must think you despise him. It would be good if you gave him some reassurance."

Already headed for the door, Reznik smiled sardonically. "You're right. I shouldn't abandon my friends, after all."

He left without waiting for a reply, closing the door behind him as Renard remained seated silently.

Epilogue

(988.2.21)

Reznik, Madeline, Renard, and Glen stared out across Lake Sanmoria. They stood on the western bridge halfway between the western shore and the Crossway. It was a cloudy night; thousands of solistones bobbed up and down in the lake surrounding Aldova. Their soft glow cast an ethereal veil upon the landscape. In the distance, the huge Coranthian flags atop the roof of the fortress were clearly visible in faint solistone light emanating from the base of the flagpoles. Small pools had recently been dug into the rooftop to achieve this exact effect at night.

"It's been more than a year since we arrived," Madeline said.

"It feels quite a bit longer," Renard said.

Madeline looked past Reznik, to see Renard smiling softly as he gazed out at the lake. In the ten days since he made the momentous decision to leave the military, his vigor had significantly returned. The worried creases on Renard's face had softened, and his eyes were no longer bloodshot. Madeline could not recall the last time she had seen him in such good spirits.

After several reps, he removed the silver captain's pin from his uniform and rolled it around in his hand, staring at it thoughtfully.

Glen shook his head. "It won't be the same without you."

"You look better, Renard," Madeline said, "and I know this is what you want, but I still feel selfish. I don't want you to leave."

"I don't like it either," Reznik added flatly.

Madeline glanced uneasily at him. Reznik and Renard had barely spoken since the night Renard resigned. She knew Reznik was still irritable about the situation.

Renard chuckled sadly. His gaze lingered on the silver pin as he turned it over in his hand. "You make it sound like we will never see each other again."

"I'm sure we will," Madeline said. "I just didn't expect this. I thought we'd stick together. I know it sounds silly, but didn't we all agree to that?"

Her voice prompted Renard to lift his head. He was seized by the light reflected from moons and solistones that swirled and danced in the emerald pools of her eyes.

Seeing Renard hold his captain's pin, she reflexively grabbed at the crimson one around her own neck.

"And now you're just leaving," she uttered before taking a moment to steady her breath.

Without looking at her, Reznik gave her hand a quick squeeze, trying to comfort her as inconspicuously as possible.

Renard folded his hand into a fist around his pin. "We haven't really been together since all this started," he said. "I'm not even talking about the military as a whole. I'm talking about us."

"What do you mean?" Reznik asked, continuing to avoid eye contact with anyone.

"I've barely seen any of you this past year. Maddy, you make it sound like such a big deal, but you probably won't notice the difference."

Madeline stared glumly into the water; she had nothing to say in return.

"In fact, I may even see you more if I'm not here. I know we all had an image of how we wanted things to be. Things never work out exactly as you envision them though. And the ends no longer justify the means for me. Or perhaps I simply feel destined for another path."

"Is Vice Captain Stradt taking over the 21st?" Glen asked, reluctant to continue in the current direction of conversation.

"He'll get the job done. We weren't friends, but we worked well together."

Reznik finally turned toward Renard. "There are plenty of people like him in the military. We need more people like you."

Renard's smile became pinched. "No, Rez, we need more people like *you*. I don't belong in a uniform, I'm afraid. I have no doubt about that now."

"Well, maybe you shouldn't have joined the military to begin with," Reznik retorted.

Despite the warm spring air, Madeline shivered.

Renard was now completely serious. "Listen to me, Reznik. Our lives have always been very different, it's true. But don't think for a second that I'm giving up. We are still working toward the same thing. I just don't believe the path of a soldier is suitable for me. I don't regret my time in the military, but who knows, maybe I would have been better off without it."

The corners of his mouth curled upward slightly.

"Honestly, there's no need to get bent out of shape about it." He tried to sound jovial. "You guys will be fine without me."

"Damn it, Renard," Reznik shouted, "what kind of bullshit is that? Do you honestly think any of us would have made it this far without you?"

Renard's eyes widened as he unconsciously took a step back. Madeline and Glen stood in stunned silence.

"The only reason I stood up to Adrian at Tellisburg was because I knew you had my back. Was I mistaken?" Reznik said.

Renard stared at Reznik in silence for several ticks, but before he could get a word in, Reznik continued. "You were always one step ahead of everyone. You gave me someone to chase, someone to motivate and inspire me. Who the hell knows where I would be if not for that?"

Renard was shocked and stung. "I'm sorry," he said. "I guess I was being insensitive."

"Maybe I was wrong. Clearly I'm wrong now, anyway. Wrong about that, wrong about you. But I guess it doesn't matter to you, does it? Everything's better for you now that you can just walk away. What's that in your hand?"

The question caught Renard off guard. He uncurled his fist to reveal his silver captain's pin tucked inside.

Without warning, Reznik snatched it from his hand and held it up between them.

"You're the one who first explained to us what this stands for and why it's important. Thirteen years ago. Look at Madeline's pin, Renard. Look at it!"

Still speechless, Renard glanced at Madeline's necklace.

"She's worn it every day since. Have you forgotten? Or is it that after all this time, we're no different from everyone else you smooth-talk?"

He grabbed Renard's hand and forcefully returned the captain's pin. "For whatever this is worth to you."

Madeline attempted to return Reznik's earlier gesture by grabbing his hand. It was partly to comfort him and partly to quiet him. He wriggled out of her grasp and backed away from the group.

"I'm not doing this," he said. He spun around and began walking briskly toward the fortress.

"Reznik! Where are you going? Come back!" Madeline called out.

Reznik did not look back, leaving Madeline, Glen, and Renard staring after him. Renard leaned against the stone guard. Fatigue had reappeared on his face.

Madeline rested her hand gingerly over his.

"It's all right. I didn't expect such a reaction from him either. But I understand why he's so upset." She attempted a grin. "Actually, I'm a little jealous, you know."

Renard stared at her wistfully. "I'm not trying to hurt any of you. It's just something I need to do, Maddy."

"I know. Maybe he doesn't understand that you feel as strongly about this as he does about what he said. He'll come around."

"I'm glad he has you to support him," Renard nodded approvingly. "Who knows? Maybe if I hadn't been on my own out here, things would be different."

The weight of his words affected her deeply.

"I'm sorry," Madeline said, shaking her head.

The smile returning to his face, Renard reached out and pinched her cheek lightly, causing her to yelp.

Glen chuckled nervously.

"Oh, you think that's funny, do you?" Madeline challenged. "Maybe Renard should accost you too?"

Glen smiled and shook his head. "I'll pass, thanks."

"All of you really need to visit me in Kantor," Renard announced with enthusiasm. "I feel so unloved! I always drag my ass to the far reaches of the Outlands, but nobody ever comes to see me."

"Captain Renault!"

Renard, Madeline, and Glen all looked around in surprise. None had noticed the soldier approach from the west. Renard turned in the direction of the shore to find himself face to face with a guard. It was an avet who saluted when Renard took notice of him. Renard returned the salute.

"Preparations for departure are complete, sir. I am to inform you the caravan will leave for Kantor in fifteen reps."

Renard nodded. "Thank you."

The soldier retraced his steps toward the western end of the bridge where it met the shore. Several covered wagons waited beyond. Soldiers carrying rodtorches bustled about, tying down the last of the equipment and luggage for the few passengers who left Aldova overnight.

Renard looked at Madeline and Glen. "I guess that's my cue."

Without hesitation, Madeline enveloped Renard in her arms.

"Take care, Maddy," he murmured through her hair.

"You too," she whispered, squeezing him tightly.

After she finally pulled away, Renard turned to Glen and held out his hand. Glen came forward and the two men shook.

"I went to see Douglas earlier. Give him my best again, all the same," Renard said.

Glen nodded. "Good luck to you, Renard."

"And look out for Reznik too, won't you?"

"I will."

Renard stole a glance at Madeline and added, "I guess I don't need to tell you that."

Madeline smiled and nodded.

With nothing more to say, Renard turned to leave; he retrieved the small sack he left propped against the bridge guard. Though most of his belongings had already been loaded onto the caravan, he wished to keep a separate bag on his person for important papers and personal effects.

He walked westward, but about halfway to the shore, he turned back toward Aldova. A wave of melancholy rippled through him when he saw Madeline and Glen still standing in the same spot. It seemed only too appropriate to see them where he and Reznik had each set out on opposite paths. His discontent gradually faded as he came to accept that this was how things should be.

Lingering on that last vista, Renard wondered what lay in store for him and his friends. He finally turned and walked the rest of the way to the caravan, his steps more assured and resolute as he headed into an uncertain future.

Afterword

Coranox has always been a joint effort between its two authors. Its inception occurred, as one would say in Laestran, many cycles ago. Then, we were fresh-faced, newly-minted college graduates. Our past experiences with countless role-playing video games keyed us into the narrative potential of these storytelling vehicles. Inspired by a plethora of titles within the genre, we envisioned the creation of our own: a compelling war drama unique in both setting and gameplay. Tentatively titled Project Moriana, named after the fictional continent on which its tale was to take place, our initial endeavor persisted for a year and a half. Unfortunately, given our other full-time commitments and general lack of resources, it became clear that we could neither expediently nor satisfactorily realize our original concept.

Left with little choice but to shelve our gameplay designs, we resolved to salvage and mold into novel form the story we had so intricately mapped out. This migration to a different medium altogether was actually the greatest benefactor to our nascent writing process. We became even more sensitive to story elements that fell prey to tropes and contrivances. These we ruthlessly excised en route to the transformation of Project Moriana into a book series, of which Coranox represents the first volume. The resulting near-total overhaul proved far less arduous than we feared, as we were easily able to retain our core foundations of themes and characters. Now, we are more excited than we have ever been to continue the journeys of Reznik, Madeline, and Renard that began so long ago.

It has taken many years to crystallize our creative aether into the work you hold in your hands, the foundation from which the rest of our tightly coiled yarn will unspool. So much has already been set in motion for we hope will be a challenging and rewarding literary voyage. Above all else, thank you, dear reader, for gracing us with your company along the way.

Tony Gao and Brent Peckham
February 2007–November 2014
New York, San Antonio, Des Moines, Seattle, Boston

Acknowledgments

The sublime artwork in this book came to us by way of the inimitable Paul Scott Canavan.

As first-time authors, we would not have made it this far without the help of our editors. We are extremely thankful to our lead technical editor, Alice Day, as well as the team at All Ivy Writing Services, Inc.

We are also grateful to the intrepid souls who braved the earliest version of Coranox and provided us with invaluable feedback: Steve Wang, Chentian Zhang, and Jonathan Peckham.

Artist and Editor Portfolio Links

Paul Scott Canavan
Lead Artist
http://www.paulscottcanavan.com/

Alice Day
Lead Technical Editor
http://www.book-editing.com/book-consultant-bios/alice-day/index.
html

All Ivy Writing Services, Inc.
Line Edit and Other Editing Services
http://aiwriting.com/

CPSIA information can be obtained
at www.ICGtesting.com
Printed in the USA
FFOW02n1803210515
13609FF

9 780986 2555